Fran O'Brien and Arthur McGuinness
established McGuinness Books
to publish her novels to raise funds
for LauraLynn Children's Hospice.

Fran's seven novels, *The Married Woman, The Liberated Woman, Odds on Love, Who is Faye? The Red Carpet, Fairfields,* and *The Pact* have raised €250,000.00 in sales and donations for LauraLynn House.

Fran and Arthur hope that ***1916*** will raise even more funds for the children's hospice.

www.franobrien.net

Also by Fran O'Brien

The Married Woman
The Liberated Woman
Odds on Love
Who is Faye?
The Red Carpet
Fairfields
The Pact

1916

FRAN O'BRIEN

McGuinness Books

McGuinness Books

1916

This book is a work of fiction and except in the case of historical fact, or mention of historical figures, any resemblance to actual persons, living or dead is purely coincidental.

Published by McGuinness Books,
15 Glenvara Park, Ballycullen Road,
Templeogue, Dublin 16.

A catalogue record for this book
is available from the British Library.

ISBN 97809549521-7-4

Typeset by Martone Design & Print,
39 Hills Industrial Centre, Liffey Bridge, Lucan, Co. Dublin.

Printed and bound in Great Britain by
CPI Group (UK) Ltd, Croydon, CR04YY.

www.franobrien.net

This novel is dedicated to Jane and Brendan McKenna,
and in memory of their daughters Laura and Lynn.

And for all our family, friends and clients who support our efforts to raise funds for LauraLynn Children's Hospice, Leopardstown, Dublin 18.

Jane and Brendan have been through every parent's worst nightmare – the tragic loss of their only two children.

Laura died, just four years old, following surgery to repair a heart defect. Her big sister, Lynn, died, aged fifteen, less than two years later, having lost her battle against Leukaemia – diagnosed on the day of Laura's surgery.

Having dealt personally with such serious illness, Jane and Brendan's one wish was to establish a children's hospice in memory of their girls.

Now LauraLynn House has become a reality, and their dream has come true.

LauraLynn House Children's Hospice offers community based paediatric palliative, respite, end-of-life care, and the LauraLynn@home Programme.

At LauraLynn House there is an eight bed unit, and also a residential unit for families, support and comfort for parents and siblings for whom life can be extremely difficult.

Putting Life into a Child's Day
Not Days into a Child's Life

WWW.LAURALYNNHOSPICE.COM

Chapter One

In January 1916 two young men walked through Dublin city. Good friends, James Wilson and Michael O'Toole talked of war. The men's route led them past Trinity College, across O'Connell Bridge, and down Sackville Street. They were members of the Irish Volunteers and were on their way to a meeting which took place every Thursday night in the Gaelic League Hall on Rutland Square.

'Have you thought any more about joining the British army?' James asked.

'No, I've decided to stay here. What is it they say? Now that England is concentrating on the Germans we have our chance, something like that?' Michael said with a grin.

Many of the Volunteers had already enlisted and were risking their lives at the Front. Those who chose to stay behind didn't know whether there would be a call to rise up against Britain, but they were prepared for the day when it would come.

'If the War in Europe hadn't happened when it did, and prevented the Home Rule Act passing through the House of Lords, everything would be different by now,' James said. He thought of his brother Maurice fighting for England against the Germans in a place called Ypres, in Flanders. His letters only hinted at the conditions which James knew were atrocious. In this freezing winter he could imagine the men trudging through mud. Digging trenches. Facing the enemy in *no mans land.*

Diving to avoid shells which exploded over them. Watching friends die in a hail of bullets. The blood of those men and the smell of death was everywhere.

James didn't talk about the Volunteers at home. By day, he worked with Michael, both clerks in a solicitor's office, dealing with litigious cases and breathing in the dust of old files. But being involved in the Volunteers was something completely different. It got them out into the fresh air. Marching. Drilling. Target practice. And always that romantic vision of fighting for an independent Ireland free of the yoke of Britain. That spurred them on.

Chapter Two

Kathleen O'Toole wagged her finger at her son, Hugh, as he ate his bowl of porridge. 'I've said to you before, this is your second year in the United Services Club, and it's no time to become lazy. You're doing well and you have to keep that up in the hope that you'll get a better position, and earn some more money. The people there are in a different class to us, always remember that.' She wiped her hands on the white apron she wore over a black skirt.

He nodded, finished the porridge and then tucked into fresh soda bread and raspberry jam.

'Tea?' Kathleen poured.

'Thanks Mam.' Hugh drank it quickly and then he hurried upstairs.

His younger brothers still lay in bed head to toe among rumpled blankets. Hugh shook them. The seven year old raised himself up on his elbow and stared at him. 'When will you be back?' he asked, his blue eyes wide, curious.

'Next week.'

Up against the other wall was a bigger bed where he slept himself with his elder brother. He pulled at his foot, and received a groan by way of response.

He put on the grey tweed jacket his mother had made him, and picked up the cotton bag which held a spare shirt, underwear and socks. He rushed downstairs. His mother came to the front door with him. Her arms reached out and she pulled him close to her ample body and held him there for a moment, even though at sixteen he was much taller than herself. There were tears on her cheeks and when she kissed him he could feel their moisture.

It was busy on this bright January morning as Hugh trudged along Camden Street, but extremely cold and icy underfoot. Cab wheels rumbled along the cobbles. Skittish horses trotted. Occasionally the crack of a whip could be heard and the sound of the trams. People came towards him and he had to step down into the street more than once on to the ice, very glad that it was a dry day and that he didn't get his boots dirty.

He was passing St. Stephen's Green now and walked down Dawson Street for about a hundred yards or so, then turned into a back lane and stopped at the third door along. He knocked, his fingers tight around the neck of his cotton bag. After a few minutes, the door was opened by a small man who nodded, but said nothing. Hugh walked into the kitchen which was noisy and hot. Steam escaped from large pots. Pans hissed. Cooks prepared food. Maids rushed in and out carrying trays. He went through and in the small staff cloakroom changed into his green uniform.

He worked with Peter, taking care of the cloaks, hats, and canes of the members as they came in. Carrying messages. Running errands. And double fast too. It was a busy place with both civilian and military members. The talk was all about the War these days, and Hugh and Peter overheard the names of various countries being mentioned in conversation.

'I've got a newspaper from the bin, we'll be able to read it tonight,' Peter whispered as he passed Hugh. The fight in Europe was all they were interested in. The descriptions of battles won and lost. The thousands of young men dying. It stirred something in both of them. They wanted to be among those who had joined up. The talk was that many of them had enlisted because they hoped Ireland would achieve Home Rule from England when it was all over. Although everyone knew that for others it was the lure of money. For Hugh and Peter the call of war reached something in their hearts and they couldn't wait to take that first step.

'Did you think about enlisting?' Peter asked when they had a break.

Hugh nodded. He had thought of nothing else when he had been at home.

'What about your mother and father, will they object?'

'Don't know.' Although he knew very well that they wouldn't approve at all.

'Have you said anything?'

'No.'

'Neither did I,' Peter said, with a grin. 'But let's go soon,' he urged. 'I can't wait to get there.'

'What if they don't accept me, I'm only sixteen,' Hugh said.

'I'm only seventeen and I was reading in the paper that they're taking anyone at all now once they look old enough.'

Hugh was charged with excitement.

Chapter Three

'Bring in those kids for their tea,' Mary McCabe said to her eldest daughter, Bridget. 'Although what there is of it won't fill them.' She pushed through the ragged piece of fabric which hung from a cord attached to each wall dividing the one room. It was a dark red, like something from the music hall she always thought. 'Lar, get up,' she shouted.

The man in the bed groaned and turned away from her.

'Man, you've been there all day, get up out of that.'

There was no response from her husband.

'Bloody lazy lump, God help us, not much chance of him getting work, he didn't even go down to the docks this morning, didn't bother his arse,' she muttered to herself as she scraped some jam on pieces of bread and piled them on a plate. The children rushed in and sat up at the table. Only for what she and Bridget made at the stall in Moore Street, they would be starving. She made tea in the metal pot on the fire, dark and strong, and poured it into a motley selection of containers. Some cracked cups. A couple of saucers. A bowl. They had no milk or sugar, but they didn't care. It was a hot drink. Robbie, her twelve year old son hadn't come home yet, but she had put aside a slice of bread for him, and Lar too, whenever he chose to get up. But hadn't bothered for herself. A weak stew simmered on the fire, to which she had added a fair amount of water to stretch it. The couple of pieces of meat in it were kept for Lar. He had to be fed and couldn't work on an empty stomach. She scraped the glass jam pot. This was the last of the damson jam, and she would have to wait until the summer to get another box of berries of some sort which were over-ripe and couldn't be sold. Not that it happened very often, there was always someone willing to pay a penny or two for such fruit.

'Mam, have you some bread for yourself?' Bridget asked.

'I'll have it later, must see to the child.' Mary lifted the baby from the cot. Just six months old, she wasn't thriving. Over this past week a fever had kept her weak and she was covered with a rash. Although Mary had tried many of the old cures her mother had used, nothing seemed to work.

Bridget poured a little of the watery stew for each child. 'Have a cup of tea yourself,' she suggested.

'Sure I will then.' She poured it and sat by the fire. There was still some heat although the coal was burning down. It was January and extremely cold. She would get them all to bed soon, cuddled up together there was some warmth, but she needed to keep the fire going to make sure there was always water on the boil in the kettle.

Lar pushed through the curtain. He stood there, stretched out his arms and yawned. A fine figure of a man, he stared around him. Mary could sense the sudden tension in the room. The children looked up at him, but down again, eyes hidden. He moved in front of the fire and spread his legs. 'Not much heat out of this,' he grunted.

She didn't respond.

'Bridget, a cup of tea and something to eat, I'm starving.'

The girl took a spoon and stirred the mixture in the pot. She poured it into a bowl and put it down on the table with a slice of bread.

He broke the bread and slurped. 'Any more?' he asked.

Bridget shook her head.

'Not enough to feed a mouse there. How did you get on at the market today?'

'Not good.' Mary cuddled the baby.

'Bloody hell.' He pounded the table. The dishes jumped. The children stared at him with fear in their eyes.

'What are yez looking at?' he roared. 'Scat! Get to bed.'

They scurried across the room and through the curtain.

'Lar, it's too cold for them in there. Come back to the fire,' Mary called out.

'They're warmer in there, there's no heat in that fire,' he grumbled.

'If you had gone out this morning instead of lying in bed, you might have got some work.'

'Shut your mouth,' he lunged towards her, and his fist just missed her. She cried out sharply, and swayed on the stool, trying to hold on to the baby in her arms, but dropped the tea cup which smashed on the wooden floor. There was a storm of crying from the children who had begun to sidle in again.

'Shut-up, for God's sake,' he roared.

Bridget rushed the children behind the curtain again. On the bed, they huddled together under a couple of light blankets and she sat there, comforting them. At fifteen, she was a great help to Mary and worked hard on the stall. It was their only way of earning money to keep the family fed and clothed, and pay the rent to the landlord.

Lar tried to get work on the docks loading or unloading the ships, but he drank most of the money he earned even when he did get a day's work. It was generally known that if he didn't have a few drinks in one of the local pubs each evening, out of which the stevedores received a cut from the publican, then he would be blacklisted. Like the other women Mary dreaded the appearance of a drunken husband coming home late at night. Roughly throwing himself about the small room in which they lived, and likely to take a swipe at anyone who caught his eye.

This very evening, Mary made no retort when he lunged at her. Lar was all guff and usually his aim was bad, so a quick duck and he hit the wall. But she was glad to see the back of his cranky presence when he eventually left the room, to bang the heavy door and clatter downstairs.

'The tea is still warm, will I pour you some more?' Bridget picked up the pot.

Mary nodded, stared at the floor, and regretted the loss of another cup. She sipped the tea thinking how much Lar had changed. Such a different man when they had met all those years ago at the stall. She recalled the day. Bright sunshine bathed the crowded street, and the voices of the hawkers all around her suddenly faded away as she caught his eye. Then he had smiled and she was lost.

Now they lived with their seven children in one room, with a large bed at the back, and mattresses for the children at the other end. Sixty-two men, women and children lived in the old Georgian house. It was a noisy place. Voices shouting. Drunken men fighting. Everyone living on top of each other. And all using one lavatory and water tap in the yard at the back of the house.

To get the best of vegetables, Mary rose very early in the morning. She and Bridget arrived at the Smithfield Market to pick up any bargains going. She haggled with the same man who always tried to trick her into accepting bruised products at top prices, but Mary was sharp, and he respected her.

Today she had brought the baby, wrapped in the shawl close to her breast. She prayed that the little mite would get better. She couldn't bear it if she lost another one, having already lost five, two boys still born, three girls who died young. None of them lived long enough to go to school and all were buried in the public plot in Glasnevin Cemetery. She often thought of going up there to say a prayer, but the graves had no headstones and there was no particular place to kneel and talk to those children. Mary sighed, and looked down at the baby but she didn't seem any better today, her pinched face flushed.

'She's very hot, I don't like the look of her,' Mary's sister Eileen said, gently touching the child's forehead.

'It's a fever, I'll have to try and get it down.' Mary cuddled the baby to her.

'You should take her home,' she advised.

'There will be nothing to feed the others if I don't manage to sell something.'

Eileen said nothing, but there was understanding in her expression.

'We have potatoes, onions, parsnips,' their mother, Lily, called out. 'Good taties for the pot ladies, come on now, only two pence a bag, two pence a bag.' Her sing-song drew the attention of some of the people who thronged through the street, and before long they were making sales and pocketing the money. They worked hard, coaxing coins out of the hands of the customers. Many of them were housekeepers or maids to the owners of big houses nearby and were only interested in obtaining good quality food for their mistresses.

They sold out most of the vegetables by five in the evening. Only some small potatoes, a few bedraggled carrots and a couple of onions which nobody wanted were left. The money was divvied out. A few pence for each, and money to buy more vegetables in the morning. They split up what was left on the stall and Mary went into the butchers hoping to get a bargain. One of the men caught her eye, and came over when he had finished what he was doing.

'A few off-cuts for the stew if you please?'

He nodded, gathered some small pieces of meat which littered the counter on to a sheet of newspaper and quickly rolled it up. 'Tuppence, Mary, that should do it.'

'Thanks, God be with you,' she smiled, pushed the parcel into the pocket of her apron and left. She was grateful. The men were always generous to the women who worked the street outside. Before she headed for home, she went to the dairy to buy milk for the baby, her own had long dried up. It was just a small drop, she didn't have money for more, each day was a struggle.

At home Mary heated the milk in a can on the fire, and gave it to the baby. She didn't seem to be any better, turning her head from side to side refusing to swallow it. 'Come on my love, take some, it'll do you good,' she coaxed the child. But she dribbled and cried piteously, the milk wasted.

'Let me take her,' Bridget lifted her. But her crying grew louder, and her face redder. 'She's very hot.'

Mary dipped a rag into the bucket and patted her forehead with it.

Bridget walked up and down trying to pacify her, but to no avail.

'She needs a doctor,' Mary said.

Bridget looked at her, but said nothing.

There was no money for such luxuries, and both knew it.

Mary stayed up with the baby, relieved when the crying stopped at some time in the small hours. She lay her head back against the chair and closed her eyes. But she awoke suddenly some time later and looked down with a sense of horror as she felt the chill of the little body in her arms.

Lar carried the baby in a brown cardboard box up to Glasnevin Cemetery. Bridget went with him, Mary was unable to face putting another of her children into the ground of that place and leaving her there. As usual she went to the market in the early morning, and then to Moore Street. The only difference to be noticed was a puckering of her lips as she clamped them tight shut, unable to speak about the tragedy which had just happened. Not that it was unusual, not at all. Every woman she knew had lost children. So no one wanted to speak about it, or even express their condolences on her trouble. It was too raw. So little Olive was kept in her mother's heart, another little soul. The birthday of each of her children, and the anniversaries of their deaths, always remembered.

Chapter Four

'You know I enjoy working at the hospital, it's all I want to do, Mother,' Anne Montford insisted.

'But you've wasted almost two years of your life, and having to live at that nurses' home is awful.' Eleanor stood up and walked to the window.

'I don't mind, the other nurses are all very nice.' Anne followed her mother and stood beside her. They stared out over the elaborate gardens which led down to the sea at the back of their Blackrock home. A gardener weeded flower beds. Another pushed a wheelbarrow.

'I've moulded you into a beautiful young woman. You could make such a good match if you'd only take some notice of the men who come to call. You need a husband,' Eleanor said. 'And you have to marry first, Catherine and Rhoda can't be expected to wait.'

'Let them go ahead, I don't mind,' Anne retorted.

'That's easy for you to say, but they must get married, they're not interested in spending their time in a hospital, no well brought up lady should be interested in such things.'

'I've always wanted to be a nurse, you know that. Ever since I was little.'

'I won't have you go to that place where they're fighting, I forbid it. I've one child already over there, and I don't know when he's coming back, if ever.' Eleanor turned to her, eyes blazing, suddenly angry. Her eldest son, Stephen, had qualified as a doctor and followed in his father's footsteps. But when the War had begun in 1914 he had immediately enlisted, in spite of the objections of his mother.

'I'm not qualified yet, the War will be over by then. Don't worry so.' Anne tried to appease Eleanor. She was glad to be living in the nurses' home. It meant she only came home when she was off and didn't have to endure endless harassment from her mother.

'No-one knows what will happen, we pray for your brother but there's been so many soldiers injured and killed already it will be a miracle if he returns unscathed. And the same applies to his friends. It's so quiet around here without them all, my heart is broken.'

There was a knock on the door, and it was pushed open by a serving girl carrying a tray. 'Tea, madam,' she said, and set out the china on a low table. She spooned tea leaves, poured hot water over them, then scalded the cups and served.

Eleanor ignored the maid and continued speaking. 'All I want is for you to make a good match. You've met enough young men. Why can't you just settle down and be happy?'

'I told you why.'

'Do you want to be alone all your life?'

'Of course not, but I don't want to sit here waiting for some man to propose. Someone I don't even know. The thought of that is just ...' She shook her head, a look of aversion on her face.

'But if you showed any interest, you could have made friends with any of the men you've met. Why, Harry Finch is most handsome and attentive too. He's escorted you to enough balls and parties. Let's hope he comes back safe.'

Anne didn't reply. Secretly she was very fond of Harry.

'His mother indicated to me that he was quite interested in you and serious too.'

'He doesn't know me at all. We've only talked on a very superficial level.' Anne wasn't going to let her mother know how she felt, otherwise she would be rushed up the aisle on his next leave, and then her plans to qualify as a nurse would disintegrate.

'What does that matter? Once he has enough money to keep you and your children ...if you are blessed with them.'

The door opened. A stocky red faced man entered hurriedly.

'Tea, Clarence?' Eleanor asked.

'Just a quick cup, I have to get back to the hospital.'

'You're never out of that place, and your daughter is the same.'

'We need good nurses.' He sat down. 'And Anne is doing very well according to Matron.'

'A hospital is no place for a lady, she has to do the most obnoxious things every day.'

'Many a lady has given her life for such work. All they wanted to do was to help people. If I had my way, I'd like Anne to be a doctor.' He glanced at his gold pocket watch. 'Follow in my footsteps. What do you think, Anne?' he asked, smiling.

She stared at him, astonished.

'A doctor? Are you mad, Clarence?' Eleanor's face flushed an even deeper shade of puce.

'She would make an excellent doctor.'

'It is out of the question.'

'It can be decided when she qualifies as a nurse.'

'She will not be a doctor. What will people think?'

'Who cares?' he shrugged.

'I care. Her sisters care.'

'We have one daughter who can think independently, and has intense feelings about making her way in life, we are lucky for that. We should be thankful,' Clarence declared.

Eleanor shook her head so strongly her elaborately arranged hair wobbled. 'She'll be joining a suffragette society next.'

‘And why not?’ Clarence said, with a grin. ‘Wouldn’t you like to have a vote to elect a government?’

‘You’re losing your mind, I have no interest and she shouldn’t have either.’

‘It will happen ...eventually. This is the twentieth century. There will be many changes over the next decades, in my own field particularly. I have a few ideas myself if I only had the time to develop them.’

‘As it is, you spend most of your life at that hospital, or in your laboratory. I can’t even find you when I need you.’

‘Anne and I may well do a lot of work there,’ he smiled at her.

She put her hand on his shoulder. ‘I’m looking forward to it.’

‘I’m outnumbered it seems,’ Eleanor grimaced.

‘I think you’re going to be very proud of our girl.’

Anne thought of Harry. His last letter had been from Flanders where the War continued, relentless. She was worried about him, and her brother too. Admittedly, they were in the Royal Army Medical Corps and not fighting, but still either one of them could catch a bullet at any time. She had become very fond of him since he had expressed his own feelings for her before he went back after Christmas.

‘Let’s get engaged,’ he had suggested as they stood in the conservatory during a send-off party at his home. He put his arms around her and quickly his lips were on hers, his breath warm. Her pulse raced. This was the first time she had been so close to a boy and her heart danced.

‘I love you, Anne,’ he whispered, his mouth pressing softly.

She let herself sink into his embrace, aware of the slight roughness of his chin. The cool touch of the buttons on his uniform. The scent of his cigarettes. Hesitantly, she embraced him, her fingers caressed.

'Anne, are you out here? The dancing is beginning.' A voice echoed.

Harry pulled her behind some plants and the two of them stood there until her sister Catherine had gone back inside exclaiming that she couldn't find her.

'Close,' Harry laughed, his voice low, his lips immediately on hers again, so enticing.

But she moved away from him a little. The spell had broken for her, to be replaced by the fear of being discovered. She didn't relish the thought of explaining to her parents and sisters why she was out here with Harry.

'We'd better go inside, Catherine's looking for me,' she whispered.

His arms tightened around her. 'Wait a few more minutes,' he begged.

'Do you want my father out here?' she giggled.

He smiled, his expression rueful. 'Might give me a chance to talk to him.'

She was unsure of his meaning for a moment, but then realised exactly what he meant.

'Should I do that?' he asked.

'No Harry, not yet.' She was taken aback.

'Many of my friends have got married while on leave, why don't we do the same?' His eyes searched hers. 'My apologies, I haven't even proposed to you yet.' Quickly he bent down on one knee. 'Will you marry me, Anne?'

This was totally unexpected. 'It's too soon, Harry,' she stuttered, her blue eyes alarmed.

He stood up, his arms around her again. 'But we know each other over a year now. I love you. All I want is to spend my life with you,' he insisted.

'I'm not qualified as a nurse yet, that will take some time,' she tried to explain.

'But you can continue while I'm away.' He stroked her fair coiled hair.

'I'm not sure if they allow married women to train,' she struggled to find excuses.

'You won't need to work when we're married, I'm going to set up my own practice, we'll be comfortably off,' he persuaded.

'I'm sorry, Harry, but I'm just not ready yet. Please try to understand.'

He was disappointed, she could see that in his downcast expression.

'Maybe on my next leave you'll feel differently?' he asked.

'Until I finish training I won't be in a position to marry,' she said, firm now.

'But that's years away,' he burst out.

'I know, but it's what I want.'

'Don't you love me?'

'Of course I do, Harry.' She hated refusing him. She did love him, but couldn't explain exactly how she felt about her nursing. That was something special. A dream come true and she just didn't want to relinquish the joy of helping the people in that hospital.

'What if I don't come back?' he asked.

'Don't say that, Harry,' she said softly. Tears clouded her eyes.

'Would you care?'

'Of course I would, how could you even think that?' She clutched him.

'Anne ...Harry ...are you out here?' It was Catherine again.

They looked at each other, and slowly moved apart.

'We were just taking some air,' Anne explained and walked towards her sister. Harry followed.

‘I think the two of you were canoodling behind there,’ she giggled as she took Anne’s arm and they made their way into the ballroom.

She had only received one letter from him since then, and read it over and over as if it brought him nearer to her. At times deeply regretting her reluctance to become engaged, and at other times glad that she had not agreed. She missed him very much and worried every day about his safety imagining the hell he had to endure. Her brother Stephen was in the forefront of her mind too. They were entwined together, these two men she loved.

Chapter Five

James leafed through an Irish grammar. He loved the language, his own language, but one he couldn't speak openly, restricted to those Gaelic League classes he attended, the only time he could share a few words with other like-minded people. That fact riled him. Fired him up against the oppression of England over the centuries, and made him think of his grandfather, and great grandfather, men who worked secretly for the establishment of an independent republic in Ireland. But his own father, Matt, had no interest in politics. They were a family of seven, and his father worked in the Dublin office of an engineering company which had its factory in Cork. A strict man, he insisted that all his children study hard at school, particularly his sons. He would have preferred James to join the army with Maurice, rather than the Volunteers, so James kept quiet about what he did in his spare time.

At the table these days the conversation was always about the War.

When they had finished eating, Maurice's latest letter was read aloud by his father.

> "*Dear Father, Mother, brothers and sisters,*' Matt hesitated for a moment, and then continued. '*I hope this letter finds you all well, as it leaves me. I can't say much, but just to tell you I am still alive and kicking as they say. I met a few fellows from Dublin and we would all give*

anything to be at home. But I am glad I joined up to fight. The weather conditions are bad. There has been a lot of rain, and heavy snow too which makes life even more difficult. But enough of that. Hope your winter hasn't been so hard and that Dublin is still as merry as ever. I know you read reports in the papers, but don't dwell too much, particularly Mother, I'll survive and be back among you before long. So pray for me, as I do for you. Until we meet again. Your loving son, and brother, Maurice. PS I met an Irish priest out here, it's been grand to talk to him."

Matt folded the letter carefully, and put it back in the envelope. Then he placed it in front of him, and stared at it, his eyes suddenly full of tears. There was a silence at the table. Liliane stood up and began to clear away the dishes, immediately helped by her two young daughters.

When the women had left the room and gone into the scullery, Matt turned his gaze on James.

'Maybe you should be there with him.' His voice was low, but the point of his words was quite clear.

James was silent. He wished he was with his brother, but his heart was here with the Volunteer movement. He was working for something different. He couldn't explain that to his father. 'May I read the letter?' He held out his hand to Matt, but the older man didn't reply, just pushed back his chair and left the table. James took the letter from the envelope and read the simple words. He did that twice, finding so much more in between those lines.

He remembered taking the oath in the Irish Republican Brotherhood. He wished he could tell his father but it would mean confessing that the oath was a promise to take up arms for Ireland and that was the reason he had not joined up to fight for England. Although the more logical side to his personality was content to wait until Home Rule was granted by the British after the War ended.

Suddenly, he wanted to be with his brother. His father's words had cut deep, and he felt guilty. He thought of how it must be for Maurice. The awful conditions he only hinted at in his letters. But James knew enough about war. It must be hell on earth. Even if he joined up now, they would never be together. It would be impossible. He returned to his room, picked up his book, but threw it down again. A feeling of uselessness caused a shadow over him. Was he a coward? Was he using his passion for their struggle here to avoid the fight in Europe?

Chapter Six

'Hugh tells me he is getting on all right on the job and hopes he'll be given more responsibility soon.' Terence O'Toole drank porter from a bottle.

'He's sensible.' Kathleen kneaded dough. 'And enjoys working there. A job in the United Services Club, all found, is a great chance for any boy to have. But I'm not worried about him, it's Louise.'

There was a questioning silence between them.

'What about her?' Her husband's voice was sharp.

'This business with Cumann na mBan.'

'They support the Volunteers. We're working from the same hymn sheet,' he grunted.

'She's only a girl.' Kathleen stopped what she was doing.

'We need young people to support the cause.'

'The cause?' she snapped.

'You know what we want.'

'You'll never have success. All you're doing is practicing at being an army.'

'It's our aspiration, to be achieved by whatever means, violent or political, it remains to be seen.'

She shook her head dismissively. 'Louise shouldn't be involved. I want her to meet a nice man, get married and settle down.'

'She wants more than that.'

'Are you saying marriage is not enough? Sure what else would a girl want only a good husband?'

'She can have both.'

'If she's still alive.'

'Don't worry so much.'

'How can I help it?'

'Mam, have you ironed my good white blouse?' Louise came in.

'Yes, it's airing.'

'Thanks,' she disappeared.

'I'm going to forbid her to go.' Kathleen went after her.

'Don't, she'll go anyway, you'll be wasting your time,' Terence said.

She moved back into the room with an air of resignation.

'I'll look out for her,' he said.

Kathleen didn't believe her husband. She worried about him as well, although she understood his belief in the cause for Irish freedom. His idealism was something which had been handed down from his father and his before him.

'How do I look?' Louise paraded in front of her.

'Nice, love.'

'You're not looking,' she accused.

'Of course I am.' Kathleen raised her head.

'So, you approve of my new hair style?'

Kathleen nodded, aware that she hadn't even noticed the more severe look. But it wasn't too drastic and didn't require censure.

'I won't be too late.' Louise put on her hat and coat.

'Where are you going?'

'A meeting.'

'Cumann na mBan?' Kathleen glanced across at her husband who was now reading the paper. 'Yes,' Louise said. Flat. Factual. And without doubt, defiant. 'We'll be doing signalling tonight, and first aid. And making final arrangements for the concert next week. You'll be there won't you?'

'Signalling, First Aid? What a thing for a girl to be doing. What about finding a husband, wouldn't that be more in your line? Some chance of meeting a nice boy when you're involved in this activity, you're more like a man.' She pursed her lips.

'Mam, just because I'm interested in Irish freedom, doesn't mean I'm a man. Although I wouldn't mind being one. It would be much easier, don't you think?' Louise asked.

Kathleen shook her head in disbelief. 'Go to your meeting, girl.'

'Thanks, Mam,' Louise said with a smile and kissed her mother.

Chapter Seven

Anne had to admit that her mother was right in some ways. It was tough working at Mercer's Hospital trying to reach Matron's exacting standards, and she enjoyed the wards better than the classes, with lectures on anatomy and other subjects.

'How do you put up with working every day?' Catherine asked as she embroidered a piece of linen.

'I enjoy it,' Anne lowered the book she was reading. Even when she was off duty and came home, she always spent some of the time studying if she could.

'What do you do exactly?'

'Look after patients, make beds, clean floors, help the senior nurses, there is an endless list of duties, but I love it.'

'And what about operations?'

'We get to watch, it's fascinating.'

Catherine shivered.

'The studying is the most boring part, but it has to be done too,' Anne explained.

'It sounds much too difficult to me, I'd give it up.' Catherine put down her embroidery on a side table, and stood up. 'Why not enjoy life?' She stretched her arms wide and, murmuring the melody of a tune, circled. Pointing her toes with precision, she danced slowly around the room. 'Leave, leave, leave. Mother would be so happy.'

'No, I'm not going to do that, just to suit everyone. This is what I want,' Anne raised her voice.

The door opened suddenly. Their mother stood looking at them.

Catherine stopped moving instantly. Both girls stared at Eleanor.

'Why do we have to listen to loud voices? What is the reason for that?' She was vexed.

Neither spoke.

'I'm expecting Mrs. Sanders and her son at any moment. Why are you not ready?'

'We won't be long.' Anne ushered Catherine ahead of her and they went upstairs. At the top they burst into a fit of the giggles, and disappeared into their rooms.

Anne knew why Mrs. Sanders and her son Trevor had come around to visit. Eleanor regularly paraded a selection of possible suitors for her and her sisters. They knew many of the young men in Dublin society, having met at various functions in the social calendar, but so far there had been no proposals except for when Harry asked Anne to marry him, and that was her secret.

They sat and sipped tea. Eleanor and Mrs. Sanders talked between themselves, occasionally drawing the young people into the conversation. But Anne left the chatting to Catherine, who seemed to get on well with Trevor. Her sister smiled, simpered, pleased with herself. Anne was relieved that for once all the attention wasn't on her. She sat there, bored, and would have preferred to be still reading her book, or spending time with her father. At Sir Patrick Dun's Hospital Clarence specialised in children's illnesses, and spent all his free time conducting experiments in his laboratory. In the evenings she sat with him and he explained his ideas, and she became fired up with enthusiasm also as he talked about consumption, diphtheria, meningitis, measles, and many other diseases which she came across every day. She was happiest looking after children, and really pleased if she was on duty in that ward. But to see the life snuffed out of the little ones was hard to bear and Anne knew she should not allow herself to be so emotional. A good nurse must be objective, and would be no help to a patient if she became too involved in their lives. So far, this was the most difficult hurdle she had to climb. But Anne simply hadn't been able to stand back. She brought every problem home with her. Not least the worry about children who hadn't made it to hospital, and who died quickly at home without any help.

Chapter Eight

This evening James had been invited to Michael's home for tea, before going to a fund-raising concert being organised by Cumann na mBan. Meeting the O'Toole family for the first time, and anxious to make a good impression, he had dressed in his good navy blue suit, and put on a clean shirt, collar, and dark tie. Before he left the house, he took time to polish his black boots to a high shine. Just twenty-two years of age, James cut a fine figure of a man as he crossed the River Liffey and walked towards South Circular Road.

James and Michael sat at the table with Michael's father, Terence, who worked on the railway at Inchicore. His mother, Kathleen, and sister, Louise, served the cold meal. Ham. Boiled eggs. Tomato. With freshly baked bread. And tea.

He was immediately taken by Louise, a beautiful girl with shining dark hair, deep brown eyes, and such a sweet smile.

'Well, James, I've been hearing a lot about you lately,' Terence said.

'Hope it's all good, Mr. O'Toole,' James smiled.

'You're of the same mind as ourselves, and that's what we like to see.'

'The cause is important to me.' He helped himself to ham.

'What brought you to join the Volunteers?'

'Why wouldn't I join, same as you?'

'Good answer,' he said, laughing.

'My grandfather was involved in the struggle so I suppose it's in the blood.'

'A family history, as it is here too. And your own father ...?'

'No.'

'That's a pity, it's always good to have the support of the family.'

'I don't really talk much about it at home,' he had to admit. 'But I'm hoping that Home Rule will be granted when the War is over.'

'Ah, you're more of a politician then?' Terence asked.

'Perhaps ...'

'So the idea of rising up against the English doesn't appeal to you?'

'If the Volunteers rebel then I'll be there with them,' he said, aware that Terence was at a much higher level in the organisation than he was.

'Would you like more tea?' Louise waited, holding the pot.

'Thank you,' he held out his cup and she poured. Their eyes met. His heart raced. He was immediately attracted to her.

'What do you do when you're not working?' Terence asked.

'He throws a good ball in cricket,' Michael said, with a grin.

'I played in my time,' Terence nodded.

'I enjoy it.'

'In the Phoenix Park?'

'Yes. But I haven't much opportunity these days. There's a lot happening as you know.'

'Plans are set,' Terence said.

James stared at him, taken aback. 'Is there a date?'

'We're still in discussion about that.'

The concert was held in the Ancient Concert Rooms on Great Brunswick Street which was packed that evening with supporters of Cumann na mBan. There was a varied programme, and the musicians and singers received rousing applause after each performance. James enjoyed the entertainment, but even more than that, to be so close to Louise was wonderful. What was this, he wondered. How could one woman affect him so? He thought how pretty she was in her navy skirt and white lace blouse, and was aware of a delicious scent of lavender. There were girls in his social circle, sisters and relatives of friends, but no-one he knew had affected him like this.

At the interval, he took the opportunity to go outside with Michael to have a smoke, as Louise busied herself selling raffle tickets. They resumed their seats, but this time Michael sat between them. James was disappointed. Still aware of her at a distance, seeing her out of the corner of his eye. Although only a couple of feet, it seemed she was a mile away.

He insisted on walking home with the family although it was in the wrong direction for his own home. But what was a bit of a walk when he could stay with Louise for even a few minutes longer? The night was cold. They talked about the concert and the people who had been there. Laughing at those funny unexpected moments. The fine performances. How many standing ovations there had been. More than once, Louise's brown eyes met his, and he couldn't help wonder how he might meet her again, and whether she would be allowed to do so by her parents. He wasn't sure of her age, but guessed she was about nineteen or twenty. Not too much of an age difference, he decided, not too much at all. He had to say goodnight as soon as they reached their house. In full view of the family, he took her hand, formal, not the way he wanted at all.

Chapter Nine

Hugh walked through the United Services Club. The opulent drawing room with red and gold decor. The library with thousands of books towering on shelves which reached up to the elaborate cornice. The reading room where men sat deeply engrossed in their newspapers, not a sound to be heard other than the rustle of paper. The bar where there were always a few stalwarts laughing over an early evening drink.

'Lord Beakonshire, Lord Beakonshire,' Hugh called out the name in a sing-song voice. He didn't think he was a good singer, but felt he could just about manage to do this, and enjoyed it. He had been working here for almost two years now, and hoped that he would receive training in different departments eventually. He found Lord Beakonshire with a group of other men in a corner of the bar and handed him the message on a small silver salver, bowed sharply, and went back to the reception desk to pick up his next message.

Peter and Hugh read the newspapers from cover to cover in their spare time, and all they talked about was the War. In the streets they were fascinated with the propaganda posters which were hung around the city to attract young men to join the British Army. Some posters listed jobs offering what seemed to be enormous pay. Others called out to their emotions and reminded them to remember Ireland's fighting spirit and enlist.

When he was home, Hugh had wondered about telling his father what he was thinking. He would have given anything to talk to Terence, but knew that his reaction would be an instant refusal to even consider sending one of his sons to fight for England. And his mother had been so proud of him when he had been taken on at the United Services Club, she wouldn't be at all pleased if he decided to leave. It was such a great chance for him, she had reminded more than once.

'When are we going to enlist?' Peter asked when they had finished work and sat talking in the attic dormitory. The long bare room held a row of narrow iron beds covered with grey wool blankets. A large wardrobe stood at one end, and at the other was a washing stand and mirror. The windows had cotton blinds which always had to be pulled down. There were rules in the United Services Club, and none of the young men dare break one.

'Let's go soon,' Hugh said.

Peter's blue eyes were wide with enthusiasm, and his fair hair stuck up in untidy stalks since he had removed his cap.

'I've been thinking I might just leave a letter for my father and mother explaining how I feel,' Hugh said.

Peter pulled a packet of cigarettes from his pocket. He offered one to Hugh. Then he struck a match and they lit up.

On his next half day, he went home as usual. Hugh always looked forward to seeing everybody, and this time was no different. He still hadn't worked through his misgivings about enlisting, and hadn't been able to imagine how he might approach his father and mother. He wanted to make a difference. That was all he knew. To play his part.

In the evening, they gathered together for tea. The younger boys were first, eating bread and butter before being hustled off to bed. Michael, Louise and Hugh sat together with their parents. Terence ate slowly, carefully, and there was no conversation. Just the clink of a knife on a plate, a slurp of tea.

The clock on the mantle ticked, a loud reminder of time passing. Hugh had made up his mind. He would speak to his father tonight. He finished the scrambled egg his mother had cooked. She always managed to put up something good for tea, particularly when he was home. When Michael had left, he tensed and looked at Terence. 'Father?'

'Yes?' He didn't look up, packing the bowl of his pipe with tobacco.

'I want to ask you something,' he said, nervous, staring at Terence's bald pate.

'And what is that?'

He hesitated, aware of his mother and Louise clearing away the dishes, but then decided to plunge in. 'I want to enlist in the army.'

There was a sharp intake of breath from Kathleen.

Terence's head snapped upwards, and his eyes bored into Hugh's. His brow furrowed. He said nothing for a moment, just sat back in his chair, lit the pipe and inhaled. 'In the British Army?'

Hugh nodded.

'You are under age. You must be eighteen to serve in the army, and nineteen to go abroad.'

'But I want to go to war and fight.'

'You'll be annihilated.'

'It's what I want,' Hugh said fervently.

'That goes against our own choice. You're only a boy and you don't understand what's going on.'

'I'm a man.'

'If I say you're a boy, then you are.' Terence crashed his fist on the table.

'I can still join up. They need men now.' Hugh stood.

'How dare you argue with me?'

'It's a pity I have to do that, why can't you just agree with me?'

‘I don’t have to answer that,’ Terence said.

‘You do,’ Hugh insisted.

‘No one tells me what I must do,’ he roared. ‘Least of all you, a skelp of a boy.’ His complexion darkened. Even his bald head shone pink. ‘I never thought I’d see the day when one of my sons would stand up to me, and argue the toss like a guttersnipe. I should take the strap to you.’ His mouth worked. Spit foamed at the corners of his lips. He looked as if he might explode with anger, got up and left the room, marched through the small kitchen and banged the door behind him.

Hugh was left standing there, shocked at his father’s reaction which was far worse than he had imagined.

‘What were you thinking, Hugh, to argue with your father?’ Kathleen asked, her face pale.

‘But I just wanted to explain ...’

‘I know. But your father loves you, he doesn’t want you to go to war, it will break his heart, it will break all our hearts.’ She put her hand across her mouth. Tears glimmered and trickled down her cheeks.

‘I’m going. It’s what I want. Can’t you understand, Mam?’ he begged.

She nodded. A look of resignation on her features.

‘You’re mad, Hugh, do you know what it’s like out there?’ Louise whispered.

‘Of course I do.’

‘You could be killed, do you understand that? Thousands are being mown down every day, blown to bits in the trenches. And many will never come home to put their arms around their mothers or fathers, or sisters or brothers, or say how much they love them, never ...’ her voice broke. ‘And all for England, what a waste.’

He was silent.

‘Don’t go, Hugh, please?’ Kathleen implored.

‘I’m sorry, Mam,’ he muttered.

The club was packed with army and navy servicemen as well as many civilians. There was much discussion and laughter too and a celebratory air about the place. As Hugh worked, he imagined himself wearing one of those uniforms. The brass buttons. The stripes. The smart cap. He was tall and broad for his age and knew that he could pass for eighteen or nineteen, as could Peter.

When they had their evening break, the boys walked through the streets talking about their plans.

'I'm worried that we won't get through. If the recruiting officer asks for our birth certificates then we're finished.' Hugh was downcast.

'They're not asking for them, you just fill in the form and that's it,' Peter explained.

'I wouldn't put it past my father to go down to them and prevent me from joining.'

'He'd never do that.'

'You didn't hear him.'

'Was he mad?' Peter asked, with a grin.

'That's a mild description.'

'My father's normally the same. Lashes the hurley about if he's angry. We have to get out of his way before we catch a wallop. And Mam is in the middle shouting and screaming, it's a regular pantomime,' he laughed, and pulled on his cigarette. 'Although he doesn't seem to mind if I enlist.'

'My father doesn't hit us, but if he was reading you could get a book flung at you. If he really loses his temper you'd certainly know about it. When we were kids we were put upstairs and kept up there until he cooled down. No dinner. No tea. No matter how much we cried.'

'I'm looking forward to getting away,' Peter said.

'So am I. It's exciting. We'll be out there helping the boys to beat the Germans. We have to do our bit. To stay here is cowardly. And we'll get paid much more money than at the Club. We'll have a few bob for once in our lives.'

'Let's go by the Army Recruiting Office, see what's going on.'

They walked down by the side of Trinity College on to Great Brunswick Street.

A crowd of men hung around outside, and a queue straggled through the door of the building.

'There are lots of boys our age. They can't all be nineteen.'

'We look older than many of them.'

They laughed.

'Will we go in?' Hugh looked at Peter.

'Yes, come on.' He walked across the street.

'Have we enough time?'

Peter looked at his watch. 'We've half an hour before we're due back.'

'Let's hope they're not asking too many questions,' Hugh said.

They walked through the crowd of men, and joined the queue. It didn't take too long before they were inside the door and through into an office, each called over to a desk.

'Name?' the burly soldier asked.

'Hugh O'Toole.'

The man wrote on a piece of paper with painstaking care. 'Address?'

'Three forty two, South Circular Road.'

He didn't look up at any point.

'Age?'

'Nineteen.'

He continued on, until finally he slid the sheet around to face Hugh. 'Sign,' he said abruptly, and handed him a pen.

Hugh dipped it in the inkwell and slowly wrote his name. He turned the page around to the soldier again.

'Report here on Monday. Eight o'clock in the morning.'

Hugh straightened up and walked out. Peter was outside, waiting.

They grinned at each other.

'We're in the army,' Peter said, and laughed.

Hugh couldn't believe he had actually done it. A mixture of elation and fear burst through him. His heart beat wildly and there was perspiration on his forehead.

'Roll on Monday.' Peter punched his arm.

'I wonder will we be sent over together?' Hugh asked.

'Don't know. But it would be great to be in the same battalion.'

'I hope so.'

They hurried back to the United Services Club, just there in time.

'We'll have to tell them here that we've enlisted,' Hugh said.

'They're delighted to know of people joining up.'

And he was right. No one queried their ages or anything else, and they were wished well, and told to come back if ever they needed a position again.

'We're soldiers now, away to war,' Peter laughed.

Hugh wrote a letter to his mother and father, apologising that he hadn't told them when he was leaving, but that he loved them both dearly and would miss them very much. He posted the letter on his way to the Army Recruiting Office on that Monday morning.

Chapter Ten

Louise hurried up the back stairs to the first floor. Lady Erskine would be arriving shortly with her family and the suite needed to be checked. There should be nothing out of place. Bouquets of fresh flowers mustn't have a dried petal or a withered leaf in view. God forbid if one had drifted down on a shining surface. She repositioned the cushions on the couches, tweeked the table cloth just a fraction and looked around the rooms until she was finally satisfied that everything was in order.

This was the Shelbourne Hotel. That place in Dublin where anyone who was anyone could be found. Society families. Foreign tourists. Businessmen. Since the beginning of the War, there were parties to say goodbye to those young men going to war. Parties to celebrate others who had come home on leave. Parties for any reason. She locked the door, and continued on down the corridor to the next suite. Brigadier Molyneaux was booked in also and she had to go through the same routine, until all the rooms were up to standard. She glanced at the watch pinned to her uniform to check the time. It was silver and had been given to her as a gift by her aunt just before she died. Louise valued it very much. She took her large bunch of keys and knocked on the door of the next suite. The hotel was fully booked this evening, and there was a shortage of chambermaids, so she had to check the larger suites herself.

'Housekeeping,' she called out, and waited.

'Come,' a voice said from inside.

Louise pushed open the door to see a young woman in the sitting room.

'Madam, is it convenient to check the room now? Or do you wish me to come back later?'

'You can turn down the beds, and pull the drapes. We're going now anyway.'

'Thank you, ma'am.'

There was another woman standing in front of the long mirror in the bedroom, adjusting her hair.

As Louise worked she thought how beautiful the two women looked, such elegance in their clothes and jewellery. There was a sense of envy in her heart.

'Come in and tell me how I look?' The woman in turquoise called of the other.

'Beautiful,' she pronounced, and adjusted a pleat at the back of the evening gown.

'And me?' She twirled, and the silver creation billowed out.

There was a knock on the door.

'That must be them now,' the women giggled, and one rushed to the door to admit two young men, handsome in their evening clothes.

'Good evening, ladies, are we ready?'

They picked up their handbags, took the arms of the men and left.

Louise finished what she was doing and locked the suite. She was surrounded by people of the upper classes every day, and just couldn't imagine how it must be to live like they did.

Normally she didn't actually turn the beds down herself, that was usually done by the maids and she followed to inspect. There was no-one in the next suite and everything was in order. Satisfied, she continued on from floor to floor. The Head Housekeeper, Miss Cunningham, expected her to check everything before she left in the evening.

She looked into the dining room. There was a buzz of chat and a quartet played classical music at the far end of the room. The waiters moved discreetly. Being Assistant to the Head Housekeeper her responsibilities were many and varied. She hurried through to the room adjoining the ballroom. There was a reception before the ball this evening, and a great air of joviality among the guests, everyone trying to forget the War.

Louise was meant to attend a Cumann na mBan meeting this evening, but knew now it was too late, as it was almost ten when she had finished and left the hotel by the side door. At least her mother wasn't expecting her any earlier, but she was disappointed to have missed the meeting.

'Louise?'

A voice cut across her musings, and she looked up to see James Wilson standing in front of her.

He smiled. 'It's very late to be out on your own.'

She explained the reason why.

'Let me walk you home.'

'Do you live near us?'

'It's not too far.'

She wrapped her scarf tighter around her neck.

'Are you cold? Would you like a cup of tea? We might be able to find somewhere still open.'

'No thanks, my mother will be expecting me. If I'm too late, she'll have someone out searching for me.'

'Let's walk.' He held out his arm. She took it.

'I missed my Cumann meeting this evening unfortunately. We were very busy in the hotel.'

'Packed with visitors by the look of it,' he said.

Louise looked back and could see groups of people still coming and going. Carriages were pulled up outside the imposing entrance. Guests climbed out of a shining motor car. She smiled, glad to think someone else could look after them.

'There's a ball on this evening. We were run off our feet. Just as well really, keeps me in a job,' she laughed softly.

'You go to regular meetings of Cumann na mBan?' he asked.

'Countess Markievicz is such a wonder to us all. Firing us up with thoughts of Irish freedom,' she smiled.

'She's an amazing woman.'

'And prepared to fight too if it should come to that.' Her face was animated.

'I don't think we have much of a chance taking on England. But some people feel that if we let the War go by without making a stand, then we might as well give up the hope of achieving independence.'

'My father feels the same way.'

'Some Volunteers who have stayed here want to take a shot at the British. But then there are others who want to wait until the War ends, whenever that will be, and our men return. I'm of that mind myself.'

'I hope I have the courage when the time comes,' Louise said, shivering at his tone.

'You won't be involved.'

'I want to be. We talk about the need to fight the oppressors. To sacrifice ourselves. And we drill and march, we are an army too.' She was aware of being a little over-enthusiastic, but couldn't help herself.

'I don't want you to sacrifice yourself,' he smiled, and moved a little closer.

A thrill burst through her. Did he like her especially, she wondered. Or was his offer to walk her home just politeness because he was a friend of her brother?

'My mother doesn't approve of women being involved, she's very much against it,' Louise admitted.

'My father doesn't approve of my interest in the Volunteers either,' he said.

'What a pair,' she laughed.

They walked along South Circular Road, passing Wellington Barracks on the other side of the road. Soldiers stood guard outside the gates. James looked at Louise, but neither spoke.

She stopped at her front door. 'Thanks for walking me home,' she said, feeling shy.

'Would you like to come out with me one evening?' he smiled.

She stared into his blue eyes. Her pulse raced. She hesitated. Knowing that she would have to receive her parents' permission. 'Yes, I'd like that.'

He grinned broadly. 'Do you have a half day?'

'It varies, and as the Housekeeper is away at the moment, I'm not sure when that will be.'

'What time do you usually finish work?' he asked.

'It's supposed to be eight o'clock, but now tonight it was ten, so it's hard to say.' She felt awkward, hating that she had to make such excuses, and hoped he wouldn't get the impression that she wasn't interested in seeing him again.

'I could meet you tomorrow night after work?'

'That would be nice.'

'I'll see you at the top of Kildare Street, the same place we met tonight.'

'But what if I'm delayed?'

'Don't worry, I'll wait.'

She nodded, and stepped inside.

Immediately her mother's voice echoed. 'Is that you, Louise?'

'I'd better go in,' she said.

'Until tomorrow night,' he smiled.

Chapter Eleven

Mary stood at the stall on Moore Street, and called out the day's offers. Her voice a hoarse croak because of tiredness. She had been up all night with two of her younger children who were now ill. A high fever had taken Emily and Dan, much the same as the baby who had been buried only a few days ago, and their bodies were covered with a red rash. She had left Bridget with them with strict instructions to wipe them down with cold water as often as she could, terrified that it was the scarlet fever. The other children were all right, but she was still worried that they would all catch it.

'Why don't you take them to the hospital?' her mother, Lily, asked, pulling her black shawl around her against the east wind.

'The Union?' Mary snapped.

'They'll look after them.'

'No, they'll never get out of that place, and I could lose them forever.' Mary shook her head. She knew enough about the Union, or the workhouse as it was more commonly known, but for people like her, to go there was a last resort.

'Well, go somewhere else.'

'They'll throw me out.'

'You'll have to do something ...' Lily turned to serve a customer.

Mary busied herself displaying the produce they had for sale. Apples, oranges, pears and all the usual vegetables were at a good price. 'Maybe they might be better when I get home.'

'Say a prayer then.' Lily crossed herself.

People thronged through the street, and the adjoining alleyways, pushing their way among the stalls which flanked each side from Henry Street to Great Britain Street. They had to avoid the horses, carts, donkeys and other animals which were being shunted from one end to the other, forced to place their feet carefully to avoid stepping on the dung which piled up. The smell was pungent.

'How are they?' she asked Bridget the moment she saw her.

The young girl shook her head.

Mary ran to the mattress on which the two usually slept. 'Where is Dan?'

'I moved him inside,' Bridget said, her face ashen.

Mary pushed aside the curtain. Tears filled her eyes as she leaned to take the slight body in her arms and hold the five year old close. Longing for him to open his eyes and smile up at her. 'Dan, wake up love, wake up.' She pressed her lips against his forehead, but there was no response from him, his little body already cold. 'Where's your father?'

'He went to the docks this morning to see if he could get work on one of the ships.'

'Maybe he's been lucky, thanks be to the good God. And where's Robbie and the twins?'

'Gone collecting coal.'

'What will we do about Emily, Bridget, must I take her to the Union?'

Bridget shook her head.

'Maybe we could go to Mercer's, would they look at her?'

'Do that, we can't let her ...' She looked at Dan.

'I'll chance it, they can only throw us out. It's the nearest.'

Little Emily cried.

'Bridget love, will you wash Dan, and get him ready? I'm taking Emily.' She bent down and wrapped the child in a blanket. 'Make some stew and feed yourself and the others and don't forget to leave some for your father.' She stopped in her rush, and pressed her hand on the soft cheek. 'Don't tell them about Dan. Just say he's asleep.'

Mary stood outside the hospital holding Emily. Her heart thumped in her chest as she pushed open the door. At first, the brightness of the place almost blinded her and she hesitated for a moment, but then continued on. In a room off the hall there were a number of people sitting on benches.

A middle-aged man came slowly towards her.

'Where are the doctors?' Mary gasped.

'Down there.' He pointed.

She went that way, and met a young nurse.

'My boy has died and my baby is sick and I must get some medicine for her. Please?' She held Emily out to her.

The nurse stared at the flushed face of the child.

'How long has she been like this?'

'Three or four days.' Tears filled Mary's eyes. 'Help her, I beg you?'

'Wait here,' she opened a door into a small room. 'I'll talk to my superior.' She hurried away.

'You'll be all right, my love, I promise.' Mary hugged Emily. The little one started to wail.

The nurse returned followed by another. She was older, and Mary suddenly had more faith in her. They looked at Emily. The second nurse put something in her mouth, held her wrist and stared at the watch which hung on her uniform.

Mary watched them, full of fear. If they didn't give Emily some medicine soon then surely she would die ...' she tried to control her tears.

The two nurses talked together for a few minutes, then the older woman came over to her.

'I think your child has scarlet fever. She should be in isolation,' she said.

'Is she going to be all right?' Mary asked.

'We don't know.'

They walked away together without another word.

Mary kissed Emily, confused. What was she going to do?

The young nurse came back. 'I'll take her to another ward.' Gently, she took the little girl from Mary. 'She'll be all right,' she said, and smiled. 'Please go out to the Almoner's Office, you will need to fill in an admission form.'

Mary nodded.

She followed the nurse for a bit, and then lost sight of her. She turned back and made her way to the front hall, but then remembered that she had been told to do something. She stood and pondered. A nurse marched past, but then stopped.

'Are you all right?' she asked.

'My child is sick ...the nurse told me to go to an office ...'

'Have you filled in an admission form?'

Mary shook her head.

'Go over to that counter.'

She stood waiting. There was a woman there writing in a large book and she took no notice of Mary. After some time she lifted her head and peered at her. 'Yes?' she asked.

'My Emily is ...'

'Has she been admitted?'

'The nurse took her.'

'Fill in this form.' She slid it towards her.

'I can't, I'm sorry.' Mary felt ashamed.

The woman sighed and pulled it back. 'All right, I'll do it for you. Name?'

Mary gave her the details she wanted, and wandered out of the door, but stood outside, not knowing what to do, which way to turn. Her child was in there and Mary didn't know when she would see her again. Leaning back against the wall she hugged the shawl around her, and thought of little Dan and her other children who lay in Glasnevin Cemetery, and prayed that Emily wouldn't die as well. Tears drifted down her cheeks.

The door opened.

She looked around. It was the young nurse she had met earlier. 'How is my Emily?'

'Don't worry, she's in safe hands.'

'Thank you,' Mary was very grateful to her.

'How many children have you in family?' The young woman asked.

'Six,' she said and then. 'No, five.'

'And where do you live?'

'Cuffe Street.'

'That's close by, isn't it?'

'Up that way,' Mary indicated.

'How are your other children?'

'My little boy died.'

'From the same illness?' She seemed shocked.

Mary nodded.

'Would you like me to look at the others, and see how they are?'

Mary's eyes opened wide with surprise.

'It shouldn't take long.'

Mary couldn't imagine bringing a lady of such standing into her home. Ashamed of the dirt of the house. The smells. The noise. And at this time of the year, the bitter cold. 'My house, the room where we live, isn't very nice ...' Her voice tailed off, she couldn't explain.

'Don't worry.' She patted her arm. 'My name is Anne Montford,' she said.

'Pleased to meet you Miss Mont ...ford,' She found it difficult to get her tongue around the name. 'Sorry, I'm Mary McCabe.'

'Call me Anne.' She shook her hand.

They climbed the stairs. A child cried. There was an argument. It was loud and had the threat of violence in the voices.

'Be careful, miss, mind your footing,' Mary warned.

'I'll be all right,' the nurse said softly.

Two floors up, Mary stopped at their door, and pushed it open. The room was quiet and dark. She took a candle from a shelf inside the door and struck a match. The wick flared, and the place was illuminated somewhat. Mattresses were laid on the floor, children stretched out in sleep.

'They're asleep, and I don't want to disturb them,' Anne said. 'Are any of them feeling ill?'

'I don't think so.' Mary twisted her hands worriedly.

'If I come back tomorrow evening could you keep them up a little later?'

'Yes, nurse,' Mary replied, amazed at the goodness of the woman.

'I'm particularly worried about the younger ones.'

Mary blessed herself.

'Where is the little boy?'

'He's behind there.'

'Can I see him?'

Carrying the candle, Mary led the way around the mattresses and held up the curtain so that the nurse could see Dan.

She looked at the still body in the flickering light, his face pale now, glistening. 'How sad,' she murmured. 'So young.'

She turned to Mary. 'I'll take special care of Emily.'

Chapter Twelve

Anne went home. She had the following day off and was due then to begin her week of night duty. She knew life was hard for the poor in the tenements, but to see how they lived at first hand was shocking to her sensitive nature, and she couldn't get the image of that house out of her mind. Her own upbringing had been very different to the way this family lived, all crowded into one room. To have to endure the cold with hardly any fire in the grate. To sleep on mattresses on the floor without proper bedclothes. The smell of the hallways. The noise of the other people who lived there. And worst of all, the dead child.

By contrast, her own home was a haven. All the lights in the windows were bright. She climbed the steps, unlocked the door with her key and went into the hall. The maid appeared immediately.

'Miss Anne,' she took her coat.

In the drawing room her mother sat with her two sisters. A warm fire leapt up the chimney and the heat was almost unbearable. Anne sat down in a chair by the window.

'Why don't you change out of your uniform?' her mother enquired.

'I think I'll go straight to bed if you don't mind.'

'That job is too much for you,' Eleanor snapped. 'You're exhausted.'

'I am this evening I have to admit.'

'Your father isn't home either.' She sniffed.

At that moment, the sound of the front door banging closed could be heard, and the maid talking with Clarence.

'Ah, he's here at last. Do you want to eat? Cook will prepare something.'

'No, I couldn't ...thank you. I'll talk to Father.' She stood up and left the room, going into his study. 'Heavy case load today?' she asked him, glad to have a chance to chat.

'Yes.' He was going through his papers. 'I'm only home for a short while. Must go back to the hospital later to see a patient. Tricky case.'

'Can I get you anything before you go?' she asked.

'I'll just have a cigar,' he said, with a grin.

They sat talking, discussing the hospitals, the patients, and about the woman Anne had met today, and her children. She was careful not to mention that she had gone to the house, knowing he wouldn't approve.

'I'm worried about some of the poorer people, they live in terrible conditions in the area around the hospital. I see them all the time,' she explained.

'There are huge numbers of people living in overcrowded houses.' Her father took a deep drag of his cigar, and exhaled the scented smoke.

Anne liked the smell. It was so masculine, and would always remind her of Clarence. As a little girl she had spent all her time with him and followed him around in preference to playing with her sisters. She showed no interest in dolls or teddies, or in playing house. No interest in anything but hanging on to his coat-tails. In his study she asked endless questions about his books and papers. What he was doing. Always such a curious child.

'It must be very hard for them to get through their lives with so little,' Anne said.

'You'll see a lot of poverty.'

'Before now I didn't notice. I passed poor people in the streets. Saw children barefoot, hanging out of their mothers, and homeless beggars lying in the wet. But I didn't care, not really, none of us cared. It's only now that it means anything to me. Mother doesn't notice either, or anyone else I know. They're all above it, on some other plane. I hate myself.'

'You'll become more objective. That's all part of being a nurse. You can't let it get to you.'

'I don't want to be objective.'

'You'll never get through otherwise.'

'I will,' Anne said, stubborn.

'All our nurses are objective, but they do excellent work and run our hospitals like an army. We couldn't do without them.'

'No, I suppose not,' she smiled. 'Sorry I'm a bit ...'

'It will be all right, girl.'

'Thank you.' She was surprised at her outburst. But seeing how Mary McCabe and her family lived in Cuffe Street was a shock. 'When I'm qualified I really want to work with the poor rather than people like ourselves,' she said, hesitantly. It was how she felt, deep inside.

'But if you're planning to go on and do medicine, that wouldn't be sensible,' her father cautioned.

'I don't know if I want to do medicine now, I'd prefer to be close to the people.'

'But you can cure them if you become a doctor,' he pointed out.

'Most of them can't afford a doctor.'

'They'll see one at the Union.'

'They're afraid to go to the Union, there's still a huge stigma from those places, they're reminded of the old workhouses,' she tried to explain.

'I can understand how you prefer to help the poor. It's admirable.'

'You do?'

'But I don't think your mother will.'
She looked at him, her eyes worried.
'Let's keep it to ourselves,' he smiled.

Chapter Thirteen

Kathleen picked up the letters on the mat. She flicked through them, glad to see one from her sister in England, and another addressed to Terence and herself in a familiar hand. But she was puzzled. The handwriting was Hugh's, she was quite certain of that, but couldn't understand why he needed to write them a letter. Immediately, she wanted to open it, but as it was addressed to Terence as well she couldn't do that. This was the first post and she would have to wait until he came home in the evening before she could find out what was contained in the letter. She fingered it and a dreadful sense of foreboding swept through her.

She found it hard to hide her anxiety from the children, and was ragged by the time Terence arrived home. The moment he came through the door, she handed him the letter. He stared at it.

'Who's this from?'

'Hugh.'

He said nothing, just tore it open and pulled out the single sheet of paper. He read through it quickly and then twisted it in his fist.

'What?' Kathleen gasped.

'He's gone.'

She sank into a chair and burst into tears.

Terence went out the back door and banged it behind him.

It took a while before she managed to gather herself, mopping up tears which continued to fall no matter how hard she tried to control her emotions. She stood at the range and prepared the tea.

'Where's Father?' One of the boys asked.

'In the shed,' she said.

'I'll go out.'

'No, leave him be.'

Terence didn't come in. After a while she went out and knocked on the wooden door of the shed. This was Terence's own domain, his retreat, a place where he could spend time on his woodwork, a hobby he really enjoyed.

'Would you like something to eat?'

'No,' he grunted.

Kathleen waited up for him that night. But when he came in there was no conversation and he went straight to bed. This was a harsh cross for him to bear, for all of them.

The following day she went to the Army Recruiting Office. She walked down Great Brunswick Street, keeping to the opposite side. But she was suddenly startled as a fire brigade swung into the street from the station and roared past her, firemen hanging on, the bell clanging as it raced to a fire. She stared in shock and blessed herself.

There were a lot of men standing around in groups outside the building, and a queue through one door. Soldiers stood to attention. Kathleen actually felt afraid as she approached, and stopped. She would have to cross the street, and make her way through them, and that was daunting as there wasn't another woman in sight. Confused, she gripped the handle of her umbrella with her gloved hand, and now didn't know what to do as it occurred to her then that if it became known to the army that Hugh had lied about his age, it might only get him into trouble. He could be arrested, imprisoned, and maybe even hung. Anything could happen. Tears moistened her eyes as she bent her head and walked away. There was nothing to be done. Her boy had left her.

Terence continued to be out of sorts and everyone in the family suffered as a result. Kathleen warned them that they should keep their mouths shut, and no answering back if Terence was there, but it was hard on the children. Edward loved to help him in his shed where he carved wooden animals out of any bits of wood he could pick up. Now the boy spent his time outside the shed door, playing with the two little horses Terence had made for him. When he was out of sight, Kathleen knew immediately where she would find him.

'Edward, come in, it's cold.'

'Waiting for Pa.'

'He's not home yet.'

'He's in the shed.'

'No, Ed, not yet.'

The boy stood up and knocked on the door. There was no reply.

'It's time to go to bed.' Kathleen took him by the hand, feeling sorry for him.

That night Terence came in after attending a Volunteer meeting. For the first time this week, he sat in his usual chair. The younger children were all in bed, and Michael and Louise were out as well.

'How was your meeting?' Kathleen asked.

'We're planning the rally for St. Patrick's Day.'

'That will be a big demonstration.'

'Yes, and we want every last man out, and looking spick and span too, every button shining.'

'I'll check your uniforms.'

'Do that ...' he hesitated. 'Thanks Kathleen.'

'I'll get them out now.' She stood up.

'I'm sorry for being so ...' He looked shamefaced.

'Don't worry, I know it's hard on you.'

'I can see there's little point in taking it out on all of you.'

She put her arms around him. There was silence. A moment of reconciliation between them. It wasn't often they disagreed over anything, but there was a great sense of relief in Kathleen, she couldn't have managed to get through each day without the support of her man.

She was very upset that Hugh had gone to the War. What possessed him to leave his good job and enlist? The question echoed in her head over and over and she had no answer. Already she imagined her dear son being blown to bits on the fields of France or Flanders. She had never heard the sound of gunfire but was certain it must be dreadful, and knew very well about the terrible conditions of the trenches. She had a horrible vision of her own boy being lost out there, and deeply regretted that she hadn't an opportunity to make sure he was well kitted out when he set off.

The following day she took out her wool bag, and began to knit socks and gloves for Hugh, and any of the other boys with him. It became an obsession with her. Something which she managed to squeeze into her busy day looking after everyone in the house, cooking, cleaning, and doing all the other domestic chores.

Every day she waited for the post anxiously, praying for another letter from Hugh. Where was he? What was he doing now? Were the army looking after him? She often picked up the family photograph on the mantel which had only been taken last year. Tears always filled her eyes when she kissed the glass, praying her boy hadn't grown cold without her, and that she would have him back home soon, the most affectionate of all her children.

Chapter Fourteen

Louise lay in bed that night. She couldn't sleep. Her heart beat fast, and her imagination painted pictures of a life with James Wilson. A life? The question was stark. How could she think that his simple request to meet again had to be anything more? But in spite of that logic, her mind still took her to places she had only ever dreamed of in secret moments. She thought of the arguments with her mother about finding a husband, but since meeting James she had changed her mind about that. She couldn't understand herself. What was this emotional turmoil she felt now? She turned in the narrow bed. As the only girl in the family she had the luxury of her own room, and she loved that. She sat up and pulled the blue satin eiderdown around her, the soft fabric was smooth on her skin and comforting.

She moved close to the window, pulled back the curtain which hung near the bed, and stared out into the night. A huge full moon shone down out of the dark sky, and caught the silvery edges of frost which clung to surfaces. Dark shadows transformed the sharp lines of the shed and the privy, the leafless branches of the tree thrown in relief over the area, creating a strange alien place. She looked up. A million stars twinkled. In the room it was bright as day, and Louise felt suddenly that the world was full of promise.

She slept eventually, even in that intensity, and awoke to hear the sound of footsteps on the stairs, and her mother's rap on the door as she passed. She climbed out of bed immediately. She would see James this evening. Her heart leapt in excitement, but then a dampening of her enthusiasm. There had been no opportunity to tell her mother and father about him, and now wasn't the time. Hugh's enlistment in the British Army had upset everyone in the family. Kathleen fussed even more than usual and her father was very quiet, so she decided to say nothing until she could speak to both her parents together. Perhaps it would be good to wait until this evening, and James had met her as he promised.

At the Shelbourne, carriages and motor cars constantly arrived and departed, leaving their passengers in the capable hands of the porters who ushered them inside to the reception staff who would take care of their needs. The foyer was packed.

Louise had served her time in all sections of the hotel over the years. Beginning in the kitchen and working her way up to Assistant Head Housekeeper. It had been a lot of hard work but she was always confident and certain she could do the job. Her one wish was to make Head Housekeeper. That would be the height of her career, and she wanted it above all, but she was aware that it could be many years before that might happen, if ever.

The day dragged, her thoughts with James in his office. She wondered was he thinking of her, and looking forward to seeing her. Her mind took her with him into private places. Quiet. Intimate. Lost in some wonderful world of love.

She finished work on time and spent a few minutes in the staff cloakroom redoing her hair and positioning her hat. She was nervous now. Very much so. She left and walked outside and saw him immediately standing just a little way down the street.

'Louise?' There was a broad smile on his face. 'It's lovely to see you.' He took her hand and held it tight.

She was taken aback. Surprised at his enthusiasm, and also that he was actually waiting for her as he had promised.

'I'm glad you finished work on time, although it wouldn't have mattered if you had been delayed.'

'I was lucky to get away this evening.'

'Would you like to have something to eat, are you hungry?'

'I can't, I'm afraid. I had no chance to ask my parents about us, so I'll be expected home.'

'Pity,' he said, softly. 'Do you think they will agree to our walking out together?'

'I'm certain it will be all right, although you will be the first boy.' She could feel herself blush, embarrassed at such an admittance.

'I don't mind that, in fact it's nice to think that there have not been many before me.'

'What did you expect? Did you imagine that there might have been a long string of boys coming to our door?' she could feel a bubble of laughter explode inside.

'Of course not.'

She laughed, unable to hold it in any longer.

'Are you teasing me?'

'A little.'

'Minx.' He pushed his arm through hers and covered her gloved hand with his own. 'I suppose we had better walk on, if you're late I'll be in the bad books of your parents, and then we'll have no chance at all.' They walked along two sides of St. Stephen's Green, up Harcourt Street, and on towards South Circular Road. They talked of their lives. Of the little things, and the big things too. Most important being their political views.

'Will you be at the Volunteer rally on St. Patrick's Day?' he asked.

'Of course I will, if I can get the time off.'

'I'll definitely be there, it's very important.'

'You're lucky, I couldn't tell anybody at the Shelbourne. They'd be shocked. To be involved in a women's political group is just not acceptable. A lot of the staff at the hotel are foreign, and come from various parts of Europe. They wouldn't have any understanding of our aims.'

'I'm a member of the IRB,' he said slowly. 'I feel I should tell you, before ...'

She nodded. 'Father and Michael are members too.'

'If we could only see into the future, how much easier it would be,' he said, with a grin.

'We're two very small cogs in a big wheel,' said Louise. 'What will happen will happen, and we'll have no control over it.'

'We'll obey orders, whatever is decided by the High Committee.'

'Do you really think there will be a rebellion?' Getting to know this man, Louise wanted his opinion.

'To be honest, I don't know. Your father mentioned plans being made but I'd prefer to have Home Rule by peaceful means, in the long run it would be better for the country.'

As the night was cold, they had instinctively hurried. Their feet moving in rhythm. Although she didn't want to arrive home, didn't want to leave him.

'Hallo James, Louise?' There were footsteps behind them.

'Michael?' She turned around to see her brother.

'Thought I recognised you.' He drew abreast.

'James is seeing me home,' she said awkwardly, trying to loosen the grip James had on her arm, but he wasn't letting her go.

Michael grinned, and raised his eyebrows. 'Something going on here?'

'I wouldn't mind if there was,' James said.

Louise blushed. She said nothing. But was annoyed with Michael for passing the remark. It was none of his business.

'Don't worry, I'll keep your secret,' he said, and winked at her.

'There's no secret,' she retorted furiously.

'Don't know about that, you seem to be very anxious to deny it.'

'Mick, stop, don't tease your sister,' James intervened.

'I don't need anyone to fight on my behalf,' she snapped and glared at James.

The two men glanced at each other.

'Louise, I'm sorry, I shouldn't have said that.' James turned to her.

'Our Louise is a very independent young lady,' Michael said, laughing.

She glowered. Rage swept through her. The evening was spoiled since her brother had arrived. And it wasn't up to James to take Michael on. It was her place to spar with him. There was a friendship between the two of them which excluded her, and she didn't like that. The look which passed between them angered her.

They continued walking in silence. Sullen, Louise stared at the odd pedestrian coming towards them. Had an inordinate interest in the occupants of carriages which clattered by. She turned her head to stare into the distance but all the time she was very aware of James. They still linked arms. She hadn't the courage to remove hers, in case it caused another remark to be made by Michael. The hot surge of fury in her heart subsided a little and she regretted her outburst. Why was it that she couldn't control her impetuous nature. There was always some consequence of her thoughtless words which she had to address and apologise to whoever had been the target of her venom.

Soon they would arrive at the house and she wondered what would happen then. Would she have to go down on bended knee to the two of them and ridicule herself. No. Immediately that possibility was cast aside. Let them apologise to her. But then she realised that James had already done that, and it had been swallowed up by Michael's following remark. But still she couldn't look at him, unforgiving.

'Finglas is arranged for Sunday manoeuvres, will you be there?' Michael asked James.

'Yes.'

'I'm looking forward to it.'

James nodded.

The house was just a hundred yards away. Louise dreaded the moment when she would have to turn to face James and was unable to think of what she would say. She was counting her footsteps now, her eyes on the ground ahead as they passed neighbouring houses. The Roches. The McGinleys. They came to a halt.

'See you tomorrow, James.' Michael pushed open the gate, and walked up to the front door.

James turned to Louise. Their arms parted. She stared into the middle distance of front gardens which stretched away along the street.

'I'm so sorry for upsetting you, Louise, I shouldn't have spoken to Michael in that way. Can you forgive me?' He looked at her, his blue eyes concerned.

For the first time, she raised her head. A glimmering steel hardened her heart. 'I must go in.'

'Louise?'

'Goodnight.' She walked up the pathway, pushed open the door and went inside.

Chapter Fifteen

Mary McCabe walked through the wet streets. There was no let up in the heavy rain and wind but she had almost become used to the discomfort. Her shawl hung heavy around her shoulders, boots squelched, and the water had seeped up into her skirt which flapped around her ankles.

The house was a large imposing residence on a corner of Mount Street. She hesitated, always daunted by such opulence, and had to force herself to go around and knock on the side door. There was no reply at first and she tried again, harder this time, feeling so self-conscious standing here in the light of the gas lamp, afraid someone would notice and ask her what she was doing. After a time, the door was opened by a thin weedy man who stared at her unsmiling. She knew him by his title, although she didn't know his name. Not that it was important. He was the *money-lender*.

'Yes?' he said, his voice low. He glanced past her, and to each side.

'I want a loan,' Mary said, hating to be in this position. She watched him, detested him, but needed him. He bled the people dry. Once you were in his clutches he never let you go. His men came around and demanded payment every week. If a person couldn't repay the money, which increased with interest, vicious bully-boys would take anything in the house that could be sold and left the people destitute. She had paid up in total at Christmas and had resisted the temptation to take out another loan when one of the men came around and offered her more money.

'I need a shilling.'

'That all?' he sneered.

She nodded, anxious to get away from his obnoxious presence.

He took a notebook and a stub of pencil from inside his jacket. He licked the lead. 'Name?'

'McCabe.'

'Address?'

'Nine, Cuffe Street.'

He rooted in his pocket and handed her the coin.

'Thanks.'

He banged the door in her face.

She hurried home. There was something else she had to do tonight.

'Just a small box, Dick, he's only five,' she said softly, the enormity of it all only beginning to dawn on her now.

'Aye, Mary, surely.'

'Maybe you might have a few pieces of wood you could nail together, I don't want anything fancy.' Tears flooded her eyes.

He tipped his hat in respect. 'Let me see.' He went around to the back of the workshop which was filled with half-finished stools, tables, chairs, and other bits and pieces of wood. In a corner a couple of coffins were stacked one on top of the other.

Mary drew her eyes away from them.

He came back carrying some lengths. 'Let me see if I can make up something for you.' On the work bench he laid them out. Mary couldn't see how he would manage with what he had, but in a matter of minutes something resembling an oblong box began to take shape.

'Thanks,' she whispered.

He worked rapidly, nailing the pieces together, his hammer flying. After a short time he was finished.

'That's grand,' she murmured. 'How much do I owe you?' She took the shilling from her pocket, praying that it was enough.

'Mary, I only used some leftovers, tuppence will do. I'm sorry for your trouble, I know your boys from playing around.'

'Thank you very much, Dick.' She couldn't believe he had charged her so little, and was very grateful to him.

'Go on now, can I help you carry it?' He counted out the change.

'No thanks, but I'll come back with the pram.' She took his hand and clasped it tight. 'I'll say a prayer for you.'

'I need a few of them.'

'You deserve the very best in life.'

He opened the door. The night yawned dark and stormy. 'I'll take the coffin around for you, it's too bad to come out again.'

'I couldn't put you to that much trouble.'

'I'll get my coat on.' He disappeared around the back and came back muffled up.

Together they walked the short distance. At the door he handed her the box. 'You watch yourself now, Mary.'

'Thank you.'

'It's nothing,' he said.

She carried the box upstairs. The children were all asleep, huddled together on the mattresses. In the quiet she could hear their breathing, Robbie coughed, the cinders in the grate glowed and shifted, but there was little heat. She picked up an old page of newspaper and held it in front of the fireplace, hoping the draught would get the fire going again. When it glowed brighter she piled on the small amount of slack in the bucket. Then she heard a scrabbling noise from a corner, and went over to a hole in the floor and stuffed a rag into it, cursing the rats which gnawed their way through anything she managed to push down. Her mother always said broken glass was the best thing, but fearing that one of the children might cut themselves, Mary wouldn't do that.

On the bed behind the curtain, was her child. She lifted him up and held him to her breast for a moment, kissing the little face, longing for him to make some response to her touch, but his body was stiff and cold. Gently she put him into the crude coffin and touched his dark curly hair with her hand. Her tears were hot, but not hot enough to bring him back to life. He was gone from her to another place.

Dick had hammered some nails around the edge of the top and she took a metal rod she used to clean out the fire and banged the nails into position. The coffin was closed now and she would never see her boy again.

Lar came back late, singing a song as he thumped unsteadily up the stairs, and pushed the door open. Mary put her finger to her lips, but he took no notice and stood by the fire. He was dirty. His clothes and body covered with soot after a day unloading coal on the quayside.

'Not very warm,' he grunted.

'It'll take up soon.'

'Is there any food?'

'I'll heat some stew for you.'

'I expect it to be ready,' he retorted.

She put the pot which contained what was left of the stew on the trivet, and covered it. 'Dan died.'

He stared at her. 'When?'

'Earlier today.'

'Where is he?'

'Inside.'

He pushed the curtain back and stood looking at the coffin on the bed. 'I won't be able to go to the cemetery, I'm hoping to get a second day on the coal boat.'

'I'll take him.'

After he had eaten, he shambled through the curtain, moved the coffin to one side of the bed, and then without another word he lay down and closed his eyes. Before Mary slept, she threw her old coat over the coffin so the children wouldn't notice it in the morning, then draped her shawl and skirt on the chairs in front of the fire to dry.

Chapter Sixteen

James turned away from Louise's house and walked down the road. He was reeling after what had happened, and blamed himself entirely. How could he have been so stupid? The relationship between Michael and himself was light-hearted, and they constantly bantered and sparred with each other, without ever a thought of offence being taken by either one or the other. But women were sensitive beings, he thought, and even more so nowadays.

Louise's passion for Cumann na mBan, and the Volunteers showed that she was a very independent person, as Michael had said. And that was what James liked about her. To have an understanding of what they were all about was so refreshing. Now he didn't know what he was going to do. Had Louise lost interest in him so quickly? Had he imagined that there was anything at all between them in the first place?

He walked home in a vague way, not seeing anyone. Filled with dread that this desire would take over and he would be left unfulfilled. How was it possible to feel so strongly about a person he had only just met? He stood on the bridge. Leaned over and stared down into the slow moving water of the Liffey. It was murky, and the street lights were reflected. It didn't smell good and was as dark as his own soul. He walked on, still angry at himself and Michael. At home he went to his room immediately, he couldn't have faced anyone.

He closed his eyes. Louise took hold of his mind, his deepest self, a part of him that he hadn't known before. He longed to be with her again, to know, to find, so disappointed that their brief journey was cut short so abruptly.

He didn't sleep well, and got up very early. Somewhere in the night, he had vacillated between going to see Louise as soon as he could, or staying away altogether. He wanted her, desired her, tortured by his emotions but couldn't bear her rejection.

At work he spoke with Michael as normal and gave no sign of the pain inside him. They had lunch at a local park and ate their sandwiches while reading the newspaper.

'Sorry about last night, James,' Michael said as they packed up.

'Don't worry,' James didn't look at him.

'Louise will come down off her high horse, she always does. Next time you see her it will be as if it never happened.'

He couldn't believe that Michael was so blasé about it, and wasn't able to think of an appropriate reply.

'Are you keen on her?' Michael asked, with a grin.

James nodded.

'Thought as much. Can't keep much hidden from a brother,' he roared with laughter.

'It's not funny,' James knew he sounded churlish.

'Take it easy. Do you want me to arrange a meeting with her?'

'No, I can do that myself.'

'Then just go ahead. I'll hide in the bushes and be there to give you both a little push in the right direction,' he laughed again.

'What about your parents? Do you think they'll approve?'

'Yes. See no problem there.'

A sense of relief stole over James. Michael's light-hearted attitude took away the anxiety which had dominated him since last night. He had gone overboard, he decided. If Louise liked him at all, then surely a small tiff wouldn't separate them before they had even got started?

That night he was waiting outside the Shelbourne Hotel again. He didn't know what he would say, other than to apologise once more and hope that she would forgive him. Reminding himself that if she didn't want to have anything to do with him then he would have to accept that. It was a clear night, and he watched the door she normally used. The streets were busy. Carriages passed. An occasional motor car. It had been raining earlier but it had stopped now. A young boy pulled at his coat, and held out his hand. He looked down at him.

'I'm hungry, mister, got a halfpenny?'

James put his hand in his pocket and took out some change. He gave the boy a penny. His eyes lit up in the thin dirt-streaked face, and he ran quickly out of sight. Aware that he had taken his attention away from the door, James looked quickly in that direction, excitement sweeping through him when he saw Louise. A couple of people walked between them and he waited until she came closer.

'Louise ...' he called.

She stopped and stared at him.

He stood in front of her. 'Louise, I just want to say how sorry I am about last night, I hope you'll forgive me.' He waited for her response, very anxious.

'I must apologise to you, I really regret what happened, will you forgive me?' She seemed apprehensive, and her expression showed every bit of that.

He smiled. 'Of course, you don't need to ask me that, if you only knew ...I thought I'd never see you again.'

'I was the same, hating myself for flying off the handle. It's my bad temper, I just can't control it.'

'I'll be more careful of what I say in future,' he promised.

'I think we have to say what we say and hope for the best. Otherwise we'll be too stilted and it would be unnatural,' she smiled for the first time.

'This is such a relief, I can't believe it.' He took her hand.

'For me too, I couldn't even sleep last night.'

'What a pair. Let's decide never to let that happen again. So we'll argue, express ourselves as we wish, but we won't go home in anger.'

They continued on, talking about what had happened in their lives that day. The crowds staying at the Shelbourne were a source of little snippets of gossip. Louise described the panic when something went wrong and one of the guests hadn't received exactly what they ordered. 'They get into such a tizzy over the smallest thing. A woman lost an umbrella and demanded that we send for a constable. It took a deal of pacifying to calm her down, and I found the dreaded thing under the chair. The children run wild. Up and down the stairs with the nannies chasing after them, hiding in corners, under tables, you can't imagine what it's like.'

'Sounds fun. Much more interesting than my dull day.'

'Michael seems to enjoy working at the firm.'

'We get on well, and it's very busy. No more than yourself.'

They fell into a relaxed silence as they came up to Kelly's Corner.

'Since last night, Louise, I feel ...' he hesitated. Not sure whether he should tell her exactly what was in his heart at this point.

She didn't say anything.

'Did you ask your parents about me?'

'I had no chance yet,' she said softly.

'I hope they approve.' He reached across and kissed her on the cheek.

'James,' she rebuked but laughed at the same time. 'We're in public. Let's hope no-one spotted us.'

'Don't care,' he said.

Chapter Seventeen

Bridget went to the market for Mary the following morning, and bought the vegetables and fruit they would need for the stall. The rain had eased. Lar went to the docks. Having some time to spare, Mary scrubbed down the room. The walls. The floors. The fireplace. She shook out the bedclothes made out of flour bags, and an old tattered eiderdown her mother had given her. She poured the last of the tea in the pot. It was strong, black, and went down a treat. There was just a half piece of bread left and she ate that dry, and felt better able to face the day.

About half past nine, she wheeled out the pram on to the landing.

'Mary, what are you doing here at this time?' her neighbour, Tilly, asked, as she passed her door.

'I'm taking Dan to the cemetery, he's ...' she lowered her head.

'Sorry for your trouble.' Tilly blessed herself.

Another neighbour overheard, and did the same thing. They were sympathetic, but every one of them had been in the same position over the years. There was little to be said, nothing to be done, a child's loss was sad, but normal.

Mary brought the pram stair by stair into the entry below. Then went back up, and carried down her child in his coffin to begin his last journey from home.

More women had gathered by then, and their children gazed with big eyes as she passed by. She put the small box on the pram and walked to Whitefriar Street Church, pushing it down the aisle to the front seat and sat there waiting for the priest. When he came out to prepare the altar, she went over.

'Father Kennedy?'

'Yes, Mary,' he smiled.

'My Dan's died,' she indicated the coffin. 'Could you bless him?'

'Of course, Mary. Bring the pram closer to the altar steps and we'll say mass for him. I'll make a note of his name in the register.'

'Thank you so much, Father.' She felt so grateful to him, but it was difficult to express it in words. He was a lovely priest and she had known him since she married Lar and liked him. When the rest of the congregation arrived, he came out on to the altar dressed in his vestments. Mary knelt, listened to the words he spoke, but had no understanding of Latin. But still she liked the sound. That this mass was especially for Dan meant everything to her. Her darling boy was already in Heaven with little Olive and her other children who had died. The priest splashed Holy Water on the coffin, and said the prayers. Afterwards, some of the congregation came up to her and expressed their condolences.

She made her way to the cemetery. It took some time to walk the distance, but eventually she arrived and spoke with the man in charge of graves.

'A pauper's grave?' he said, roughly.

'We have no money.'

'You'll have to pay the grave digger.'

'How much is that?'

'You can do the deal with him, go up there to the back.'

She walked past the rows of headstones. Mary couldn't imagine how expensive it would be to have one of those stones for their own family. There would be nothing standing over their graves, no one would know who was in the ground, they would be lost forever.

In a large open area a couple of men were digging. She went up to them. 'I have to bury my child.'

The men came over. They looked at the coffin.

'How much will it be to bury him?' Mary asked.

'Only a child ...' One looked at the other. 'How much have you got?'

'Ten pence.'

'Six pence will do.'

'Thank you.'

One of the men lifted the coffin and carried it over to where they were working. They dug down into the earth, lifting shovelfuls of dark brown earth to one side, until Mary could only see the tops of their heads. Her heart was broken for all of her children who were buried in this place, and she prayed for them and all of the other people here too.

The man scrambled up, took the coffin and handed it to the other who laid it down. None too gently, in Mary's opinion. They climbed out then, and began to fill in the grave. That harsh sound of earth and stones clattering on wood echoed. She blessed herself, and whispered a decade of the Rosary. A final goodbye to her little Dan.

She paid the men, and thanked them. Then she turned and walked away, anxious to leave this place of death.

Mary went straight in to Moore Street from the cemetery. She found it hard to chat to customers, thinking about poor little Dan lying in the cold earth in Glasnevin. Business on the stall hadn't been as brisk as usual because of the damp weather, but the normal contingent of regulars still arrived sheltering under umbrellas to choose whatever they needed quickly before rushing away again. Mary's voice was hoarse from shouting out their offers to attract customers. But they still managed to make a few pence each and as usual she bought some pieces of scrag end. Always the same thing, day in, day out. How nice it would be to eat something else, Mary thought, but reminded herself that she was lucky to have stew, very lucky.

Today she had to buy flour as well and that took the rest of it. She still had the four pence left over from the money she borrowed, and while she was very tempted to use it for coal or other things they needed, her sensible side warned that if she could hold on to it then it would go a big way towards paying back the loan. The moneylender's man would be there every Friday night, hand out for his penny, for the next twenty-four weeks.

When she arrived home, the children met her at the front door of the house.

'Get in out of the rain, you'll all get your death.' She hunted them into the hallway.

'Mam, we found some wood around the back,' Robbie said, excited.

'Where?'

'We'll show you, come on.' They ran out.

'Get back in here,' she yelled, but they took no notice and she had to follow them out of the house and down a nearby lane. They ran ahead of her, jumping across deep puddles, into a derelict area where there was an old house in a bad state of repair. They went to the back gate which had already been broken in places, and Robbie squeezed through a gap. The other children waited to follow his lead.

'Stop, you can't be going in there.' Mary held on to them.

'Mam, we were in before,' they protested.

She peered through the gap into the back yard of the house, but could see little in the darkness. 'Where has Robbie gone?'

'He's gone into the kitchen, he found a way in.'

Mary waited nervously.

'Mam?' Robbie put his head through the gap in the gate.

'Did you break in there?'

'No, it's always like this, but the dog is gone.'

'What dog?' She pulled her shawl over her head, her dark hair, prematurely streaked with silver, was soaked by now.

'There's always been a big dog here and we couldn't get in.'

'You can't break into places, the police will throw you in jail.'

'But there's all these bits of wood lying around outside the kitchen, if we could get something to carry it we'd have a great fire.' He held out a length of wood which looked as if it came from an old door. 'I'll go back and get the pram.'

'You will not, come out of there now. I've always told you not to be stealing. Let's go home.'

'But Mam, it will be so warm if we burn the wood?'

'All right, then, just take as much as you can carry, but hurry about it.' Although she knew it was wrong, she couldn't resist.

Robbie grinned. Threw out the wood on to the ground and disappeared inside again.

That night they had stew to eat, and fresh bread which Mary had baked. Most of all, they were warm. It didn't take much to make them happy.

'Now, I don't want you going around there again. You'll be picked up and never seen again,' she warned.

They giggled among themselves.

'I'm going out to Mercer's now,' Mary said. 'I've to meet the nice nurse.'

'Will you bring Emily back?' Bridget asked.

'I don't know, but I'll take some food over for her.' She poured some of the stew into a tin cup. Cut a slice of bread and wrapped it in a piece of cloth. 'No-one is to go to bed, and

Bridget, will you tidy up the place, and say the Rosary while I'm gone.'

Mary hurried downstairs. Passed a couple of her neighbours standing in a doorway chatting. There were some very young children still playing around the entry, and she thought that they should be in their beds. However poor Mary was, she looked after her children as well as she could, and made sure they behaved themselves. No hanging around late at night. Always at school on time. What little clothes they had were patched admittedly, but were as clean as she could get them. But what were they up to when she couldn't see them, she wondered. Children will be children, but stealing? She was aghast. But then realised that she was guilty too. She crossed herself and said the Act of Contrition.

It was raining again. Mary felt embarrassed stepping into the hall of the hospital, her footsteps leaving wet impressions on the shining floor. There was a different woman at the counter, and Mary went over, and stood there wiping the water which dribbled on to her forehead from her shawl. The woman didn't look up. Doctors walked past. Nurses wearing crisp white cotton aprons, and stiff little caps swished by. Eyes glanced her way, but she was ignored.

'Yes?' the woman's voice was sharp.

Mary immediately felt sure she was in the wrong place. 'My child, Emily, is here and I want to see her.'

'What is the name?'

'McCabe.'

She opened a large ledger. Her finger went down a list. 'She's in isolation.'

'How is she?' Mary asked. She didn't know what *isolation* meant.

'How do I know?' The eyebrows were raised. The hair dipped in a sharp widow's peak.

'Where is she?'

'I told you, she's in isolation.'

'Can I go there? I've brought some dinner for her,' she explained.

'They won't let you in. Anyway visiting time is over.'

'When is that?' Mary was beginning to feel desperate. Was she ever going to see Emily?

'Two to three.'

She was confused.

Another person came up to the desk, and engaged the woman in conversation.

Mary stood there, wanting to shout out loud and demand to see her child. But she stayed silent and decided to wait and ask the nurse when she met her. There was no budging this woman.

She went outside and stood a little to one side trying to shelter from the rain.

There were a lot of people coming in and out of the hospital and she kept her eyes on the door, hoping she wouldn't miss the girl. But she needn't have worried, Anne arrived a short time later and immediately called out to her.

'Mrs. McCabe?'

Mary smiled.

'How are you?' She pushed up an umbrella and held it above them.

'I'm all right, but it's Emily I'm worried about. The woman in there wouldn't let me in.'

'It's because she's in isolation.'

'I don't understand what that means, could you tell me?'

'That means she's on her own in a room because her illness is infectious.'

Mary put her hand to her lips, very concerned.

'That means others may catch it,' Anne explained.

'How is she?'

'She's doing well, but it will be another few days before she's turned the corner.'

'When can she come home?'

'I'm not sure.'

Mary crossed herself and whispered a prayer in her heart.

'She's getting good care and that's the main thing,' Anne said, comfortingly. 'Now will we go to your home and check the rest of the children?'

'Can you?' Mary could hardly believe this was actually happening.

'Of course, come on.' They walked quickly, Mary enjoying the luxury of an umbrella, something she had never had before.

They climbed the staircase. Small ragged children still hung around. Mary pushed open her own door, relieved to see all the children kneeling around the fire which burned brightly. They were just finishing the Rosary and reciting the Hail Holy Queen.

'Come in, miss,' she said, reluctant to interrupt the prayers by speaking too loudly.

'Thank you, and call me Anne,' she smiled.

Mary nodded and smiled back. 'Anne, would you like to sit down? Can I get you a cup of tea?' she offered.

'No, thank you, I'll be having something to eat later.'

Relief flooded Mary when she thought of the collection of cups she had to offer such a lady.

The Rosary was finished. The children blessed themselves and stood up silently.

'This is Miss Anne, and she is a nurse. My eldest girl, Bridget.' She bobbed respectfully. 'And Robbie, my best boy. And all my other little darlings. This is Brendan, and the twins Maureen and Peggy.' Two little girls, about seven, hid behind Bridget. The boys shuffled awkwardly. 'Stand out there in a line and let Miss Anne look at you.' Shyly they lined up each one wearing a flour bag nightshirt.

'I'm only a trainee nurse, and I don't know very much. But tell me, have any of you got a sore throat?'

They shook their heads.

'Stick your tongues out for me?'

They did as she asked.

Anne looked closely at them. 'Have you noticed the rash on any of them, Mary?'

'No, only on Emily and Dan.'

'The children look well,' Anne said, smiling. 'I think they're all right.'

'Thanks be to God,' Mary made the sign of the Cross. 'Say thank you to the lady,' she said.

'Thank you, lady,' the children chorused, wide smiles on their faces.

'Bed now.' Obediently they went to the other side of the room and climbed on the mattresses.

'I can't thank you enough, you're very good to us.' Mary was grateful to this woman who seemed like a saint come down from Heaven.

'The children look to be in good health, although they are malnourished and underweight,' Anne said.

'That's a blessing,' Mary said, although she didn't really understand the words the nurse used, but was glad to hear that the children were all right.

'I suppose money is a problem. Does your husband have a job?'

'He had a day's work yesterday, and today, and that means we'll have a few pence, but sometimes there is no work.' She shrugged, despondent. 'But I work on a stall in Moore Street with my mother and sister, so I get enough vegetables to feed us, and buy a bit of meat for Lar, but there's the rent and other things too.'

'Life is hard then?'
Mary nodded.

Chapter Eighteen

James's feelings for Louise, which had exploded since meeting her that first night, had rushed him into a strange new place of elation. He loved her. This was the girl he wanted to marry.

After he had left her last night he had walked home in a dream. She dominated his mind, his soul, and he remembered the touch of her skin on his lips when he kissed her. It was delicious. And her laughing beautiful face told him she enjoyed it too. Now his senses were intensified, he couldn't wait for her to appear.

She was late. He checked his watch. Ten minutes. Fifteen minutes. He grew frustrated. Had she left by another door? He folded down the umbrella he carried worried if perhaps she had not recognised him and passed by. He didn't care about the rain. Twenty minutes. Panic surged within him, and he imagined she didn't want to meet him again or that her parents had forbidden her to have anything to do with him. Twenty-five minutes. His heart darkened.

And then suddenly, with a sense of wonder, he saw her come through the door and he walked quickly towards her. 'Louise?'

'I'm sorry, I was delayed.'

'It's of no matter, I'm just glad to see you.' He felt awkward, longing to put his arms around her and press his lips on hers, but held himself back.

'As usual, there was a dinner this evening, and a lot of guests, I had to check everything before I left,' she explained with a little smile of apology.

'It's not too late. Do you have to rush home or can we spend some time together?' he asked, hesitant. Although that wasn't the question he wanted to ask.

'Yes, I think we could ...' her eyes twinkled.

'Have your mother and father agreed to us walking out together ...' he burst out.

She nodded and giggled.

'That's wonderful.' He took her arm which was the closest he could get to her at this moment. 'I can't believe it, I'm sorry I should have put up the umbrella, you're getting wet.' He held it over them and they walked down Kildare Street. He was very aware of her body which was so close to him. How intimate was this little space under the umbrella. The raindrops loud above. A musical cascade.

They went to the DBC in Sackville Street. It wasn't too busy and he chose a table in a corner by the window. He wanted privacy. To have her to himself. Talk of the things that mattered to him and find out what mattered to her. He ordered coffee and pastries. The waitress brought a tier plate of luscious creamy confections.

'These are gorgeous,' Louise smiled. 'Will you have one?'

'I'll just have coffee, I don't have a sweet tooth.'

'And I can eat all of these?' she asked with a smile.

'If you like.'

'You're spoiling me.'

'I'm looking forward to doing that. I'm so glad your parents have allowed you to come out with me.'

'They like you.'

'I'm relieved.'

'Michael has talked about you before, so it's not as if you're a complete stranger, I've often wondered what you were like,' she giggled. 'But I imagined you very differently.'

'What did I look like?' he asked, with a grin.

'I thought you were skinny, and small, with a big nose, and very little hair,' her eyes twinkled.

He laughed out loud. 'I hope I'm a bit of an improvement then?'

'Definitely.'

'That's a relief.'

'Sorry, I was only joking,' Louise admitted.

'Getting your own back?'

'Maybe.'

Louise forked some of the cream pastry. 'This is delicious. You should have one.'

'I'll just look at you enjoying that.'

'I have such a sweet tooth, I'll be the size of a house one of these days.'

'Not at all, you're slim and beautiful. Go ahead, enjoy it,' he smiled, very comfortable in her company. He didn't feel he needed to say anything. Was that what loving someone was all about?

Suddenly Louise stepped eating, the fork held just at her mouth. There was a horrified expression on her face.

'What's wrong?' James asked.

'I shouldn't be eating, it's Lent, my mother will have my life.' She put the forkful of pastry on the plate.

'What your mother doesn't see she won't worry about,' James smiled.

'No, I can't finish it, I'm sorry. And you'll have to pay for it.'

'Don't worry, at least you enjoyed a few forkfuls.'

'I feel guilty, why didn't you remind me,' she said.

'Bring a girl out and tell her that she can't have anything to eat, doesn't sound like she's going to have a very pleasant evening.'

'I wouldn't have minded. Just hope my mother doesn't find out.'

'I'm not going to tell her, I promise.'

They smiled at each other.

Tell me about your own family?' Louise asked.

'Mother, father, two sisters, two brothers, one who is in Flanders, fighting.'

'So is Hugh.'

'Michael told me.'

'He's only sixteen, I worry about him.'

'My father thinks I should have enlisted with Maurice.'

She looked at him, surprise etched on her face. 'Will you go?'

'No.'

'Can he force you?'

He shook his head. 'But he makes me feel guilty that I'm not there also.'

'Does your mother want you to go as well?'

'She has never said. My mother is an unusual kind of woman and she never stands up to my father, not in front of us anyway, although she has very strong opinions.'

'War is terrible. So many men have died and no one seems to know how long it's going to last.'

The waitress came to clear the table.

'My mother spends all her time in the church praying for Maurice.'

'Mine too. It's very hard on those left at home.'

A silence yawned between them. He changed the subject, sensing her concern about Hugh. 'What are your favourite pastimes?'

'Reading, music ...'

'Maybe we might add a few more. Have you ever been to the theatre?'

'I enjoy concerts mostly.'

'Would you like to go to the Abbey Theatre one night?'

'Yes, I'd love that.'

'We'll choose something good and book tickets. I also like the Empire for music hall. And the Theatre Royal. Although maybe your parents mightn't approve of the English comedians.'

'I can always ask.'

It was a consent to their future. She seemed so sure. He found it astonishing. He looked into her large eyes and was lost in their limpid depths. The dark pupil surrounded by the brown golden flecked iris, fringed with incredibly long lashes. Suddenly, he wanted to be close to her again, like before, she was too far away from him now.

'Shall we go?' he asked softly.

She nodded.

He called the waitress and paid the bill. Then stood up and ushered her ahead of him, holding the door open.

It still rained, and he was full of gladness that there was a reason to put up the umbrella.

'The rain isn't that heavy,' she said.

'I can't have you getting wet,' he took her arm. 'Although perhaps we should catch a tram?' he suggested.

'No, I prefer to walk.'

They went slowly. He felt protective. Happy to look out for her. He would let nothing intrude on this newly discovered world in which he found himself and never wanted to let it go.

Chapter Nineteen

Anne thought about Mary and her whole family living in that one room. The place was clean, the table, chairs and benches scrubbed, the water buckets which stood in the corner shone bright, the crockery stacked neatly. But she couldn't imagine living in such a place. The cold, the noises from outside, the smells, she shuddered.

She opened one of her wardrobes in the dressing room and stared at the clothes. There was enough to clothe half a dozen people. She flicked through. Each wardrobe held a different item of clothing. Dresses. Skirts. Blouses. Short coats. Long coats. Day shoes. Evening shoes. Boots. In the tallboy, her underwear, petticoats, and nightdresses, were neatly folded, and gloves, scarves, handkerchiefs of every description in the dressing-table. What an array, she thought, looking through them. Anne was a pretty girl and, like any other, loved to wear beautiful clothes. Some of them she didn't like because they were chosen by her mother. Others were just slightly out of fashion and couldn't be worn without taking the chance of someone whispering a critical remark.

Mary McCabe was roughly the same size as herself, although slightly shorter. But Anne was sure that the woman would have no trouble taking up the hem until it was just right for her. She pulled out a lovely red dress, richly patterned, and thought how nice it would look on Mary, but then hesitated. The women who lived in those tenements all wore dark clothing. It would be impractical to give her something so bright which very likely she would put away and never wear. She flicked on. Coming across a dark brown day dress her mother had bought her. She pulled it out and held it against herself. It had a very detailed pleated design, with a wide band at the waist, and the collar was lace trimmed. That would suit.

She turned her attention to the skirts. Here there were much more possibilities. Navy. Dark green. Black. Plain and simple. She chose one of each. Next, she looked through the blouses, matching them to the skirts. Looking back into the dress section, she found two more. A dark maroon with velvet buttons, and a grey with black trim. As she folded them in a valise, she remembered to put in some white cotton nightdresses, knickers, camisoles, petticoats, stockings. Shoes were more of a difficulty as she didn't know what size Mary wore. Still, she took a pair of soft black leather boots which should stretch if her feet were bigger, and if they were suitable, then she could give her some more. At the last minute, she chose a heavy black overcoat which she had worn at her grandmother's funeral. When everything was ready, she suddenly thought about the children. It was a pity there were none in this house as Mary's children were literally dressed in rags, so she planned to enquire and see if she could find some clothes for them.

The following week she was back on day duty and left the house so early no one took the slightest notice of the bag she carried on the back of her bicycle. She left it into the nurses' home and that evening went over to Cuffe Street. The rain had cleared and the weather was more pleasant. Walking up the stairs with the heavy bag wasn't easy and she was followed by a group of small children all looking at her and giggling. Some women stood in doorways and watched her pass, their eyes followed her curiously. A couple of men talked together, sharing a smoke, and turned to tip their caps as she passed. Anne thought she would never get to Mary's room.

At last she stood outside, and knocked. She could hear the children talking inside, but the racket was quickly shushed and the door was opened by the young girl.

'Hallo Bridget, is your mother here?' Anne asked, with a smile.

'Who is it?' Mary appeared, wiping her hands on her apron.

'I just called around to ...' Anne began.

'Is there something wrong with Emily?' Immediately Mary put her hand to her chest, fear quite apparent in her face.

'No, she's fine,' Anne reassured.

'When can I take her home?'

'She will need a lot of care, so it may be some time, but I'll look after her, I promise.'

'Thank you,' Mary said. 'Won't you come in?' She glanced along the landing, and seemed anxious for Anne to come inside quickly.

There was a reasonable fire in the grate this evening and the children were gathered around it. Mary offered her a chair to one side. 'Sit down, please. Can I get you some tea?'

'No, thanks, I'll be having something to eat later.'

Mary nodded, took her shawl off the other chair, and sat opposite Anne.

'I've brought some clothes for you.'

Mary's eyes widened in surprise.

'These are just a few things which I hope you can use.' She opened the valise, and took out the first thing to her hand. It was the heavy black coat and she handed it to Mary.

She stared down at the coat, astonishment on her face. Her hands stroked the velvety wool like it was something very precious. 'But I can't take this beautiful coat, it's much too good for me.' She handed it back.

'No Mary, I've a lot of clothes, more than I can ever wear, and I want you to have them,' Anne insisted. 'I'm just hoping it's going to fit you. Try it.'

'Yes, Mam, do, it's beautiful,' Bridget added and helped her mother put it on.

Mary stood there. The coat looked very well, and was only a little too long.

'If you think it's a bit big you could move the buttons.'

'Yes, I'll do that,' Bridget said.

'I'd be afraid to wear this down the market.'

'Keep it for Sunday,' her daughter suggested.

'That would be nice,' Mary said, smiling for the first time.

Anne took the petticoats and underwear from the bag. 'I'm sorry but I've probably worn these only once or twice, but they're freshly laundered.'

'How beautiful.' Mary caressed the lace frills. 'I've only ever seen things as nice as this in a shop.'

Bridget held a petticoat over the dark skirt she wore and swung around in a circle with an excited whoop.

'Now, here are some dresses, skirts and blouses, so there is something for both of you. But you might have to adjust the hems so that they will fit properly.'

'I can't believe this, you are so good.' There were tears on Mary's cheeks, and she flung her arms around Anne and held her close. 'This is the best day in our lives.'

'I'm glad that you like them, and hope they're of some use. Here's a pair of boots as well, let me know if they fit and I'll see if I have any others which might suit.'

'Mam, you look so different.' Robbie came over, and hugged his mother.

'I will let you know if there is any change in Emily. But don't come around to the hospital, they won't let you in to see her.'

'Thanks for looking after her,' Mary whispered emotionally.

'Not at all.' Anne turned to leave.

'Do you want to take the bag with you?'

'No, you keep it.'

'Thank you.' They all crowded around the door as she went down the stairs, and waved to her from the landing.

Chapter Twenty

At dawn, Hugh marched out along a narrow road in northern France. The men in his battalion had welded together, at first training hard in the camp which was somewhere in Wales with an unpronounceable name, and then sailing across to France where they trained for another week until at last they were ready to be sent up to the Front line.

Hugh felt this was why he had joined up. He was excited, challenged. All the men were tough, hard, and determined to fight the Germans. To his disappointment, his friend, Peter, had been allocated to another battalion, and he had no idea where he was now. But he liked the other men and although he was younger than most, he was tall and strong and none of them passed comment.

It was still dark when he climbed out from under canvas, ordered to make his way up to the trenches. The noise of the gunfire was tremendous, echoing over and over, the sound magnified. German SOS signals went up, coloured rockets bursting in the sky. The men continued onwards in an effort to retake their own trenches which the Germans had taken the day before. The mud underfoot caused them to slip and slide. Rain soaked them. Their hands were wet on the rifle butts, trying to aim at the German soldiers. It was the closest Hugh had been to action. The first time he had confronted the enemy, a face blackened with mud, eyes white and staring. Raising his gun Hugh retaliated at once, took aim and shot. The soldier fell in front of him. He didn't know whether it was his bullet which had done the damage, but he kept on in the face of rifle and machine gun fire. One of his friends took a shot and collapsed forwards into the mud, and another to his left. Hugh wanted to see how badly injured they were but knew there was no time. He was under orders which had to be obeyed instantly, you didn't think for yourself.

Some time later, Hugh was relieved, and threw himself against a bank to eat some bully beef and biscuits. But in the fading light, they were told to *fall in* once again. As they went, Hugh found that his eyes were affected by something which drifted towards them. It was a gas of some sort and he hadn't experienced this before. It was uncomfortable. He pulled on his goggles, but they were no help and he took them off again until gradually the affect of the drifting stuff diminished. They entered a trench and it was difficult to make their way along in the darkness. They were only able to see ahead when the enemy's flares lit up the sky. Shells tore up the earth which showered down on them. Bullets whizzed past. Hugh found it difficult to keep his footing, and was unable to see, occasionally bumping into the soldier in front, and finding the man behind doing the same. Against the noise, it wasn't possible to hear the shouts of the wounded, but the man ahead of Hugh fell quickly, and in the dark he found it hard not to step on him, or on the other bodies of men who lay ahead. He was scared, such fear he had never known before. Sweat dribbled down his body. He shook, and found his legs sinking into mud. He dragged himself up, but then had to drop down again to protect himself, and lost his balance, his head muzzy. Unable to clamber up again as the boots of the men following crunched across his body. He let a shout out of him, and grabbed the leg of a soldier. The man pulled him upwards and he stumbled on.

Chapter Twenty-one

Louise was affected by the mood in the house after Hugh had enlisted. Almost guilty that she felt so happy, while her mother and father were obviously upset. That last night she had met James had been wonderful, and she couldn't believe how much he seemed to like her. He was the first man she had met that she liked especially, and she had to try and stop herself thinking about what might happen between them. Her mind swooped and took her like a bird to that moment he kissed her, remembering how soft his lips were, warm, moist, she couldn't escape from it. Her nights spent restlessly tossing and turning in her bed, sleep disrupted by dreams where his face and blue eyes followed her around in vague inexplicable situations. It was unusual for her to be so distracted. Normally, she would sleep the moment her head touched the pillow, exhausted from her long day's work. But now, regardless of turbulent nights, she still rose in the morning full of joy and longing to see him again.

This was Thursday, and she knew the Volunteers met that night, and it would be unlikely James would come to meet her after work. Still, she persuaded herself perhaps they would meet on Sunday which she happened to have off this week. But then remembered Michael was always out in the country on manoeuvres on that day, so probably James would be with him.

She was disappointed, looking forward so much to spending an afternoon or even longer with him.

But on Friday she received word that there were manoeuvres arranged for Cumann na mBan on Sunday also. So there was no chance at all of seeing him. She would have to march and drill in preparation for the rally on St. Patrick's Day. While she really enjoyed the manoeuvres, she was frustrated, her heart pulled both ways.

'Louise?' Mr. Quinton called her.

She turned. 'Yes Sir?'

'There's a large group of guests arriving and they will need help at the desk.' He whirled away, black coat-tails flying.

Louise glanced quickly in a mirror to check her hair and make sure the crisp white collar on her dark dress was in position. She could see that the man who normally ran the reception desk was indeed having difficulty dealing with the crowd gathered in front of him. The guests were a large group of English people, mostly couples, and she concentrated on allocating rooms.

'I don't think that is the same suite we had on our last visit. It was on the second floor overlooking the park, and I do so want the same one,' one particular dowager demanded. 'And we were here at this time last year.' She was a large lady, dressed in green, her face rather flushed. 'I particularly requested it, isn't that so?' she appealed to her husband, a small, ferret-faced man who simply nodded.

'Let me check.' Louise looked up the ledger for the previous year. Normally, this was done automatically as guests usually preferred to stay in the same room, but she wanted to keep the woman happy. 'Actually, you have been allocated the identical suite as last year, and it is one overlooking the park,' Louise smiled.

'Oh ...' she was taken aback. 'I'm sorry, I was so sure.'

'Look here, we can't all wait in a queue while you have discussions about a particular room?' A man poked his head between the couple. A look of extreme irritation on his pallid features. Louise rang the bell. A boy came over immediately and she instructed him to escort the couple to their suite, and handed him the key. To appease them, she personally walked over to the lift and made sure their luggage was ready to follow in the next few minutes.

When she returned to the desk, she could see that the other man was becoming even more irritated with the delay. 'I'm sorry, but I'll have your key for you in a moment. And we'll send up a bottle of champagne and some flowers,' she smiled at the woman by his side, who seemed pleased by this special treatment.

'Thank you,' she nodded.

'Yes, yes,' he conceded.

She rang the bell again. Handed the room key to the boy, and he led them away. The woman turned around and gave a little wave to Louise who only noticed it as she glanced up to make sure they had arrived at the lift. She smiled and then continued dealing with the next person standing in front of her. The rest of the people were much more amenable, with a lot less complaining and fuss.

When they had all been taken up to their rooms, another group sailed through the door and when the woman caught sight of her she made a beeline.

'Louise, how are you?' Eleanor Montford beamed at her. 'We're meeting some friends for dinner, but I wanted to introduce you to my youngest daughter Rhoda who hasn't been here before so late in the evening.'

Louise put out her hand and the young girl shook it shyly.

Mr. Quinton approached. Smiling, obsequious. They all made acquaintance and were joined at that point by Dr. Clarence Montford who had been talking with someone he had met outside, and the enquiries into each other's health bounced between them.

'Would you like me to put your coats in the cloakroom?' Louise asked.

The ladies nodded, and followed her to the room where she helped them divest themselves of coats, and scarves, and then rejoin Doctor Montford. Louise had got to know the family quite well, particularly the elder daughter, Anne, as they were frequent guests at the Shelbourne.

'How are you, Louise?' Anne asked.

'I'm very well, Miss Montford.'

'Maybe we'll have a chance to have a chat later?' the girl smiled.

'That would be nice,' Louise said. But it was so busy she doubted that it would happen.

She led them to the dining room, and then she hurried back to the reception desk, and found that the man who normally dealt with guests seemed to be receiving the people left in the foyer fairly rapidly, and the queue had diminished. Between them they made sure everyone was happy, and turned to each other when that was done.

'Thanks Louise, you were invaluable,' he said with a grin.

Louise threw herself into the manoeuvres on Sunday with enthusiasm, enjoying marching and drilling in tight formation. They had to be as perfect as possible in front of the public at the rally on St. Patrick's Day. On her arrival home she noticed the gas lamp was lighting in the parlour. She wondered who was inside and pushed open the front door. Immediately she heard voices and a wave of male laughter. She stopped abruptly as her heart began to thud. Was that James? She pressed her hand against her chest to calm herself. At the same time she felt her face grow hot. Don't let me blush, she whispered a prayer, dreading the thought of entering the room looking like she had been sitting by a fire. She took a deep breath and tried to steady herself. At that moment the parlour door opened and her mother came out.

'Louise, what are you doing standing there?'

She said nothing.

'Go on in, James is there,' Kathleen smiled.

She forced herself to go into the room. James sat with Michael and Terence at the table, and the three were in deep conversation. But as soon as she appeared, James stood up immediately and smiled.

Her father and Michael looked at her. Louise felt very self-conscious and wished that she hadn't come in, but there was no choice now but to sit down.

'How did it go?' her father asked.

'Good.'

'All ready for Friday?'

She nodded. Feeling embarrassed in the presence of her father and brother, and aware they both knew how she felt about James.

'The march will give us an opportunity to show the country who we are,' James said, and his eyes met hers. She nodded, but looked away quickly.

'That's what we want,' Michael made a fist of his hand, and banged the table. 'The British will know what they're dealing with.'

'This is our chance and we will take it soon. They won't have an inkling of what's ahead of them,' Terence said slowly.

'Yes,' Michael yelled.

'It's why we're marching on Friday,' Terence said.

'I'm looking forward to the day,' Louise smiled. Her soft voice changed the mood.

'You girls love a parade,' Michael said, with a laugh.

'Do you think that's all we're interested in?' Louise asked, suddenly irritated with him.

'Little girls in uniforms,' he grinned.

'Don't talk like that to me.' She leaned forward towards him, suddenly angry.

'Michael ...' Terence's voice was stern.

'You're too damned sensitive, that's the trouble, and I don't think women are going to be any good to us if we ever ...bloody useless in a crisis.' He lit a cigarette and stared at her through the blue smoke haze, pushing the packet across the table to his father and James.

'You know nothing, Michael O'Toole, nothing.' She stood up.

'Go Louise,' Terence muttered tiredly. 'And Michael, shut your mouth. I want to hear no more.'

Louise wanted to scream out loud, so angry at being told to leave the room by her father.

'I suppose I'd better be going, it's late,' James said.

'It's been good to see you,' Terence reached and shook his hand firmly. 'I'm glad you're with us.'

James nodded.

Louise walked into the hall ahead of him and Michael.

'Sorry sis, got carried away,' Michael said, with a crooked grin on his face.

She didn't reply.

'Louise,' James turned, put his hand on her arm and smiled.

She managed to return his smile, but was still angry with Michael. He spoiled everything between James and herself. Her brother had made her feel so small in her own parlour, as if her life was nothing. She was as passionate about rising up against the British as he was. And she could hold a gun, dismantle it, clean it, and aim at a target just as well as he.

'Are you working tomorrow?' James asked softly.

'Yes.'

'I'll wait for you.'

She smiled, feeling better.

Chapter Twenty-two

Bridget held the brown dress up against herself. 'Isn't it beautiful, Mam. Feel the material, it's so soft. And look at the cream lace.'

'It's lovely,' Mary stared at her daughter, and could see how pretty she was. What a difference clothes made.

Bridget picked up a skirt, and pulled it on over her own. Held a white lace blouse over it and twirled. 'What do you think, Mam?'

'It's so nice on you, Bridget.'

'I'll wear this on Sunday and keep the dress for a special day. Mam, why don't you try on one of the other dresses, or this blouse?'

'All right,' Mary took off her black skirt and blouse, and Bridget helped her on with the maroon dress. They smiled at each other.

'This is posh, Mam.' Bridget walked along by the fire in a mincing fashion. 'Madam, would you like to take your carriage to town?'

'We'll have tea and cakes,' Mary laughed.

After that, they tried on the other clothes, which mostly fitted. Some were a little long and would need to be taken up but they didn't care.

'People won't recognise us, they'll think we've won a pile of money.' Bridget flounced.

The door opened and Lar appeared. 'What's this?' he barked, staring balefully at the two of them.

Mary could immediately see he had had a few drinks, and that meant arguments and possibly worse until he went to bed and slept.

'Someone gave us clothes, she was very generous.'

'Who's that?' He was suspicious.

'The nurse who is looking after Emily.'

'Looks good.' He took hold of the black coat and twisted the smooth wool. 'Should get a few shillings for it and the other stuff.'

'What do you mean?' Mary gasped.

'I'm taking them to the pawn shop.'

Mary was taken aback. She hadn't thought of what Lar would say, and had simply been enjoying the moment with Bridget. It wasn't often they had such fun. Now she was very disappointed.

'But Pa, don't you like this skirt on me?' Bridget asked with a smile.

'Too good for you, take it off and I'll go around now with them. Have a bit of dinner cooked when I get back.'

They went behind the curtain and changed into their old clothes. They were silent. There didn't seem to be much to say now.

'The pawn shop will be closed,' Mary said.

'I'll knock him up. Is this the bag she brought them in?'

Mary nodded.

He pushed the clothes into the valise. 'Give us those boots.' He grabbed them too and went out.

Lar wasn't out for very long. Mary didn't have the courage to ask him how much he had received. He probably wouldn't have told her anyway.

'Is the food ready yet?' he grunted.

'In a minute.' She stirred the mixture until gradually it came to the boil. Then she poured some into a bowl, spooning the couple of pieces of meat which were at the bottom of the pot.

'Go to bed Bridget, we've to be up early in the morning,' Mary said.

The girl went over and lay on the mattress pulling the coarse sheet over her. Underneath it, she pulled off her outer clothes and lay them on top of the sheet for warmth.

When Lar had finished eating, he went into the other half of the room. Threw off his clothes and lay on the bed. 'Come in here to me,' he called to Mary.

'I'll be there ...' she banked down the fire. Knowing what he wanted and delaying, praying that he would fall asleep.

She checked the children, and bent to kiss Bridget. 'I'm sorry about the clothes, love.'

'Doesn't matter, Mam,' she whispered. But Mary noticed a glimmer of tears in her eyes, patted her shoulder and blew out the candle. The room darkened. She stood looking down at her children, each one so precious. Then she thought of Emily, and her heart contracted. Would she ever see her again? Would she get better? It was so hard, particularly as they wouldn't even allow her in to see her. As Anne had advised, Mary decided to stay away, although she missed Emily sorely and prayed she would have her home soon.

She walked to the curtain and looked inside. Lar lay with his mouth open. He was snoring.

Mary was very grateful to Anne for her generosity in giving her the beautiful clothes. But she dreaded meeting her again and having to explain why she was still wearing the same old skirt and blouse that she always wore. She didn't care so much for herself, she had one blue blouse for Sunday and took great care of it. But more than anything, she regretted that Lar hadn't allowed Bridget to keep something. Even one blouse or skirt would have made her happy. It was unfair. The boots were very different to what they normally wore on their feet and she thought that they would have fitted Bridget perfectly. Their old boots of hard leather chafed their soft heels and toes, particularly if they were caught in the rain. They were worn down, and to try and make them more serviceable, Mary pushed in pieces of cardboard although that broke up after a few days and she had to look around for more. She was despondent.

Lar still snored, and she felt safe from his attention. She sat by the fire, enjoying the heat from the embers. She would doze here for a while and keep out of his way. If she was in the bed beside him, he could wake up suddenly and then she would be for it. Mary thought about the man she had married. He had been such a charming character. What had caused such a change? Nowadays, none of them could argue the toss with him, or even try to persuade him to change his mind about anything. They simply had to bow down and obey. He would tolerate no opposition to anything he wanted to do.

She wondered what lay ahead for all of them. Would they live like this for ever? The families she knew around her, generation after generation, never seemed to be able to fight their way out of the mire of poverty. No matter how they struggled to escape, it was impossible to improve their lot, kept in their place by the upper classes.

Mary was a clever woman although she had little schooling and couldn't read or write. She had worked on the stall in Moore Street for as long as she could remember, and anything she had learned at school was soon forgotten. But she was good with figures, able to add, subtract, multiply and divide in her head, and come up with the correct answer. Mary was the one on the stall who worked out the prices of their products. Her mother and sister always looked to her for the answers.

Her own children still went to school, and she made sure that they always did their lessons. Although she couldn't manage to read the words on their slates, each evening she made them go over what they had learned that day. Bridget was bright and could read and write, and Mary was sorry she couldn't leave her at school, but Lar wouldn't agree. Women didn't need to know anything more than looking after their husbands and children, he would declare, and if Bridget could earn some money on the way then let her at it. Schooling was a waste of time for women.

Twelve year old Robbie was good at school too, and Mary prayed hard that Lar wouldn't force him to leave. Even another year at the Christian Brothers would help him. Still, once they all stayed healthy she was happy. So many children died. Every week she heard of at least one death. From babies up. She thought of little Olive and Dan lying in the cemetery, their bodies cold. Then she bent her head and prayed for Emily. It was a long time before she slept, but Mary stayed there in that uncomfortable position. It was better than taking her chances with Lar inside. Let him have the bed.

Chapter Twenty-three

Hugh's battalion was sent into *no man's land.* Through that terrible place of dugouts and barbed wire. Most of the action was at night. Out of the shadows came flashes of gunfire and shells cut through the earth which sprayed skywards in huge arcs. His friends fell, and there was no one there to help them in their last moments, and no priest to whisper a prayer. Hugh and the other men huddled in dugouts, faced by an enemy they couldn't see. Time meant nothing out there. Hugh aimed his rifle, shooting at vaguely imagined shapes, unable to hear the report against the thunder of their own guns and that of the enemy.

They were ordered back to the support trenches. The mud was home to rats and other vermin. Hugh hated the rats most of all, dreading the touch of the little feet when they crept across them. Hugh lay against the side of the trench and tried to get into a comfortable position, constantly scratching his body. He was infested with lice, as were most of the men. They lived in their dirty clothes and even though the clothes were deloused occasionally, it made no difference. They had got used somewhat to the smell. The rotting corpses. The latrines. Their own bodies. It was part of trench life.

Today, Hugh was refilling sandbags. The condition of the trench was bad. Other men pumped away the water which had collected due to the heavy rain. He was glad to be back here, away from the worst of the action, but was still aware that he could be mown down by a bullet even in this position. He thought of home suddenly. Dublin. Imagined his mother and father sitting at the table in the evening. The soft light from the lamp casting a gentle aura. In his mind, Louise was there too, and Michael. His thoughts took him upstairs to where the younger boys slept together, their baby faces innocent in slumber. His heart filled, and suddenly he wondered if he had made the right decision when he joined up.

To his regret, he hadn't met Peter since he had left the Welsh training camp and didn't know whether he was dead or alive. Or whether he himself would be alive tomorrow. He humped a sandbag on his shoulder and pushed it into position, glancing at the man beside him. Doug and he had become friends and when he grinned at him, Hugh felt better, and punched him on the shoulder as they lifted another bag each. If he could just get through the next few minutes. That was as far as he would look ahead.

Suddenly, there was a loud explosion. Doug was flung towards him. Shrapnel rained down. Hugh fell into the trench. The other man on top of him. And there was blood everywhere. In a red haze he struggled to get out from under his friend. He yelled, and pushed himself up. He reached down and put his hand on Doug. He could see bone protrude through his uniform. He stared at his own body and was horrified at the blood which spattered across it. He shouted his friend's name, but he didn't move.

Unable to feel any pain, Hugh didn't know whether he had been injured. His mind registered that his legs were holding him up, but with the amount of blood he could see there was always the possibility that shrapnel had entered his body. The explosion had affected his ears and he couldn't hear properly. He looked at Doug's body. At the poor bloodstained man that he had befriended. He bent his head and vomited.

Hugh awoke lying on a stretcher in the hospital tent. The pain in his shoulder was intense. A nurse came over.

'How are you feeling?'

'Thirsty.'

She gave him a drink of water. 'We'll be transferring you to a barge hospital later.'

'My friend?' he asked.

'What is his name?'

'Doug.'

'You were together?' she smiled. A pretty red-haired girl.

He nodded.

'I'll check if he came in at the same time.' She patted his hand.

As he lay there, images of the explosion swept through his mind. The noise. The blood. He began to shake. Tears filled his eyes. He wanted to go home. Back to his mother and father. Mam would look after him. Tuck him up in bed. Bring him hot drinks. He cried out for her.

The nurse came back later but never said anything about Doug.

'Did you find him?' he asked tearfully.

'I'm sorry, perhaps he wasn't injured.'

'He was, it was terrible, the shell ...'

'Perhaps it was only something minor.' She checked his dressing.

'No, no, I saw him.'

'I'll keep looking, there are a lot of men here.'

'If you see him, tell him I was asking for him.'

'Of course I will,' she reassured gently.

'Is my mother here?'

'She may come later.'

'Will she be able to find me?'

‘I’ll make sure of that. Now go to sleep. It will do you good.’

He closed his eyes, and thought of home.

Chapter Twenty-four

Louise was excited. She had arranged to have some time off on St. Patrick's Day as a special favour from Miss Cunningham. She had asked politely if it was possible to make up the hours later and to her surprise, the woman had agreed. Louise couldn't believe it. She thanked her profusely.

In the morning she dressed in her dark green uniform, and left the house with her father and Michael, all three going to join their respective companies and march to College Green. There were a lot of Irish Volunteers on the streets, and she caught up with some of her friends in Cumann na mBan. But at the same time, she watched out for James, often mistaking some other Volunteer in uniform for him. Each time, her heart dropped inside her in a moment of disappointment, but the closer they got to College Green, she was swept up in the excitement of this tremendous gathering of Irish Volunteers and Cumann na mBan. There were crowds of curious people watching from the sides of the streets, the lines stretched all along Dame Street and into College Green. Nothing like this had happened for a very long time, if ever.

Louise joined her company and they marched in tight formation to their position led by Countess Markievicz, presented arms, and stood to attention. The troops were reviewed. When it was all over, they marched proudly back up Dame Street to the point where they had started. Louise felt so happy to be here, and regretted that she had to go back to work and couldn't enjoy the excitement of the day.

The Shelbourne was full of people all celebrating the holiday, many of them trying to avoid the throngs which had gathered in the city to watch the rally. Mr. Quinton spotted her immediately and drew her into his office. 'Louise, thanks be to God you're back, it's chaos here. Will you go down to the kitchens and tell me how things are going there. We need to speed up the service of food. People are beginning to get very tired waiting for their orders.' He pressed a crisp white handkerchief on his brow.
It was as he had described. In the kitchen chefs fell over each other as they rushed around. Waiters stood with hands out waiting for plates of food to bring up to the restaurant. The Maître Chef, Monsieur Pierre, stood in the middle of it all inspecting the dishes as they were completed and sending them back to be prepared again if they weren't up to his high standards. At the same time, he yelled loudly, using words in French that certainly Louise couldn't understand, although she had some knowledge of the language.

She had a look at the list on the board just inside the door, shocked to see so many unfulfilled orders, but certainly wasn't going to say anything. She stood watching for a moment, and went back to Mr. Quinton.

'Are things any better downstairs?' he asked.

'They're coming along,' she said, reluctant to describe the scene too vividly.

He sighed. 'There's not much we can do. Monsieur Pierre will take no notice of anything we say. You may go on with your usual work.'

Louise was relieved. She didn't want to get involved in the problems in the kitchen. Her mind full of the day's events, and wondering if James would be waiting for her outside the hotel tonight. But because of the number of guests there, she had no idea what time she would finish, it could easily be after midnight.

Chapter Twenty-five

Anne walked down the long white corridors of the hospital, quiet now at this time of the morning, and went into the small room where Emily lay sleeping. The child had made improvement, and the rash had faded on her body. Maybe she was well enough to go home, Anne wondered, but she wasn't directly involved in the care of the child and couldn't make suggestions to the staff on this floor. She hadn't seen Mary since she had brought over the clothes and hoped everything was all right.

She tiptoed across to the cot. The child immediately sat up. 'Emily?'

'Want Mam.' Tears spurted.

'She'll be here soon.'

'Mam?'

'Soon, pet.'

The door opened. 'What are you doing here, this child is contagious.' A nurse Anne didn't know marched towards her.

'I thought that the stage of contagion had passed?'

'It's not up to you to decide that,' the woman snapped.

'So she's not allowed a visit by her mother yet?'

'Definitely not.'

'How long do you think?'

'The doctor will decide that. It's not up to us.' She stood and waved Anne out of the room.

'Bye Emily,' she called to the child, who wailed even louder.

'Look what you've done, now we'll have to get her quiet again and that won't be easy,' she admonished.

'I'm sorry. But I know her mother and I said I'd call to see how she was.'

'You know her mother?' There was shock on the nurse's face.

'Yes.'

'I'm surprised, I've seen the woman. Surely she wouldn't be in your class?'

'What has that got to do with this child?' Anne was irritated.

She sniffed disapprovingly. 'On your way now, I'm sure you're meant to be on duty.'

'I've finished now,' Anne smiled. 'But thanks for looking after Emily so well.' She didn't want to be at loggerheads with any of the staff in the hospital.

The woman nodded and closed the door.

Anne changed out of her uniform in the nurses' home and cycled along by St. Stephen's Green, amazed at the numbers of Irish Volunteers on the streets this St. Patrick's Day. There were throngs of them making their way towards the centre of the city She had never taken any interest in the movement, or the women's Cumann na mBan either, but now was curious. She followed the crowd down to Dame Street, watching as they gathered and began to march. She stood among the onlookers very impressed by the review, and general salute.

At home, she went in to find her mother and sisters in a state.

'We were going into town to have lunch and literally could not drive through all those men. They marched along with their guns, and no sign of the DMP, or any soldiers to put them down. I was horrified. We had to turn around and come back,' Eleanor announced when she saw her.

'It was quite terrifying,' added Catherine.

'I thought it was exciting,' Rhoda's cheeks were pink.

'They have a right to march,' said Anne.

'You'd have gone over and joined in, I suppose?' Catherine accused.

'Why not? They were marching for Ireland.'

'How do you know what they were marching for?' her mother asked.

'I heard them talk.'

'When was that?'

'Today.'

'You shouldn't have been taking any notice of what those hooligans were saying.'

'It was the women I heard.' Anne wasn't sure if she ought to admit that.

'That's even worse. Women wearing such clothes, looking like men, and some of them even carrying guns. No better than suffragettes. Never heard the like. We can't even walk through our own streets now.'

'Some people resent the fact that the Irish are not allowed to rule their own country. They don't want Britain to be running things,' she pointed out.

'The Irish wouldn't be able to rule themselves. Everything they have is provided by England. And there's a war going on, and men needed to fight. What are these men doing here? They should be out in Flanders fighting with Stephen,' Eleanor snapped.

'Still, a lot of countries want independence.'

'Where is all this coming from? You're a young girl. You know nothing.'

'I read father's newspapers. It's all there.'

'Well, you won't be doing that for much longer,' Eleanor announced.

'You can't stop her from educating herself about what is going on in the world,' Rhoda said.

Anne was astonished to hear such things from her youngest sister.

Rhoda smiled.

'There's a pair of you in it.' Eleanor was dismissive.

'Life is changing, mother, women's role is changing,' Anne pointed out.

'It won't change in this house,' her mother flashed.

The girls looked at each other.

'Get me some tea, I need something to calm me. And I suppose there's no sign of your father?'

Catherine shook her head.

'To be married to such a man is a penance.' She sighed loudly. 'Never there when you want him. Who's bringing me tea?'

'I'll ask Sally to make some.' Anne went downstairs to the kitchen, glad to get away from her mother. Even talking about the Volunteers and Citizen Army had excited her, and she wanted to know more.

Chapter Twenty-six

'Would you mind washing my uniform shirt please, Mother, there will be manoeuvres on Easter Sunday.' James handed it to her.

'I'll have to keep it out of sight of your father, lately he's been very much against you being involved in the Volunteers.'

'I suppose it's because Maurice is fighting in Flanders, he doesn't understand the way I think.'

'Your brother is giving his life for us. No-one wants Germany to take over. Imagine what that would be like?'

'I'd give my life for Ireland,' his eyes gleamed.

'Ireland will never survive on its own without Britain. We depend on them for everything.'

'But we should be self-sufficient,' he insisted.

'Everyone should be self-sufficient.' She bent down and pushed the shirt into one of the presses. 'I was intending to go to university and that would have meant I'd have had independence but my life changed.'

James's mother, Liliane, was an intelligent educated woman. Her father was a judge, and the family lived in a large house on Ailesbury Road. But they had become estranged, and their mother had never spoken about it.

'What do you mean by saying your life changed?'

'I met your father.'

He smiled.

'But my family didn't approve of Matt, so against their wishes we secretly married and the following day I brought him over to meet them.'

He stared at her, so astonished he couldn't think of anything to say.

'I was hoping that when they met Matt everything would change, but that didn't happen. My father was very angry. I'll always remember his words ...' she bent her head.

'Mam, you don't have to tell me if it's upsetting you, I understand.' James pressed his hand on hers.

'No, I want to tell you,' she insisted. 'Anyway, he said he didn't approve of your father and that by getting married I had alienated myself from the family.' There were tears in her eyes.

He listened.

'I argued with him. Told him how much I loved your father but he wasn't interested.'

'How awful for you.'

'He said I wasn't welcome at home any longer, and that I should just leave.'

'What did Father say?'

She smiled. 'He said that it was to his advantage, and then he took my hand and we left. I never went back.'

'It's a wonder he didn't punch him,' James said with a wry grin.

'Your father isn't a violent man.'

'He never lifted a hand to any of us.'

'But you should be careful with your father,' Liliane said to James. 'He has strong opinions and if you go against him, you might lose him for ever. I lost my own father. I lost my life. I had to remember my mother and sisters, remember my home,' she paused for a few seconds. 'And the wonderful times. You don't realise how many ways you will be affected. You're young now and it's only as you grow older that the loss of a family makes itself felt.'

'You must have been very lonely for your home, and not to have seen your mother and father again was very hard,' he said.

'Yes,' she admitted. 'But I never regretted my choice. We've been very happy ...' Her voice was soft. 'And my sisters kept in touch.'

'How was it we never met them?'

'It wasn't possible. But they were true to me and I love them dearly, although I haven't seen them very much in recent years.'

'Maybe there's a chance now?' James said hopefully.

'My parents died within a few weeks of each other just last December, so I'm hoping I'll see more of my sisters.'

'I would really like to meet your family if you ...if you wanted it too,' he stuttered, embarrassed, wondering if he had crossed a line with his mother. He dropped the subject. But the conversation signalled a new level of closeness between them which he would treasure. 'There's something I want to tell you,' he said slowly.

She smiled, and waited.

'I've met a girl.'

'That's nice.' There was a twinkle in her eyes. 'I'm glad for you. There should be something else in your life apart from the Volunteers. Tell me who she is?'

'Her name is Louise.'

'And where does she live?'

'South Circular Road.'

'Sorry, I'm being too inquisitive. But how long do you know her,' she laughed. 'There I go again.'

'Just a few weeks,' he had to admit that.

'So you've fallen in love?'

'She's the girl I want to marry,' he admitted, suddenly feeling shy.

'You must follow your heart, son. I did. So you have my support.' She reached across the table and kissed him.

That chat with his mother made him feel good. Now all he could hope for was that Louise would agree to marry him and that her parents wouldn't have a major objection like his own mother's family.

'I'd better get on with tea.' She rose from the table.

A little stiff lately, he thought, watching her move.

'I'd prefer if you didn't say anything about Louise to the others, and especially Father,' he said.

'How long do you think you can keep her a secret?' she laughed. She was still an attractive woman, only a few grey strands in the dark hair. 'I want to meet my future daughter-in-law. When will that happen?' She busied herself at the range.

'I haven't even asked her yet,' he had to confess. They both smiled at each other. He was unaware how alike they were.

Chapter Twenty-seven

Kathleen tucked her young sons into their beds. She came downstairs, and into the kitchen where her husband sat by the fire reading the newspaper. 'There's something going on, Terence, why don't you tell me about it?' she asked. He didn't raise his head from the newspaper.

Michael came in. 'I'm starving, Mam, any chance of a bite?'

'You know it's Holy Thursday, you've had all you're going to eat for today.'

He sat beside his father with a groan.

'Offer it up,' Kathleen advised. 'And go to bed early, you'll forget how hungry you are when you fall asleep.'

'Get as much rest as you can, you'll need it,' Terence spoke for the first time.

'I can't wait,' he grinned at his father.

There was a glint in the older man's eyes.

'Have you told Mam?' Michael nodded towards Kathleen, who stood at the range, her back to them.

She turned immediately.

'This is between us and is to go no further,' Terence spoke quietly.

'Have I ever spoken out of turn?' Kathleen asked.

'There have been meetings going on this last while.'

'Don't I know it, sure you're never home.' She sat down at the table and looked at the two of them.

'An uprising is planned,' Terence said.

'What?' She was shocked.

'Yes Mam, for next Sunday,' added Michael.

'Easter Sunday?'

He nodded.

'My God, that's sacrilege.' She took her Rosary beads from her pocket, blessed herself and kissed the crucifix.

'The Citizen Army flew the Irish flag over Liberty Hall a couple of weeks ago, that was the first blow,' Michael said excitedly.

'What Irish flag?' Kathleen asked, puzzled.

'It's green with a gold harp on it and to see it flying there was just ...' He ran out of words.

'That doesn't sound like an uprising is planned. Didn't you have marches arranged for Sunday anyway?' There was criticism in Kathleen's voice.

'Yes, and we have to arm ourselves well,' Michael said.

'Terence, tell me this isn't true?' she demanded.

'Michael, you'll have to go to Confession,' Terence grunted.

'I'll be going anyway.'

Kathleen stared, white-faced. For the first time, the gravity of the situation dawned on her. 'Where is this going to happen?'

'We can't say.'

'Why not? Haven't we all got to prepare ourselves, and the children,' she gasped.

'You'll be all right, it will be over in a couple of days, the British won't know where they are, and will probably crumble under our assault. It's the last thing they'll be expecting.' Terence seemed to be very confident. 'And you are not to breathe a word of this to anyone, if you do it could destroy everything.'

'How many guns have you?'

'We have enough.'

'Mam, we've been training for a long time now, we're well able to take on the British,' Michael said, with a wide grin.

'And are you a good shot?' she countered.

'Of course I am,' Michael said.

'And have you thought about getting killed?' Kathleen was angry.

'God will protect us,' Terence said.

Chapter Twenty-eight

Michael and James met on Holy Saturday in the city.

'Is there any further news?' James asked.

'There's a meeting at our house tonight.'

'A lot of planning to be done no doubt.'

'The GPO is the headquarters. And we should take the whole of Sackville Street, all that area,' Michael explained.

'And hold all the other positions across the city. It's a hell of an undertaking.'

'The whole country will rebel. The British will be on the run. They won't be expecting this. Not on an Easter Sunday when they're all enjoying themselves, I can't wait,' Michael said.

'I'm still doubtful about the possibility of success,' James said.

'I'm going to buy a bayonet,' Michael said. 'Come on around to O'Lawlor's in Fownes Street, we'll get them there.'

James stared at him for a few seconds. 'Do we need bayonets?'

'Hand to hand combat,' Michael said.

'Being mown down by British guns is more likely.'

'They won't be able to defeat us once we get going.'

'No country as small as ourselves has ever succeeded in bringing down the might of the British Empire, they'll wipe us out.'

'If we can hold them off for long enough, then they'll turn and give us what we want.'

'Do you think it will be as easy as that?'

'Yes. The British are all bluster.'

'Does Louise know about the plan for tomorrow?' James asked. 'I haven't seen her very much this week.'

'Father felt it was better not to talk about it in front of her.'

'I'm sure Cumann na mBan are involved. I'll wait for her tonight after work,' James said.

They arrived at O'Lawlor's but the word from the men gathered outside was that there wasn't a bayonet or a sword to be had, they were all sold out.

'I've missed you,' he put his arm around Louise and kissed her as soon as they met.

'And I you,' she said, smiling.

'Have you heard the news about tomorrow?'

'I know the uprising is happening, and it's my day off which means I don't have to ask for special permission to be absent.'

'I hate the thought of you being in danger.' He tightened his embrace.

'I won't be in danger. We've to gather in St. Stephen's Green. What about you?'

'GPO.'

'It's happening at last, I can't believe it,' Louise was excited.

'I don't see us defeating the British.'

'You're too negative.'

He found it hard to share her enthusiasm.

'It will change our lives, don't you see?'

'Maybe I am a bit cynical.'

'You are. Just be positive. We'll achieve what we want ...the Irish Republic.'

Back at South Circular Road, they were met by Michael at the door. 'Tomorrow's off,' he said, obviously disgruntled.

'What do you mean?' James was astonished.

'Do you know why?' Louise burst out.

'No. Father just received a letter earlier to say that the manoeuvres on Easter Sunday are cancelled.'

Chapter Twenty-nine

Mary pulled out the tin bath and with the help of Bridget she made many trips up and down the flights of stairs to the water tap in the back yard. They boiled the water on the fire, and Mary managed to half-fill the bath a couple of times so that all of them could have a wash. She left herself until last, but enjoyed the feeling of cleanliness after scrubbing herself all over with a rough cloth. There was only one very small piece of *Sunlight* soap and by now it had almost melted. Many's the time she had no soap at all, so it was a novelty and she still felt the better of it. She put out clean knickers and petticoats for herself and Bridget, and clean drawers for Lar and Brendan, admittedly all patched and worn, but it was important that they wear their best on Easter Sunday.

Lar came home late. The children were in bed.

'You must have been working on the coal boat again?' she laughed when he appeared, his face black.

'Aren't we lucky I was taken on?' he grinned, his teeth white against the grime.

'You look like a chimney sweep,' she laughed. 'Have a bath.'

'I hate washing,' he groaned.

'Come on, I'll heat the water again, you're last in line, Robbie took the twins down to stay with Eileen for the Easter, so it's not that dirty.'

'Doesn't matter.'

His mood was unusually affable and she was glad of that, this being a holiday and all.

When he climbed out of the bath looking more like his normal self, she made him a cup of tea, without milk or sugar. It was Holy Week and as Mary was deeply religious, she held strictly to the Lenten rules. One meal a day and two collations. Not that it made much difference to them. The diet Mary fed her family was like being on a Lenten fast all year around, except for the bit of meat she gave to Lar to keep his strength up.

'I got you something.' He went to his coat. 'One of the lads on the banana boat picked one up.' He handed her the rather bruised fruit.

'Thanks Lar.' She was astonished. It was seldom he gave her anything for herself. Occasionally they sold bananas on the stall but never had any left over, people would buy bananas no matter what they were like. 'I'll keep it for tomorrow.' She put it away in the press knowing by then it would probably have blackened and regretted that it wasn't possible to eat it now.

'Give us a bite,' he asked.

'This is Holy Saturday, it would be a sin.'

'Aw, for God's sake,' he grimaced.

'And I'm going to the Vigil soon and if you want to commit a mortal sin then you can, but I'm not,' she said. 'And you should be coming with me.'

'I'm in need of sleep, woman, and you should be in bed with me,' he grunted, throwing himself down.

'Was there a few lumps of coal to be had?' she asked, pulling on her shawl.

'A few, not much. Come in here before you go off,' he ordered.

'How could you say such a thing and I going to see the Lord. And keep your voice down, the children are asleep.'

Mary could hear him muttering angrily from behind the curtain as she left the room. He would have her soon, she knew that. She had tried hard to avoid his attention lately, but she was running out of excuses, and prayed that she wouldn't find herself expecting again.

When she arrived home, to her relief Lar was asleep and she felt safe getting into the bed beside him. But he suddenly turned towards her. She froze and held her breath, lying quite still until he drifted off again.

She went to Mass with the children the following morning, although Lar didn't come with them. Rolling out of bed he just managed to get last Mass and then went into the pub for a few drinks with his friends. It was a lovely sunny day, and Bridget and Mary took Brendan for a walk around St. Stephen's Green in the afternoon. There were a lot of people out taking the air, and it was pleasant to follow the pathways between the trees, admire the beautiful spring flowers, and watch the antics of the ducks in the ponds. People fed them pieces of bread, although Mary felt it was a sin to waste such good food, but laughed with everyone else as the ducks fought with each other over every little piece.

Because the weather was so warm, she hadn't needed to wear her black shawl and felt less conspicuous among the other people there in her dark skirt and only good blouse. There was quite a fashionable crowd today, all showing off their Easter bonnets.

'I wish I could look like some of those girls, Mam,' Bridget said softly.

'One of these days, love.'

'If we could only have kept some of the clothes the nurse gave us I'd be so happy.' Bridget stared at a young girl of about her own age dressed in a pretty lemon gown.

'They're all in the pawn shop,' there was an edge of bitterness in Mary's voice. She had hoped that Lar might have given her some money as he had been working the last few days, but the argument the previous night had probably put paid to that hope as most of the money would be spent in the pub over the holiday. She had managed to gather a few more vegetables, and bought some end cuts of meat and an ounce of ham parings over the week as people were not buying so much because of it being Holy Week. Yesterday the butcher had given her a lump of dripping, so she had something to put on the bread for later along with the blackened banana.

'Do you think we'll ever have anything?' Bridget asked.

'Sure we will,' Mary said. 'Soon.' But she had little faith in her assurance, very much aware of the unfairness of life.

Bridget smiled, but there was a sadness in her eyes.

'I've been talking to Father Kennedy and asked him about you,' Mary confided.

'What do you mean?'

'About getting a place as a kitchen maid in one of the big houses.'

'What did he say?'

'He said he would make enquiries and let us know. I'm praying hard.' She put her arm around the young girl's shoulders.

'Mam, there's a band playing,' Brendan rushed towards them.

'All right, we're coming.' Mary and Bridget followed him to the bandstand. They sat on the grass, watched and listened. The bandsmen wore smart red uniforms with bright glistening buttons and braid. They played brass instruments, and the music swung along and children ran about in the height of enjoyment. She smiled at Bridget, and their previous dark mood vanished.

'Happy Easter love, this is a lovely day.' Mary took her hand. 'And I'm hoping we'll have our Emily home with us soon.'

Chapter Thirty

On Easter Sunday, James bought the Sunday Independent and sat reading in the garden with his father. His sisters helped Liliane to cook dinner. His younger brother kicked a football up against the back wall, the sound of which had a monotonous regularity which got on his nerves. He leafed through the pages of the paper, surprised to see a notice of the cancelling order of the manoeuvres printed there.

After dinner, he set off to South Circular Road to see Louise. It felt odd to have time on his hands on a Sunday, it was usually spent with the Volunteers as they carried out manoeuvres on the outskirts of the city. When he arrived, he found the family gathered together, and he was made very welcome. Louise looked particularly pretty wearing a pale green dress, but James had no chance to talk to her as Michael immediately engaged him in conversation.

'What do you think of this state of affairs?' he asked in an undertone.

'I don't really understand it. I haven't heard any more,' James said.

'There was a disagreement between the leaders.'

'About what?'

'Some of them felt today wasn't the right time to go ahead.'

'They might choose another date.'

'But I wonder if we will ever build up such fervour again,' Michael looked disgruntled. 'All our company were for it.

They'd have taken on the Empire itself not just the few soldiers here.'

'What are you two whispering about?' Louise came over.

'Nothing,' Michael said abruptly.

'You're talking about the cancelling order, aren't you?' Louise smiled.

'What do you know about it?' Michael asked.

'In Cumann na mBan we know everything. And we'll fight too whenever it happens,' she announced.

'Not if Father has anything to do with it.'

'He's just being protective because I'm a woman. He talked to me this morning. I know how he feels.'

'Women would only be in the way in any fight,' Michael grunted.

'That's your opinion and you're entitled to it, but I have very different ideas as has Countess Markievicz,' Louise said.

'Don't argue, there's nothing to be gained,' James intervened. He immediately regretted speaking, realising that he could be drawn into an argument between Louise and Michael. But neither of them spoke, and so he continued in a reasonable tone. 'Maybe just as well it's cancelled. After the War we'll achieve Home Rule and that will be the first step towards freedom.'

'Britain won't release us, not ever, unless we rebel,' Michael spoke vehemently. 'We're too valuable to them. They'll hang on, it's the way they do things.'

Louise turned to James and smiled. His eyes met hers and that same feeling swept through him as had happened on the night they had been in the DBC. 'Would you like to take a walk?' he asked.

'Yes, I'd love to.'

James turned to Michael. 'Want to come along?'

'No thanks, not with you two love birds, I'd only be in the way.' He seemed churlish.

'Thanks Mick.' Louise reached to kiss his cheek.

'Go on then,' he said, with a grin.

James and Louise walked arm in arm towards town. There were a lot of people on the streets taking advantage of the fine weather. The city of Dublin basked in sunshine under a brilliant blue cloudless sky.

'It's so nice to be on our own, we've had so little opportunity lately.' She hugged close to him.

'And wonderful to have you to myself,' he said softly. 'Last night was too short.'

She smiled. 'Usually, you're involved with the manoeuvres on a Sunday, and it's seldom I have Sunday off.'

'Let's make the most of it then,' he grinned down at her.

'Father is very disappointed about the cancellation of the uprising,' she said.

'And Michael too.'

'All of us in the Cumann were building up to it. We were so sure our lives were going to change.'

'That's a dream, Louise.'

They were walking on Camden Street. Stopping every now and then to peer into shop windows. Louise pointing out things which she particularly liked and he, foolishly, promising that he would buy her whatever she wanted.

'You're so generous, thank you,' she giggled.

They continued along Aungier Street, and turned on to South King Street, passing the Gaiety Theatre.

'*The Gondoliers* will be on next week, I love the music.' Louise gazed at the posters outside.

'Would you like to go?' he asked.

'Of course,' she exclaimed.

'I'll book tickets,' he promised.

'I'll have to check when I have a day off as I can never be sure of the evenings, I'll let you know.' She turned to him, her face animated.

James was entranced by the beauty of this girl.

'You're so good to me, James, thank you,' she whispered, a sudden blush on her cheeks.

'Why wouldn't I?' he asked. 'Let's walk in St. Stephen's Green.'

'I'm so glad I was off today, imagine if I was over there looking out.' She gazed at the Shelbourne. 'How awful it would be to see you here alone.'

They followed the pathways through the trees. From time to time they were alone although voices could be heard from nearby, and the sound of a band playing in the distance. James was so glad to have the opportunity to spend time with Louise. He wanted to hold her. To kiss her. They were in among the trees now, and quickly he pulled her close to him. 'Louise,' he whispered her name, and touched her lips tenderly with his. His heart beating wildly as he felt her respond with a slight tremor. More confident now, he pressed her lips slightly open very much aware of the warmth of her breath, the moistness of her mouth, and the enticing aroma of the perfume she wore. Holding each other close, they stood there in silence. After a time, he stepped back a little and looked down at her. 'I'm sorry, I've let my feelings take over,' he murmured.

She shook her head, but made no move away from him. Suddenly, voices could be heard and he took her arm once again, just in time to avoid the curious eyes of a group of children who ran into view.

Louise laughed.

James pressed her hand. 'I think I'll have to tell you how I feel. I wouldn't like you to think I would take advantage in any way.'

She smiled.

'I know it's a bit soon, but ...' he turned to her again, clasping her hands in his. This time completely oblivious as to whether there were any onlookers.

'Will you marry me Louise ...please? It would make me so happy, and all I want is to make you happy too.' He waited on tenterhooks.

She nodded.

'You will?'

'Yes James, I will.'

Chapter Thirty-one

Anne cycled home from the hospital on Easter Sunday evening. There were lots of people out and about enjoying themselves, and she regretted having to work on a holiday but was glad that she had been granted Monday off duty. Anne loved her work so much it really wouldn't have upset her unduly if she had to attend to her patients every day.

As soon as she had come in the front door, and was making her way upstairs to her room she heard her mother call from below.

'You're late, Anne,' Eleanor's voice was sharp.

'I'm sorry, Mother, it was very busy at the hospital.'

'Your aunt and cousins have arrived.'

'I won't be long.'

'Don't be.'

Her maid filled the bath with hot water and she soaked in the scented suds, feeling much more refreshed when she dressed and went down.

But, as ever, she found the rather gossipy chat of the family hard to tolerate and her mind dragged her back to the people she had treated today. Her probationer duties had expanded and she was given much more responsibility now, although Matron and the nursing staff kept a strict eye on her and the other girls. Her special interest was the little girl, Emily, who had made a good recovery in spite of being severely malnourished and on the point of death when she had first been admitted.

Anne had met the child's mother, Mary, more than once since but had never seen her wear any of the clothes she had given her. But she had learned a lot about her pride. The poorer the people were, the prouder, and none more so than Mary. Perhaps there were other reasons why the woman couldn't wear the clothes, she decided. It was such a pity as her extensive wardrobe was unused in the most part, particularly now that she wore a uniform to work and her opportunities for socialising were curtailed. Sensing that it might not be appropriate she had not brought over any more clothes.

'Anne, don't you agree?' Eleanor cut across her daughter's thoughts in a strident tone.

'I'm sorry,' she hadn't heard the remark which had been addressed to her.

'There you are, head up in the clouds as usual,' Eleanor said with a hint of laughter in her voice. 'Your cousin Belinda has asked you to join them at Wicklow next Saturday and Sunday. There will be all sorts of activities, and she thought you might enjoy the festival with your sisters.'

'Thank you Belinda, but ...'

'It will be wonderful fun, Anne, picnics, a treasure hunt, and lots more, I can't remember all the events but we'll have a great time. And we could take the horses out in the morning if you like. Please come. Catherine and Rhoda have already agreed.'

'I'll be on duty then, I'm afraid. I'd love to be there but ...' Anne made her excuses. It was all true anyway.

'Can't you just ask them to let you off, if you explain exactly surely they wouldn't say no?' Belinda beamed at her.

'Yes, you must do that,' added her mother.

'No, I'm sorry, it wouldn't be possible.' Anne knew she sounded abrupt but almost laughed inside as she imagined approaching her immediate superior. There wasn't the slightest chance it would be allowed. 'It's very strict in a hospital and Matron rules with a rod of iron. Father will tell you that.'

'I'll ask him to intervene,' Eleanor said.

'I wouldn't like my girls to do nursing. It's just not suitable for young women to see such sights. I can't imagine how awful it would be to have to help sick people. It's altogether too horrible. I don't know how you do it, Anne,' her aunt said.

She didn't reply. Such a remark didn't deserve one.

They drove away in their motor car a little later and Anne was glad to see the back of them, but was aware that she faced a telling off from her mother before the night was out and wasn't to be disappointed. Eleanor had just begun a tirade when her husband arrived, and she switched her attention to him.

'If your brother-in-law was here, you would have had to be home. But since he wasn't you didn't even bother to appear.' Her face was red with annoyance. 'And imagine coming in at ten o'clock, what sort of time is this?'

'He wasn't here, so I didn't have to be home.'

'You don't care about my family,' she sniffed with displeasure.

'Don't be silly, Eleanor, you know that's not true.'

She pouted.

'Forget about it. We'll be going out tomorrow to lunch at the Shelbourne, so that will cheer us all up,' Clarence said, with a wink at Anne.

'I'm putting my foot down, this nursing business is at an end. If you keep it up you will be on the shelf. No man is going to want to have anything to do with you. I know from all my friends. Their attitudes are all the same, and certainly none of their sons will want to marry you.'

'I don't care, Mother,' Anne stiffened her resolve.

'So, being an old maid doesn't bother you? You'll have no husband, no children, no home of your own. What a prospect. I can't imagine your father would want that for you.' She looked at Clarence. 'Tell me you wouldn't?' she demanded of him.

'Of course not. But I'm sure Anne will meet a nice man one of these days.'

'Where will she find him?' She sniffed. 'I told you what my friends think.'

'There's more people in Dublin than your friends,' Anne retorted.

'Don't speak like that to your mother,' her father rebuked her unexpectedly.

'But she doesn't understand.'

'She has your best interests at heart.'

'Are you on her side?' Her eyes blazed.

'Really, Anne, such rudeness cannot be tolerated,' Eleanor exploded.

'I'm beginning to think your mother is right,' Clarence said, his forehead creased with irritation.

'But Father ...' Suddenly she found her one ally beginning to drift away.

'I'll have to reconsider. Perhaps I made a mistake in giving you so much freedom.'

'I thought you believed in what I do. I'm the same as you, I want to help people too.' She tried to bring him around to her side.

'Maybe it mightn't suit you after all.'

'Father, please don't stop me training, it would break my heart. It's all I want to do.' She could feel herself losing control and wondered how she would persuade both of them if they decided to jointly stand in her way.

'Enough about it now.' He stood up.

'But Father ...'

He raised his hand, and left the room.

She ran after him.

'Father, can I help you in the lab?'

He said nothing. Simply strode down the corridor and disappeared.

Chapter Thirty-two

James was exultant on that Easter Monday, planning to go over later in the day to ask Louise's father for her hand in marriage. It had to be formally done and he hoped that his own father would agree, he couldn't bear a refusal. He hung about the kitchen as his mother prepared the dinner. His sisters had gone out walking with their friends and his young brother was playing in the street.

'I'm surprised to see you around the house, you're normally gone off on a day like this,' she said, rolling pastry for a tart, her hands floury from the rolling pin.

'No manoeuvres.'

'It's good to have a day off for a change,' she said.

'I mentioned something to you the other day ...' he paused.

She glanced up at him with a little smile.

'I've asked Louise to marry me and she said yes,' he said in a rush of emotion which he couldn't hide.

'I'm glad of that.'

'I will ask her father later, he should be at home as it's a holiday, although Louise is working at the Shelbourne.'

'I wish you all the best, son, this will change your life.'

'I know,' he was sheepish.

'What about your politics?' She placed the rolled pastry on an enamel dish and trimmed the excess around the edge with a knife. A quick expert move. Then she rolled the ribbon of pastry up and added it to the other ball she was using for the top.

'Louise shares my hopes for Ireland, all her family feel the same way.' He couldn't hide his enthusiasm.

Liliane put in the chopped apple, tossed sugar in and added cloves.

James picked a piece of apple and popped it into his mouth with relish.

'Cheeky,' Liliane laughed, flipped the top on, spread beaten egg, and crimped the edges together. Finally she stabbed the top with her fork in a couple of places. 'Right, into the oven.'

'Can't wait to have a slice of that.'

'Maybe you might mention Louise to your father, you know how he likes to be informed about what is going on.'

'Do you think he'll approve?'

'He may feel you're a bit young, but he wasn't much older himself when we got married, so that's in your favour,' she washed her floured hands in a bowl of water and dried them on a small towel. 'Go on now, he's in the parlour.'

James felt suddenly uncertain now about his plans. What if his father didn't approve?

'Father ...' James stood in the doorway.

Matt lifted his head and stared at him over gold-rimmed spectacles.

'I've something to ask you.'

His father waited but said nothing.

'I'm thinking of getting married,' he decided to come straight out with it.

Matt's eyes showed surprise.

'And I'm hoping you'll give me your approval.'

'Do you think you can support a wife and family on your wages?' There was a slight edge in his voice.

'We won't be getting married just yet, we'll wait and save up until we have enough.'

'Who is this girl? Do we know the family?'

'No, but I could bring her over and introduce her to you.'

'Do that.' His eyes went back to his newspaper.

'Thank you.' James felt relieved and walked to the door.

'You don't think I'd refuse to allow you to marry? You're over twenty-one,' his father said with a grin.

As James went down the hall, a decided spring in his step, someone knocked on the front door. He turned back and opened it, surprised to see Michael outside.

'Word has come down. The *Rising* is on again,' he said quietly.

'But I thought it was cancelled?'

'We're to report to the GPO. Get your rifle and ammunition, don't bother about the uniform. I have my bicycle. Come on ...'

James rushed upstairs, and took the bag which contained his gun from under the wardrobe, and then went down to the kitchen.

'Mother, the manoeuvres are on again.' He kissed her quickly.

'So much for your day off,' she said.

He hesitated. His mother knew nothing of any uprising and suddenly he felt he should tell her. He couldn't just go off and disappear. 'It's more than that ...'

She stared at him. 'What do you mean?'

'There will be an uprising.'

Her face paled.

'It's what we've been waiting for, I couldn't tell you before now, didn't really know myself.'

'My God, James ...' she whispered.

'I haven't time to explain.' He kissed her. 'But I'm sure it won't last long and I'll be back soon.'

She grabbed hold of him. 'Don't go, please?'

'I'm sorry, I must, Michael is waiting.'
'You'd better talk to your Father.'
'You tell him ...please?'

James and Michael rode quickly into Sackville Street. People were on the streets although the shops were closed, but there was a definite holiday air about. James wondered whether anything was happening at all. They swung into Princes Street, left the bicycle up against the wall, and knocked on the side door of the GPO. A uniformed Volunteer opened the door holding a rifle.

'We've been ordered to report for duty.'

'Why aren't you wearing your uniforms?'

'We'd no time,' James explained. 'Just got word.'

'Right, lads.' He opened the door wider. 'Go downstairs and into the first room on the right and see Sergeant O'Connor.'

'Our manoeuvres have brought us to something worthwhile at last,' Michael said, with a laugh.

The Sergeant checked their ammunition. He grinned. 'I'll put you on bomb-making. Down there to the last door on the left. The men will tell you what they want.'

James was struck by the fever of activity in the place. There were men everywhere, carrying guns, bayonets, and all sorts of other implements. Some in the uniform of the Volunteers, or Citizen Army, and others, like themselves, just in their ordinary clothes, having had no time to change. Anything which could be used was taken to barricade doors and windows. Every now and then he saw someone he recognised, but the majority of the men in other companies were unknown to him. At the same time, men carried boxes of food from the Metropole Hotel nearby and took them down to the rooms which were being used as a kitchen. Others carried piles of linen and mattresses which had come from the hotel as well.

They were both instructed to make up bombs. There was a large amount of empty tins, and these were to be filled with gunpowder, a piece of string then inserted which would be lit just before the tin was thrown at the enemy.

'Mind yourselves with that gunpowder, and no smoking or you'll blow us all up,' the man who was directing the operation said.

The two grinned at each other.

For the first time James felt he was involved in something real, and his previous doubt that there was any chance of success diminished. The *Rising* would strike a blow for the people of Ireland as their commandant had said many a time.

'Is your father here as well?' he asked Michael.

He nodded, carefully filling a tin with gunpowder.

'Louise is working, isn't she?' He asked the question hoping that she hadn't been summoned to join Cumann na mBan before she went to work.

Michael nodded.

James was relieved.

'Stop talking to me, I have to concentrate on this,' Michael muttered, his mouth clenched.

'Sorry.' James paid attention to what he was doing himself.

Under pressure to get through all of the tins, there was a sudden explosion and a shout. One of the men put his hand to his face, blood flowing through his fingers. James used his handkerchief to stench the bleeding and took him to the area where the women had set up a first aid station. They were already busy tending to a man who had been shot by another volunteer whose gun had gone off accidentally. Michael and he were very careful after that. Not a word between them. Very much aware that they could be the next victims if they didn't take care.

When they finished all the tins, there was a general air of relaxation, and someone cheered.

'Sorry for talking,' James said.

'I was shaking like a leaf.'

'Men, Patrick Pearse has gone out to talk to the people outside.' A man put his head around the door. They rushed into the corridor and up the stairs.

'What is he saying?' James asked.

'He's reading the *Proclamation of the Irish Republic*,' someone said.

Men stopped what they were doing for a moment. Although he strained his ears, James couldn't hear what Pearse was saying, and regretted he was out of earshot. But after a short time, there was a loud cheer and as he joined in with the rest of the men, suddenly James knew that whatever the outcome he was prepared to give up his life for Ireland.

Chapter Thirty-three

Louise was so happy this morning. Her dreams had come true when James asked her to marry him. She couldn't wait to see him later on and hear whether her father had given them his blessing.

On any holiday the Shelbourne was crowded with guests and on an Easter Monday especially so. She was passing the front reception desk when the Manager, Mr. Quinton, called her over.

'This note was dropped in earlier for you.' He handed her a brown envelope, her name roughly scrawled in pencil on it.

She put it into her pocket, suddenly wondering if it was from James. Had something happened to upset their plans? Her heart pounded and her hand itched to open it now, but she had to go upstairs and check the linens immediately. She did that and before anyone else called her, she headed to the staff cloakroom which thankfully was empty. Quickly, she opened the envelope, pulled out the single sheet of paper, and read the contents. She was shocked to be summoned at once by Countess Markievicz to the Harcourt Street corner of St. Stephen's Green. The *Rising* would happen today at noon. Panic set in. It was past that now. How could she leave her work just like that? Neither the housekeeper, Miss Cunningham, or the Manager, Mr. Quinton, would be pleased, and especially if she left on such a busy day. She didn't know what to do. Had her father, Michael and James been called up also? Perspiration bathed her forehead, and she poured water from the jug on to her handkerchief and dabbed it on her face. She stared in the mirror, and took a moment to consider what to do. She would have to respond to the call no matter what the consequences. Having to explain to Miss Cunningham that she must leave immediately would mean without a doubt that she would never be employed at the Shelbourne again.

She hurried back upstairs and walked into the foyer. Lunch parties were now arriving and she saw Doctor and Mrs. Montford come through the front doors followed by their three daughters. Immediately, they acknowledged her and she was forced to smile pleasantly and welcome them.

'How lovely to see you.' She shook hands with each. 'And all looking so pretty in your Easter bonnets.'

'I'll take you into the dining room, but first would you like me to put anything in the cloak room for you?' asked Louise.

'No thank you, but I'd like to freshen up,' said Anne.

As the Montford family were frequent visitors to the hotel, the two girls had struck up an unlikely friendship. On one occasion, Anne had been taken ill and Louise had arranged for her to rest in an unoccupied bedroom and stayed with her until she had recovered. Since then, they had become firm friends considering the social strata in which each of them lived.

'You're looking very pretty today,' Louise said when they went to the cloakroom.

'And how are you?' Anne asked.

'I'm ...' Louise hesitated. She suddenly found it hard to hide her concern about what was happening.

'Is there something wrong, you seem worried,' Anne asked.

'I've just had some unexpected news,' Louise admitted.

'Is there a problem?'

Without thinking, Louise took the letter from her pocket and handed it to Anne. 'I'm in Cumann na mBan.'

'What does this mean?' Anne read through the letter.

'There is to be a *Rising*, a call to arms.'

Anne's eyes widened. The two girls stared at each other.

'You will need nurses?'

Louise nodded.

'Then we'll both go together.' She took off her flower trimmed hat decisively. 'But I can't work in these clothes.' She stared down at her pale blue lace dress.

'I've a spare uniform, it should fit you.'

'Quickly, there's no time to waste,' Anne said.

'What about your parents, how will you explain where you are going?' Louise asked.

'I'll just say I have to go back to the hospital, Father will understand, Mother certainly won't.'

'And I have to tell Mr. Quinton and Miss Cunningham,' Louise rushed to the door. 'Thank you so much for your support, I'm very grateful to you,' she smiled at Anne as they left the room together.

To say Miss Cunningham was horrified was an under-statement.

'What are you talking about, girl? I never heard the like. You want to leave your job to march with the Volunteers? To tell you the truth, I'm sick and tired of seeing them on the streets.'

Louise had deliberately avoided mentioning the word *Rising*. 'It's very important, and I'm deeply sorry for going on such a busy holiday.'

'When will you be back?' she asked with an air of suspicion.

'I'm not sure, to be truthful.'

Miss Cunningham humphed loudly. 'Well, if you must go, you must, I suppose.'

'Will I still have my job?' Louise asked tentatively.

'We'll have to see about that.'

'Thank you Miss Cunningham, thank you.'

'Mind you, it won't be up to me, remember that, it will be Mr. Quinton's decision. Off with you now.'

Louise left the office as quickly as possible, unable to believe her good fortune. In the cloakroom Anne was closing the buttons on the uniform.

'Does it fit?'

'I'm a bit bigger than you, I think, but I can manage if I hold my breath,' Anne said, smiling.

'Is it that small?'

'I'm joking, it's all right.'

'I'll put away your things for safe keeping.' Louise hung the dress in the wardrobe and left the hat and gloves on a shelf. 'What did you say to your mother and father?'

'That I had to go back to the hospital.'

'Did they ask how you received the message?' Louise asked.

'No,' she said, with a laugh. 'I didn't give them a chance, and just ran out of there.'

They smiled at each other.

'Let's leave by the side door.'

Chapter Thirty-four

Mary walked down the hall to the door. There were a number of people gathered there.

'Mary, did you hear about the fighting?' Tilly asked.

'What?'

'It's the Volunteers, they're shooting the English.'

Mary had often seen the men going around in their green uniforms, and slouch hats. But was too concerned with her own hand-to-mouth existence to pay them much attention other than to think they had little else to do.

'You can hear the noise of the guns down by the Green, and someone saw them turn cars and vans over on their sides at the end of Leeson Street,' one of her neighbours said, peering out the door.

'Jesus, Mary and Joseph, what's upon us at all?' Mary crossed herself.

'And there's women out there too, they must be mad.'

Mary's eyes widened at the possibility of that. 'I was just going over to Mercer's to see if they will let me take our Emily home.'

'I'd watch yourself if I were you,' a man said.

'I'm sure they're not going to bother shooting me, I'm no use to them. But before I go I'd better tell Lar.' She hurried back up the two flights of stairs to their room. Lar lay in bed and she shook him. 'Man, there's fighting on the streets. Wake up.'

'What are you talking about?' He opened his eyes a little. They were bloodshot.

'Men shooting the English, that's what,' she snapped, irritated at his slow response.

'Is it the Volunteers?' He sat up now, fully awake.

'Yes. And Bridget took Brendan to St. Stephen's Green. God only knows what will happen to them.' She walked up and down the room in a state.

'They'll be all right.' Lar was pulling on his work clothes over his drawers, and pushing large feet into cracked brown leather boots. Then he slung his braces over his shoulders and rushed downstairs. Mary could hear him quizzing the group of people at the door.

Lar had never got involved with any political grouping, too lazy in the first place and too fond of his drink to do anything which required dedication. Now he thumped back up the stairs. 'Mary, I'm joining them.' He picked up his old coat from the bed. 'Have you anything to eat?'

'There's bread there.' She went to the kitchen press and took out the soda bread she had made this morning. She cut a few slices and spread dripping on them. He chomped while she poured a mug of strong tea.

He ate one slice and stuffed the rest into his pocket. 'Don't know when I'll be back, look after yourself.' He disappeared.

She followed him down to the front door.

The men and women gathered there watched his progress, passing shops and pubs along the street. 'What d'ye bet he dives into one of them pubs and doesn't come out again for weeks?' a woman asked, and the others laughed.

Mary said nothing, but agreed with their comments.

'And my man as well. Maybe they'll all use the excuse of fighting to go and live in a pub,' another woman added.

'Give me a chance and I'd do the same,' one of the few men there grunted.

'Off you go then.'

'It's my bad leg, I wouldn't be able to make it, might get shot.'

'Coward.' They burst into raucous laughter. But their merriment stopped abruptly as a bullet whined past and thudded into the frame of the front door. At that, they pushed and shoved past each other to get inside.

'Close over the bloody door,' someone yelled, and they leaned against it to ensure it stayed that way.

'Watch a bullet doesn't come through and kill one of us,' a bright spark said.

They stared at each other in shock. No-one had really considered the possibility of one of them being killed.

Mary hesitated now about going over to Mercer's. She went back upstairs to her room. She stood at the window and looked through the piece of net curtain which prevented the whole world from staring in. The street below was empty. One half in shadow, the other in bright sunshine. It was so unusual to see it like that. Cuffe Street was always a busy place with numerous public houses and shops. The street itself thronged with horses and carts, people going about their daily business, and even an odd motor car pushing its way through.

Mary was worried about Lar. While she constantly complained about him, he was her husband and she depended on him and still loved him the truth be told. There was the sound of footsteps on the stairs and she went outside. A few of the men and women on her landing had gathered towards the back of the house. 'We'd better keep away from the front windows,' one of the men said. 'Maybe put up something against the glass to protect ourselves,' he suggested.

'I'm going to push my dresser over,' a woman decided.

'And mine too,' another said.

They disappeared immediately.

'Bloody Sinn Feiners,' muttered a man.

'And you can be sure that the Citizen Army are mixed up in it too,' someone else added.

'I was a member of the Citizen Army in 1913 after we were locked out. Are they out there?'

'My son is fighting in France, God knows where he is by now.'

'And here they're fighting against the English. A lot of the men stationed here are Irish so that means Irishman will be fighting Irishman. Killing each other.'

'For what?'

Mary recognised Bridget's voice and pulled open the door. The girl flung herself into her arms, and Brendan grabbed hold of her. She held them close. 'You'll be all right, I have you now, stop crying.'

'They made us get out of the Green, and they had guns. I was frightened,' Bridget cried. 'What's happening, Mam?'

'It's the rebels, the Volunteers, they're fighting the English.'

Bridget gasped. 'We saw women there and they had guns too.'

'They were real guns,' Brendan said.

'Not like your old wooden one?' Mary laughed.

He shook his head.

'It took a long time to come home.' Bridget was shaking.

'We were afraid.' Brendan threw his arms around her neck, and she could feel the moisture of his tears on her cheeks.

'Would you like some bread and dripping?'

He nodded.

'You take him, Bridget.' She kissed her daughter, and quickly made them something to eat. They were badly shocked and she was very relieved that they had returned safely to her but was still worried about Robbie and the younger ones. But to her relief he arrived shortly afterwards.

'Robbie?' She looked behind him. 'Where are the twins?'

‘Aunt Eileen took them out to Aunt Agnes.’

‘Thanks be to the good God.’ Mary blessed herself. ‘Why didn’t you go yourself?’

He shrugged. ‘I heard of all sorts going on in town. People with guns. Fighting.’

‘How did you get through it?’

‘I came the back ways, it’s all happening around the GPO.’

‘Has your Gran gone to Agnes as well?’

‘No, she wouldn’t move. She said she was born and bred in Moore Street and she wanted to die there too, so there’s no budging her,’ Robbie grinned. ’What’s it been like here, Mam?’

‘Some guns firing but it’s not that bad. People have left but I’m like my mother I suppose, I’m not going. This is our home.’

‘Where’s Pa?’ he asked.

‘He went down the street to see what was going on and didn’t come back. Said he was joining the Volunteers.’

‘Hope he’s all right.’

‘He will be, don’t worry. What’s Moore Street like? Do you think we’ll set up the stall tomorrow?’

‘Don’t think so, Mam.’

‘We’ll need to buy food,’ Mary was suddenly worried.

‘I’ll go out in the morning and scout around,’ Robbie said.

‘I haven’t much money, except the few pence left over from the moneylender.’

‘Granny sent up some food, but it isn’t much.’ He handed her a small bag of vegetables.

‘That will keep us going, but I don’t know for how long.’

There was a loud crash. Mary rushed across the room.

‘Mam, get back, you could be shot.’ Robbie stood in front of her.

‘I should have blocked the windows like the others, let’s move the dresser over.’

‘I’ll do it.’

Helped by Bridget, they emptied the contents and between them dragged it across to the window.

'It's almost the same size. We could stuff something down the side to fill the gap,' Robbie said.

'What will we use for the other window?' Mary asked, staring around the room.

'A mattress,' Bridget suggested.

'Right,' Robbie pulled one from the floor and pushed it against the glass.

'It's going to slip,' Mary said.

'No, it won't.'

'We'll stand the table against it.'

They cleared away the miscellaneous crockery, carried the table over, and pushed the top of it against the mattress.

'It seems to be holding.'

'Use some of these flour bags for the gaps.' Mary picked them up from a shelf.

There was a loud report of gunfire.

'Where is it coming from?'

'Seems like it's coming from the Green.'

Mary and Bridget blessed themselves.

Chapter Thirty-five

Lar ducked into a doorway. Cuffe Street was almost deserted, and he didn't know what was happening. Then he saw a small group of Volunteers march towards him and break down the door of a public house he used to frequent. Quickly, he ran that way and followed them inside. A rifle was pushed into his face.

'Hey don't shoot ...' he raised his hands. 'I want to join you,' he said.

'Good man,' the Volunteer said. 'Our post is at Jacobs biscuit factory,' he said. 'And we're to hold this place for the moment. Have you a gun?'

Lar shook his head.

'Here's a couple of bombs, go upstairs and if you see the enemy, light that string and throw.'

He went through the bar carrying the tins, and his eyes slid past the bottles of spirits on the shelves, an immediate wrench in his gut at the thought of all that drink sitting there and no publican to keep an eye on it. He continued on up the back stairs into a parlour but it was empty. There were two windows overlooking the street and he took up a position to one side. He was a big man, Lar, and was glad to be involved. His everyday life a drudge. To find enough money to live his main objective. Working at the docks when he could get a day's work, and then hitting the bottle with the few bob he earned, but having to deal with Mary's disapproval when he fell in the door at night.

This was something different. Another side to his personality had emerged. A man had been hidden behind the façade of that *divil may care* fellow liked so much by all of his friends. Now excitement swept through him. It made him feel he could do anything. He would take on these British soldiers. Blow them to pieces with his bombs. He knew all about the hopes of the Volunteers and the Irish Citizen Army. He had been involved in the lock-out of 1913, but had been too lazy to put his hand up and declare himself for either group since then.

The men remained in the pub for some time, and then received a message from a young boy to retreat. They waited a short while and then left the premises. Hugging the buildings, ducking in and out of doorways, making it safely back to Jacobs which had been barricaded using large sacks of flour in the windows.

'I need a gun,' Lar said to one of the men.

'Can you shoot?'

'No.'

'You'll be a lot of use,' the man grinned.

'I'll bloody learn, and quick,' he muttered.

He disappeared into the shadows of the building.

Lar waited. Growling to himself that if they didn't give him a gun he'd do a bunk and go back to that pub. But the man returned and pushed a rifle into his hands, and a box of ammunition.

'Thanks, I feel useful now,' he grunted.

The man took a moment and showed him how to load and aim the gun. There was a crackle of gunfire from outside, and under cover of that Lar aimed and shot at the box which had contained the ammunition. It jerked across the floor out of sight.

'All right,' the Volunteer grinned. 'Follow me.'

They joined a group of men who went outside to check on the movements of the British.

'We've got information that there is a group of military coming down Camden Street. We're to attack them.'

They gathered at the corner of Redmond's Hill.

Lar was nervous. Praying that he would not make a fool out of himself, or get himself killed through his inability to even shoot a tin can. A cardboard box hardly counted. He regretted not joining the Volunteers before now.

As soon as the group of British soldiers appeared, they opened fire, including Lar. The officer who led them and a number of soldiers fell to the ground. Lar couldn't believe it. A rush of satisfaction seared through him as the rest of the soldiers fled out of sight. His group rushed back to the shelter of Jacobs.

A quick meeting was called by the commandant. A messenger had arrived from headquarters at the GPO with a copy of the *Proclamation of the Irish Republic*, and news of what was happening in the Sackville Street area. It was only then that Lar realised what this was truly all about.

Chapter Thirty-six

Louise and Anne left the hotel cautiously but it seemed quite normal outside. There were plenty of people about, and the girls cut across the street to St. Stephen's Green and followed around the square to the Harcourt Street entrance. There was a barricade of trees and branches erected across the gate and a number of well armed men on guard.

'I am Cumann na mBan, Company C, and this is my friend who wants to join with us,' Louisc said.

'I'm a nurse. I'll do whatever I can,' Anne said.

'Good, we could do with you, although thankfully we have no wounded yet. You'll have to climb over the gate. I'll give you a hand when you get to the top.'

They managed to pull themselves up and over with his help.

'Be careful, we don't want you to fall,' he said.

A large number of men were digging trenches on each side of the pathway which led into the Green itself parallel with the railings. It looked heavy work.

As the girls stood there, a well-dressed man and woman with their children stopped to stare at the barricade. A number of other people also gathered to watch.

'What's that?' A small boy pointed.

'Come away,' his mother grabbed his arm.

'Who are they?' another asked.

'Can we go into the park by this gate?' A man enquired.

'No, you're in the middle of a *Rising*,' a Citizen Army man said.

They stared at him, shocked.

'But we planned to have a picnic ...'

'If you've any food to spare we'd appreciate it,' he said.

The woman looked at the man.

'I don't hold with this,' he said.

'Be off with you then.' The Citizen Army man waved his gun.

'We could let you have something.' The woman lifted the basket.

'Thanks.'

The man ushered the children away.

'But what is it all about, Mother?' One of them asked.

'We're fighting for the freedom of Ireland,' a man inside the gate yelled.

The family rushed away.

One of the men climbed over the gate and retrieved the basket.

'I'll join you.' A middle-aged man offered.

'No-one's refused,' they said from inside.

A young man helped him, and then climbed over himself. 'I'm with you as well, men.'

'Which way should we go?' Louise asked one of the men.

'Straight down there, Miss ffrench-Mullen is in charge of the food and first aid.'

At that moment, a woman dressed in uniform and carrying a rifle, hurried towards them. 'Come with me, girls.'

They followed deeper into the park where a group of women were setting up a kitchen of sorts. They introduced themselves.

'We're the kitchen detail, but we'll need some women who can handle a gun. Are you a good shot?' One of them asked Louise.

'I'm not bad,' she admitted.

'I'm a nurse so I have no experience of guns,' Anne added.

'Don't worry, we'll need you.'

Louise was given a rifle and ammunition, and sent with a few other women to join the men at the Harcourt Street gate.

'Get out there and stop those motor cars.' The order came.

They were helped over the gate.

Louise's heart was thumping. This was it now. She raised her rifle, and with the others, crossed the road in front of the oncoming vehicles. A large blue motor car screeched to a halt when the driver saw the men and women with the guns. Someone fired a shot in the air. Louise ran to a second car which stopped behind the first. 'Get out,' she pointed her gun at the occupants. So close to them she was nervous, her hands gripping the rifle were wet with perspiration.

'We will not. Who are you to tell us? I'm going to get the police.' The man shook his fist at her.

'Get out or I'll shoot.' She tried not to show how anxious she was, and moved closer.

The two women in the back seat screamed.

The man gave up his defiance and opened the car door. They all climbed out and ran down a nearby laneway, the women holding on to their hats.

There was a crowd of people gathered at the end of Harcourt Street, watching what was going on, but when they heard the gunshots, they moved back up the street. As soon as the occupants of the motor car had disappeared the men joined the women and they swung the motor back and forward until it fell over on its side with an immense crash of broken glass and metal. Then they went to the other vehicles which had been stopped and did the same, creating a barrier across the road. A tram appeared and the women held their guns on it. The driver didn't resist. He pulled up and got out smartly, shouting at the passengers to do the same.

Louise and the others retreated back to the comparative safety of the gate. The barricade of cars and the tram was holding. Anyone coming down Harcourt Street was now turning around and driving back up, although people still wandered past. Couples arm in arm. Families. Children peered in and laughed. It was quite bizarre, Louise thought. To be here in St. Stephen's Green holding a gun on the people of Dublin.

Chapter Thirty-seven

Eleanor Montford and her two daughters, Catherine and Rhoda, were still in the Shelbourne Hotel. She was very annoyed that Anne had left. And Clarence had followed her later. It simply was the last straw. Now she decided that she would put her foot down, and finish this nursing nonsense. For the first time satisfied that Clarence now felt the same as she did herself. After they had finished lunch, they went into the sunlit drawing room to sit and chat until afternoon tea was served. There was much merriment as the crowd increased, no-one taking the slightest notice of the occasional bullet which thudded against the front of the hotel until there was a crash of breaking glass. Eleanor screamed. Men jumped to their feet. Catherine and Rhoda stared. An officer in uniform immediately came over.

'Ladies, are you all right?' he asked with concern.

'What's happening?' Eleanor was confused.

Men were now examining the wall.

'The glass in the window was shattered by a bullet,' someone exclaimed.

Eleanor fainted.

'Mother?' Catherine and Rhoda bent over her.

Mr. Quinton appeared beside them, shouting for smelling salts, which were produced within a few seconds by one of the staff and held under her nose. A moment later, she responded and was helped to sit down again, and handed a glass of water by Miss Cunningham.

'Are you feeling better, Mrs. Montford,' she enquired.

'I simply don't know. I'm confused. What happened?'

Mr. Quinton hesitated for a few seconds. 'They are firing at the hotel, you'll have to move out of here, Mrs. Montford, Catherine, Rhoda, come with me. Lord and Lady Berenson, Captain Howard,' he ushered the guests out of the room.

'I want to go home,' Eleanor said.

'Soon, Mother.' Catherine helped her through the doors.

'Miss Cunningham, will you get us a carriage please?' Eleanor asked.

'That won't be possible just yet Mrs. Montford,' she replied.

'Why not?'

She led them towards the back of the hotel. 'There has been an uprising against the government,' she explained. 'St. Stephen's Green has been taken over.'

'We must leave at once. My husband has gone over to the hospital but he'll be home later and expect us to be there.'

'He will know that we are looking out for you and that it would be far too dangerous for you to attempt to travel to Blackrock. At any rate, there is no transport, all the trams have been cancelled.'

'But our chauffeur will drive in with the motor car, he brought us over this morning.'

'We can try and telephone your residence. I will call you if I can make communication,' she promised.

'I wish I knew what to do.' Eleanor fluttered her hands in a distracted fashion.

'We will take good care of you here and I'm sure this whole escapade will be over by morning,' she assured.

'By morning?' her expression was shocked.

'Calm, Mrs. Montford, calm.' She moved away to deal with another group of people who were anxious to leave. Gave instructions to various staff members, and tried to control the general pandemonium.

The porter had already closed the heavy front doors, and the inner doors as well.

Mr. Quinton was on the telephone and Eleanor went over to him.

'I must get home, Mr. Quinton, you don't understand, I don't feel safe.' She grabbed his arm.

He put his hand over the mouthpiece of the telephone. 'Don't worry, Mrs. Montford, I'm calling the police and the army, Miss Cunningham?'

She hurried across the foyer.

Eleanor turned to her. 'Please let us go home, I'm afraid to stay here,' she appealed.

'We'll have you home as soon as it is safe, Mrs. Montford, now you must come with me. You will be perfectly all right, I promise.'

Miss Cunningham had an amazing ability to calm the most fractured of nerves, particularly of those female guests who had no understanding of what was going on. The men, on the other hand, were loud in their condemnation of the rebels and wanted to go out and help the soldiers in whatever way they could. Many were military and felt they could put down this petty little rebellion in a matter of hours.

'Make yourselves comfortable in the Writing Room, and tea will be served as quickly as we can,' Miss Cunningham announced.

Catherine handed her mother the smelling salts if she felt faint. They had no idea what was happening, and Eleanor had them as nervous as herself. The other people in the room were more relaxed. Ladies and gentlemen chatted and enjoyed the novelty of this enforced stay in the luxurious hotel. Not that they were able to use most of its rooms being cooped up here at the back, but there was a certain excitement about it and the general feeling was that as soon as the army arrived to protect them everything would be fine and they would be quite safe.

Chapter Thirty-eight

'I don't believe this,' James's father Matt shouted. 'Where is he?' he rushed out of the parlour.

'He's gone with Michael,' Liliane said.

'Where?'

'To the GPO.'

'Did he say there was going to be an uprising?' He was furious.

She nodded.

'You mean ...fighting?'

'I'm not sure.'

He ran out of the house and stared down the road. Then he went around the side, leapt up on his bicycle and sped away. Fast down Infirmary Road, and then on to the quays. As he went along, he tried to get his mind around this business.

He didn't approve of the involvement of his son with the Volunteers, particularly as his eldest son, Maurice, was fighting for England against the Germans. Now if Liliane had got it right, James was going to fight against the English. It made his blood boil. How on earth did a few Volunteers think they could take on the might of the British Empire? It was complete nonsense.

He glanced around him. It was a lovely sunny day. There was no sign at all of anything untoward happening. It was like any other holiday, everyone out to enjoy themselves. He put his foot on the ground and stopped the momentum of the bicycle.

Maybe Liliane had got it wrong, the Volunteers were probably just doing their usual manoeuvres. But he set off again along Bachelor's Walk, and turned on to Sackville Street. Here it was different. There were a number of people standing on the Clerys side of the street staring at the GPO, and in front of it a larger crowd had gathered. He left his bicycle up against one of the columns in front of the building, and moved through the crowd. Noticing only now that the windows in the Post Office were smashed and barricaded. A group of men wearing green uniforms stood at the main door. One of them was reading aloud from a sheet of paper. Matt couldn't quite understand what he was saying as there was much muttering among the people. But then the man finished and they went back inside. The door opened a moment later and a notice was nailed to the door which was closed again with a bang. The people surged forward to read it. Matt peered over the heads in front of him but was unable to get close enough.

'Shoot the Sinn Feiners,' a man shouted.

'Traitors.'

'Up the Republic,' another yelled. There was a scuffle as that man was turned upon by the others.

It began to look dangerous, and Matt decided to get out of there. He was shocked. It was an uprising and James was involved. He was too young to be caught up in this. Maybe he should go in there and haul him out, but Matt knew that he couldn't do that. James was over twenty-one and entitled to make his own decisions, regardless of what his father thought about it. He retrieved his bicycle and walked through the crowd. He stopped at the Metropole Hotel and stared back. Out of the door of the hotel, Volunteers carried a motley collection of mattresses, linen, boxes and bags, into the side door of the GPO on Princes Street. Back and forth they ran, helped by young boys. It looked like they were preparing for a siege, Matt thought.

He hurried back home, now very worried about James and the family. His son would be in danger, and if other parts of the country had risen as well, then all of Ireland could be devastated.

Chapter Thirty-nine

James and Michael were posted to one of the rooms on the third floor of the GPO. Here they smashed the glass in the windows and barricaded them using the furniture. Then they knelt down and covered the street below with rifles waiting for a response from the English. Suddenly, a company of British Lancers on horseback trotted into view, wearing their colourful uniforms. They reached Nelson's Pillar. James looked at Michael, a question in his eyes. They took aim. But they weren't the only Volunteers shooting at the Lancers and there was a loud volley of shots. A number of the horsemen fell to the ground, and two of the horses. James stared in shock. This was the first real sign of war he had seen.

That Monday night, the gunfire diminished and James lay on the floor, gun by his side. Michael and he took it in turns to get some sleep during the night. He was hungry, and hadn't had anything to eat or drink since the morning when his mother had given him the usual breakfast of porridge, and a slice of bread and marmalade. 'Michael?'

He turned his head.

'You sleep for a while, I can't.' James pushed himself up.

'I don't think I can either.'

'Anything stirring out there?' he asked.

'No.'

He knelt at the other window. Pushed his rifle out through the glass splinters at the end of the window. Outside it was pitch black. There were no street lamps lighting, and James felt he could be out in the countryside it was so dark.

Tuesday dawned, the street bathed in sunshine from the east. He watched the beauty of the morning light creep over the rooftops opposite in delicate hues of pink and blue, chasing the night away. Louise had been foremost in his mind all night. Imagining their lives together in the future. First he would buy her an engagement ring. But he had to save up for that. He had a few shillings in the Post Office but that would never be enough to buy Louise the ring she deserved. It had to be something beautiful. A glittering stone to signify how much they loved each other.

Suddenly he was jerked out of his dream by the sound of a tremendous burst of gunfire. It echoed through the building. The surface of the front of the GPO was peppered with bullets. He trained his gun on the area below. Sackville Street was being swept by heavy machine guns, with gunfire from snipers on the tops of other buildings. Lines of communication had been set up between the various posts held by the Volunteers and the GPO, and a telephone connection enabled those on the roof to report back what they saw happening.

He could see no soldiers and felt frustrated by that. The street was empty except for an occasional hurrying civilian. Where were the English? 'I can't see them,' James yelled to Michael, during a slight lull.

'They can see us.'

Bullets whizzed past his head. He ducked. And could hear them thud into the wood panelling of the door behind him. His pulse raced. Perspiration dribbled down his face. He knew they should try to reinforce the barricade in the windows. Block every opening. But if he stood up now he could be mown down, the gunfire constant. He crawled along the floor. Pushed his rifle out the side of the second window. Thinking that maybe he would get a better view from here. He could see barricades down at Nelson's Pillar. Soldiers behind them. He aimed. But realised that they were too far away to get a decent shot with the old rifle he had. All they could do was to defend their position, keep the English at bay, and pray they wouldn't be shot.

An order came through for James to help fortify the area on the ground floor, and he went down, glad of the break. Anything which could be found by way of furniture, books, files, supplemented with sandbags, would protect the open areas. On the ground floor mattresses had been brought in for the leaders, but they didn't get much chance to use them. It was down here that James could see what was happening. Upstairs, he had been shielded somewhat. Shocked at the number of injuries already sustained by Volunteers who were then carried to the area where the women of the Cumann na mBan looked after them.

He was back on duty later that night in a top floor office with Michael and another man named Richard. The gunfire died down as it grew dark. He watched the street. Astonished to see gangs of people rushing past Clerys carrying clothes and other goods and then ducking down the side streets and disappearing from view. Others pushed prams laden down with booty. A group of men fought over whatever they had.

'I can see smoke,' Michael said. 'Some place is burning.'

'We've got people in most of the buildings on the other side of the street, The Royal Hibernian Academy, Hopkins and Hopkins, and on up to Clerys and the Imperial Hotel from Eden Quay, and we're in most of the places on this side of the street as well.' James pushed his gun out through the broken window. 'Hope we can hold them.'

Richard didn't speak.

'Did you see my father?' Michael asked.

‘No. There’s a lot going on down there.’

‘Where are the English, it’s like we were fighting ghosts,’ Michael said. ‘But their bullets and shells are real.’

‘They’re afraid to come too close. Afraid we’ll blast them out of it,’ James laughed. ‘Isn’t that right, Richard?’

The other man held on to his rifle tightly, but never looked in their direction.

‘Where are you from, Richard?’ James asked.

He didn’t reply.

It was strange not even to receive a jocose remark, so they left him alone.

Bullets still whizzed past them occasionally, thudding into the walls. James’s heart raced, very much aware of the danger they were in. But so far they had been lucky. He took a shot towards the area where the fire was directed at them, but in doing so, he cut his wrist on the jagged glass at the side of the window. He pulled back with a shout. Michael looked towards him, concern on his face.

‘Have you been hit?’ he asked.

‘No, just a scrape,’ he grinned, and had to put down his rifle for a moment, pull his handkerchief from his pocket and tie it around his wrist. Relieved that’s all it was. He wasn’t afraid. But he was tense. Like a taut string. Now and then he had a vague feeling of hunger. But it didn’t really bother him too much. A slice of bread this morning from one of the women had eased that. Smoke drifted in. The acrid stuff caused bursts of coughing, and stung their eyes.

They took it in turns to doze a little, but Richard still ignored them and stayed in the same position at the window.

Chapter Forty

As darkness fell, Louise went to see if there was anything to eat. In the area where they had set up the make-shift kitchen, a fire burned and a pot of water boiled. There were some basic provisions but there wasn't anything like enough to go around the numbers of men and women there. But they managed to stretch the soup by adding water.

'I never thought to bring some food from the Shelbourne,' Louise said. 'I feel so stupid.'

'Me neither,' Anne said.

'Although if I'm hoping to get my job back, I suppose it wouldn't have been a good idea. Mr. Quinton would take a dim view of us raiding the pantry, and as for Miss Cunningham, don't even think about that.'

'But how will the men and women survive if the *Rising* continues for a few days?' Anne asked.

'We'll have to go out and get food wherever we can. I'll take this billy-can of tea, and a couple of slices of bread over to the women. Did you eat?'

'I'll have something later.'

Louise returned, to be greeted warmly at the gate. The amount of bread only allowed for a bite each, and a slug of barely warm black tea, and soon she was back on duty her gun aimed at the street outside. The crowds of onlookers had gone home, but suddenly a motor car whizzed past. She held the weapon in her hand. It was heavy. Her wrists ached. Louise wondered about firing it at someone. At the Cumann meetings she had learned how to clean a rifle, take it apart and put it together again until she was completely familiar with it. She spent hours at target practice until her ability to hit the target was up to the standard demanded. But now she wondered what it would be like to discharge the rifle and for the bullet to cut through a body, hit a vital organ, blood spewing out.

Suddenly, Louise had a horrible feeling that she wouldn't be able to do this. To choose someone to be her victim at random was a terrifying thought. What if she could see the face? What if the eyes met hers? Could she bear seeing the fear in them?

It grew cold, and Louise buttoned the light jacket she had worn this morning over her uniform. While the day had been beautiful, the night was cold. She lay down with the other women on the grass close to the trench, but didn't dare sleep. They had to keep watch. To stay awake they talked among themselves about their aims, and what it would be like to have their own country, free and independent, no longer under the control of England.

'We'll put it up to them,' one of the women said.

'Pearse read the *Proclamation of The Irish Republic* in the GPO, Irish flags are flying from the roof,' another added.

'We have taken over a number of posts, and have every chance of defeating the English.'

'I can't wait to read the *Proclamation.*'

The other women's fervour inspired Louise.

'But the English will attack at some point, they're not going to take this lying down,' someone warned.

The talk tailed off.

Louise found it hard to stay awake during the night. Somewhere in the small hours she had fallen asleep for a short while, but awoke with a jerk and hoped it wasn't for too long. She straightened up, stared into the dark empty street through the trees, until suddenly, as light streaked in the eastern sky, the thunder of gunshots echoed.

'Get down into the trench,' an order was given. She climbed in. Another barrage of shots could be heard.

'There must be snipers on the buildings,' whispered Louise to no-one in particular.

'Defend our position.'

They crawled closer to the gate, pushed themselves up and aimed their guns. Although cold, damp, and hungry, these women were determined to hold off the English troops.

Chapter Forty-one

Robbie crouched low at the end of Coles Lane. The sound of gunfire echoed all around him. A group of other boys appeared.

'There's a lot of stuff to be had,' one of them said.

'Where?' he asked.

'Nobblett's sweets ...we're going down there now, and Lawrence's shop has exploded,' a boy laughed. 'All the rockets going up in the sky. My Mam has got bucketloads, and no peelers ...'

Robbie was galvanised and with the gang of boys he joined the looters, which included young children, and grown-ups too. Breaking through doors into shops the like of which he would never have put a foot inside before. He went to a man's clothing shop and picked up a jacket. He put it on the floor and into it threw whatever else he could find. His mother would be delighted.

He left the building, determined to get what he had home and come back later. On his way, he came upon a crowd of men and women drinking outside a public house.

'You took my whiskey,' one shouted.

'I did not,' another replied.

'You bloody did. Give it here.' They immediately began to fight over the bottle. Within seconds, mayhem had broken out, all of them trying to get whatever the others had.

As he passed one of the doors of the GPO, suddenly one of the Volunteers came on to the street. 'Stop this disgraceful behaviour, you should be ashamed to be Irish,' he shouted at the people.

There was a volley of shots from somewhere opposite. Soldiers appeared around the corner, and the Volunteer went back into the building. The people scurried away carrying their plunder, and Robbie put his head down and ran.

'Where did you get all that stuff?' Mary demanded when he threw down the jacket and all the other items of clothing tumbled out.

'In the shops. Everyone's there grabbing anything they can. You should go down. And there's plenty of drink to be had for Pa.'

'I can well imagine. But your father is fighting somewhere. You'll be lucky if he escapes with his life. Then where will we be? Now unless you want us all arrested, you'll have to bring all this stuff back.'

'But the shops are open, anyone can walk in. You never saw the like, Mam.' Robbie was excited.

'It would have been worth your while to have looked after yourself, did you not think you might have been killed in the fighting?'

'I can dodge bullets, Mam,' he joked.

'If you came back with a loaf of bread it would be better, what are we going to eat?'

He stared at her, taken aback. 'Sorry, there wasn't a bread shop open. Everything's on fire.'

'Maybe we should go somewhere else,' Bridget said.

'Where?' retorted Mary.

'Maybe Aunt Agnes out in Clondalkin?'

'I'm not going anywhere. If we leave, there will be someone else living here when we come back and then what?'

'I'll go out again tomorrow,' Robbie promised.

'What happened to the money I gave you?' Mary demanded.

He fished in his pocket and handed it to her.

She pursed her lips with annoyance. 'That's something at least. We're depending on you, Robbie. I can't have Bridget wandering the streets with all those soldiers hanging about, you never know what might happen to her.'

'Aren't you worried about my skin?' he asked, with a grin.

'I'll give you cheek.'

She went to whack him one, but he ducked and succeeded in widening the distance between them.

'Mam, Robbie, stop,' Bridget yelled. 'Let's think about what's happening instead of fighting about it.'

Mary pushed back the dark hair which had loosened out of the tightly coiled bun. 'I'm fit to be tied,' she sighed. 'We need food.' She went to search the press, opening the two doors and staring into the dim recesses. 'There's flour but no buttermilk.'

'Is there any milk?'

'Only some for Brendan.'

'Let it go sour and we can make bread tomorrow,' suggested Bridget.

'If there's any fire.' Mary poked the embers.

'I'll get sticks, there's still some around at the old house,' Robbie said.

'You're going nowhere,' Mary admonished.

'We're like prisoners here,' Bridget said slowly.

Chapter Forty-two

The gunfire was intense. Sharpshooters were positioned on the buildings around St. Stephen's Green. A machine gun thundered from the top of the Shelbourne Hotel and raked the Green. Commandant Mallin and Countess Markievicz decided that the place should be evacuated, and they would take over the College of Surgeons instead. Louise stayed on duty at the Harcourt Street gate with a couple of other women, while the others went to help shift the provisions and equipment they had. When some of the women had made their way across the street safely with a number of the men, dodging the snipers, Louise was ordered to help carry the wounded. Anne was among this group as well, and they helped the men make their way through the trees to the gate nearest to the College. They waited for a lull in the speed of the gunfire to rush across the road and were lucky to get over safely.

While Louise had trained in first aid, nothing had prepared her for the sight of the wounds sustained by the men. While they were not all life threatening, to look at skin which had been torn open, shattered bones and extensive bleeding made her sick to her stomach. A doctor came over from Mercer's Hospital and attended to the injured. Louise worked in the makeshift hospital with Anne. The rooms they had been allocated at the back of the building were very dark, with sandbags at the windows keeping out natural light. Out on the roof were the best shooters, picking off snipers they thought they could see at the other side of the Green, or shooting in the direction of the machine gun fire being directed at them from the Shelbourne Hotel.

In the evening, Louise helped Anne replace a dressing on a man's wound, and suddenly they looked up and stared at each other, surprised to hear the sound of a man singing softly. It was one of the wounded men. A patriotic song about Irish men giving their lives for Ireland. The two girls stood listening for a moment and there were tears in their eyes as they went back to their work.

'Imagine he can sing even though he's injured.'

'I've never heard that song before, it's beautiful,' Anne murmured.

'My father used to sing it, but I can't remember the name,' Louise said. She was emotional, and regretted that they had heard the song.

'Are you worried about him,' Anne asked.

'I worry about them all, especially James,' Louise admitted.

'He's your beau?'

She nodded.

'A nice boy?'

Louise smiled.

'Are you going to be married?'

'Yes, he has asked me.' She blushed.

'Then it will happen. Nothing will come between you,' Anne reassured. 'I persuade myself that Harry will come home from the War. That God will protect him and send him back to me.'

Louise turned away, and looked into the shadows of the room, longing to see James there, smiling, waiting for her like he had done so many nights outside the Shelbourne.

Chapter Forty-three

At the Shelbourne Hotel, Eleanor Montford lay on the bed in the small room. 'How much longer is this going to last?' she moaned. 'It's so warm, I feel like I'm going to expire.' She closed her eyes.

'Mother, will I get you some cold water?'

'Yes, please.'

Rhoda rushed away.

Catherine sat on the bed and held her mother's hand. 'It will be over soon.'

'But all our plans for this week have collapsed, and I was so looking forward to going to *The Gondoliers* at the Gaiety, the tickets have already been delivered. And do you think the Spring Show will be on at the Royal Dublin Society?' she asked.

'I'm not sure.'

'And we were invited to the garden party given by Lord and Lady Burroughs at their castle in a couple of weeks. Now everything will have to be cancelled. It's such a pity. And all because of a few men with guns who want to kill us all. And we don't know where your father and Anne are, I hope they are safe.'

'They are looking after their patients at the hospitals, and nothing's going to happen there,' Rhoda said, coming back into the room carrying a tray with a jug of water and some glasses.

'Drink this, Mother, you'll feel better.' She poured and handed a glass to Eleanor.

'Let's go downstairs. It's easier to talk in the Writing Room, much quieter,' Catherine suggested, trying to speak over the noise of the gunfire.

'Come on,' Rhoda encouraged.

'Get Mr. Quinton for me, I must talk to him.'

The Manager appeared some time later. 'I'm sorry for the inconvenience, Mrs. Montford.'

'I thought you said it would be over by today?' she demanded. 'Or someone said.'

'I'm sorry, but this is completely out of our hands.'

'Did my husband telephone?'

'We have no telephones. And no gas. We only hope that we have enough candles to keep us going. This is war, Mrs. Montford.' He rushed out of the room in a state of alarm.

'Well, have you ever heard the like? I'm not returning to this hotel again, they don't deserve our business. Clarence is going to be very upset when I tell him.'

'Mother, don't worry so, we'll look after you.' Catherine kissed Eleanor.

'Some chance of you two empty heads doing that.'

'We have to make the best of it. Some people are arranging card games. And there are good singers here and they'll entertain us. We have to try and behave as if this is normal.'

'Are you saying this terrible noise is normal?' There was a crash of gunfire from above. 'What's happening? Are they the rebels or the Germans? Who are they?'

'Mother, calm yourself. Why don't you come downstairs? If we talk to some of the other guests it will help pass the time,' Catherine persuaded.

'All right.' She nodded.

In the Writing Room a number of people were gathered. Some read newspapers in the dim candle light, and others peered at books. A group sat around a circular table. Children played in a corner.

'That's a medium over there. One of the other girls was telling me. The woman's name is Signora Bartolini and she communicates with the dead,' Catherine whispered and glanced across the room.

'Really?' Eleanor's attention was suddenly diverted away from herself.

'I've always wanted to attend a séance. Let's do it, Rhoda,' Catherine suggested.

'No, I'm scared.'

'Please?'

The door opened, and Miss Cunningham entered. An imperious woman, she stood surveying the guests in the room, her hands clasped together in front of her dark uniform. At first, conversation continued, and then slowly petered out as attention was given to her.

'I'm sorry to disturb ...' she hesitated. 'But, as you know we are in a difficult situation. Yesterday, we were able to supply a certain amount of food which had already been prepared, but unfortunately today the situation has changed. Some of the staff have been unable to come in, and we wondered if any of you could help?'

The faces which stared back at her were blank. The guests looked at each other with an air of horror.

'We need people to help the chefs in the kitchen. We have some food, and the menu will be quite simple,' she explained. 'And if there was someone who had some knowledge of wines we would be grateful. And after that, we need waiters, and chambermaids, but you don't have to be experienced.' She stood looking at them, an expectant smile on her face.

'I'll help,' Catherine immediately responded.

'You will not,' Eleanor said sharply.

'Someone has to do it, otherwise we'll all starve,' Catherine laughed.

'Yes, that's true,' Lady Teesbury agreed.

'I forbid it. I didn't raise you to work in a kitchen.' Eleanor put her hand on Catherine's.

'Maybe it's time to learn? I think it's up to all of us to pull together. We don't know how long this rebellion is going to last, we could be here for some time. What do you think?' She threw the question out to the gathered assembly.

There were nods of assent.

'I'm not sure if I could do anything, I've never been in a kitchen in my life.' A glamorous woman said from the direction of the séance group.

'If anyone likes Italian cooking then I can do that if we have the ingredients,' Signora Bartolini smiled expansively. Her dark eyes excited. 'It is many years since I have had a chance to play the mama, so I would be very happy if that would please you?'

'Thank you so much, Signora Bartolini, we would be very glad of your help.' Miss Cunningham seemed quite pleased.

'I could wait on tables,' one of the men offered.

'Thank you so much,' she gushed.

There now seemed to be a great deal of enthusiasm.

'Mother, please, I want to help, both of us do,' Catherine smiled at Rhoda.

'But what am I going to do while you're down in the kitchen?' Eleanor whimpered.

'You'll be fine. Why not help as well?' Catherine insisted.

'And dirty my hands?' she shrieked.

'Well, I'm offering ...' she stood up. 'Miss Cunningham, I'll do whatever you need.'

'Thank you so much, Catherine.'

'I don't know what your father will say,' Eleanor muttered.

'I'll make up a list of the various jobs to be done and maybe you will all come to my office and we'll have a discussion about how we are going to arrange things,' Miss Cunningham said.

They were divided up in three groups to help the few chefs who had been able to make their way in to the hotel. One would help cook the breakfasts. Another, the lunch. And last but not least, the dinner. Catherine was in this group. Rhoda had offered to wait at table. And others chose to help in various ways. Everyone was very enthusiastic.

Dressed in a white jacket, and a big apron, Catherine followed the others into the kitchen which had big scrubbed wooden tables. Ovens. Sinks. Cookers. The walls were covered with brass pots, and pans. Off the kitchen were various rooms which contained meats, poultry, vegetables, fruits and other foods.

Catherine found the heat of the place oppressive. Ovens belched heat. Pans hissed. Pots steamed. She was given a large container of potatoes to peel. It was difficult at first, Catherine's delicate hands were unused to grasping the large potatoes and scraping off the skin, but eventually, with practice, she managed to speed up her progress. When the potatoes were finished, and they were put into large pots to boil, she had to help bake a number of apple pies for dessert with a Mrs. Drumgould. This she really enjoyed. The pastry chef was a stickler about the way they should sift flour, mix butter, and make the pastry. That wasn't easy, as Catherine found the sticky stuff hard to handle, and was unable to get it off her hands and apron. Mrs. Drumgould had more experience and finally between them they managed to make enough. Then they had to peel, cut and chop the apples, and the chef returned to see their progress.

'I don't know how these apple pies are going to taste.' He stared critically at their efforts. 'The guests won't be happy.'

Catherine was taken aback. 'I'm sorry but I've never made a pie before.'

'They'll have to put up with it. They're lucky to get anything to eat.' Mrs. Drumgould was a mature woman and well able to take on the excitable chef.

He shouted something unintelligible and disappeared.

'Take no notice of him, Catherine, we're doing fine. Let's put the pastry into the dishes, and then the apples.'

They worked well together, and soon the pies were ready for baking.

The other people who had offered their services did their best, and at last the food was prepared and served up to the guests. Next it was washing the dirty dishes. Another task Catherine had never done. She didn't find that a very pleasant occupation, but had to join in with the rest of the guests on kitchen duty. Later, they sat around the table and ate their own dinner so casually it was like they were children. They talked, laughed and enjoyed themselves so much, their merriment actually made them forget where they were.

Chapter Forty-four

Kathleen stared into her kitchen cupboard. She had a good store of flour in, but not much milk. Wondering how her neighbour was doing, she went in next door.

'Are you all right,' she asked the middle-aged woman, a spinster who lived alone.

'I tried to go out to get some messages yesterday but some soldiers sent me back home. I'm afraid to go out today.'

'Have you enough to eat?' Kathleen asked.

'Yes, I have,' she said, nervously fingering her Rosary beads. 'Is the rebellion still going on?'

'I'm sure it won't affect us here. We'll be all right. Do you want to come inside to us, the children might cheer you up?'

'Thank you.' She seemed pleased.

'I'm going out to see if I can buy food, so if you could look after the two boys for me, I'd be very grateful.'

'How long will you be? I don't want to stay away from my house for too long.'

'As quick as I can.'

Kathleen climbed up on her bicycle and headed towards Leonard's Corner in the hope of finding some shops open. But most of the ones she knew were closed up, and she continued on to Rialto. But it was much the same there. She wondered what to do, and decided to cycle up to Crumlin. The village was out in the country, a place they often took the children on a summer Sunday.

It was an uphill ride, but eventually, after stopping a couple of times to take a breath, she arrived at the village. Here the place looked much more normal with people going about their business, although she was aware of a hurried air of tension in the women who were gathered outside shops on the main street. She joined the queue at the butchers.

'He'll be sold out at this rate,' the woman in front of her commented.

'Sure we don't know how long this rebellion will go on. Could be dead and buried by that time,' another laughed.

'What possessed the Sinn Feiners? A rebellion? Never heard the like. Do they think they can take on the British? Are they going to send them back home and run the country themselves? We'd be in a right pickle then. My husband isn't too pleased he can't go to work.'

'What are we going to do for money?'

'They should throw them all in jail.'

Kathleen nodded in agreement. If the women found out that her husband, son and daughter were all involved, then she might be hunted out of the village. She fingered the money she had in her pocket. She had raided her savings box and took some of the money she had received from the army for Hugh. She hated doing that, but knew he wouldn't mind.

Inside the shop now, she stared around her to see what the butcher had. She wanted as much as possible, so decided to buy the cheapest cuts. She still nodded and agreed with the women who talked around her and by the time it was her turn she felt more confident.

'I'm staying with my sister and with the two families we need quite a lot ...' she explained to the butcher. 'It's all very worrying.' Kathleen felt guilty telling a lie.

'There's terrible goings on to be sure,' he agreed.

She got out of there as quick as she could, her bag bulging with bacon, pigs feet, and sausages. Then she joined the queue at the grocery, and bought as much as she could there as well, until she had just a few pence left.

Chapter Forty-five

'I'm sure that's not very comfortable,' Louise said to the young man. He had been injured, and was carried from St. Stephen's Green into the College of Surgeons, and was now lying on a mat on the floor. A couple of the other women had gone searching for some trolleys or something else they could use for the wounded, but hadn't returned.

'I'm all right, miss,' he said.

'Are you in much pain?' Anne asked.

''It's not too bad,' he said with a grin.

There were three more men who had suffered injuries and they took care of them too, although one man had been killed on the steps of the College in the evacuation of St. Stephen's Green.

The woman in charge of the kitchen called the girls together.

'If anyone has any money, we'd be grateful if you could spare some of it so that we can buy food. We have very little here and our fighters need something to eat to give them strength. Brid will be going out to see what she can forage, although there are not many shops open. We'll be passing around the hat among the men also.'

Louise and Anne handed her whatever money they had in their pockets. Louise had a sixpence, but Anne had the most, two shillings. As there was little food left, Louise didn't have much to do. The men had scattered around the building, creating barricades out of anything they could find. The best shooters were up on the roof, and in the windows and they were determined to hold the College against the British. Louise would have given anything to be with them. Defending St. Stephen's Green had made her feel really useful and she had managed to put her earlier misgivings about killing someone to the back of her mind deciding to cross that bridge when she came to it. If she worried too much she would just run home and leave her friends to carry the burden and that just wasn't something Louise would do.

She went to her commanding officer.

'Could I help the men? Make bombs maybe. I want to do something.'

'No, we're more use down here, we have to look after the men, feed them, care for them.'

'Maybe I could take messages, or look for food like Dettie and Brid?'

'Well, maybe so.'

'I'll feel like I'm contributing something.'

'Wait until the women come back, and we'll see if there's any money left.'

Brid and Dettie returned some time later, and immediately the women began to cook the food on a fire. There was bacon and vegetables, and they made a soup which they shared around between the men. Some bread and tea completed the meal but it wasn't much, and there was little left for themselves.

As there was still some money left, Louise offered to go out later. She knew the area fairly well and was certain she could pick up some food while the others concentrated on delivering messages to other posts. A bicycle was procured from somewhere, no one knew the source, and Louise set off towards her own home on South Circular Road using the back alleys. After a while, she came out on to Clanbrassil Street unintentionally and to her horror saw a group of English soldiers march towards her. She stopped, unsure of what to do. Her heart thumped with fear. She pulled out her white handkerchief and waved it in the air.

'Where are you going?' an officer demanded.

'Home,' she whispered.

'Where is that?'

She pointed vaguely in the direction. Reluctant to give them any information. Now suddenly face to face with an English soldier, she wished she had a gun with her.

'Be on your way and don't come out again,' he ordered.

She wanted to argue with him. How dare he tell her what to do in her own city. Anger flared inside her, but she said nothing.

She hadn't seen any shops open so far and decided to call in to her mother, who when she opened the door and saw her standing there, burst into tears and threw her arms around her.

'Come in, child.' Kathleen brought her inside. 'You're looking so tired and pale, what have you been doing?' She sat her down.

'We're in the College of Surgeons.'

'I've been so worried about all of you, have you seen your father and Michael?' she asked anxiously.

'No, they're in one of the other posts we've taken.'

'So they could have been injured or ...?'

'No, no, let's not think like that, we're holding the English at bay. We're beating them, Mam, it's the way we've always imagined it would be. Soon we'll be free of them. Imagine what that will be like?'

'I'm making you something to eat, you look as if you could do with a good meal.' Kathleen immediately began to heat a pot of soup.

'No, Mam, I couldn't.'

'There's plenty of food, I was lucky to find shops open in Crumlin.'

'Maybe I should go up there, we haven't got much food for the men. They just had a mouthful of soup today and there really wasn't enough to go around. I couldn't eat a big meal while men like Father and Michael and James are starving. Can I have something to take back if you can spare it?'

'I boiled a piece of bacon and there's some potatoes, an apple tart ...' Kathleen was searching in the pantry. 'Pigs feet, sausages.'

'Thanks Mam, that's great. Would you have any flour, or oatmeal?'

'Yes, we won't need that much.' She gave her a bag of each.

'Thanks so much, Mam.'

'But how will you carry all this?'

'I have a bicycle with a carrier, I'll tie it on.'

'Before you go, have a bowl of soup at least, and some bread.'

'Well ...' Louise hesitated. The sight and aroma of the soup sent her stomach into spasm. She was extremely hungry.

Kathleen poured the soup, and buttered the bread.

Feeling guilty, Louise ate quickly. 'It's wonderful, Mam, thank you.'

'There's no need to thank me, love, I only wish I could feed your father, Michael, James, and all the others as well.'

'What you've given me is going to make such a difference.' She threw her arms around her mother, both in tears as they hugged close.

'You look after yourself, I love you, and I want to see you back here safe and well when this is over.'

'I will be back, Mam, don't worry.'

At that moment, the back door burst open and her two young brothers rushed in.

'Mam, there's smoke in the sky,' Edward shouted.

'And we could hear bangs, they were loud ...' Martin added.

'Let me alone, boys, I'll be out in a minute.'

'There's another bang,' they charged out again, not even noticing that Louise was there.

Kathleen put the food in old flour bags, and together they tied them on to the carrier of the bicycle.

'I'll try to keep in touch if I can but I don't know how ...' Louise was suddenly very emotional. Her mother's tears had affected her and she was close to breaking down again.

'I've just thought, Mam, it's very cold at night. I'll take my winter coat and something for a friend of mine, and would you have anything we could use for bandages?'

Kathleen immediately found a clean sheet which she cut up with her scissors, while Louise went upstairs and took a couple of coats from the wardrobe. She put one on over the other.

Finally, she was ready to go, the bike heavy with the weight of all the bags on the back, and hanging out of the handlebars as well. She kissed her mother once more, and set off down a nearby lane. Her mind immediately thinking of the route she would take, and hoping the English soldiers wouldn't see her again. She prayed, whispering the old familiar words, constantly watching out for barricades. She rode along a deserted lane, but was aware of curtains being pulled, and eyes peering at her. The bicycle had developed an annoying squeak from the front wheel, and that made her even more self-conscious. She wasn't really worried about people, it was the soldiers, and she was terrified that they would notice her. Perhaps take her into custody. Maybe even kill her there and then on the street.

She remembered her thoughts about shooting someone, but knew now that faced with a gun held by a soldier she would shoot him to save her own life.

She stopped to get her bearings at a corner.

A group of young boys and girls gathered around her.

'Where are you going, missus?' one of them asked.

'Home.'

'What's all that stuff?' Another started to pull at the bags on the carrier.

'Get away from me,' she shouted and climbed up on the bicycle again.

They ran after her.

Was she to be tormented by children, she wondered, and pedalled furiously, but they stayed close until suddenly there was a burst of gunfire up ahead. She turned down a lane, and cycled quickly away. There was a shout from the children, but they had gone running in the other direction. Louise was relieved to see the back of them.

She had to retrace her way more than once, but eventually came close to York Street. She waited around a corner. Suddenly a machine gun roared. She stiffened with fright and pressed herself into a closed door, staying there until finally she took a chance, pushed the bike the last few yards and banged on a side door of the College. But there was no reply. She banged again and threw herself against it. 'Open up, please, open up.'

At last, a man peered out.

'Let me in quick,' she said and pushed through.

'Are you all right?' he asked.

She nodded, already taking the bags off the carrier and hurrying downstairs.

'You have some food?' Nancy, the girl who was in charge of the kitchen, was astonished.

'It's not that much, I'll go out again,' Louise explained.

'Are there shops open?'

'I didn't see any, my mother gave me the food.'

'Where would we be without our mothers,' Nancy smiled.

Louise nodded, but doubted that she would go back home again. If the English watched her, then it would only bring the family into danger, and anyway, her mother needed food for herself and the boys, she couldn't take it all.

The bags were opened. 'This is wonderful, thank you for taking such chances with your life. Come on girls, get cooking. Our boys will have something decent to eat tonight,' Nancy smiled.

Chapter Forty-six

Unable to go to Moore Street, Mary cleaned the room. Robbie had gone out to find some food as he had promised and she had given him a couple of pence. She had boiled the vegetables and now had something for them to eat. Bridget helped, both of them glad to do something to pass the time, and try to get the sound of the popping of rifles and the boom of machine guns out of their heads. Robbie had explained the difference between the guns and she wondered how he knew about that. There had been no guns in the house, ever. And now Lar was caught up in this rebellion. She was confused. He had never done such a thing before or ever shown any interest in the Volunteers or the Citizen Army. She decided that more than likely he was in McCluskeys public house, as had been suggested by her neighbours who had watched him go down Cuffe Street and disappear into the doorway of the pub. She sighed, preferring to think of him lying drunk on the floor rather than risking his life.

'I might go across to Mercer's and see if Emily is all right,' she said later.

'But Mam you could get killed,' Bridget warned.

'Think how a little girl feels listening to all that noise?'

'The nurses will look after her.'

She shook her head. 'I want to see her.'

'Don't bring her back, we can't look after her here, she'll only get sick again.'

'I won't, I just want to put my arms around her,' insisted Mary.

'Mam, don't go, please.'

'I won't be long.' She flung her shawl around her shoulders.

'We'll be praying for you.' There were tears in Bridget's eyes.

She hurried towards the door. 'They're not going to shoot a woman going by.'

Mary went on to the landing and knocked on Tilly's door. As a close neighbour, they supported each other over the years and now in this situation even more so. The door was opened and her pale face appeared, small children gathered behind her.

'Are you all right?' Mary asked.

She nodded.

'Have you got food?'

'Not much.'

'Why didn't you knock over to me?'

'I was afraid, the guns, the noise, it's terrifying.'

'I don't know if there are any shops open, but I'm going out now and hope I can buy something for both of us.' Mary put her hand in her pocket but knew that the tuppence she had there wouldn't go very far for two families.

'Could you buy me something?' She went inside and Mary could see her take a jar from the mantle and search in it. 'Here's something, get whatever you can.' She threw a few coins into her hand.

'Why didn't you go over to your mother?'

'My sister is there with her brood, so I felt it was too much to land any more of us on top of her.'

'I think most of the people in the house have gone, there's only ourselves and old Mr. Keenan downstairs.'

Mary took the stairs to the ground floor. It was strange to find the place so empty, no children gathered around the various landings and in the entry below. No screaming and shouting, footsteps, doors banging, footballs bouncing down stairs, skipping ropes flapping. Just the noise of the guns and an occasional eerie silence.

There was no reply when she knocked at Mr. Keenan's door. The old man lived alone. He was in his eighties and all the women in the house kept an eye on him, bringing him something to eat if there was anything to spare. He had a son who lived on the north side of the city, but he didn't often come by to check on his father.

'Mr. Keenan?' Mary knocked again. And then, worried that the soldiers might come in, turned to close over the front door which was slightly ajar. The hall darkened. Originally painted a dark brown the lower half of the walls were now marked with scuffs, scrapes, and children's drawings, and the wooden floor was covered with a thick layer of mud brought in on the feet of the numerous people who lived here.

She listened at the old man's door, worried now about him. But after a moment she heard a shuffling sound, the key turned in the lock and finally she saw the wrinkled face stare at her. 'How are you, Mr. Keenan?'

'Grand, thanks,' he rasped, and began to cough.

'You don't sound so good, that's a bad dose you have.'

He smiled.

'Have you enough to eat?'

He nodded.

'I'm going out to try and get some food. Tilly and her children are the only people in the house, and ourselves, so I'll get you something as well if I can. I'm sure you could do with some milk for your tea.'

He waved at her to wait, disappeared into his room and came back a moment later. 'You'll need some money.' He handed her a half crown.

Mary stared at the bright shining silver. 'I couldn't take that, it's too much,' she protested.

‘You’ll need it for Tilly and yourself, and you must feed the children.’

‘I’ll bring you back the change,’ she whispered, astonished at the generosity of the man. Tears suddenly moistened her eyes.

‘There’s no need, keep it, and look after yourself out there.’

They both listened to the thundering sound of guns which didn’t seem to be too far from the house.

‘I will and thanks again.’

He went inside and closed his door, and Mary stood in the hall waiting for the noise to subside. After a few minutes, she opened the front door a little, stood to one side and looked out. The street was deserted in front of her but she was unable to see either end and didn’t know what was happening there. The guns were quiet for a few seconds, and she slipped out the door and pulled it behind her, flattening her body against it. On her right towards St. Stephen’s Green she could see some carts blocking the road and at the other end a motor car was pushed over on its side. She wondered if it was safe to cross and cut through one of the narrow lanes, which would lead her down to the hospital. She muttered a prayer to Our Lady, pulled the shawl over her head and dashed across the road.

Chapter Forty-seven

Lar was in the thick of it now, among a group of Volunteers who were sent to occupy a hardware shop on the corner of Grantham Street. On the other side of the road a group occupied a haberdashery. Lar felt he was contributing something to the *Rising*. He could shoot better now, and was ordered to position himself in the upper floor of the building with a number of other men, and to keep his eyes on the approaches. Sharpshooters were on Jacobs roof and had a good view of the surrounding streets. The men bedded down, using what could be found on the premises to barricade the windows, determined to hold the post.

The following day, the streets were almost deserted except for the odd pedestrian hurrying past.

'They're probably looking for food,' Lar said.

'Taking their lives in their hands.'

'We live up the street, my wife is probably out as well. We don't have much.'

'Everyone has to eat.'

'Don't mention food, I'm starving.' Lar had shared the last of the bread and dripping with the other men and they had eaten what they could find in the house.

Suddenly, a hail of gunfire spattered against the building.

'Where's that coming from?' Lar asked.

'Redmonds Hill.'

The men moved to defend their position.

Lar pressed himself against a side wall, and managed to get a good view of the corner. A number of British soldiers gathered there were attacking the two shops. Immediately Lar was on the defensive. Lying on the floor of the upper room, his rifle pointed through a large hole he had punched in the glass pane of the window, he shot in their direction. But the soldiers' return fire shattered the rest of the windows. Glass cascaded down and he rolled into the centre of the room to avoid it.

There was an order to retreat from the Volunteer in charge. Lar followed the other men. They made their way to the back of the building and out into the yard. Kicked down the gate. Then ran and crouched at the corner, able to hear the reports of gunfire and a loud explosion from the hardware shop. They moved quickly and finally managed to get back to Jacobs without harm.

Unfortunately, by then a number of the positions held had been lost, but the men in Jacobs were in high spirits, determined to hold on. Among them, Lar made his presence felt. He was fearless, and was now convinced by the men he had met in Jacobs that Ireland must be free.

In quiet moments, he worried about Mary and the children. Cuffe Street was just a short distance away, and he hoped that they had enough food, and were safe. His mind no longer dulled by alcohol, this was a new Lar.

Chapter Forty-eight

Matt got up the following morning, washed, shaved and dressed in his dark suit.

'Do you think the office will be open today?' Liliane asked when she saw him come into the kitchen.

'I'm going to work. I go there every day. It's how I earn my living. I'm not going to let a bunch of Sinn Feiners interfere with my life,' he said bluntly, and sat down at the table.

Liliane put a bowl of porridge in front of him, and poured a cup of tea. 'But it's dangerous in the city. I was talking to the neighbours and they've heard that the soldiers are everywhere and people have been injured.'

'If I don't go to work, how will we eat?'

'We have some food in.'

'But how long is this upheaval going to last?'

'I don't know, Matt.'

'Is this a war, Pa?' Daragh asked.

'Eat your breakfast,' Matt snapped.

'Don't go, love please?' she begged.

'Where are the girls?'

'I left them in bed, I'm sure there's no school.'

'Let them laze, they're probably delighted to be off,' he smiled, finished his breakfast, and stood up. 'I'm off now, I'll see you this evening.'

'Take care of yourself.' She followed him to the front door.

The closer Matt got to Sackville Street, the more deserted the city became, and the sound of gunfire grew louder. He turned into Jervis Street intending to cut through into Middle Abbey Street where his office was situated. He had the keys, and worried if he was late all the staff would be waiting outside. He increased his pace.

'Don't go up there, you'll be blown out of it,' a man running in the opposite direction shouted at him.

'I'm going to work,' he muttered.

'Get out of here,' a woman screamed as she ran past holding on to her hat with one hand, and dragging a small child with the other.

He ignored them and continued on into Abbey Street. But then he had to stop. Staring up towards his office he saw a barricade erected across the street. It was made up of upended vehicles, and enormous rolls of white printing paper probably taken from Independent Newspapers. He hurried along the street, forced to avoid a group of people running past him carrying bed clothes, tablecloths and other white goods which they had looted from the shop below his office. He climbed off the bicycle, and pushed it along the footpath quickly and could see that the window of the shop had been smashed. He was furious with them. Taking it personally because he knew the family who owned the shop.

He reached the small hallway which led to his own office, pulled the bunch of keys from his pocket and opened up. Shoved his bicycle inside, and followed, banging the door behind him. He stood there for a moment, breathing heavily, and listening to the noise from the adjoining shop. He had wondered should he intervene. Try to get rid of the looters and so protect the stock. But his quick look as he passed by had told him that there was very little left there now, and that the mood of some of the people had turned rough, the women, in particular, fighting over the pickings. He hurried upstairs.

Everything was as normal up here, and he immediately went to his desk, determined to do his day's work now that he was here, even if no-one else came in.

He wondered where his employer and the other staff were. It was surprising that none of them had made an appearance. He opened the ledgers and began to work. But as the hours passed, the noise of the gunfire began to get on his nerves. The building was quite near the corner, and he could feel the walls shake as shells landed and exploded along Sackville Street. One o'clock approached, and his stomach told him that it was time to go over to Wynn's Hotel and have dinner as he usually did. He locked up and went downstairs, but was shocked to see a much more violent scene on the street now. There would be no dinner today. Matt was a very precise individual. Breakfast was at eight o'clock. Dinner at one. Tea at seven. Supper at ten, except during Lent. Maybe he should head home, he thought, if things become any worse here ...for the first time he was worried about his own safety.

He went back for his bicycle, and pushed it out into the street, staring into the shop. He was shocked to see a small fire burning at the back. If that took hold he might have been burned alive upstairs. He ran in to see if he could put it out, concerned for all the records and paperwork in the office upstairs. But there was no water, so he just threw some old mats on the flames which were now climbing up the wooden frames of the windows. He stamped on the mats, but his efforts were ineffective. The smoke billowed out. He began to cough. The heat of the flames forced him to step back, and he decided that he may as well give up. He ran out of the shop, took his bicycle and began to ride home as fast as he could. But before he got very far, something hit him from behind and he lost control of the bicycle and fell on the footpath. He tried to get up, but a weakness came over him and he passed out.

Chapter Forty-nine

Robbie dragged the pram behind him. It bounced along on its tinny wheels, making uneven progress on the cobblestones behind Whitefriar Street church. He was going back down to Sackville Street by a roundabout route to see what he could find. Dodging through lanes, surprised to find people still around. Huddled in small groups at doorways talking about what was happening. It made him more courageous. They didn't seem to be too worried so it couldn't be that bad, he decided, and continued on. He tagged on to a group of boys, who were of the same intent as himself, and as a gang they headed into the centre of the city. Robbie had already been there yesterday and didn't think there would be much left now but he went with them anyway. They arrived into Cathedral Street and came upon a few people who had broken into a shoe shop. He went through the door which hung loosely on its hinges, dragged the pram behind him and began to fill it with boots and shoes.

'Give us them,' one of them yelled.

'They're mine,' Robbie protested.

One of the bigger fellows pushed him and tried to wrestle the pram out of his hands.

Robbie immediately turned and rushed back to the door anxious to get out of there. But he met some women and children coming in that way, and mingled with them, finding himself swept back inside again, where he grabbed whatever else he could find and filled up the pram once more. As he pushed his way out, he spotted a few pieces of wood on the ground which had been broken off something, and took them too. Loaded up, he ran for Great Britain Street, but he could hear loud gunfire and threw himself on the ground behind the pram. As he huddled there he wondered about getting back home. The gunfire eased after a short while and he stood up, deciding to go to his grandmother in Moore Street. He ran quickly, caught up by a couple of young men who were going in the same direction. The three made their way around a corner but up ahead they could see a barricade, and one of the men put his arm across Robbie's chest and stopped his headlong rush. He threw himself down again as shots rang out and one of the men fell injured in front of him. He covered his head as a hail of bullets thudded into the pram and the wall of the building.

Another person rushed to where they were. Robbie sensed rather than saw him, but as he bent over the man on the ground, Robbie heard the murmur of a prayer being said and realised that it was a priest.

'Come on,' the priest urged. 'Get out of here quick.'

He nodded.

'And you too,' he said to the other man.

'We're trying to get to our work.'

'There's nowhere open today.'

'The factory is in Rathmines, it'll be open,' he insisted.

'Maybe it will, but you could be killed trying to get there.'

'I'll make it. But I have to help my friend first, he's injured.'

'You may say a prayer for him,' the priest said slowly.

The young man's face paled.

'And don't bother going to work, go home,' he advised.

'But what about my job, I'll get the sack,' he burst out emotionally.

'Your life is more important.'

He looked at his friend lying on the ground.

'Go on, hurry.'

He ran and disappeared.

'Where do you live?' the priest asked Robbie.

'I'm going into my granny.'

'Where does she live?'

'Moore Street.'

'Be careful,' he warned.

Robbie grabbed the pram and hurried after the man. He wasn't sure what the priest would do to him if he saw the shoes, and worried that he would take him to the police. He glanced back, but the priest was gone.

He reached his grandmother's house fairly quickly, running down the lane at the back and pushing the pram through the narrow door in the wall, only then managing to get his breath. 'Granny?' he called, going up the stairs. There was no-one about. He rushed into the room. 'Granny?' he called again, and saw her lying on the bed under a blanket.

'Robbie, thanks be to the good God, don't leave me,' she wailed.

'Do you want a cup of tea?' he asked. His mother always wanted a cup of tea when she was upset so he felt it was the right thing to do.

Her eyes brightened. 'I made some earlier but I was too afraid to stay in the kitchen.'

'I'll get it.'

'Don't be long,' she entreated.

'Back in a minute,' he promised.

The fire was still lighting and tea pot hot, so he poured a cup. Carefully, he carried it in to her.

'Every time those guns roar I begin to shake.'

'Come home to us,' he suggested.

'I wanted to stay here but ...' she said slowly. 'I should have gone out to Agnes, now I'm sorry.'

'I'll take you to our place.'

Robbie threw all the shoes out of the pram and pulled it in.

'Have you got some food, Mam said to bring back anything I could find.'

'I have a bit.'

'We'll put it in the pram.'

'Are you clearing me out of house and home?' she demanded.

'Better to have it with you, someone could steal it and then what?'

Chapter Fifty

Liliane talked with the neighbours who gathered in small groups on the street outside discussing the rebellion. The majority of them were very much against it.

'What do they think they are doing? Look at the fires in the city. Our houses will be burned to the ground if it spreads.'

'And did you hear about the looting. Gangs of people and children too all breaking the windows of shops, and stealing anything they can get.'

'It's disgraceful.'

'And there's no police around, they've disappeared.'

'People are buying up all round them too, just in case we're going to be short of food I bought some flour and oatmeal to keep us going.'

Liliane listened. She didn't dare mention that her own son had joined the Volunteers in the GPO. Being so concerned for her husband and James put the thought of buying up extra food completely out of her head.

She waited for Matt to arrive. He was normally home at about six-thirty. And that never changed.

'Are we having tea yet?' Patricia asked.

'When your father comes home.' She went into the kitchen, reluctant to let the girls and young Daragh see how worried she was.

'I'm hungry,' Angela complained.

‘Can we go outside?’ Her daughter Patricia wandered towards the door.

‘No,’ Liliane snapped.

‘But there are other people on the street,’ Angela said. ‘Why can’t we?’

‘Because there is trouble in the city, and it could easily come this far, so we have to take care.’

‘What does it mean, trouble?’ Daragh played with his toy train on the floor.

‘I can see smoke.’ Angela stood at the back door.

‘It’s getting bigger.’

‘Is there a fire?’

‘Let’s go and see it,’ Patricia said, excited. ‘It will be like the Halloween bonfire.’

Liliane said no more. It was after eight o’clock now. She wished she could go into the office to see if Matt was all right, but she couldn’t leave the children on their own and was frustrated.

‘Mam, I’m hungry.’ Daragh stared up into her face.

‘I’ll get you something to eat.’ She cut slices of bread, and spread her own home made jam. Then she made cocoa and they sat down at the table, still chattering.

For herself, she couldn’t eat a thing, just poured a cup of tea and sipped it. Her mind following Matt as he had gone into Abbey Street, imagining the worst that could befall him.

Chapter Fifty-one

Mary took a dash down the street, hugging the walls of the houses for shelter. The sound of gunfire echoed, and it was so loud her ears popped, and she wondered if it would deafen her altogether. She pressed her hands against the side of her head for a moment, and then ran on until she reached Mercer's Hospital. She pushed against the main door, but it was locked. She banged against it with her fist, but no-one answered. Then she ran around the side of the building, and tried another door. A nurse walked across, visible through the glass pane and Mary rapped again, louder this time. The nurse stopped and stared.

'I must get in to see my child but the door is locked, can you open it, please?' Mary asked.

The woman looked blankly at her.

'It's my little girl, Emily, she's sick, let me in please?'

The nurse shook her head, and murmured something, her expression severe. Mary couldn't understand what she was saying.

'Please?' she begged.

The woman waved at her to leave, and Mary turned away, suddenly terrified by the sound of gun shots whizzing past her. She flattened herself against the wall, her heart beating. Then she crouched down, pulled the shawl over her head, crossed herself, and whispered a prayer, as the guns continued to splay bullets across the area. It continued for what seemed like hours, but eventually the noise diminished a little. She stood up, stared around her, and rushed back around the building, praying that someone would leave and give her the chance to slip inside. But there was no-one about, except a couple of mangy dogs sniffing at something on the cobbles. She waited, sitting at the side of the steps, and remembered that her intention had been to buy some food. She fingered the money in her pocket and pushed herself up, darting quickly down a narrow laneway. It was deserted, and she felt exposed, not knowing from which direction the bullets had come from earlier, and fearing that she would be cut down at any moment.

She reached Aungier Street, and could see that at each end there were barricades, and groups of soldiers gathered. Around the Carmelite Church she searched for shops which might be open, but they were all closed. She was frustrated. What were people eating? She talked to herself as she hurried up to the canal. But gunshots were coming from the direction of Portobello Bridge and she turned back into the maze of small streets of *Little Jerusalem,* so called because of the Jewish people who lived in the area. Suddenly, as she turned a corner, a woman appeared on the path ahead of her. She was carrying a parcel.

'Any shops open around here, missus?' Mary asked.

She pointed to a narrow courtyard.

'Thanks,' Mary could see it now and pushed open the door.

'I'm closing,' the man behind the counter said roughly.

'Please, I just want something, anything, we've nothing to eat, please sir, please? And I have money, look,' she held out her hand and showed him Mr. Keenan's half crown.

His eyes brightened.

A short time later, Mary left the place carrying a bag of provisions. She couldn't believe her luck. There were more people around here now, and she felt self-conscious at the glances she received. A few boys gathered at a corner up ahead. She bent her head, and tried to hide the bag under her shawl.

'What have you got there?' The biggest of them stepped into her path.

She ignored him, but was forced to slow her pace.

'Looks like you've got a right bag of stuff.' He came closer.

'Grab it.' The others yelled, and surrounded her. One reached for it.

'Go home,' she snapped.

'What's in it?'

'None of your business, cheeky brats.' She held on tight to the bag.

'What's going on here?' A man appeared. It was the shopkeeper. 'Away with you, boys, or I'll have the police on you.'

They looked at each other, and scooted back up the street.

'Are you all right, lady?' the man asked.

'Yes, thank you.' She pressed a hand on her chest, her heart thumping with the fright of it.

'Which way are you headed?'

'I've to get back to Cuffe Street.'

'That's right in the middle of the fighting,' he said. 'You'd better be taking care.'

'People are depending on me to bring back some food,' she smiled.

'Go quickly.'

'God will be with me, thanks for all your help. Go back to your own family, they'll be needing you.'

'You're a good woman,' he said.

Mary took a deep breath and walked down a narrow street, praying the ruffians wouldn't come back.

Turning a corner, she saw a group of soldiers behind a barricade of packing cases. One of them looked around and saw her. 'What are you doing, woman?' he asked. 'Get away from here.'

'I must get home.'

'You could catch a bullet,' he warned.

'I won't be a minute crossing over, please?' she begged.

'If you want to risk your life, then it's on your own head. Go over there by the side and get out of here quickly.' He waved his rifle at her.

Mary did as he ordered. She ran. There was a sudden burst of gunfire. She threw herself into a doorway, expecting at any moment that a bullet would cut through her. A picture of blood spurting came into her mind. Slowly she straightened up and looked around, lugging the bag on to her shoulder. It was heavy. The day warm. Extremely so for this time of the year. It seemed to take a long time to get back home. Seeing the barricades, and having to retrace her steps more than once and choose another path. Coming closer to Aungier Street, there were a few people about, most of whom were going into the back entrance of the Carmelites. The worst part of it was crossing over the main street again as the gunfire was much heavier here. Those last few hundred yards were terrifying as she ran up into Cuffe Street, just a few doors from her own house. Breathing heavily now, she pushed through the front door and banged it behind her. She lay against it for a moment, catching her breath, and then took the stairs. She had to get out of sight, and was terrified that she had been followed. She knocked on her own door. It opened a little. Bridget stared out through the gap.

'Let me in girl, let me in for God's sake.' Mary pushed through.

Chapter Fifty-two

Every time James saw the women hurrying to help an injured man, he was reminded of Louise. He didn't know where she was, his stomach sick at the thought of his darling girl being injured, or God forbid, killed. The gunfire grew heavier, and thundered from the buildings which the British occupied. Shells landed. Explosions caused walls to collapse. Tons of brick cascaded down into Sackville Street. James was ordered to join a group of Volunteers and crossed the street to help the Fire Brigade put out fires in the stables at Clerys, Tylers and other buildings on the side of the road opposite the GPO. But it was hard work. The smoke and fumes poisoning their lungs as they were beaten back by the flames again and again. James hung on to a water hose, trying to keep the stream of water directed on the fire. The heat was intense. But they had some success and the fires died during the night. They were recalled to the GPO, their clothes and faces blackened from smoke.

'Where have you been?' Michael asked when they met later.

'Putting out fires across the street. Feel like I've been fried,' James said, laughing.

'I've been up on the roof. Could see it from there.'

'The wind changed, but there's huge damage. How are we doing, do you think?' James asked.

'Hard to say. From above it looks like the British have brought in extra men, but if we can hold all our posts there's still a chance,' Michael said, with a grin.

'We have proclaimed the Irish Republic as a Sovereign State,' James said. 'And to be part of that in itself is an honour.'

'And some have given their lives.'

'And others have been injured,' James added. 'Where is your father?' he asked.

'With the leaders mostly.'

'I saw them talk.' He hesitated for a moment. 'Have you any idea where Louise might be?'

'Hope she's still in the Shelbourne.'

'I doubt that. If she knew what was going on she'd definitely be involved,' James said slowly.

'The women are looking after the wounded and the food. If she is in one of the other posts she'll be all right and in no danger,' Michael assured. 'Now, I've just a couple of minutes and then I'm back up on the roof.'

'Have you changed your mind about the women?' James grinned.

'I suppose they are useful,' he admitted.

'Better not let any of them hear you speak like that, you'll be left to starve.'

'I'll just give them a wink and they'll be only too glad to feed me,' Michael laughed.

'You'll be lucky.'

James settled down in the room he had been in previously. Richard was still there. Kneeling down, his rifle pushed through the same window.

'Hallo Richard?' James smiled. 'Has it been rough up here?'

The man didn't respond.

James thought his lack of conversation or any acknowledgement that there was anyone else in the room was a bit odd.

The gunfire began again at dawn. Machine guns thundered. Rounds of fire scattered across the GPO, shots whined past them and thudded into the wall behind, spinning, chewing up the plaster. The smell of cordite all around. James aimed in the direction of the shots, and fired a couple of times indiscriminately. However, he stopped then. It was a waste of ammunition to do that, he realised. Stocks had to be conserved if the *Rising* was to continue.

Suddenly Richard stood up and backed away from the window where he had been kneeling.

James turned, wondering was he injured.

The man lifted his gun and pointed it towards him.

His heart thumped. His mouth was dry. He was numb with shock. Slowly he lowered his gun to the ground, stood up and raised his hands. He could almost feel bullets whizzing from the other weapon and smashing into his chest. He stared at Richard.

The man's eyes were blank and he didn't seem to know where he was.

James couldn't speak. Fear swept through him. Sweat gathered on his forehead and dribbled down the sides of his face.

Richard swayed. His finger gripped the trigger.

James watched as the skin stretched white across the other man's knuckles.

Time passed. Seconds. Minutes. James knew that he had to do something. 'Richard, put down your gun, I'm not the enemy,' he said, slowly.

The man stared at him, eyes dark-shadowed.

James took a chance and with slow measured steps moved a little nearer to him, although he didn't know whether the man would take a shot at him or not. Richard backed away from him.

'It's time for a break, aren't you hungry?' he asked.

The other man nodded.

'Then let's get some food. We'll go downstairs.'

A round of machine gunfire echoed. Richard jerked his head around to stare at the window, a look of sheer terror on his face.

James had almost reached him now, and was preparing to grab the gun if he could at all, but it was still aimed at him. He wished Michael was here, to be alone with someone who seemed to have lost his mind was terrifying.

'Get back,' Richard spoke for the first time.

'We're relieved. Off for a while. Time to rest. God, we need it,' James said, forcing a smile. He never felt so vulnerable, unarmed and defenceless. Then he took a chance, and threw himself at Richard. His body weight pinned the other man to the door with a crash. He gripped the gun with his two hands, and tried to wrench it from his grasp. But he wouldn't let go. They struggled.

'Give me the gun, Richard,' James urged. 'You don't have to shoot anyone any more. It's over. Don't you hear me? It's over.'

Bullets continued to spatter against the frames of the window, as if to belie his words.

'You can go home. Your mother is waiting.'

Suddenly tears filled the other man's eyes.

'I'll take the gun,' James said, and tightened his grip on the weapon.

They stared at each other, two men teetering on the edge of an abyss.

James pulled the gun away from Richard. Almost losing his balance as he flung it away, hearing it clatter on the floor behind him.

He grabbed Richard's arm, opened the door and forced him out on to the landing.

There was no resistance in him now, his body soft and floppy, hardly able to put one foot in front of the other.

A Volunteer walked towards them.

'This man isn't well, he can't have a gun in his hand, somebody has to look after him,' James burst out.

'What happened?'

'I told you, he's not well.'

'Has he been injured? Can I help?'

'There's no cover in that room now, but I'll be back up as soon as I ...' He supported Richard.

The man took his other arm and together they managed to get him downstairs and to the back, leaving him with the Cumann na mBan women.

James searched then for his own commandant. It took some time but eventually he found him in the main hall. He explained the situation, and it was arranged that a soldier be ordered to keep Richard under guard in the event that he would again become a danger to himself or anyone else.

He went back upstairs to the room on the top floor, settled himself at the window, using both weapons. Now that it was over, he found that he was shaking, astonished to think that Richard had pulled his gun on him. What if he hadn't been able to control him and he had gone berserk, shooting indiscriminately? The possibility of that was horrifying. He couldn't believe he had escaped, and had almost lost his life to another Volunteer, while the British were blasting them both to bits at the same time.

Chapter Fifty-three

Kathleen prayed a lot. Feeling so utterly useless, confined to the house and not knowing what was happening to her husband and children. She bent her head and asked God and his Holy Mother to protect her family. Her young sons didn't understand what was going on and certainly resented being kept inside the house. But that was necessary. There was still danger. She could see dark clouds of smoke massing in the sky, and during the last couple of nights an alarming red glow. She didn't know whether there would be enough food to feed her boys if the fighting went into the next week.

She checked the quantity of food in the press, and cooked anything which might turn bad. Boiled the pigs feet, the sausages, potatoes and carrots. Heated the soup to keep it fresh. Baked a meat pie, and made soda bread using some of the sour milk.

There was a knock on the door. Her heart jumped and she rushed to peer out through the sitting room curtain. She couldn't see anyone outside, but forced herself to open the door, a crazy hope in her heart that it might be Louise again.

'Kathleen, let me in.' It was a woman who lived further down the street. 'How are you for food?'

'I have some.'

'Mrs. Dunne has very little, I'm going around to everyone to see if we can get something for her. Even a little if you can spare it.'

'Let me see. I've just made bread, I could give you some of that.' Kathleen cut a quarter, wrapped it in a piece of paper. Then gave her some of the bacon and vegetables in a dish, and half of the pie. 'This should help.'

'You know the town is burning?'

'I can see the smoke. It looks terrible.' She thought of Terence in the middle of that. And his breathing wasn't good. How would he manage if he got a fit of coughing?

'What do you think of the goings on, isn't it terrible?' The other woman asked.

Kathleen didn't know what to say. Her family felt that their dream of a free Ireland was worth fighting for.

'Did you ever hear the like. Trying to take over the country and throw the English out.' She was angry. 'And my man is in France fighting. And that's where all those men who have taken over the city should be as well. Oh, I'm sorry, your man is in the Volunteers, isn't he?' Guilt flashed across her face.

'Do you think there's enough for Mrs. Dunne?' Kathleen indicated the bag.

'It will keep her going for a day or two, nine children need a lot of feeding.'

'Let me know if you hear anything about the fighting,' Kathleen asked.

'I just pray that a shell doesn't land on us. Then we'll know all about it. Thanks for giving so much, everybody is short, but she'll be relieved she has something to give her children.'

She left quickly.

Kathleen went into the kitchen where the boys threw a ball from one to the other.

'Lads, you can't play in here.'

'Where can we play?' Edward groaned.

'Go down the hall.'

'Can't we go outside?'

'No, will you have sense. You know there's trouble, you have to be careful.'

They went into the hall, and she could hear the ball bounce from one side to the other. Terence certainly wouldn't be pleased about that, she thought. He had put up fresh wallpaper only last year. Still, they had to be kept occupied. If she wasn't careful they would get out of the house, and then what would she do if there was trouble. She felt a draught and realised that the front door was open and the boys had already gone.

'Get back in here,' she ran after them. 'I told you not to go out.'

'Aw, Mam, we won't be long. Just a few minutes,' they shouted back from the gate.

She watched them join other children playing football. Maybe they would be all right. It was almost impossible to keep them in especially as the weather was so good.

But as she turned back she saw a few people gather a little way down the street.

'Your crowd are fighting, aren't they?' a man shouted.

She didn't reply, disliking his tone.

'They're Sinn Feiners. Look what they've done to the town. And we can't go to work, can't earn a penny, what about that?' another asked.

'You don't care about us,' a woman spat.

'My son is out in Flanders fighting, and yours might as well be shooting a gun into his heart.'

'Traitors,' someone yelled.

The rest of them took up the chant. 'Traitors. Traitors. Bloody traitors.'

'Edward, Martin?' Kathleen shouted to the boys. 'Get in here.' She had to walk on to the street to get their attention and eventually hunted them in, trying to calm her racing heart. She didn't know those people. They didn't live on this street. Scared, she closed the front door, trying to control the tears which threatened to overcome her. The boys hadn't heard and she was glad of that, but prayed that her close neighbours wouldn't turn against her.

Chapter Fifty-four

Robbie peered out into the lane. He could hear the sound of gunfire. And it wasn't very far away.

'Granny, you just follow me. I'll push the pram.' He took her hand.

They came out into Moore Lane. He glanced at his Granny, her eyes stark in her white face. 'It'll be all right, don't worry,' he reassured. She nodded. They went through a narrow alleyway and came out on to Great Britain Street. Children ran past, carrying the results of their looting. Outside a pub, a group of men and some women too staggered around, drinking.

Robbie crossed the street to avoid them, aware that his grandmother was pulling out of his hand. He turned back.

'I can't keep up, you're going too fast, my legs ...' Her breathing was heavy.

'Gran, we must be quick.'

'I don't think I can go on any longer, take me back,' she begged.

'It's not safe there.'

'It's not safe here,' she muttered.

'Climb into the pram.'

'I'm not a child,' she exclaimed.

'Just for a few minutes, you'll feel better.'

'I'm not going into that. What if someone saw me?' She stared at him, belligerent. 'And do you want the bit of food to be squashed? And what about those bits of wood?'

'Doesn't matter,' he pushed the bag down to the end of the pram, and took the lengths of wood out. 'Get in, Granny,' he persuaded.

She leaned against the wall of a building.

'Hurry,' he encouraged.

'Well ...' She stared at the pram, and slowly took a step towards it.

'If you put your foot on the wheel, I'll get you up.'

She did as he asked, and he helped her to sit in.

'Oh my God this is awful.' She wriggled around trying to make herself comfortable.

'Cover yourself with the shawl, and hold the wood in your lap. No-one will see you then.'

She pulled it over her face.

'Right, hang on,' he grinned, and speeded up. The pram bumped over the cobbles, and his grandmother shrieked loudly every time it careered over a rough patch. They came out into Middle Abbey Street, crossed over behind the barricade and then ran past a group of youths who were breaking into a hardware shop. They had smashed the window and shards of glass were spread all over the ground. They were dragging everything out of the window. The wheels of the pram crunched. One of the boys turned.

'Hey, what have you got there?' he yelled.

Robbie continued on.

The boy ran after them. 'Come back here.' He grabbed Lily's shawl.

'Get your hands off ...' Robbie stopped and took a swing at him.

Suddenly, Lily pushed herself up and wielding a length of wood, climbed out of the pram, and hit the boy. He gave a shout and fell on the ground. Robbie grabbed hold of the handles of the pram, and dragged Lily after him around a corner. They ran on.

'Stop, stop, I can't breathe, give me a minute.'

'Will you get back in, Gran, we'll never get home,' Robbie said.

Just then he noticed a bicycle thrown in a doorway. A bicycle. That would get them home quicker, he thought, and he could tie it to the pram. He lifted it up, and leaned it against the wall, only noticing then the body of a man who lay face downwards on the ground. Gently he turned him over. Lily bent down to touch the man's face.

'Is he dead?' he asked her.

'No, but we'll have to get him to hospital quickly.'

'We'll put him in the pram, and bring him up to Jervis Street.'

Between them they managed to lift him into it, and he lay sprawled, one leg dragging out, his face white, deathly.

'Granny, can you hold one side of the pram, and I'll take the other side and his bicycle,' Robbie asked.

She nodded, and together they pushed him across Liffey Street, and up to the hospital. Lily stayed outside, and Robbie ran in.

'There's a man outside, I think he's been shot,' he said to the first nurse he saw.

'Bring him in.'

He went back to Lily, told her to watch the bicycle, and pushed the pram in.

The nurse immediately asked a porter to bring a trolley and they lifted the man on to it, and disappeared through a door.

Lily still stood where he had left her.

'Should we leave the bicycle for the man?' he asked.

'We don't know his name.'

They looked at each other in silence for a few seconds.

'There's no point in leaving it here, it will only be pinched. We may as well keep it,' she said firmly.

With Lily back in the pram, and wheeling the bicycle, Robbie brought them close to home. At every turn, he saw groups of soldiers. The crash of gunfire continued to echo around them. He stopped on Adelaide Road outside the Eye and Ear Hospital and stood in the shadow of the pillars each side of the gateway and tried to decide which was the safest way to go home. Finally, he headed down Harcourt Street, cut into Harcourt Lane, then into Montague Lane and stopped in a doorway.

'Granny, you just sit there and I'll check up ahead.'

'You're leaving me here?' she asked.

'Just for a minute.'

She stared at him in horror.

He ran down towards Aungier Street. When he reached the corner, he looked out. It was deserted. Only a group of soldiers gathered at the junction below. Suddenly, there was a number of shots. The noise resounded all around him. He fell. Hit the ground with a crash, his leg doubled up underneath him. He tried to push himself up, but was unable to put any weight on the leg. Then he felt something warm and looked down. Blood seeped on to the pavement. It was strange. There was no pain. None at all.

He dragged himself back to the laneway. His leg was heavy. 'Granny?' he called out. 'Granny?' He could see the pram up ahead with the dark shawl covering his grandmother, and the bicycle beside it. Suddenly, he groaned as pain whipped through his leg, and he found himself unable to move any further.

Chapter Fifty-five

'Louise?' Anne shook her arm. 'Wake up.'

She sat up. 'What is it?'

'A man has been injured, I'll need your help. The doctor is attending Margaret Skinnider, she was wounded earlier and he can't help this man just yet.'

'How is she?' Louise adjusted her dress, and tied back her hair which had fallen loose as she slept.

'He thinks she'll be all right.'

'Thanks be to God,' Louise blessed herself and whispered a prayer for her.

A large framed man was laying down the injured fellow on a rough mattress when she came through the door. She had a strange thought that he was so gentle he looked as if he was carrying his own child.

Louise bent down beside the man. He had been shot in the upper arm and the shirt he wore was bloodstained.

'I'll have to try and cut out the bullet,' Anne said. 'The doctor usually does that and says the man's life can be saved if he succeeds in removing it.'

'We were upstairs on the roof,' the man explained.

She cut open the shirt to reveal the wound beneath the shoulder.

'Try to do something for him please? He's a brave man,' his friend said.

'You're all brave men,' Louise said with smile. 'Can you help us keep him still?'

'I'll ask the doctor for some chloroform,' Anne rushed away.

Louise cleaned the wound with disinfectant. The man winced as she touched it, moving from side to side in pain. 'I hate hurting him, but this has to be done, and if he keeps moving the bleeding will only get worse.'

Anne came back carrying a small bottle. 'The doctor said I should only use a little of this, and that I must be very quick.' She poured a drop of the liquid on a white pad, and held it over the man's nose and mouth. Within a few seconds, his body had relaxed, and quickly she picked up a sharp knife which lay among a number of surgical instruments on a tray.

Louise felt her stomach clench as Anne cut into the man's flesh. Every time an injured man came in, she imagined that it might be James who was lying in front of her. She soaked up the blood but it continued to gush and she couldn't manage to stem its flow. 'What if we aren't able to stop the bleeding?' she whispered anxiously.

'This man will die if we can't find the bullet, I'll just give it another try.' Anne continued to search.

With bated breath, Louise stared at her as she worked. The man began to come around, groaning loudly. His friend and Louise held him down.

'I've got it,' Anne whispered, picked up a pincers and removed the blood covered bullet.

Louise put a bandage on the wound. It was immediately suffused.

'He'll need stitches, I'll get the doctor.' She disappeared, and after a couple of moments came back with him.

'You'll be all right,' Louise comforted him.

The doctor examined the injury. 'You've done well. I think we'll just have to stitch him up.' He took what he needed from his bag.

'Pity we don't have some whiskey,' the man's friend said, a grin on his face.

The doctor carefully joined the edges of the wound, his stitches neat.

Louise, Anne and the friend tried to keep the man quiet.

'The bleeding isn't so bad now,' Louise said.

'Clean it up,' the doctor instructed.

Louise tried to be gentle.

'Put a dressing on it.' He left the room.

Anne cut some strips from a sheet and carefully the two girls put a thick pad on the wound and held it secure with strips around the shoulder.

'I'm needed back up on the roof. Thanks for helping him, girls,' he said, with a wide grin.

While Anne was helping the doctor, Louise sat by the injured man for the rest of the night. She leaned up against the wall. Her eyes closed every now and then as sleep overcame her. It was quiet now, and only an odd burst of shooting occurred during the night hours. Even if she didn't get much sleep, the peace and quiet in itself was a relief.

Anne sat beside her later.

'How is Margaret?' Louise asked.

'She's sleeping.'

'And the other men?'

'Most of them are all right.'

'God help them,' Louise said.

Anne took her hand. 'God help all of us.'

Chapter Fifty-six

The following morning, James was on duty at the side door of the GPO which led into Princes Street. Someone knocked. He tensed. Held his gun tight in his hand and waited a moment. The knocking continued. He opened the door slowly, just a few inches.

'Hey mister, let's in,' someone shouted. A childish voice.

James looked down to see a dirty face staring up at him.

'What do you want? Go on home, you shouldn't be hanging around here.'

'I've brought Pa's dinner.' The skinny undernourished boy tried to push past him carrying a tin can.

'You won't be able to find your Pa. I can't let you in, away with you.'

'Go on, mister, I was here yesterday, I know where he is.' The cheeky urchin ducked under the gun and disappeared into the shadows.

'Hey?' James shouted after him.

He was gone.

Someone else knocked on the door.

He opened the door again, expecting it to be another boy with a dinner, and had almost decided to take it himself he was so hungry, but, to his surprise, he saw Louise standing outside. He stared at her in astonishment.

She smiled at him, out of breath.

'What are you doing here?' He couldn't believe his eyes.

'I've a message.'

'You shouldn't be out there, it's very dangerous. Where are you coming from?' He drew her inside.

'College of Surgeons.'

'What's it like up there?'

'We're being bombarded from the Shelbourne, which is rather odd I suppose,' she smiled. 'How are you,' she gazed at him, dark eyes searching his.

'All the better for seeing you.'

'Are Michael and Father here with you?'

He nodded.

'Are they all right?'

'Yes, both of them.'

'I must deliver my message and get back.' She reached up and kissed him. 'Look after yourself.'

'I love you,' he whispered.

She smiled. 'I love you.'

He moved closer to her.

'Is it this way?' she pointed.

'Yes, someone will direct you, sorry I can't leave my post.'

She blew him a kiss and disappeared.

He was excited at seeing her again. It gave him a huge boost. She was safe. His love was safe. That was all that mattered to him.

She returned a few moments later, and he was just about to kiss her when the boy who ran in earlier with his father's dinner flashed past.

'Open the door, mister.'

He did that.

'I'll go, must get back.' Louise touched his hand, and followed the boy.

Later he was posted upstairs again. He could see a pallor of smoke hanging over the city. Flames leapt from buildings, red and angry. There were two other men in the room with him. Shells burst against the building and exploded. Suddenly, there was a crash above, and a large section of plaster fell down in a cloud of dust from the ceiling. Lengths of wood which had been wedged into the windows collapsed into the room. They threw themselves on the floor. One of the men let a shout and crumpled up. James, who was nearest, dragged him out on to the landing. The other followed.

'How is he?' They stared down at him.

'We'll have to get him downstairs.'

Blood spread down his face.

James took hold of his shoulders, and the other his legs, and they staggered down the stairs and into the room which served as a makeshift hospital. The women were busy caring for wounded men. Some had minor injuries and sat, although others lay prone, much more seriously wounded. A priest bent over one man, anointing him. After he had blessed him, he moved to another.

They put the man down, and tried to make him comfortable. One of the women came over to attend to him. They stood up and looked at each other, both covered in white plaster dust. The other man grinned wryly as he wiped some of it off his face. James did the same but he couldn't share the humour, particularly as he had noticed James Connolly lying injured as he came down the stairs. He had an immediate urge to go over and see how he was, but he was asleep. A sense of dread swept through him as he returned to his post.

They hauled a table and a bookcase from another room and barricaded the windows again. In the midst of all the chaos, James suddenly became frightened. For the first time his bravado deserted him, and he questioned the affect of all this destruction on his city. Later that night when he was told to take a brief respite from his post by his commandant, he met

Michael's father, Terence, as he walked through the central hall, which was packed with men trying to get some sleep.

'Michael is on the roof,' the older man said. He looked exhausted. A grey pallor on his face. His eyes sad.

'I know,' James said.

'He's fighting for Ireland, and that's all he ever wanted.' Terence glanced above.

James nodded. 'How is Connolly?'

'He's holding his own.'

'I saw him earlier.'

'He's strong, no fear of James.'

'How are the other posts doing?'

'It's not looking good, communications have been cut.'

'But we'll fight on?' James burst out.

'To the last, lad.' Terence put his hand on James's shoulder. 'While the flag of a free Ireland flies above us.'

Chapter Fifty-seven

Eleanor lay in the bed, her eyes closed. Her head ached from the sound of the guns, in particular the machine gun which had been positioned on the roof by the British Army. As it fired round after round, the walls, floors, the very place itself, shuddered. For her daughters however, it was different. Eleanor knew that Catherine found the heat and steam of the kitchen hard to endure, and Rhoda was run off her feet as she waited tables, cleared away and washed dishes, but both stayed downstairs all day helping in any way that they could. Their mother couldn't understand how they seemed to enjoy the work. She bitterly resented that they didn't have any time for her, only rushing upstairs with her meals and disappearing just as quickly.

'There you are. Get me some iced tea, this heat is intolerable.' She fanned herself with a newspaper. Her forehead was dotted with perspiration, and her plump cheeks glowed a deep pink.

'The kitchen is closed now,' Catherine said, and poured cold water into the glass on the bedside table, and handed it to her mother.

'If I don't get home soon I will die,' Eleanor sighed.

'It won't be long now.'

'You've said that so many times I don't believe it any more. What if we never get out?'

'Don't be silly, mother, this can't last.'

'How do you know?'

'No-one believes that it will. They're surprised that it's continued for so long.'

'Who's they?'

'There are a lot of military people here, and they know what's going on.'

Eleanor sniffed disparagingly.

'Now I'm going to the singsong downstairs.' Catherine checked her appearance in the mirror.

'Are you going to leave me here?' Eleanor was aghast.

'Why don't you come? Rhoda said the singing is really good, and everyone enjoys themselves. It helps to forget what's going on outside, and the guns are not firing in the evening,' she said.

'How could you ask me that when I'm in such a state. A singsong? The very thought of it ...' She fanned ever more vigorously.

'I want to go down as well,' her sister demanded.

'It's my turn, I stayed with Mother last night,' Catherine said.

Rhoda sulked.

'There's a bridge game going on too. Why not join in? You used to play.'

Eleanor shook her head.

'You could help ...' Catherine continued on, hoping to persuade her mother to do something which would help pass the time for her. 'You could talk casually with people who are all in the same position, I'm sure they would appreciate it.'

She sniffed.

'Why not?'

'Catherine, go down to the singsong, I can't bear to listen to you any longer, Rhoda will look after me.'

'All right.' Catherine flounced out of the room.

Rhoda made a face at her departing figure.

The following morning Eleanor actually rose at seven o'clock, instead of lying in bed until lunchtime.

'What are you doing up so early, Mother?' Catherine asked.

'Never you mind. Shouldn't you be in the kitchen?'

'I'm going now.'

Eleanor positioned her hat.

'Are you going somewhere?' Catherine asked.

'Really, you are such a pest, can't you mind your own business?' She settled her collar.

Rhoda hurried out.

'Go on, Catherine, leave me be, go with Rhoda.'

'All right, then, if you're sure.'

Eleanor made her way down the richly carpeted staircase. On the way she passed some of the other guests. She nodded politely but didn't stop to make conversation. During the night she had done some serious thinking. When she considered the work her daughters were doing, she had felt ashamed of her own behaviour. Spending all her time moaning about the situation in which they found themselves. She reached the hallway. The noise of the guns was deafening. She stood uncertain and stared around, searching for Miss Cunningham or Mr. Quinton. But it was chaos down here and Eleanor couldn't see either of them. She was about to go back upstairs, when an injured soldier was carried on a stretcher in front of her. He was taken down a corridor. She followed and went into a room where a couple of women were looking after some men who had been wounded.

'Can I help?' she asked, removing her gloves and hat.

Chapter Fifty-eight

Lily couldn't see her grandson. 'Robbie?' she called, her voice tremulous. She threw the wood out and climbed out of the pram with difficulty and had to force herself to walk down to the corner, afraid of what she would find. Her eyes widened. Robbie lay on the cobblestones at the end of the lane. She bent over him.

'It's my leg, Granny. I can't get you home,' he whispered.

She pushed up her black skirt, and tugged at her white petticoat. It wouldn't tear at first but in a few seconds it gave way. 'Let me tie this around your leg, it'll help stop the bleeding.' She wrapped the strip of cotton a couple of times around his leg, tight.

He grimaced.

'I'll get the pram.' She wheeled it to where Robbie lay. Then awkwardly took him by the arm and helped him climb in.

'Don't forget the wood,' he reminded.

She wedged it in. 'You're turn now,' she said with a smile and put her weight on the pram handle.

'Thanks Granny, sorry, I'm supposed to be looking after you,' Robbie said, and groaned.

'What about the bicycle?' she asked.

'Have to leave it,' he sighed. 'Pity, I would have liked a bicycle.'

'I'll try to push it along,' Lily said.

He compressed his lips.

'Have you a terrible pain?' she asked, one hand on the handle of the pram, the other trying to hold on to the bicycle and keep the wheels straight.

He shook his head.

'Poor fellow.' Lily struggled. She was in her late fifties and not in the best of health. While she could still work on the stall, much of the harder work was now done by her daughters. But she was silent about her health, and reluctant to let anyone know just how tired she was these days. She managed to get the wheels moving on the uneven surface of the lane, breathing heavily. A couple of women appeared out of a doorway, and hurried towards her, their shawls flapping.

'Give us a hand, girls,' she smiled at them.

'It's Lily, what are you doing up here?'

'Robbie's been shot and I'm trying to take him home, and we found a bicycle and he'd love it ...' She coughed, her chest wheezy.

'Here, give me the bicycle and I'll push it for you.' One of the women took it from her.

'The soldiers are shooting at anything that moves, and our lot are just as bad, picking them off. They're forgetting all about us. Here we are terrified out of our skins, looking for food, children starving.'

There was a burst of gunfire from behind.

The other woman grabbed the handle of the pram, and pushed it along the alley until they reached Cuffe Street.

Robbie cried out.

'We're nearly there, boy,' Lily patted his cheek.

'Good luck to you,' the women ran back.

Lily stared out into the street. 'Right boy, home to your Mammy.' She left the bicycle up against the wall, glanced left and right and hurried across, praying they wouldn't be shot. 'Sorry Robbie boy, I can't get you up the steps, I'll be back in a minute.' She clambered up and pushed open the door. 'Mary, Mary?' she yelled.

'Who's there?' Mary looked over the banisters from above.

'Robbie's been shot.'

'My God.' She clattered down, followed by Tilly with whom she had been talking.

They both helped Robbie out of the pram and carried him into the hallway. There was a trail of blood behind him.

'How bad is it?' Mary asked.

'I'll be all right,' he managed a grin.

'The pain is something fierce,' Lily said.

'It's not that bad, Granny.'

'You told me it was terrible,' snapped his grandmother.

'Let's get you up to bed and we'll have a closer look.' Mary lifted Robbie in her arms, and made her way up the two flights.

'Be careful, mind his leg,' Lily warned as she followed.

'Mam, what's wrong with Robbie?' Bridget gasped.

'Hold the door open.' Mary struggled along the landing.

She lay him on the bed, but as she took her hand from underneath his body it was covered in blood.

'My God, he's been hit in the back too.' She lifted him. He groaned.

'Get scissors from my sewing bag, Bridget.'

She ran for it and handed it to her.

'I'm sorry Robbie pet, but I'll have to see what's wrong.' She cut through the shirt, and was shocked to see the injury. 'We'll have to stop the bleeding. Bridget, get me a clean flour bag and pour some hot water from the kettle into the dish. I hope we have enough wood to keep the fire going, we're going to need it.'

'There's some in the pram, I'll get it, and the bicycle,' Lily disappeared downstairs.

'This is going to be a bit sore, Robbie, but we'll have to clean it.' Mary did that as gently as she could. All the time the boy moaned. After a few minutes she folded a pad and put it on his back. 'Now, let's look at the leg.'

'I tied a bit of my petticoat around it,' Lily said, as she put the wood on the fire.

'Good job, Mam.'

'Cut up another flour bag in strips for bandages, Bridget love.'

It took some time, but eventually they had Robbie more comfortable. Lily made tea and they all had a cup sitting around the bed. But he was only able to take a little and before long was sleeping.

'I'm glad Robbie brought you here, you must have been scared stiff down in Moore Street?' Mary busied herself stirring the soup she had made.

'He threw out all the new boots and shoes he had in the pram and made me get into it,' she screamed with laughter, joining her hands together.

'Shoes?' Bridget asked.

'He'd got a load of them from somewhere, they're in our back yard.'

'Wonder would any of them fit me?' She stared down at the old worn boots on her feet.

'I'd like to know where he got them,' Mary retorted.

'Don't ask me,' her mother laughed.

'He took some stuff already, but that will all be sent back.'

'I don't know anything about it,' Lily said, with a grin.

Mary was annoyed.

'Don't send the stuff back, Mam, please?' Bridget begged.

'I'd send him out now to return them only he's not able. But as soon as he is, mark my words he'll go back with everything and be ready to say he's sorry too.'

'It's a pity about the bicycle,' Lily said.

'What bicycle?' asked Mary, surprised.

Lily explained how they had found it. 'But when I went back across the street it had gone, some other lucky person had put their eye on it.'

'If we get our boy well we're not going to be worrying about a bicycle,' Mary said, and tucked one of their few blankets around Robbie's shoulder.

'That soup smells lovely,' Lily remarked with a sigh.

'I just have to give some to Tilly and Mr. Keenan, and then we can sit down ourselves.'

There was a sudden burst of gunfire from somewhere outside.

Lily screamed and rushed to the door. 'Are they coming in here?'

'No Mam, but be careful, don't go near the windows.'

'It'll be under the bed I'll be.'

The noise increased.

'Get down on the floor,' Mary shouted, blessing herself.

Chapter Fifty-nine

Liliane sat in the front window of the house. She could see the smoke billowing upwards over the city, and could even smell it on the air. Dublin was burning. And James and Matt were in the middle of all that mayhem. She prayed God would keep them safe wherever they were. And her eldest son, Maurice too. She couldn't even imagine what it was like to be caught up in a war. There was no difference between her two children. No difference between a small war or a big war. One fighting a mile or two away, another in Flanders. The danger in either situation was equal. She worried about them both all of the time. Now for Matt to be missing was just too much. And she didn't know where he was. Ironic too that he had no sympathy with the republican cause. In fact, James had been a member of the Volunteers for quite some time before he had ever mentioned it at home. Liliane had often wondered if Matt resented the fact that James had not told him, although she knew that in his heart he would have been glad if Ireland was ruled by the Irish and not the British.

Since he had gone out on Tuesday morning she had waited for him to come home, always sitting at this same window.

'Mam?' Young Daragh dashed in from the street.

'Yes?'

'It's Pa, it's Pa.'

The girls, who sat with her, jumped up immediately and ran out of the house after Daragh, calling excitedly for their father.

Liliane followed.

In the distance, she could see that a man was walking up their street wearing a dark business suit, and pushing a bicycle. He did indeed look like Matt and she hurried after the children, overjoyed. But the nearer she got to the man her excited rush slowed, and her heart dropped when she realised that it wasn't him.

The children were closer now, still running, shouting out loud, and waving their arms, but she could see their footsteps lag as they slowly came to a halt in front of the man.

'I'm sorry, but I thought you might have been my husband, Matt ...' she said as he reached her. The children were silent, just staring.

'Not at all.' He nodded his head.

'Who is he?' Daragh asked.

'I don't know.'

'Maybe Pa will come home tomorrow?'

'Maybe.' She put her arm around him, and they walked back home.

It was such a trial for them all, this never ending waiting. And not being able to go into the city to search for Matt was frustrating. But the word on the street was that it would be extremely dangerous to go anywhere near Middle Abbey Street, and she had to think of the children. He could still be in his office, unable to leave because of what was going on around him. She prayed that this was the case.

She worried too about food, trying to eke out the amount in the larder. She always kept a good store of basics in the pantry and so far they had enough, but she prayed that this rebellion would be over soon. She wanted all of her family home.

Chapter Sixty

Louise and Dettie left by the side door of the College of Surgeons, and cut into Proud's Lane. They carried an important message about the food situation at the College which was to be conveyed to the commandant at the GPO, but also had been ordered to pick up any provisions they might come across on their way. This time they had been issued revolvers, and it made them feel much safer even if they never used them. It was difficult trying to avoid the British barricades but they finally managed to make their way to Sackville Street unscathed.

Dettie went in with the message.

Louise followed, moving around the rooms searching for James, or her father and brother. After a while, to her joy she saw her father in conversation with another man and rushed over to him.

As soon as he saw her he threw his arms around her. 'Louise? What are you doing here?'

'I've come with Dettie, we badly need a supply of food at Surgeons.'

'How are things up there?'

'We're holding our own.'

'Take care of yourself, James told me that you were taking messages from one post to another.'

'We have to make our contribution,' she insisted.

'We've been given some food.' Dettie appeared at her side.

Louise introduced them.

'We must go,' Dettie said.

'Where are Michael and James?' Louise asked her father.

'Both here, safe and well.'

Relief flooded her.

'Give them my love when you see them,' she whispered, and kissed her father.

They hurried out of the hall to the door, where a Volunteer waited with provisions. The man on guard checked outside. 'The gunfire seems to have eased, get yourselves away quickly.'

'These bags are very heavy,' Louise shifted one on to her shoulder.

'We'll get there,' Dettie laughed. 'A bicycle would have been a help.'

Two boys ran past.

'Hey there, stop,' Louise shouted.

The boys turned around.

'Help us with these bags and we'll pay you,' Dettie offered.

Their faces lit up and they came back.

'Have you any money?' Louise asked Dettie.

'Only a penny.' She put the bags down on the ground and searched her pockets. There was a loud burst of firing nearby. They stepped into a doorway.

'Do you think we should waste it?' Louise asked.

'Can't buy much with a penny.'

'Where are you going missus?' the taller of the two asked.

'College of Surgeons.'

'Lot of firing going on up there.'

'We'll give you a halfpenny each.'

They took the bags from them and charged off.

Louise and Dettie exchanged grins, and they followed the boys as they ran down Princes Street.

They made their way back by a new route, led by the boys who seemed to know every back alley. 'Remember where they've taken us,' Louise said to Dettie.

'I'm trying to make a note of it in my mind.' She breathed heavily, the boys were setting a rapid pace.

On a narrow street by St. Patrick's Cathedral, they came across a cart selling potatoes to a crowd of men and women and stopped in their tracks.

'Boys?' Louise shouted after them. 'Wait a minute while we get some potatoes.'

They went over to the cart, pushing their way through the crowd.

'Sorry, we're in a hurry,' they apologised.

There was an immediate uproar from the people.

'Wait your turn. We're here first. Go on out of that.' They jostled them.

'We need it for the men in the College of Surgeons,' Louise explained.

'They should be over with our husbands and sons in France, not here making us suffer, take yourselves off some place else,' a woman shouted. The rest of them joined in, pushing and shoving, directing lewd remarks at the girls.

Suddenly, Louise pulled her revolver. There was an immediate silence. The people moved away, a sense of fear among them.

'We want a bag, we have no money now but we'll see that you are paid,' Louise said quietly to the man selling the potatoes.

There was a growl from the crowd.

Louise took a deep breath. She had pulled the gun from her pocket without thinking, and tried hard to hold the firearm steady and hide her anxiety.

The man filled a bag. Louise moved closer, put the gun in her pocket and took the potatoes. 'What is your name?' she asked.

'Ryan, Tallaght,' he muttered.

'Thank you.' She turned, worried that the people would try to take the bag from her but there was no move from them as she followed Dettie and the boys.

To their great relief they were back at the College much quicker than they expected, and everyone was glad of the provisions they brought. Some of the men hadn't eaten much at all, particularly those who held some of the buildings in York Street. Immediately the food was prepared it was distributed. For the numbers of men it wasn't a great deal, but it seemed to rejuvenate them and they took to their posts with renewed vigour.

Louise and the other girls left themselves to last. They ate a little of the tinned sardines, and a couple of small potatoes between them. They didn't want to finish all they had entirely, some food had to be kept for emergencies and to feed injured men who needed sustenance to enable them to recover. But for the girls, it was something and the gnawing hunger diminished a little. They had also received a bag of flour which could be used to bake bread when the milk they had soured so that would take care of the following day.

Chapter Sixty-one

James heard the first sound of gunfire. It was Friday, the end of a momentous week, and he tried to stay positive. But all day the British machine guns pounded. Bullets bombarded the building. Shells exploded. Groups of scouts went outside but were cut down as gunfire scattered among them, some of them limping back, bloodstained, others lay still where they fell. The bodies of civilians huddled there too. Shot as they attempted to loot, search for food, or just simply escape.

As a result of the fierce shelling fires erupted on the roof of the GPO and quickly took hold of the upper floors. Angry flames licked walls and ceilings. James, Michael and the others dragged hoses up and fought the fire. Water overflowed everywhere. All the time the snipers' bullets whined past them, and men were picked off. James's eyes stung, his throat narrowed from the affects of the black smoke, and he found it difficult to breathe. The heat was tremendous and forced them back and downstairs to another floor where they tried to keep the fire from spreading further.

'If we don't get it under control it will finish us,' James yelled hoarsely.

Michael grabbed him. 'Get out of here.'

James shook him off.

'Come on,' Michael shouted.

They stood there, pulling against each other. There was a roar, and the ceiling of the room where they were was suddenly engulfed in flames. Michael managed to drag James out on to the landing and they finally had to retreat to the ground floor, but the fire had already taken hold at the back, and the ammunition stored below exploded. There was a hellish stench of sewage, and the smoke was so thick and black they could barely see.

Then the order came to evacuate the building and charge through Henry Street, and take some of the houses in Moore Street. James was instructed to assist a priest who was there to transport the wounded to Jervis Street Hospital. The walls in houses adjoining the GPO on Henry Street had already been broken down as far as the Coliseum Theatre, and James helped carry the men in blankets through those houses. He had been fighting beside one of them earlier in the week, although he didn't even know his name.

'Damned English caught me with a bullet,' the red-haired man grimaced.

'It's going to be hard to get to the hospital. Can you bear it if I lift you as far as the theatre?'

'Do your worst. And don't forget to get me a drink in the bar, I'll need it,' he managed a weak grin.

James had a sudden image of being in that same theatre with Michael one night enjoying the jokes of some English comedians. Although a few months ago, it only seemed like yesterday.

'I'm going back to join the move, I'll continue on for the two of us, twice as hard,' James assured him.

Michael and the other men were gathered at the side door on Henry Street. Among that group were some of the leaders, and the only three women still there. As the position had worsened in the GPO the other women of Cumann na mBan had been sent away for safety. James and Michael were in the last group to leave. Among them Connolly waited to be carried over. In the red glow of the flaming building, James listened for the order to move, and when it came he ran out into Henry Street with the others through a barrage of bullets from the British barricades. They returned fire, covering those who carried Connolly, and crossed into Henry Place. A number of men were wounded, staggering helplessly along the street until finally falling to the ground. James was horrified to see Michael fall just before he reached the house in Moore Street. He crouched over him and shook him. But he lay there, eyes closed. Blood seeped out of his mouth and dribbled slowly down one side of his chin. 'Michael?' James shouted.

Bullets whistled past him, squealing, exploding against the walls of the houses and spattering off the cobblestones. He took hold of Michael's arm and dragged him into the house, threw down his rifle and knelt by his friend. He put his hand on his neck to check for a pulse and was relieved to find his skin still warm. But he couldn't feel even the flutter of a heart beat and a dreadful roar of anger swept through him. He lifted the gun and rushed back to the door. The area outside was still being strafed with gunfire. He took aim at the barricades and discharged a volley of shots.

'Get in here,' someone yelled and dragged him inside again.

'Break down the walls of the houses, we have to move further down Moore Street,' an order was shouted. 'Use anything you can find.'

The men were packed into the house, and James had to react to the order. With the others he searched the house and back yard. They found a pickaxe, hammers and other pieces of metal which they used to break through plaster and stone into the next house. All through the night they worked, from house to house. It was tough going. Their bodies were studded with sweat. James summoned greater vigour as he thought of Michael. He would get his revenge on the bloody Brits for killing his friend.

Chapter Sixty-two

Eleanor sat by the bed of a wounded soldier. She was wearing a large white apron and hated the roughness of the heavy cotton against her skin. But was glad that it served to protect her lilac silk gown which was what she had been wearing on Easter Monday when they came to lunch here, looking forward to enjoying the last day of the holiday.

As it was, she had every intention of throwing out the dress when she went home, that's if she ever saw her dear house again. Tears moistened her eyes. Down here, it was the smell that got to her. A mixture of blood and other unmentionable things. Nausea swept up through her and she pressed her hand over her mouth.

'Mrs. Montford, will you say a prayer with Nigel?' One of the women who had been nursing the wounded asked.

Eleanor took a deep breath and nodded. She had been shocked to see the men here, and guilty too that she had lazed about doing nothing while everyone else seemed to be helping in some way or other, including her daughters. She regretted her selfishness, and went over to where the man lay and took his hand. He was hardly more than a boy really, only about eighteen or nineteen years. 'How are you feeling, Nigel?' She asked that most inane of questions when it was quite obvious that he was seriously wounded.

There was a slight tremor in his hand and a flutter of his eyelids.

'Shall we say the *Our Father* together?' She didn't know whether he understood or not, but went ahead and whispered the words close to his ear, hoping he could hear her and that it provided some solace.

A woman came to change the dressing on his wound and Eleanor moved to another young man.

This soldier was awake. He held her hand tightly and she twisted a towel in a bowl of water and patted his forehead with it.

'Would you write to my mother?' he whispered.

'Of course, let me get some paper and a pen.' She went across to where one of the women sorted clean linen, and asked if there was any paper. The woman pulled a small notebook and a butt of a pencil from her pocket.

'I keep this in case ...' she said.

Eleanor nodded, and went back to sit by the young man. 'Tell me her name? Where are you from?'

It was a relief to get back to the small room she shared with her daughters. Neither of them were there, and she lay on the bed glad to have the place to herself. Faced with death around her, she was conscious of a sense of mortality for the first time in her life, and was more worried than ever about her husband and Anne. Where were they? How were they? She cried then, exhausted.

Eleanor's life was a gentle existence. Work of any sort was abhorrent. Her personal maid brought her breakfast each morning, put out her clothes, helped her bathe and dress, arranged her hair, and took care of her every need, as did all the rest of the staff at home. She did nothing for herself, or anyone else.

'Mother, are you all right?' Catherine bent over her.

Eleanor stared at her through a mist of tears, and held out her arms.

Catherine hugged her.

'I didn't know what was happening, and then I saw them and it was terrible ...' her voice broke.

'What do you mean?'

'The young soldiers.'

'Where?'

'Downstairs, I went to offer ...' she gulped.

Catherine looked at her, shocked.

'I hope that I was of some assistance to them.'

'Mother, you were helping?'

'Why shouldn't I?'

'I thought you were afraid?'

'I was, but when I saw them I had to ...'

'You're so good.'

Eleanor held her tight.

Chapter Sixty-three

Louise lay on a chair. She would have given anything to have a bath. There was minimal water for washing and all of them felt the same way, but no-one said a word. Who cared about such things under the circumstances. Their hair pinned back untidily. Clothes dirt-stained. Blood-stained. Collars and cuffs no longer pristine. What did it matter?

The men were still at their posts, the women looked after the wounded, and tried to eke out the diminishing stock of food. It was becoming more dangerous to venture out, but they continued to carry messages from post to post, and tried to pick up food on the way. But there was none to be had now and hunger stalked all of them.

Louise thought about the loss of life, and all the injuries suffered in this week of violence. James was always in her mind. Her love. Who might at this moment be injured or even dead in the GPO, like those who had died here were already lying on the seats in one of the lecture theatres at the back of the college. A gunshot could change the course of James's life in seconds, and she might never see him again. Never feel the soft warmth of his hands. Never know the touch of his lips. So sensual she was taken to another place, somewhere she had never known before.

Knowing sleep was impossible now, she took a walk around. Anne was asleep, leaning up against the wall. Soldiers slept on the floor among the injured. Commandant Mallin and

Countess Markievicz were sitting on the far side of the room among a group of people. She wondered what they were talking about. She would have loved to be at the hub of things. To know what was going on. As it was, people like her knew nothing, all decisions were made by others.

She thought of her brother Hugh who was in France. In the newspapers she had read the descriptions of life in the trenches. It sounded horrendous. He was in the same position as she was and obeyed orders without question, not knowing why. Hugh didn't know when the War would end. He was caught up in a fight which had gone on since 1914, far longer than anyone expected. And no-one knew who would triumph. Louise didn't know when this rebellion would end either. But the Irish Republic had been proclaimed at last. The Irish flag flew above the college, and the GPO and other posts, and to all the people in Ireland who had taken up arms that was all that mattered.

Chapter Sixty-four

'He fought the good fight,' Terence said, staring down at Michael's body. The older man's shoulders were hunched, his face white. He knelt down on one knee and blessed himself.

'I'm sorry ...' James murmured.

Terence looked up but didn't seem to recognise him.

James blessed himself also, and said a silent prayer.

That was the only opportunity they had to be with Michael, and they quickly carried him into one of the rooms and laid him down, covering him with an old coat which was hanging on the back of the door.

James found it hard to accept that Michael was dead. He would miss his friend so much, the young man he met every day who shared his longing for a free Ireland. His loss cut deep. James was exhausted after the heavy physical work, sleep deprived, his mood low at this point of death and retreat. Wondering whether their small army would succeed in bringing down the British and force them to accept their demand that they get out of Ireland and leave it to the Irish. If they achieved Home Rule it would have been a great step forward, but now even that might not be possible.

'We'll get away from here, set up a new headquarters, I want to fight on,' James growled.

'Keep on breaking through these walls and God knows where we'll end up,' one of the other men said.

'We're well hemmed in,' someone else commented.

'Barricades at both ends of the street.' James peered out through the torn lace curtain which covered one of the windows. He could hear a loud rumbling. A crash of masonry. And thought that it could well be the final destruction of the GPO. It was a bad omen.

'We must take them on. Never give in.'

'Bloody Brits, bloody Brits,' James muttered to himself as he bent forward on one knee, his rifle pushed through the lace curtain.

On Saturday morning, Terence stood in the doorway.

'Men ...' They turned to look at him. Something about his voice gave James a sudden sense of dread.

'We've had a Council of War, and it has been decided ...' He bent his head. 'To surrender.' He took a deep breath. 'There have been too many deaths, and we are surrounded here.'

Shock waves swept through James. He couldn't believe it. The word *surrender* something it was impossible to contemplate. Was this an end to it? All their hopes and dreams?

The men were silent.

'Elizabeth has offered to go out to meet with the British under a white flag, so make sure you keep her covered.'

Terence saluted and left the room.

'We can't let them have victory,' James appealed to the others. 'We must keep on fighting. We have a chance now, they can't move us from here.'

'There has to be a reason for surrender. Pearse and Connolly know. They wouldn't give in unless they had to. We've fought so hard, so long, all this week, night and day, without sleep and food ...' One of the young men choked.

'But we're throwing it all away. Our flags fly above the GPO. We established The Irish Republic. It has to mean something.' James felt tears in his eyes, and he lowered his head. 'We can't give up hope.'

'The flags are in flames now.' One of the others said slowly.

'And why is Elizabeth going out there alone?' James burst out. 'They'll mow her down.'

He stood up immediately and went to the door.

A group of men stood on the landing watching the woman walk down the stairs. Terence among them.

'Sir.' He saluted. 'I'll go with Elizabeth.'

'No, James, she's safer alone.'

'But ...' he wanted to argue with him.

'Go back to your post.'

He saluted again, went back into the room and knelt at the window. 'They wouldn't let me go with her,' he muttered.

'They must know what they're doing.' One of the men said.

'But a woman alone ...' James saw her leave the house carrying the white flag. She marched down Moore Street, her head held high. He couldn't believe her courage.

She walked out of sight. The gunfire eased. It was very strange. They could hear someone walk past the half-open door behind them and back again more than once. Time passed slowly. They didn't look at each other, all eyes riveted on the street, hands held taut around rifle butts. It was some time before they saw Elizabeth return with a British officer walking beside her.

Now they looked at each other.

'What does this mean?' James asked.

'Why is that Brit with her?'

'I'd love to put a bullet through him.' James aimed his gun at the officer.

She came close to the house. They parted.

James listened to her quick footsteps come up the stairs and pass the door.

Voices in argument were heard next door. It went on for some time.

Elizabeth left the house again and once more the eyes of the men were on her, their rifles held in readiness.

'What's happening?' James burst out. 'Why is she going out there again?'

'There's some reason for it. I suppose they wouldn't harm a woman,' the man beside him said.

'Wouldn't put anything past them, they've shot enough men this week and probably women and children too no doubt.' James was angry.

They waited. Still. Tense. Until she came back into their sights again, and entered the house.

'She's all right.' The apprehension in James eased just a little.

They could hear more discussion and raised voices.

James glanced at the man beside him. It was obvious things had stepped up a pace. Footsteps passed the door. His heart raced. And then crashed down as he saw Commandant Pearse and Elizabeth leave the house together and walk towards Great Britain Street.

James marched with the other Volunteers behind the leaders. Now those with whom he had spent the last week in the GPO were like brothers and sisters. They had fought side by side to overthrow the stranglehold the British had on their country. And while they had failed, lives had been offered up for the cause and he was prepared to sacrifice his life as well. Whatever was demanded of him he would give freely.

They arrived in front of the Gresham Hotel on Sackville Street. He took his rifle and threw it on the large pile of arms already surrounding the Parnell statue. They stood in line. Some in uniform, others like himself, still in their civilian clothes. All were dishevelled, with a few days beard, but marched with shoulders straight and heads high refusing to be cowed by the numbers of armed soldiers around them.

'Name?' An officer held a pad and pencil in his hands.

'James Wilson.'

Slowly the man added his name to the list. 'Address?'

'Twenty-seven, Sullivan Street, Infirmary Road.'

'Slow down,' the man snapped in a heavy English accent. He wrote down the words.

James waited.

'What's that again?'

'Twenty-seven, Sullivan Street.'

'That's all right, go on with you,' he motioned him away.

Another soldier pushed him towards the green area in front of the Rotunda Hospital.

James's group were gathered among others already there.

The soldiers stood in front of them but took little notice.

'Were you in the GPO?' he asked a man beside him.

'Church Street,' he replied.

'How was it?'

'We stood up to them, held to the last, until the order to surrender was brought over. We didn't want to give in to them. We wanted to fight on,' he muttered.

'So did we,' James said.

'Give me one of those guns and I'd blast through a few of them, feel better then.'

James nodded. He stared at the soldiers standing guard. 'We're outnumbered ten to one now. They've brought men from everywhere, shipped over from England. Men who probably thought they were heading for France ended up here.'

'We all have to obey orders.' The other man lowered his head.

The night was cold and James couldn't sleep, full of regret about the surrender. His heart sore at the death of Michael.

There were a few hundred men there that night, including some women, and he searched for a glimpse of Louise, and Terence, but couldn't see either among the crowd. He was very worried about Louise, wondering where she was now and what had happened in the College of Surgeons.

Chapter Sixty-five

At the College of Surgeons, Louise and Anne changed the dressing on the wound of an injured man.

'Is that all the bandages we have?' Louise snapped.

'Yes.'

'How are we going to be able to look after the men with so little?'

'Don't let it upset you. There's nothing to be done,' Anne murmured softly.

'If we can't take care of our wounded, then they'll die,' Louise was tearful. Tiredness had got to her and she had a permanent headache. Food was still a problem, but they had almost become used to the empty gnawing in the stomach.

'I'm so afraid one of them will die from gangrene because of the conditions here, I can't bear it.' Louise wiped her eyes.

'They're all doing well under the circumstances. Why don't we go around and check on them?' Anne took her hand and together they went to each man. Some were awake and others asleep. But they held their hands and murmured soft words, hoping they were comforted. Margaret Skinnider had made some recovery and they held her hand and said a prayer.

'There's something strange ...' Louise said as she washed her face in the small amount of water they had.

'What do you mean?' Anne asked.

The two went upstairs into the hall.

'I can't hear the guns. What's happening?' Louise asked the first man she saw.

'Don't know,' he shook his head.

'This could be a trick,' Louise said. 'They want us to think they're retreating.'

'And then they'll burst in on us,' he yelled. 'I'm going back to my post.'

'We'll have to look after our men, in case the British do attack.' The girls returned to their patients.

But before long they were ordered back to the main hall. There they gathered. Men came down from the roof and all the other parts of the building which they had occupied for the last week and from York Street where houses had been taken.

Countess Markievicz and Commandant Mallin stood there. He spoke to them about the order which had been received from the GPO, and read the shocking word *surrender.*

Louise felt tears in her eyes, and immediately Anne threw her arms around her, and they both hugged each other, as did the other women there.

'We don't want to surrender,' a man shouted.

'We've given it everything, the fight must go on.' Others waved their firsts in the air.

'No surrender,' they yelled.

There was a strange relief in Louise.

'It's a pity all our efforts were for nothing,' Anne said mournfully.

Louise took her gun from her pocket and stared at it. 'It's going to feel very odd to be without this. That day I held up the cart I could have held up the whole of Dublin.' She looked around the room. 'There's still some home-made bombs over there, look. They should all have been used.'

'This has been like a dream and I'm so glad I was part of the struggle. If I hadn't been in the Shelbourne last Monday, I wouldn't be here.' Anne took her hand. 'I'll never forget this. It will change my life entirely.'

'The dream of an Irish Republic will be with us forever,' Louise murmured.

They stayed there, not knowing what to expect. A door opened. A group of British soldiers came in. There was a low angry murmur from the men.

'Throw down your weapons,' an officer ordered, his polished voice echoing.

The company of soldiers held their guns on the Volunteers, an attitude of menace about them.

No one moved.

'Drop your guns,' the officer shouted.

Louise stared, her heart beating. She didn't know what to do.

The seconds passed.

Then, Commandant Mallin moved. With slow deliberate footsteps he walked to the centre of the room and threw down his rifle on the floor. Bent his head, went towards the door and stood there. Countess Markievicz followed. They spoke with the officer.

There was no further resistance.

Louise added her gun to the pile on the floor. She and Anne followed the others, left the College of Surgeons and made their way down Grafton Street guarded by soldiers.

'Bastards.' A raucous voice echoed.

'Traitors.'

Others joined in shouting vile insults.

Louise was shocked.

They were marched towards Inchicore. Louise was tired, and unsteady and it was an effort to walk. More people stood by and watched now, but they were silent. A wind blew up. It was cold. Suddenly people gathered at a corner began to throw things. Louise refused to be intimidated by them and stared straight ahead. One of the soldiers caught a bottle which had been slung and his retort wasn't polite.

The dark edifice of Kilmainham Jail threatened as they were marched across the yard. Inside the building, they were pushed along dark dank corridors by the soldiers. Cell doors stood open and Louise was shoved inside one of them with Anne, Dettie, and a girl called Joan. The smell in the place was foul. Damp and mould stained the walls. The door was banged shut and locked, and they were left there with one candle. They stood in the middle of the small room and threw their arms around each other.

Later, a soldier came and gave them blankets. Another followed carrying a billy can of tepid tea and biscuits. They immediately ate and drank and then sat on the one bench and huddled together for warmth until the candle flickered and eventually extinguished. Louise leaned against the wall and dozed, but it was hard to sleep. Listening to the noises in this place. Voices. Footsteps. The banging of heavy doors. As the night went on it grew quieter, but then she could hear other small sounds. The squeak of small creatures as they scurried across the floor. This week Louise had had to steel herself to face many unpleasant things which she had never experienced before, and now scolded herself for her timidity.

Chapter Sixty-six

Eleanor awoke and realised that she was still here in this cubby-hole of a room in the Shelbourne Hotel with her two daughters. She sighed, wondering if she would ever see her home again? Ever escape from this imprisonment? Then she remembered the injured soldiers who lay below, and felt guilty. God help them.

'I'm going down to the kitchen.' Catherine tied up her hair.

'What's for breakfast?' Eleanor asked.

'Porridge and tea if you're lucky. I'll bring some up,' Rhoda said with a smile.

'I hate porridge. I'm never going to eat it again,' Eleanor groaned.

'Better than nothing,' Catherine laughed, and the two girls hurried away.

Eleanor pushed herself up, and decided to face the day. Her lilac gown hung limply in the wardrobe. It looked awful, and smelled as bad, she thought, and would have given anything to wear fresh clothes. She poured water into the bowl, and washed herself. Then had the unpleasant task of dressing in her used clothing. She stood in front of the mirror, and tried to adjust the gown. She missed her own maid, and hated dressing herself. Her hair was a fright, tangled after her night's sleep and she had difficulty making it look anyway decent.

Rhoda came up with the porridge and tea which she ate quickly, horrible though it was. Then she went downstairs and sat with the young soldier, Nigel. She had grown fond of the lad although he still lay unconscious, and made no response to her voice. She pressed his hand, and thought of her own son, Stephen. His letters told nothing of what it was really like at the Front, and she understood that they were censored by the military. Since she had come down here to this make-shift hospital at the hotel, she had been forced to think of what it must be like for Stephen, who was looking after the wounded in much worse conditions, and how he risked his own life every second. Now she hoped that if he should be injured, there would be some person there to hold his hand and comfort him. This week had brought it all into her mind in ghastly detail. Guns roared in Flanders too. But louder, much louder. Huge explosions shattered the landscape, and the injured men lay in the most terrible of conditions, many of them lost in *no man's land* never to be found or even given a decent burial. Families were left grieving the loss of their sons who had gone to fight and never returned.

She sat there with the soldier. Her head ached. But she didn't want to leave, praying that the boy's eyes would open and that he would show some signs of life. The doctor came later and checked him. But there was little he could do, and the young soldier was too ill to move to the hospital.

After the doctor had left, there was a disturbance. The women who had been taking care of the wounded ran outside. Eleanor could hear shouts and screams and wondered what was going on, astonished to see them run back waving their hands in the air.

'It's all over, they've surrendered.' They danced around, kissing and hugging the soldiers.

'What?' Eleanor was puzzled.

'The rebels have surrendered.' A woman came close and shouted the words into her ear.

She burst into tears.

Chapter Sixty-seven

Robbie lay on the bed, still asleep. Mary put her hand on his head. 'He's burning up,' she murmured, and rushed to pour some water from the bucket into a dish. Swilled a cloth in it and pressed it on her son's forehead. Then she opened his shirt and dabbed it on his neck and chest.

Mary and Bridget had stayed up all night with Robbie, trying to keep his fever down, while Lily and Brendan slept. It was cold and they wrapped their shawls around them to keep warm. Their hands were red from squeezing the cloths in the water, but this morning he was no better. She put her hand out, stroked his face, and then blessed herself and whispered a prayer.

Bridget pressed a damp cloth on his brow.

Mary put her arms around her son and held him close.

The young girl stared in horror at the large bloodstain on the bed. 'Mam, he's still bleeding.'

Mary gasped. 'We'll have to get something to stop that.'

Bridget folded a piece of cotton and inserted it under his back.

They watched him. Fear in their eyes.

Mary patted his face.

Slowly, in front of their eyes, there was a change in him. He couldn't catch his breath and began to choke.

'Robbie?' Mary screamed.

His breathing was hoarse. Laboured. And they had to watch as he fought painfully for breath, the time between each effort growing longer until he took one last gasp and his body lay still.

They cried then, deep gulping sobs, their arms tight around each other. The much loved son and brother now lay as if in a gentle sleep. All traces of pain had disappeared.

Mary wiped the tears from her eyes. 'I can't believe he's dead, and Lar away somewhere not knowing anything about it. I'll go over to the church and talk to Father Kennedy,' she said, pulling her shawl around her. 'We never got Mass this morning, I forgot it was Sunday.'

'Watch yourself,' Lily warned. 'You can't afford to get shot as well.'

'The guns aren't firing.' Bridget peered out the window.

'I heard a few shots early this morning, but it's been quiet for a while now,' Lily said.

'There's a couple of men walking on the street,' Bridget gasped. 'And they're strolling as if there's nothing up.'

'Surely they're taking their lives in their hands?' Lily asked. 'I'm not going near that window, come away you two.'

'I'll go down and see what's happening.' Bridget rushed to the door.

'You will not.' Mary immediately ran to stop her.

'Don't worry, Mam, I'll be all right.'

'Stay here, Bridget, if it's safe I'll go over to the church.' Mary ran out the door.

Lily and Bridget followed and leaned over the edge of the banister.

Mary peered out the front door. It was chilly. Grey skied. A light rain fell. A group of women stood together at a neighbour's door. 'What's happening?' Mary asked.

'They've surrendered at the GPO, bloody crowd,' one replied angrily. 'And the soldiers took the Surgeons lot down Grafton Street earlier. Come on,' she laughed, following the other women and children along the street.

'Thanks be to the good God,' Mary blessed herself. Now I'll be able to bury my boy, she thought, but was still nervous and glanced over her shoulder as she walked along not knowing what was happening. She could hear gunshots in the distance, but people had reappeared on the streets and gathered in groups talking. She made her way to Whitefriar Street church, going in by the side door, relieved to find the priest in the sacristy. 'I'm sorry to interrupt, Father Kennedy, but my son has died ...' she said helplessly, suddenly unable to explain exactly what she wanted to do.

'There are many people who have died during these last few days,' he said slowly.

'Can I bring Robbie to the morning Mass tomorrow?'

'Of course, but there will be others here also.'

'I don't mind.'

He wrote his name down in a small notebook.

'Thank you.'

She made her way back. Slower this time. Thinking of Robbie. Suddenly the enormity of what had happened this last week swept over her. She didn't know where Lar was. He could have been lying somewhere, his body shot to pieces. And how were her other children? She prayed that Agnes was taking good care of them. She stopped suddenly and leaned against the wall, head in hands and cried for Robbie. She hadn't wanted to upset Lily, Bridget or Brendan too much, so had bottled up her sorrow. Now she couldn't keep it in any longer.

'Missus, are you all right?' A woman put a hand on her shoulder.

She nodded, wiping her eyes.

'I feel the same way myself, it's been hard, my husband was in Jacobs and I don't know whether he's been injured or not, I'm going that way now to see him, someone told me the soldiers are taking them out.' She rushed away.

'I don't know where Lar is either.' Mary said and followed her. They ran up the street and she was shocked to see a column of Volunteers marching between lines of soldiers. Some of them seemed ill, stumbling a little, white-faced. Others marched with heads high, defiant. She stared at them. Her heart thumped. These were the rebels. The men who had stood up to the British. She felt proud. Then suddenly she saw Lar. There with the rest of the men. Striding out, taller than she had ever seen him.

'Lar?' she called out, running alongside. He didn't hear at first. She shouted, 'Lar?'

He turned his head and saw her, smiled widely and waved.

Mary was so glad. So glad he was alive.

A crowd had gathered at a corner. They yelled and shouted at the men.

'Kill the bastards.'

'Hang them.'

Something rotten splattered on a man's uniform.

Mary was filled with rage. How dare they? These men had fought for them and they didn't appreciate it. She wanted to shout back, but there were more of them and she was alone. They continued to heckle and this time it was horse dung which flew through the air, and she had to dodge to avoid the onslaught. They reached Dublin Castle where they were herded into the courtyard and disappeared.

When Mary pushed open the door of the work-shop, she was taken aback by the sight of rows of rough-hewn coffins standing against the wall, and stood silent for a moment.

'Mary?' Dick smiled at her.

'I can see there's a need for you,' she said grimly.

He nodded, his expression sad. 'I don't want this work.'

'I'm sure you don't.'

'But it's necessary.'

'Robbie was killed.'

'What, young Robbie?' Shock flashed across his face.

She rubbed her hand along a length of wood on the work bench. It was rough. Small splinters caught in her skin. 'Would you have spare?'

'To be sure, poor Robbie, I'll miss him coming in and out.' He stood staring at the row of coffins, and then reached to lift one out. 'This size should suit, he wasn't that tall.'

'But that's too expensive, I only have a few pence.' She put her hand into her pocket.

'Don't worry, Mary, this is the least I can do for the boy, sure many's a time he helped me in here when I needed a hand.'

'But you always paid him in wood for the fire.'

'This is a bonus. But I never thought I'd be doing this, I thought he'd put me down.'

Mary stared into the wooden box, and could see her darling son lying in it. She dabbed at the tears which moistened her eyes. 'I'll go back and get the pram.'

'This is heavy. A good one. You won't be able to carry it. I'll take it around for you.'

'Thank you so much Dick, I'm very grateful to you.'

He carried it out to the cart, and harnessed the horse. They went back to the house and he took it up to the room. Some of the tenants had returned and were hanging around the entry now, silently staring, and blessing themselves.

'Who?' It was Tilly.

'Robbie,' Mary said softly.

Her whispered words were heard by everyone and there was a low murmur.

Mary pushed open the door, and Dick carried in the coffin.

Bridget, Lily and Brendan watched them.

'Where is the boy?' Dick asked.

Mary pulled back the curtain. Robbie's body was wrapped in one of their few blankets.

She lifted the slight body and gently laid it in the coffin. The others came close. Dick fixed the top in place, put a few nails between his lips, and one after another, hammered them into the wood. When he had finished, they made the sign of the Cross, and together said the *Our Father,* three *Hail Mary's* and the *Glory Be.*

'I'll come back in the morning and take him to the church and on to Glasnevin,' Dick said.

Mary was overcome. 'Thank you so much, I'll never forget this.' She pressed his hand. 'Will you have a cup of tea with us, we've no milk, but it will heat you up.'

'No thanks, Mary, I must get back to work, there are a lot of people who have deaths in the house.' He pulled the peak of his cap and left, his head bent.

Chapter Sixty-eight

On Sunday, James and the men who had taken the houses in Moore Street were marched from the green in front of the Rotunda. They had given in to their enemy. It sickened him. Physically. He had vomited a number of times but there was nothing in his stomach, and all he spat up was bile, evil tasting.

He questioned his own motives, and compared them against the loss of life. Was war ever worth such sacrifice? He wondered now if this defeat meant that the Irish flag would never fly again.

He longed to see Louise and hold her in his arms, but he knew very well that that might never happen again either. He was dejected but held his head up high, and had to force himself to march at his usual smart pace, as did many others who were exhausted, stiff and sore.

Surrounded by soldiers, ahead of them and to each side, they were taken to Richmond Barracks. Stumbling into the yard they were lined up, left there to wait until their captors were ready for them growing more weary as time passed. Eventually, they were marched into the barracks. James was pushed into a large empty room with the others, so many of them crowded together they had barely room to sit down on the floor. Among the men he was glad to see Louise's father, Terence, but he looked worn out, holding his head in his hands. James managed to get close to him. 'Mr. O'Toole?' He shook his hand and sat beside him.

Terence looked at him, but there was no spark in the eyes of the older man.

'It's sad to find ourselves here after all our efforts,' James said.

'We made a stand,' Terence muttered. 'That's what we worked for. Now the British know we're serious.'

'We were able to hold them off for almost a week,' James grinned. 'They never expected that.'

'It's a start. Politics will take over now. The British can't ignore us, if they do, the next time the whole country will rise up. Michael wanted that,' he said.

'He fought hard. Too young to die.'

Food was brought in some time later. Bully beef and biscuits. James was starving and like everyone else, grateful for what he was given. Afterwards, they lay down on the floor for the night. James was restless. Disturbing nightmares passed through his mind. Images of the flames which had ravaged the GPO. The sound of gunfire. The flash of explosions. And more than anything, the fear he had known when Richard held his gun on him. He awoke suddenly and sat bolt upright, breathing heavily and staring into the darkness. What was going to happen to them here? Would the British take their revenge and kill them all? Or would they set them free? The questions whirled around in his head. He had no answers and didn't sleep again.

Chapter Sixty-nine

Louise walked slowly across the small cell. Eight paces one way. Eight paces the other. It was all the girls could do. Walk. Impossible for them to find a comfortable position sitting on the floor for any length of time, although they tried to sleep sitting on the bench and leaning up against the wall. Dozing on and off, waking suddenly when pain attacked their stiffened limbs.

On the second day, they were herded out into the yard. So glad to see some of the other women who had been in the College of Surgeons with them. They immediately began to talk but the soldiers shouted and ordered them to walk with their hands behind them and their heads down, so preventing them from making contact with each other. But it was good to get out of the awful cell and although the day was chilly they didn't care about that. Just to breathe in the fresh air was wonderful.

After exercise, they were lined up. An officer and a group of soldiers marched out.

'Give us the name of your leaders?' He asked the first woman.

She didn't answer.

'Who instituted the order to take St. Stephen's Green?'

'Who decided to move to College of Surgeons?'

He continued on asking questions about the *Rising*. Repeating them over and over in rapid fashion, and when he didn't receive a reply, he moved on to another woman and began again.

There was no response from them.

'I'm glad no one told that officer anything,' Louise said, after they had been returned to the cell.

'Can you hear someone singing?' Dettie asked.

The others listened.

'Is it in here or outside?' Anne moved closer to the door.

'Can't imagine anyone singing in here.'

'There's a few people singing together. It's a traditional tune.'

Louise hummed along. The others joined in. They smiled at each other, and raised the level of their voices which echoed around the cell.

'Let them see we don't care,' Louise whooped, jumped up, put her arm through Anne's and swung her around. They burst out laughing. Immediately they were all on their feet, dancing a reel around the small space.

The door was pushed open, and the wardress stood there. The expression on her face was thunderous. 'What do you think this is? A dance hall?' she barked.

They stopped dancing, their voices stilled.

'No more noise.' She banged the door closed again.

The girls exploded with laugher, trying to stifle the sound but failing. They hung on to each other still laughing, tears in their eyes.

'Did you ever see such a face?' Dettie asked.

'Like a monkey,' Joan said.

'I never enjoyed anything so much,' Louise said.

They tried to stay awake during the day so that they would sleep at night. But the dullness of time passing so slowly began to get on their nerves.

‘When will they let us go home?’ Joan asked tiredly.

The others stared at her. No one spoke.

‘And it’s so cold, I’m freezing all the time.’ Anne wrapped her arms around her body.

‘Why don’t we dance silently?’ Louise suggested. ‘It will keep us warm.’

‘But if the guard catches us again ...what then?’

‘We’ll have to put up with it. It’s not much worse than last week, is it?’ Louise asked softly.

‘We’re just being women I suppose,’ Joan replied.

‘Are we different to men? Weaker?’ Anne asked.

‘No,’ three voices chorused.

‘Do you think they’ll be complaining?’

‘They won’t care about their dirty clothes.’

‘Or that they haven’t had a wash in over a week.’

‘Or don’t like the rats crawling over them at night.’

‘I saw a few rats in the college,’ Louise said.

‘We won’t let the British soldiers know how much we hate it here.’

‘Our men are in exactly the same position.’

‘We have to be brave. Whatever happens.’

‘I hate the bucket,’ whispered Anne. ‘The smell is awful.’

‘At least there’s one there. What if there wasn’t?’

They laughed.

‘I’ve lost weight in the last week. I’m thinner than I’ve ever been. My clothes are hanging off me.’ Joan put her hands around her waist. ‘My mother will be so pleased. She always says young men aren’t interested in dumpy girls. On and on. Makes me wear tighter and tighter corsets,’ she giggled.

‘She wants you to have an hour-glass figure?’ Louise asked.

‘She’ll get her way now,’ Anne added. ‘Sounds like my mother.’

Joan giggled.

‘I think there’s someone looking through the hole in the door,’ Dettie said.

They were immediately silent.

‘They’re listening outside,’ Louise whispered.

‘It’s because we were singing, better be careful,’ Joan whispered.

‘Maybe they think we’re having fun.’

‘If the men were in here, it might explain it.’

‘There was one I liked,’ Dettie giggled. ‘He liked me too.’

‘Who was he?’ Anne asked.

‘The tall fellow who was repairing the guns.’

‘I can’t remember him.’

‘He kissed me,’ Dettie admitted shyly. ‘Asked me to walk out with him.’

‘And are you going to?’

‘If I ever get home.’

They fell silent, their mood quickly changing.

‘Whatever happens, we must stay positive that they will let us go.’ Louise sensed their sudden depression.

‘How is that possible in this hole of a place?’ Joan asked.

‘Will they take us to court?’ Anne was worried.

‘Will we be shot?’ Dettie asked.

They looked at each other, and no-one had an answer.

Chapter Seventy

Liliane couldn't believe that the rebellion was over. People were out on the street cheering, although there were warnings that Volunteers and Citizen Army still held some parts of the city. The red glow of fire at night had died down somewhat but a pall of smoke still hung over the city. Liliane was very concerned about Matt and James, and decided to go into town and see if her husband was in his office.

She took her bicycle, nervous and unsure of what she would find. The smoke drifted like a fog, and it caught in her throat and made her cough. A lot of people walked and cycled along the streets, and there were the usual throngs of horses and carts, and even an occasional motor car, all going about their business now that normality had returned. But army battalions were on duty at every street turn, bridge, and cross roads, guns at the ready. Watching. Waiting.

She managed to get as far as Liffey Street, but at that point, a soldier stopped her, his rifle in his hand.

'You can't go any further,' he said.

'But I'm searching for my husband, his office is in Middle Abbey Street.'

'There's very little left up there,' he said. 'Move on.'

'Can't I just have a look? He hasn't been home since Tuesday.' She found it hard not to cry.

'How far up is it?' he seemed to soften.

'Up near Sackville Street.'

'Everything's burned to the ground up there,' he said.

Liliane stared along the street, and could see that it was in a terrible state, with collapsed buildings still smouldering. She was devastated. All week she had been reassuring herself that Matt might have bedded down in the office rather than take the chance of coming home, and couldn't let them know what had happened, but now that seemed unlikely.

She was distraught, and stood for a while, now very worried that Matt may have been injured. She made her way to Jervis Street Hospital, stopped by the military again on that short journey but managing to persuade them to let her through.

The hospital was very busy. The wounded were sitting on the floor, lying on trolleys and stretchers. She stood there, feeling very much in the way, and afraid to interrupt any of the staff. She joined a queue of people waiting at an office. It took some time, but eventually she moved closer and received the attention of the woman in the window. 'I'm looking for my husband,' Liliane said.

'What's the name?'

'Matt Wilson.'

'When did he come in?'

'I don't know, he left home on Tuesday last but ...' her voice tapered off.

'I'll have to check, but I can't do that now.' She looked at the next person.

'I'll wait.'

'I'm not sure how long it will take.'

'I'll be here.'

There was nowhere to sit, but she didn't care. The hours passed. Other people were attended to. Liliane approached the woman again.

'Did you find out about my husband?'

'What name?'

'Matt Wilson.'

'No record.'

'So he didn't come in here?'

'He could be dead. Try the City Morgue.'

Liliane stared at her, speechless, unable to grasp what she meant at first. 'How can you be sure that he isn't here?'

'He isn't recorded. Can't you grasp that?'

'There could be some other explanation,' she argued.

'Look, I haven't got time for this.' She turned away.

Liliane burst into tears. She hadn't wanted to accept that Matt could be dead. Had hoped all week that there was some other reason for his absence. Slowly she moved away from the office, staring around her at the patients. She walked through them. No-one took any notice. Her eyes examined every face, longing to see Matt somewhere among them. But he wasn't there.

Eventually Liliane had to force herself to leave and wondered how she was going to get to the morgue in Store Street with all the military around. She tried to get her bearings thinking that if she could go around the centre of the city, and approach from the north side then she had a chance of getting there. The thought of Matt being dead broke her heart. She had never been in the morgue before, and her imagination painted horrific pictures.

She stopped and started. Retraced her steps. Took alternative routes. Was stopped by the military more than once. Guns pulled on her in terrifying encounters. She found herself on Dorset Street and only then turned back into the city and made her way to the morgue. There were a lot of people outside with the same intention as herself, a pall of gloom over all. Liliane joined the queue which moved very slowly.

It had begun to rain. A mist soaked everyone. Creating a darkening in the sky which mingled with the residue of smoke. She watched people coming out of the door. Family groups.

Individuals. Couples. All overcome in one way or another. She was immediately affected by their emotion, and prayed that she wouldn't find Matt. He had to be somewhere else, safe and well. She couldn't bear it if she lost him.

There was a strong smell of some sort of chemical. It caught her breath and she almost choked as she was ushered into a large room by a man wearing a white coat.

Tables stretched from one end to the other, and on each was laid a body covered in a black cover. People walked slowly. Stopping at each one and then moving on. But sometimes staying where they were as they recognised a loved one among the dead.

Liliane took her handkerchief from her purse, and pressed it up against her face.

'We'll start at the left hand side,' the man said. 'This room holds unidentified people.'

She said nothing.

'Are you all right?' he asked.

She nodded, her fingers clasped tightly around the narrow handles of her purse.

He turned back the cover, revealing the face of the person. It was an old man. His face white. Immediately her stomach went into spasm, and she felt sick.

'Take a deep breath,' he said.

She wanted to run away from this place of death, but forced herself to stay there. The man moved to the second corpse. This one was a woman. Tears flooded her eyes. They continued on. One after another. Men. Women. And even some children. That was the worst for Liliane. She lost count of the numbers of people. Became numb. Until suddenly, something hit her in the stomach. She was winded and couldn't breathe. She screamed. The man caught her before she hit the ground.

Chapter Seventy-one

Eleanor sat beside Nigel. The gunfire had ceased. The quiet was eerie, like they were in the depths of a cellar.

'Mother, we've cooked a meal, hopefully it is the last.' Catherine rushed in.

'Eleanor, go and have something to eat,' one of the other women said.

'I'm really not hungry.' She didn't want to leave the boy.

'You must eat to keep your strength up.'

She nodded.

The doctor came in.

Eleanor called him over. 'I'm concerned about him.'

He examined the boy.

'How is he?' she asked.

He shook his head. 'I'm not sure there's much to be done.'

'Can we get him to hospital?' she asked.

'He doesn't have long, there is no point.'

She stared at him. Tears filled her eyes. 'Isn't there something you can do?'

'No.'

Regardless of his grim prognosis, she continued to sit there holding Nigel's hand. Another woman came and sat at his other side. They prayed. The doctor checked the injured men and then returned. He stood there holding the boy's wrist, a watch in his other hand. After a time, he lowered his hand, and pressed his fingers against Nigel's neck.

'I'm sorry,' he said.

Eleanor stared at the young man. His face had changed. She could see it now. There was a softness there which hadn't been obvious earlier, although he had been in a coma. How tragic, she thought. His mother hadn't been here to tend to him. To speak gentle words to her boy. She bent her head and let the tears flow.

Clarence came looking for them.

He embraced her and the girls.

'How are you?' Eleanor asked.

'I'm fine, but I couldn't leave the hospital, there was a lot of shooting around Boland's Bakery and there were many injured,' his face was sad. 'And some died as well.'

'Is Anne with you?' Eleanor asked.

'No.'

'I hope she's all right,' she whispered.

'I went over to Mercer's but they said she hadn't been there.'

Eleanor stared at the two girls, horror on her face.

'They haven't been able to keep proper records over the last few days and there are so many patients the hospitals are chaotic,' he smiled. 'Don't worry.'

Eleanor was in tears. 'I'll never forgive myself if anything happens to my girl.'

'It must have been very tedious for you here. What did you do to pass the time?' Clarence asked.

'We were working in the kitchen, Father, cooking the food for everyone,' Catherine said.

'And I was waiting on the tables and helping in the kitchen as well. We enjoyed it,' Rhoda added.

'My God, cooking? That's something new,' he laughed.

'Mother was tending to the wounded,' Catherine smiled at Eleanor.

Clarence stared at his wife.

She nodded.

'My God, maybe there's a hidden nurse there.' He kissed Eleanor.

'There was one soldier, Nigel, I was with him when he died.'

'He was a lucky man to have you by his side.'

'Was it very dangerous coming over here?' Rhoda asked.

'I had my Red Cross band on my sleeve, and the soldiers let me through.'

'Is there still fighting going on?'

'No, most of the battalions have surrendered.'

'So we can go home?' Eleanor asked.

'Not yet, it would be difficult and I don't know if there's any transport. But you'll be safe here and as soon as things calm down I'll arrange for the car to come over. Now I must go back to the hospital.'

'Try and find out about Anne, Clarence,' Eleanor urged.

'If she's not in Mercer's should we go to the police?' Rhoda asked.

'Maybe she's injured?' Catherine said slowly.

There was a sense of fear in the room. Their faces paled, as each one contemplated the awful possibility that something had happened to Anne.

'I knew that nursing would be trouble, I told you, Clarence, but you wouldn't listen to me.'

'Maybe she got involved with the rebels over in St. Stephen's Green?' Rhoda asked.

'Anne knew nothing about any rebellion,' Eleanor retorted. 'We're a different class of people to any of that rabble. It's a ridiculous suggestion.'

'I'm sure she's at the hospital, probably exhausted after the week she's had.'

'But knowing Anne, the patients will come first, so stop worrying, we'll see her when all this is over,' Clarence said, smiling.

Chapter Seventy-two

Mary, Bridget, and Lily sat in the first pew of the church. The mood of the people was sombre. They had left Brendan with Tilly. Most of the people in the congregation were those who had lost loved ones, caught in the crossfire. The coffins of those who had died were lined up before the altar. The priest read out the names of the deceased, the children mentioned first. When Mary heard Robbie's name called out, she bent her head, and tried to stifle the rush of tears. How could God do such a thing. To have taken three children from her in such a short time was terrible. Her brave young son who would do anything for her had lost his life. He had no future now. She would never see his smiling face again.

They stood outside the church and watched as three coffins were loaded on to Dick's cart, and he clicked the reins and began to move slowly away. They walked behind with the other mourners. The streets were thronged with military, the barricades still in place. Mary was astonished at the sight of the ruined and burned buildings in the distance, although they were waved on to the quays by the soldiers and not allowed to walk up Sackville Street. Many buildings on Eden Quay were just piles of rubble. Suddenly a group of soldiers coming towards them stopped, and refused to allow them to pass any further.

'Open those coffins,' the sergeant barked.

Mary stared at him, aghast.

Dick got down from the cart. 'These poor people have died, we can't open the coffins,' he objected.

The sergeant raised his rifle. 'Open them up.'

'Why?' Mary found her voice at last.

'It's sacrilege,' one of the mourners shouted.

'We have to search the coffins,' the sergeant insisted. 'You could be carrying guns.'

'We have no guns,' a women burst out, in tears.

'We're just burying our dead, and two of them are children.' Mary was angry now.

'You'll go no further if you don't obey my orders.'

There was silence for a moment, then Dick climbed up into the cart, took out his hammer and began to lift the nails. It took him a while and in the meantime a crowd gathered. They grew more noisy in their condemnation of the actions of the military.

The sergeant ordered one of the soldiers to examine the coffins. Dick lifted the first lid and stood waiting. The body of a young boy lay there. The soldier glanced inside, obviously unhappy having to obey his superior's order.

'Lift the body,' the sergeant roared.

The man looked at Dick and then gently moved the body a little. There was an audible hiss from the crowd and they massed closer. Other drivers held up behind them began to protest in loud voices. Mary found herself pushed against the back of the cart with Bridget and Lily. She held the board with her two hands and tried to prevent the people behind from forcing them against it. Bridget's eyes streamed with tears.

Dick re-nailed the coffin. Then he opened the second one.

It was the same procedure, and all the while the crowd grew more and more angry. And then it was Robbie. Mary stretched to catch a last glimpse of him. But his slight body was deep in the coffin and she only caught a glimpse of the blanket which was wrapped around him.

'Don't touch my son,' she shouted at the soldier.

'Have some respect,' a man yelled from the crowd.

'Respect, respect ...' the people chanted.

The soldiers began to look uncomfortable. The sergeant waved his rifle at the crowd. 'Disperse, or it will be the worse for you.'

The soldier looked into the coffin. 'Nothing here, Sir,' he said.

To Mary's relief he didn't touch Robbie's body.

'Get down,' the sergeant instructed.

He climbed out of the cart.

'You're creating an obstruction, and there should be only one of you with each coffin. How many are you?'

No-one replied.

Dick quickly nailed down the lid on Robbie's coffin, picked up the reins, and moved forward.

The crowd parted and allowed them through.

It was a long walk to Glasnevin, but Mary didn't notice the distance. She had made that journey before and was familiar with the streets on the north side of the city. Closer to the cemetery, there were more and more people around. Many stopped to bless themselves and bowed their heads as the cart passed. They made their way to the plot. It was busy. Many people already there waiting to bury their dead. They had to take their turn. Luckily Mary had enough money to pay the gravediggers, all that was left out of what Mr. Keenan had given her for food. She had every intention of returning that money to him as soon as she could.

They joined in with the people saying the Rosary. A priest blessed the bodies. They moved near the top of the queue. Mary was overcome, thinking that this was the last time she would be with her dear son. She put her arms around her mother and daughter. The gravediggers lifted the coffin and put it into the dark earth, and quickly began to fill up the grave. Mary leaned over and peered down to whisper a final goodbye to Robbie.

Chapter Seventy-three

The Shelbourne Hotel was beginning to return to normal. Most of the staff had come back to work. The front doors were opened. The sandbags removed. All the carpenters and other labourers who could be found had been put to work to remove the signs of the conflict. And at last the Montford's car had arrived to pick them up.

Eleanor lay back in the soft leather seat. 'I can't believe it's all over.'

'There are still soldiers behind barricades.' Rhoda stared out through the window.

'I'm afraid it might start up again,' Eleanor said.

'That won't happen.'

'Why did they rise up?' Catherine mused.

'The rebels want freedom for Ireland,' Rhoda replied.

'But life isn't that bad here. Everybody I know seems happy.'

'The Irish have been occupied by the British Empire for hundreds of years,' Rhoda said.

'Maybe it was about time they rebelled,' Catherine said.

'But they were probably outnumbered and didn't really have a chance.'

'What about the boys who were injured in the hotel. The rebels didn't care about them,' Eleanor interjected. 'And Nigel?'

'Maybe the British should go,' Rhoda said.

'Don't talk rubbish, Rhoda,' Eleanor snapped. 'We're home now, look.' The motor car turned into the driveway of the large imposing house. 'Maybe Anne is here already, I'm so looking forward to seeing her.'

'It must have been tough looking after those injured people at the hospital,' Rhoda added. 'And for Father too.'

'Not as hard as it has been for us, this has been the worst time in my life,' Eleanor muttered.

'I enjoyed it, well, apart from the noise of the guns, and not having any clothes,' Catherine said. 'And we met some nice people,' she smiled.

'I want to soak in a bath for hours,' Eleanor murmured.

'And you were very kind to the young man who died,' Rhoda touched her mother's hand.

'I suppose ...' Eleanor stared across the gardens.

'You did a lot for him in his last hours.'

'If you weren't there then he would have been alone. You took the place of his mother. Such a lovely thing for a boy who was far away from home.'

For once, Eleanor was silenced.

They climbed out of the motor car. A maid held the door for them.

'It's so good to be home.' Eleanor sighed deeply and walked into the hall. 'Is Miss Anne here?' She asked the butler.

'No Ma'am, she isn't,' he said.

'Catherine, we'll have to get in touch with your father, he'll have to search for Anne, she must be found.'

'I'll send a message.'

'And quickly, I must have my girl home with me here, I can't bear not knowing where she is.'

Chapter Seventy-four

Hugh travelled on a merchant ship into Kingstown and walked most of the way to Dublin. He talked to people he met and got very colourful descriptions of their experiences during the week of the rebellion. Surprised to find that most of them were very much against the rebels.

'When will Sackville Street be repaired?' one man asked. 'It's as bad as any place in France. If you saw the buildings, they're completely burned down.'

'After a couple of days our food ran out and there were no shops open. We had nothing to eat,' a woman said. 'Imagine that, nothing. And there's precious little in the shops that have opened since.'

'None of us could go to work, so we had no wages, and the landlord isn't going to wait for his rent. We'll have to double up next week. And the shop where I work is a wreck. All the stock looted. I don't know when it will re-open.' Another man was irate.

Hugh was sympathetic.

'You coming back from France?'

'Yes.'

'That's another thing, you were fighting out there against Germany, and the Sinn Feiners here were hoping that Germany would help them. What do you think of that? Traitors, every last one of them,' he grumbled.

Hugh pushed open the front door. Walked quietly down the hall and into the kitchen. He stood for a moment. Just to be back in this house was wonderful. Kathleen was busy drying dishes, and it was only when she put them away in the dresser that she looked around. 'Hugh?' she screamed out loud, rushed across the room, and threw her arms around him.

'Mam,' he laughed, and embraced her tightly.

'It's so good to see you.' She stood back a little and stared at him, tears in her eyes. 'How are you? Is your shoulder better yet?'

'It's grand,' he dismissed it. 'How's everyone?'

'We're all right here, the two boys are out in the back yard playing.'

'Have you any news of Father, Michael and Louise? I heard all about the rebellion.'

'They're in prison. They were taken to Richmond Barracks.'

'Louise too?'

'She's in Kilmainham Jail.'

'That's a terrible place.'

'All the women are there. I'm just praying for their lives.'

'And I've been fighting for the English ...' his tone was bitter.

'You weren't to know.'

'I should have been here.' He stood up and strode to the window. 'I can't go back.'

'You must.'

'It's terrible out there. My friend was killed by a shell. I was beside him. It's a miracle I escaped although I'd prefer to give my life for Ireland.'

'I'm so glad, so glad to see you.' She put her arms around him again.

'How did you manage on your own during the week, people were saying there was no food to be had anywhere,' Hugh asked.

'We were very low on food but I found shops open in Crumlin so we're all right. Have you had enough to eat?'

'It doesn't matter about me, I'm just so glad to be home.'

'Would you like soda bread, although it's a few day's old?'

'I don't care how old it is, your bread is the best,' he said with a grin. 'I missed it.'

She smiled. 'Was the food terrible?'

'Bully beef, and hard biscuits, that was it.'

'Hopefully we'll have some decent food for you soon.'

'Whatever you make, Mam, it will be great.'

'How long will you be home?' she asked.

'I leave on Friday.'

'Pity you have to go so soon. I want to take care of you. Bundle you up. Take you away from all that pain you've gone through,' she whispered.

Hugh didn't say anything, remembering his dreams of home, and how he imagined her doing just that. He shrugged.

'Watch your shoulder.' She touched his right side.

'It's the other one.'

They laughed.

'Did you miss your work at the United Services Club?' Kathleen asked.

'Not really. Being in the army was an adventure at first. Peter and me were together in Wales, but then he was posted somewhere else and I never saw him again.' He tried to hide the emotion which swept through him.

'It's hard when that happens, but you made new friends?' She poured him a cup of tea, and cut soda bread.

'There was one fellow I liked a lot, his name was Doug, but he was the one who was killed.' A shadow came over his face.

'It sounds terrible.'

'We were together in the trench.'

She stared at him, her eyes widening.

'We had to dig the trenches out of the earth, like one long grave.'

She shuddered.

'I hate the thought of going back.'

'If you didn't, what would happen?'

'They would probably come after me.'

Chapter Seventy-five

Liliane stood by the grave. The weather reflected her own mood, a grey cloudy sky threatened rain. The priest murmured the prayers, and she placed a hand on young Daragh's shoulder. The girls were very upset, but her young son was silent and hadn't spoken much since he had heard his father had died. She missed Maurice and James very much, and would have given anything to have them both here by her side. She had heard what had been happening to those in the Volunteers who had stood up to the English, and prayed that James hadn't been killed. As it was, there was no news yet except that many of them had been sent to England for internment. She had written to Maurice about his father, but couldn't let James know.

The gravediggers lowered the coffin. She longed to look at Matt's dear face again, and found it difficult to come to terms with the fact that he had left home one morning and never came back. Caught up in a struggle with which he had no sympathy, disapproving of his own son's commitment to the Volunteers and their fight to gain Irish freedom from the English.

On the practical side, she had to arrange the wake at the house, and the funeral. Had to borrow money for that expense. All the time keeping up a front for the sake of the children. She had help from Matt's family, but no offer from her own, even though she had written a letter to tell Etta and Mimi that Matt had died. Their lack of response had hurt. Particularly as she was sure that people wondered if she had any family. But as she had always done, she put that to one side. Without Matt, everything was difficult. She had depended on him so much since they had married, feeling so strong with his support and able to stand up to her family. Now she was lost without him, and would have to survive on her own. Support her children. Feed and clothe them. She might have to get a job. The thought of that was daunting. She had never worked. Had no idea what she might do.

The heap of earth and stones was shovelled on top of the coffin. She couldn't look, and moved the children away, anxious that they should not be upset. Some people had said Daragh was too young to attend, but she insisted. He needed to be there to mark the passing of his father. For the future.

Liliane whispered a prayer, turned to walk back, and suddenly stopped. Two women stood there, dressed in black.

'Etta, Mimi?'

Her sisters embraced her.

'We're so sorry about Matt, it's such a terrible loss for you,' Mimi whispered.

'If we had known, we would have been here with you,' Etta said. 'But we've been out of town because of the trouble and only got back last night and received your letter.'

'It's so good of you to come.'

'We haven't seen you in years, and that's been wrong, but Mother and Father ...'

'I know, don't worry. Let me introduce you to my children.'

They shook hands.

'Unfortunately, my eldest son Maurice is in Flanders, fighting, and my second son, James, is in prison at the moment.' She had to say it, knowing that they would be very shocked.

Their eyes rounded in surprise.

'He was involved in the rebellion.'

'That's such a cross to bear,' Etta murmured.

'Come back to the house,' she invited. But was nervous about that. What would they think about her home? A small house which would fit into one of the rooms in Ailesbury Road.

'We would like that more than anything.'

They came back, and met Matt's family, friends and neighbours, charming them with their grace and elegance. Liliane couldn't really believe this was happening. They stayed until everyone had left and the children had gone to bed, and the three sisters sat together, the house silent at last.

'I want to meet your husbands and children,' Liliane said. 'Soon.'

'We would like that as well. Although they don't know of your existence, Father was particularly adamant that we should never speak of you, but Mother always regretted that he sent you away.'

'They never met their grandchildren,' Liliane couldn't help the slight tinge of bitterness in her voice.

'No, and that was so sad, and for us too not to have known you all before now, we should have stood up to him,' Etta said.

'But you know what he was like,' Mimi added.

There was a pause.

'Now we want to make things right, to ease the hurt. Although it's a bit late now that you have lost Matt, but still ...' Mimi hesitated.

Liliane was puzzled.

'We're selling Ailesbury Road, and although Father left it to both of us we feel it's only fair that you should have your share, particularly now.'

'I don't really understand.'

'We have arranged with our solicitors that the proceeds from the sale will be divided in three. We've already had some offers, so it means that you will be quite comfortably off,' Etta smiled.

There were tears in Liliane's eyes, and immediately she hugged her sisters. 'You are so good, thank you, thank you.'

Chapter Seventy-six

At Richmond Barracks, the men talked among each other of the week past. How things had gone against them in spite of everything they had done.

They argued too.

'We should have occupied more of the buildings on Sackville Street, and kept the British at a distance.'

'We hadn't enough men,' James said.

'Would have had if so many of the Volunteers hadn't gone to fight for the English.'

'And how many of them have been killed? For nothing.'

'They gave their lives to an English king.'

'Instead of giving their lives to Ireland.'

'Some of them will be back.'

'But how many?'

'Depends on when the War is over.'

'Will they support us then?'

'Of course they will.'

James didn't know whether the men who came back would want to get involved in another conflict after being through so much already. But he kept his thoughts to himself. It wasn't his place to put a damper on the other men's certainty that the Irish would rise again.

The following morning the door opened. An officer marched in accompanied by three soldiers. James held his breath. Was this it?

'Stand up,' one of them shouted.

They got to their feet awkwardly, stiff and sore from lying on the floor all night.

A number of names were read from a list by a soldier.

Relief flooded through James that his name wasn't among them.

'Step forward,' the officer shouted.

The men pushed their way through and were taken out.

When the door was banged shut, the others looked at each other.

'Bloody hell,' one swore.

'What's going to happen?' another asked.

'Probably be court-martialled.'

'It will happen to all of us.'

James said nothing but he was very concerned for the men who had been singled out. He contemplated a very uncertain future, if he had any future at all.

They were held there. Another night. Another day. Another night. On Wednesday morning, James pushed himself up. He still felt tired and didn't know whether he had slept for five minutes or five hours. The cold had penetrated his bones and even though this was early May the night temperature plunged during the small hours and he felt every bit of it. Richmond Barracks wasn't built for comfort.

'Did you hear, James?' the man beside him asked.

'What?'

'The gunshots.'

He looked at him, puzzled.

'There was a volley very early this morning, in the distance. Just a few shots and then silence after that. It didn't sound as if there was any response.'

'Maybe some of our men are still holding out,' James said.

'Bloody good enough for the English.'

'It's hard to keep us down once we get the bit between our teeth,' someone laughed.

'Maybe they'll come and rescue us here.'

They raised their fists.

'Would they have taken over somewhere else? Maybe Kilmainham Jail itself?'

'Did all the posts surrender?' James asked.

'Maybe they did what we wanted to do and refused to throw down their guns.'

'We had to obey the orders.'

'Could be a group from the country. The Volunteers rose up against the British in other places as well and maybe they banded together and attacked the city.'

'If we could only get out of here.' The men were growing more convinced that another *Rising* was in progress.

'Could we escape?' A couple of men stood up and began to examine the room they were in.

'What about the window?' They looked up.

'It's barred and too high. Even if we did get out, it's a hell of a drop.'

'What can we see?' One man climbed on another's shoulders and tried to reach it.

'I can just about see the sky.' The man on top stretched his neck.

'There would have to be three of us standing on each other to see anything out of that window. Anyone ever worked in a circus?' There was much laughter at that question.

'And if we managed to break the bars, and the glass, how would we get to the ground?' James asked, going along with it, even if he thought in his own heart that there wasn't a hope of escape out of a place like this. Still, it was something to talk about.

'Anyone got a rope?' There was more laughter.

'We could tie our coats together,' someone suggested.

'And swing down like monkeys,' James grinned.

'We're getting ridiculous,' another man said.

'We'll never get out of here.'

The mood of the men darkened.

'We just have to hope that we get a chance to have our say in court.' James brought things down to earth.

'Want to get justice in a British court?' It was a sarcastic comment.

The men grumbled.

'I'm still hoping the lads are out there. God is good.'

'Yes, we have to be ready to join them.'

It kept them going. That thought.

Names of the leaders were mentioned. James stared at one of his friends who sat beside him. Neither man said anything. But from the look in his eyes, James knew he was thinking the same way as he was himself. What fate was in store for all of them? He stayed awake all of the following night, in dread of the dawn light brightening the room, and hearing the gunfire as described by the others. But it was still dark when out of the silence the report of the guns echoed. He turned his face to the wall, and closed his eyes.

Chapter Seventy-seven

Louise lay on the floor. The flagstones, which were uneven and ice-cold, dug into her body so much it was impossible to find a comfortable position. Her clothes were damp, right through, and because of the lack of fresh air, had no chance to dry. She would have given anything for a hot bath to wash away the body odour which clung to her skin and clothes. Her scalp was itchy. She felt unwell. All of the girls did. The amount of food they received was barely enough for the four of them. Lumpy porridge and cocoa in the morning, watery soup and hard biscuits in the evening. And they were always thirsty, that most of all.

On Wednesday, before dawn, Louise was awakened by the harsh sound of gunshots which echoed around the building. She jumped up, rushed to the door and banged on it. 'What's going on?' she shouted. There was no sound from outside. What was happening, she wondered? Had the Volunteers risen up again? Was it possible that arms from Germany had landed? Had some other country come to their assistance?

'What's wrong?' Anne asked out of the darkness.

'They're shooting out there,' Louise said. 'Did you not hear it?'

'When I woke up I wasn't sure where I was for a minute, here or back at the College.'

'What do you think it was?'

'I don't know. But wouldn't it be marvellous if it's our men,' Anne whispered.

'Could be they're still holding some of the buildings.'

'Is there any chance of that, do you think?'

The other two girls were awake by now, and they were all excited by that possibility. They listened for more gunfire but it was quiet now.

'It's strange there were only a few shots,' Louise said, suddenly doubting her own earlier explanation. What if all of the Volunteers had been captured like themselves? She was quite unable to voice the terrible thoughts that came into her mind.

In the morning the wardress came in with the porridge. Louise stood up. 'Who was shooting in the middle of the night?' she asked.

The woman turned her head to look at her, but didn't reply.

'Please tell us?'

'You'll find out,' she grunted.

'Were they ...shooting us?' Her pulse raced as she asked the question. Fear swept through her.

The woman stared at her with a cold, appraising look. Then left the room, crashing the heavy metal door behind her, and turning the key in the lock.

There was silence in the room. No-one spoke. She could feel the tension from the others.

'What did you mean by asking her that?' Joan asked, after a moment.

Louise didn't answer.

'Us?' Dettie gasped.

'Oh my God,' Joan burst into tears.

'They can't execute us without a trial,' Anne said.

'We must have a chance to explain ourselves. Tell the court the reasons why we are doing this. If they know then perhaps it might make a difference. All my family have longed for the Irish people to be free, my father, my grandfather and back even further. What's wrong with that?' Dettie exploded.

'My family too ...' Joan added. 'I don't even know if my father and brother are still alive.'

'We'll pray that all of our families are safe.' Dettie blessed herself.

'But if anyone takes up arms against the British Empire it's considered treason.' Louise had gone so far down this road she couldn't stop. 'Maybe we'd better face up to that.'

'I might never meet that boy again,' Dettie murmured, tears in her voice. 'I liked him.'

'We all have people we may not meet again ...James and ...' Louise put her arm around Anne and hugged close. She thought of James constantly. Went over every second of the time they spent together. Remembering what it felt like when he kissed her. The touch of his lips. The aroma of his skin. Something so delicious she was swept away even now. Heart beating. Longing to be close to him again. Even for one second. She would have given her life to have that one second with him. 'I'm sure you're thinking of Harry too,' Louise said to Anne.

'I think of him all the time now, knowing what he is going through,' she said. 'And I'm sorry I didn't accept his proposal, it would have meant so much to him.'

'Next time you see him just tell him you love him,' Louise advised.

'If I ever get an opportunity.' Anne's voice was bitter. 'Stupid fool that I am.'

'Don't say that. You'll see him soon, never fear.' Louise held her close.

'I'm still hoping to meet someone, I wonder will it ever happen,' Joan said.

'Now that you've an hour glass figure they'll be queuing up,' Dettie laughed. 'Your mother will be whipping them in to view her slim daughter who doesn't even need to wear a corset.'

The girls had to smile.

'We can always depend on Dettie to give us a laugh,' Louise said.

The wardress came back later and allowed them out for exercise. To see the other women who had been with them in the College of Surgeons was wonderful. Although the wardresses tried to stop them talking, they didn't succeed, and the girls chatted among each other, refusing to follow their orders. They didn't allow them to stay out as long as the previous day, but still it was great to make contact, and they all agreed to sing and dance as much as they could to spite the British.

Chapter Seventy-eight

The newspaper had been passed from house to house. Kathleen couldn't have afforded to buy a copy for herself, as was the case with most of the other people on the road. When she received it, crumpled, and with pages out of order, she unfolded it quickly and immediately searched for the front page, praying that she would not see the name of her husband or children printed there.

Hugh took it out of her hand.

She felt weak.

He read the list of the men executed that morning and shook his head.

Kathleen sighed with relief and held on to the back of the chair. She was so glad that Hugh was here with her.

'I was thinking I might go down to Richmond Barracks,' he said. 'To see if I can find out anything about Father or Michael and Louise.'

'No, don't you dare. Do you want them to throw you into jail as well?' she retorted.

'I'm a soldier, they're hardly going to do that,' he laughed.

'You don't know. I forbid you to go,' she snapped.

'Mam, don't you want to find out how they are?'

'Of course I do, but I don't want you to go down there. It's too much of a risk.' The last few words were whispered softly. 'Maybe we'll go together.' She lowered herself into the chair wearily. The boy who had left her had disappeared for ever.

And a man had returned in his place. To have lost him so quickly broke her heart. It was like a death. Yet here he was in front of her. still just sixteen years old. But she didn't know him now. The babyish curves had gone, tightened, honed, and left an image of his father.

'I'll go out,' he said. 'See if I can get some food.'

'I must give you money.'

'It's all right, I have some.'

'No, son, you keep your money. I've already spent all of your wages that the army sent on food. I was keeping it for you, but I had to use it.'

'I wanted you to have it,' he smiled as he stood there at the door.

'I've missed you,' she whispered and bent her head. There were tears in her eyes.

He moved towards her, placing his hand on her shoulder. She touched it. They stayed in that position for a few seconds.

'Are you all right, Mam?' he asked. It was a gentle question.

She nodded. 'I'm sorry, I promised myself I wouldn't embarrass you like this.' The tears came fast now.

'I'm not embarrassed.'

'With your poor old Mam crying her eyes out?'

'Cry all you like, Mam, I've cried too.'

She looked at him, hating the thought of that and how alone he must have felt and she not there for him. That hurt most of all.

They went to Richmond Barracks the following morning, and stood outside with other people who had gathered there in the hope of finding out what was happening to their loved ones. But the soldiers stood to attention and wouldn't engage with them. She had brought some food with her from the little which was left in her pantry and asked a soldier to take it in to Terence or Michael. But even though Hugh showed him a shilling, he ignored them. They left and went over to Kilmainham Jail where the women were imprisoned. Hugh offered a soldier there the same money, but received no response from him either.

When Kathleen arrived back home, dispirited, she found it hard to put on a bright face for the boys. They didn't understand what was going on. They thought it was all over.

'Where's father?'

'When will he come home?'

'Soon, boys.'

Edward bounced a ball against the front door.

'Stop doing that in the house, go out to the back,' Kathleen admonished.

'Michael isn't here to play with us,' he was sulky. 'And where's Hugh?'

'He's gone to see some of his friends. Why don't you play with Martin?'

'Don't want to.'

Kathleen found it hard to keep her patience. 'You'll be back at school soon. No time for playing then.'

Later that afternoon, Martin ran in. 'Mam, there's a boy out there looking for you,' he burst out, all out of breath.

'What boy?' she asked.

'Missus?' The boy walked up the path.

'Yes?' She wiped her hands on her apron.

'The man at the morgue asked me to give you this.' He handed her an envelope.

Her heart began to beat uncomfortably loud. Alarm swept through her. She couldn't move and was unable to take it from him at first. He pushed it nearer and finally she forced her stiff fingers to grasp its edge. He ran down the path, picked up his bicycle which was leaning against the hedge, and cycled away.

Tears filled her eyes. Her legs shook. In torment, she rushed back inside. This was terrible news. She knew that. It had to be. Someone was dead. Martin stood in front of her. His little face concerned.

'I'm sorry love,' she pulled him close and hugged him. To be able to touch her child seemed to help her gain some control over her emotions. He pulled away.

'Are you going to open the letter?' he asked innocently.

She nodded, took her handkerchief from her pocket and blew her nose.

'Who's it from?'

'I don't know.'

She slid her thumb under the flap. There was a white square inside. She unfolded it and stared at what was written there.

A body has been found with an envelope on its person identifying this address. Please report to the City Morgue as soon as possible.

A scream curled through Kathleen, but with a supreme effort she managed to clamp her mouth shut. She stood up.

'Why are you crying, Mam?'

'I must go out now, Martin, you do what Edward tells you.'

'Where are you going?' He stood staring at her.

'Into town.'

'Can I go with you?'

'No, love, you stay here. I won't be long. Hugh will be home soon.'

'Is Edward going with you?'

'No.'

'Bring us some sweets.' He ran to the door.

She nodded, and went out the back to where Edward was playing. She called him, but he wasn't there. Out the front obviously, she decided, hurrying through the house again.

'Edward, come in here.'

'Ah Mam, I'm playing,' he complained.

‘Edward,’ the other boys called.

Kathleen ushered him ahead of her. ‘I want you to take care of Martin until Hugh comes home.’

‘Why?’ he groaned.

‘I must go out. Now please behave yourself. Tell me I can rely on my big boy to look after everything while I’m gone?’

For a minute he said nothing, staring down at the floor. ‘All right,’ he muttered.

‘You won’t leave the house?’

He shook his head.

‘You’re in charge.’ She threw on a light coat, took all the money she had in the jar on the mantle, and hurried next door to ask her neighbour to keep an eye on the boys in her absence. She regretted that Hugh wasn’t back yet. She would have given anything to have him with her now. But he had been anxious to visit Peter’s family and find out how he was.

There was a queue of people outside the morgue, but she pushed her way through and went into the office. She knocked on the glass window, and handed the letter to a woman. She looked at it, took her name, and told her to go back outside and join the queue. She stood among the people and there was very little conversation between them. It was quiet. Time passed slowly. She hadn’t allowed herself to think of who she would see here. Couldn’t even whisper a name. This wasn’t happening.

It was very slow. As the afternoon wore on Kathleen became disturbed by the sight of tearful people coming out of the morgue. She prayed. Whispering *Hail Marys* over and over. It must be a mistake, she said to herself. It had to be.

Finally she reached the top of the queue and went into the main hallway. In the office the woman handed her a piece of paper with a number on it. A man led her down a corridor into a room filled with trolleys. Each one held a covered body. The smell caught in her throat and she felt faint. The man took her arm and forced her to walk. They stopped. She didn't have any conscious thoughts. The cover was moved. She saw a face. It was a man. He was young. She knew him instantly.

'No,' she shouted and leaned over the body. 'Michael ...'

'Mrs. O'Toole, come with me.'

He supported her as she walked, led her out of that place, and sat her down. She didn't notice the other people there.

'Michael, Michael ...' she cried.

He left her for a few minutes, and then returned. 'You will need to give us his full name. I'll fill in the form and you can sign it.' He moved a small table in front of her.

She was distraught and couldn't understand at first what he was saying.

'Mrs O'Toole, please stop crying,' he spoke firmly.

Kathleen's sobs lessened somewhat.

'You should do this quickly and go home. There's no point in staying here, and I have a number of other people to deal with.'

She stared at him.

'His name is?' He dipped the pen in the inkwell and held it poised over the form.

'Michael ...' she whispered.

'Sir name?'

'O'Toole.'

'His address?'

She hesitated.

He took a crumpled brown envelope which was attached to the form and showed it to her. 'Is that it?'

She looked at it and nodded. It was an envelope which had contained one of Hugh's letters. He completed the form, and handed her the pen. 'Please sign here ...'

She took the pen with shaking fingers and scrawled her name.

'That's grand.'

She stood up. Suddenly she wanted to put her arms around Michael. He was in there all alone and she couldn't bear the thought of that. 'I want to take him home.'

He shook his head.

'But he's my boy.'

'You have to arrange for the undertakers, they'll do all that.'

'No.' She turned to run back into the room.

The man caught her arm.

'Mrs. O'Toole, you'll have to come with me.' He took her outside. 'Do you have anyone waiting for you?'

She shook her head.

'Will you be all right getting back to where you live?'

'Yes.'

'Go on now, go home.'

Kathleen stumbled over the threshold of the door, and out into the street. She walked along, and just about managed to put one foot in front of the other, wandering in the direction of the river. It began to rain. She was unaware of where she was going. The wind blew up. She reached the quayside. All she could think of now was Michael when he was a tiny baby, her first born. She loved him fiercely, and kept him with her all the time. There was a special bond between them. Always was. Now she simply couldn't imagine living without him.

Chapter Seventy-nine

Louise rubbed her arm. It was itchy and getting worse all the time. They were infested with fleas and could see the marks of their bites, but could do nothing, just scratch.

'I can't bear this,' Dettie cried. 'How long will they keep us here?'

Joan screamed.

'What's wrong?' Louise asked.

'Something crawled over me.' She scrabbled around in the gloom.

Louise slapped at the floor with her shoe. 'That'll keep them at bay.'

'Nothing will keep them at bay.' Joan shivered.

'We'll just have to put up with them.'

'I hate the things,' she murmured.

'I never thought I'd be in such a place. The English are pigs.'

There was a sound from outside. Footsteps. A metal door banged closed.

'I hate not knowing what's going on,' Anne whispered.

'How many of us are in here?'

'All of us from Surgeons, and the other posts probably as well.'

'If we're kept here for years, what will we be like then?'

'We'll die from lack of food and water. We can't survive on what they give us.'

'The people will have to protest.'

'We were fighting for them. Do you think they will rise up?'

'They didn't support us as we made our way here. They were on the side of the English, I couldn't believe that,' Louise said.

'Do our families know where we are?'

'They haven't come up to see us so they mustn't know.'

'My mother is going to be so worried,' Louise said.

'All of our mothers will.'

'There's something I can't get out of my head ...' Joan said, and hesitated for a few seconds. 'What if my mother and father never find out that I'm here?'

'That's silly, Joan,' Dettie said. 'Of course they will, sure they probably know already, all the families do. But the British won't let them in to see us.'

'I didn't hear any shots this morning, did you?' Louise asked no one in particular.

The realisation dawned on them.

'Maybe it's over and there won't be any more,' Anne whispered.

'Thanks be to God.'

The door was unlocked, and the wardress came in with the meagre breakfast. The girls ate gladly, it was better than nothing.

'There will be a visit from the Governor today, and the Medical Officer, and here's pencil and paper for you to write home for clothes.' She handed it to them, then locked the door again.

They looked at each other in surprise.

'What does that mean?' Louise asked.

'Maybe he'll tell us to go home,' Dettie said excitedly.

'How wonderful,' Anne whispered.

'But what about writing for clothes, that doesn't sound like they're going to let us go very soon?' Joan asked.

'We'll write the letters, at least our families will know where we are, and that we're all right. Who wants to go first?' Louise asked. The thought of writing to Kathleen felt so good, it was almost like talking with her.

Later, the Governor arrived with the Medical Officer. He just stood there, silent, while the Medical Officer asked the girls how they were feeling.

'We've been bitten, it's very uncomfortable.' Anne showed him the bites on her arm.

He nodded. 'Any other complaints?' he asked.

'We don't feel well in general, how could anyone be well in a place like this?' Louise took her opportunity.

He nodded but said nothing and left, followed by the Governor.

'That was a lot of use,' Louise exploded when they had gone.

'If we had said we were really sick do you think they'd have let us go?' Anne asked.

'I'm not going to let them think we're that bad,' Dettie retorted.

'That only plays into their hands.'

The visit left them very disgruntled, and angry too at their treatment.

In the afternoon, there was another visit. This time it was a priest from Kilmainham.

'It's so lovely to see you, Father.' They gathered around him.

'How are you?' He seemed very concerned.

'Awful, and the food is terrible.'

'You won't be here much longer,' he said. 'I'll do my utmost to persuade the Governor to release you.' He blessed them.

They were very grateful.

Chapter Eighty

James waited for those sounds in the early morning. He slept initially each night but always around dawn he awoke as if someone had called him. His heart clenched when he heard the distant crack of rifle fire and tears moistened his eyes. He was crushed. And felt that a bullet had been fired through his own heart, imagining how his body would be flung to the ground with the force of the shot, his blood splattered. The volleys echoed and magnified. He couldn't put that out of his head during the day, no matter how hard he tried.

Terror stalked among them now. It made it all the worse. A priest came to visit them and he told them the names of those who had been executed and they were sickened. James and others made Confession, not knowing what lay ahead of them.

The soldiers ordered them into the barracks yard. They glanced at each other for a few seconds and then marched in line outside. They were directed out through the gates and back towards the city by the same route they had come just over a week ago, guarded by a wall of soldiers on either side. All the time, James's eyes searched for Louise among the people who stood watching. He had some crazy idea that she might be there, and prayed that she wasn't imprisoned. They marched along the quays. There was a shout from a man standing on a corner.

'Shoot them, the bastards,' he yelled.

'Hang em,' another roared.

This was taken up by a few more in even more colourful language.

They passed the turn for Sackville Street. James looked at the ruins of the buildings. Blackened walls. Collapsed roofs. Gaping windows. Piles of bricks. From what he could see of the street, the GPO was just a façade.

They went down to the North Wall and were held there on the quayside. It was raining. Cold. They received no food or drink. They had to stand, line after line of them. The day dragged by until they were loaded on to a large vessel which was moored alongside. Forced down into the hold of what was a cattle boat. It was filthy, and smelled foul. Hundreds of them were crowded together in the dim cramped space.

'Where are we going?' the man beside him asked.

'Don't know,' James said, despondent.

'There's a chance we'll just be thrown into jail.'

In the gloom a hand reached across him. 'I'm Lar.'

'James.' He grasped it.

They landed in Wales some hours later, and were transported across the country. A long uncomfortable journey, at the end of which they arrived at a large black prison building. They were herded inside by soldiers. 'Get in there. At the double,' they shouted, guns held over them.

As he waited in line, James could see men climb noisily up the steel stairs, slipping and sliding as they were pushed ahead by prison guards. On the landings they were forced into the cells on the two sides of the upper floor.

James found himself in a small cell on ground level. The floor was stone, as were the walls. A narrow bed along one wall had a grey blanket on it. There was a bucket in the corner. Nothing else.

Chapter Eighty-one

The cell was gloomy. The girls huddled together. They were exhausted. Lack of sleep and food had weakened them.

'Did you hear the shots this morning?' Louise asked.

No one spoke.

'I've lost count. I can't tell how many,' Anne said.

'I feel guilty about that. They should be remembered, each and every one,' Louise murmured sadly.

'Let's say a decade of the Rosary.'

They knelt down.

'What day is today?' Dettie asked of no-one in particular.

'I can't remember,' Louise said.

'Yesterday was Sunday, girls, we went to Mass in the prison church,' Anne interjected.

'And we came here on the previous Sunday.'

'Yes, remember we surrendered and they marched us here.'

'I thought I had counted each day,' said Louise.

'So did I.'

'Is it seven?'

'I think it's nine,' Joan got involved for the first time.

'And this is Monday.'

'Did we count the Sunday as the first day or Monday as the first day?' Dettie got up and walked around, but then sat at the end of the bench again. She couldn't stop moving.

'We have to count Sunday as the first day.'

'Then what day is today?' Joan was becoming annoyed.

'What does it matter?' Anne said tiredly.

'We'll know when we're allowed out of here.'

'If that ever happens.'

Suddenly, there was the sound of a key in the lock and their attention was riveted on the heavy door. Eyes wide. Always so afraid whenever that door opened and what it would bring.

The wardress stood there. She stared at them. None of them spoke.

'You can go, you're free,' she said.

They couldn't understand what she meant at first and didn't move.

'You mean ...away from here?' Louise stuttered.

'Yes.'

They looked at each other, and together they stood up, disbelieving.

She went ahead leaving the door open, and slowly they followed her out into the dark corridor.

They walked along unsteadily. Light filtered from an archway at the end. It beckoned.

Louise smiled at Anne. They held on to each other and came out into the yard where a number of women were already gathered.

The Governor stood there with a group of British officers. One of them stepped forward. He held a sheet of paper in his hand and began to read out names. As the women were identified they walked to the gate and stood there waiting.

Louise waited with bated breath for her own name to be called. Dettie, Joan and Anne had already joined the group, and when the officer finally called O'Toole, Louise smiled broadly and rushed over to them. They held on to each other as a soldier pulled open the gate, and allowed them to walk outside.

'We're free, girls,' Louise screamed out loud, and immediately they threw their arms around each other and hugged emotionally, unaware of the curious glances of passing people. The other girls were equally overjoyed to be free at last.

'I can't believe it,' Anne wouldn't let go of Louise.

'We can do what we want, go where we want,' Dettie whooped, and she and Joan danced a jig of sorts, although they hadn't the energy to dance for very long.

'And no-one can order us around.' Louise glanced back at the gate to see two soldiers on duty there. 'Let's get out of here before they change their minds.'

'How will I get home, I've no money,' Joan wailed.

'Let's walk to my house, it's the nearest and then we can get some money from my mother,' Louise suggested.

They walked from Kilmainham to South Circular Road. There were a lot of British soldiers on the streets, but now the girls kept their heads down, and controlled their delight aware that they could be pulled in again if it was suspected they had been involved in the *Rising*.

Louise knocked on the front door. There was no answer at first. 'Mother, where are you?' She searched in her pocket, but couldn't find the key, and knocked again.

'Maybe she's out,' Anne said, a disappointed tone in her voice.

Louise peered in through the letter box. 'No, here she is, Mam ...'

The door was opened, and Kathleen stared at them for a couple of seconds, then put out her arms and embraced her daughter. Tears streaming down her face. 'Louise, my girl ...I thought I had lost you.'

Louise was in tears too.

'Come in my love ...all of you come in.' She reached for the other girls and hugged them too. They stumbled down the hall into the kitchen.

'These are my friends, Mam, we were in Kilmainham Jail, we don't know how long ...it was horrible.'

'Sit down girls, what would you like? A cup of tea, or I have some soup?' Kathleen was already stoking up the range.

'Anything Mam, the food was terrible, but I just want a drink of water, I'm so thirsty.' She took cups from the dresser, filled them from the tap in the pantry and handed them to the others.

'That's delicious,' Anne sipped the cool water.

'It's so warm in here, I thought I'd never be warm again.' Joan held her hands out to the fire.

'Now you have to tell me all. Was the food I gave you enough?' Kathleen asked.

'Yes, it was wonderful, and fed everyone that day.' Louise wasn't going to admit to her mother exactly how hungry they were.

'How about your father, and James?'

'I was down at the GPO a couple of times and met James and Father, but I didn't see Michael, although they told me he was all right.'

'Michael has ...' Kathleen hesitated.

Louise stared at her. 'Mam, don't tell me something's happened to him?'

Kathleen nodded. 'He was killed.'

Louise burst into tears.

Anne put her arm around Louise's shoulders. Dettie and Joan clung to her too.

'Myself and Hugh went down to Richmond Barracks and Kilmainham Jail with food for you, but the soldiers wouldn't take it even for a bribe, and would tell us nothing either.'

'Hugh was home?'

'Yes, he had been injured.'

'What happened to him?'

'A shell exploded and shrapnel hit his shoulder, but it's better now. He's gone back there, God help him.' Kathleen blessed herself.

'I'm so sorry I missed him,' Louise was very down. The thought of never seeing Michael again upset her deeply. 'Do you know where Father and James are?'

'A lot of men have been sent to jails in England, and some men have died,' she said slowly.

'We heard the shots but didn't want to believe it was our men who were being killed.'

'Twelve have been executed altogether, including four this morning, it's been terrible. Every day more men.'

The girls were shocked to hear their worst fears confirmed.

'They printed the names in the papers, but thanks be to God so far I didn't see an O'Toole there,' Kathleen added.

'Or a Wilson?' Louise whispered.

'I didn't see his name either.'

Louise sighed with relief.

Kathleen poured bowls of soup, and cut bread. The girls ate hungrily.

'You look like you haven't eaten in days.'

They smiled and tucked in.

'This is so good, thank you,' Anne said, grateful.

'It's wonderful, Mrs. O'Toole,' Dettie added.

The door burst open. The boys rushed in and stared at the girls, shyly standing around Kathleen.

'Hallo boys?' Louise hugged them, but they ran out of the kitchen again just as quick.

'You must tell me everything that happened,' Kathleen said. 'I was so worried about all of you. We were afraid to go out of the house as the week went on. Some of the shops have opened but what they have on the shelves wouldn't feed a mouse, although I did manage to buy some flour. A farmer came in yesterday and he had plenty of fresh vegetables on his cart so I was able to make this soup.'

'I'm sorry, we shouldn't be eating so much,' Anne put down her piece of bread.

'Not at all, girls, eat away. You're entitled to all we have, sure haven't you put your lives at risk for all of us?'

'Don't worry Anne,' Louise reassured.

'There is some help for poor families, relief vouchers are given out by the St. Vincent de Paul, but I don't feel we should take them, we'll manage. Hugh told me to use his money.'

'That's good of him.'

'You wouldn't recognise him.'

'Why?'

'He's grown up, a man now.'

'I'm sure his experience would make anyone grow up.' Louise was bitter.

'Now girls, have you had your fill? Can I do anything more for you?' Kathleen asked.

They all smiled. 'You have no idea how good it was to eat something nice.'

'I'm delighted, girls.' Kathleen cleared away.

'Would you be able to spare some money for the girls' tram fare, Mam?' Louise asked.

'The trams aren't fully running yet so I'm not sure how you'll get home. But we have a couple of bicycles here, Terence didn't take his, and there's mine as well. Where do you live?'

'I'm in Blackrock,' Anne smiled. 'And a loan of a bicycle would be wonderful.'

'I'm in Ringsend,' Dettie said.

'Why don't we go together?' Anne suggested.

'Gardiner Street,' Joan said.

'You can take the other one, then you'll all get home.'

Louise went into the Shelbourne Hotel the following morning. It looked surprisingly normal. Men worked around the building. The front door was open. Porters waited to welcome guests. She went in the side door as usual and hurried down the corridor to Miss Cunningham's office. She knocked, and tried to gather enough courage to approach her supervisor.

'Come?'

She could hear the sharp tones, hesitated for a few seconds and then pushed open the door and stepped inside, very nervous.

'Louise?' Miss Cunningham stood up and came around her desk. 'How are you?'

'I'm all right.'

'You were involved in the violence?'

'I was.'

'It must have been very dangerous for you?'

Louise nodded, afraid to say too much.

'I couldn't believe there were women with guns out there, it was quite terrifying for the guests, and ourselves.'

'There were a lot of people killed.'

'I know, and quite a few of the soldiers protecting us here were injured as well, and one even died. The whole experience was dreadful for everyone.'

'I know I left on Easter Monday without any notice, but under the circumstances I hope I may be excused.'

'Well ...' Miss Cunningham turned back to her desk and sat down.

'I like working at the Shelbourne, and would dearly love to be granted my position again.' She watched the other woman's face, and hoped the rather disapproving expression didn't mean she wouldn't take her back.

'You are a very good worker, Louise, so I'm glad to say that Mr. Quinton and I are willing to offer you the position of Assistant Head Housekeeper again,' she smiled then.

‘Thank you so much, I really appreciate it, and I promise that I will work even harder for you.’ Louise couldn’t believe her good fortune.

She went straight upstairs to the staff cloakroom, and changed into her one remaining uniform which she had brought with her. She was overjoyed, but sad too that the person she wanted to tell most of all wasn’t there. He was most likely in England by now, languishing in some prison, held by the English for doing something which any man would do for his country. To stand up and fight. Give of a life. For freedom. Then she thought of her father who was incarcerated in prison as well, and could still be shot. And Michael who was cut down at such a young age. A shadow came over her.

Chapter Eighty-two

Anne rushed into the house, using the back door.

In the kitchen, the first person she saw was Sally the cook, who immediately threw her arms around her and burst into tears. 'Miss Anne, I'm so glad to see you.'

'Where's Mother and Father and the girls?'

'They're just sitting down to dinner.'

'I'll go on up.'

'Will we set a place for you at the table?'

'No, it's all right, I'll get something later.' She went up the stairs, and crossed the entrance hall into the dining room.

There was consternation when they saw her, and they rose out of their chairs and rushed to embrace her.

'It's so good to see you home, I was really worried about you,' Eleanor hugged her tight.

'I can't believe I'm here,' Anne smiled, so happy.

'We were imprisoned in the Shelbourne in the middle of all the fighting, would you believe?' Eleanor exclaimed, and then stared at her. 'You're not looking very well. Your hair is all over the place and you ...' She put a hand to her nose with a distasteful look on her face. 'I think you should have a bath.'

'You had to stay in the hotel?' Anne asked, shocked at that, and ignoring her mother's remark.

'Yes, and it was terrible, horrendous, the guns, the noise. I thought I was going mad.'

'Our hospital was busy too, shocking injuries and deaths.' Clarence put his arm around her shoulders. 'Come sit down. Catherine, ring the bell and tell Sally to bring Anne something to eat.'

'I'm not really hungry, I had something earlier and couldn't eat any more.'

'Just have something light. Now, tell us all about it.' They gathered around the table.

'I helped cook the food at the hotel, and everyone liked it,' interrupted Catherine.

'And met some interesting boys too,' Rhoda added.

'I have two wild daughters who would take up with anyone at all. I don't even know who these boys are or where they come from. It's all too much,' Eleanor groaned. 'It will take me months to get over this. I think I'll have to go somewhere to recuperate. You'll have to arrange it, Clarence. Maybe the girls will come with me. We'll go somewhere quiet like Lake Garda in Italy. My ears are still buzzing with the sound of those guns. I don't know if it will ever leave me. How could anyone be expected to tolerate such penance?'

'You will have to wait, Eleanor, there's nothing but gunfire in Italy as well,' Clarence sipped his glass of claret.

'Oh, I'd forgotten about the War. God only knows how long it will be before we can get away.'

'It must have been hard for you too, Anne, although when I went over to Mercer's they said you hadn't been working since Easter Sunday,' Clarence said.

She didn't answer for a moment, unsure how to explain exactly what she had been doing. 'I wasn't there.'

'Where were you?' Clarence gasped.

'In the College of Surgeons.'

'What?'

'It's a long story, but I was glad to do it. I wanted to support the Volunteers.'

'You were fighting?' The girls were excited.

'I was nursing the injured, and cooking the food we had, which wasn't much.'

'You were cooking too?' Eleanor exploded. 'I don't know what my life has come to. All of my daughters are working in kitchens, like servants.'

'You're safe, that's all that matters.' Clarence hugged Anne.

'And there are letters for you.' Rhoda rushed out of the room and came back holding two envelopes. 'They're both from Stephen.'

Anne opened the first with a smile.

'You have two letters and we didn't get any.' There was a distinct note of complaint in Eleanor's voice.

They waited.

Anne took the letter out of the envelope. Her heart beat wildly as she recognised the handwriting. 'It's from Harry,' she laughed in excitement.

'Who?' her mother burst out.

'Who do you think?'

'Oh that Harry.' Realisation dawned on her.

Clarence and the girls smiled at each other.

'We've been writing to each other since he went away, but I didn't mention it.'

'Why not?' Eleanor demanded.

'Because you'd only rush us into getting married and then I couldn't continue with my nursing.'

'But surely you'd love to be married?'

'At some point, but not now, so you're not going to have a wedding very soon, unless it's Catherine or Rhoda,' she smiled at them.

'What about Harry, what does he think about it?'

'He'll agree,' Anne said, smiling. 'Don't you worry about that. Now I'm going to go upstairs for some privacy.' She was already reading the first few lines of the letter as she opened the door. She turned back. ‘And both Harry and Stephen will be home on leave at the end of the month.’

Chapter Eighty-three

Mary missed Lar very much and prayed he would return to her soon. But she was broken-hearted about Robbie. He was the one who did everything for her. She had gone down to Richmond Barracks where Lar was being held and enquired at the gate for him, but the soldiers ignored her. She talked with the other people there and found out that some of the men had been sent to prison in England, but that there were still some held in the barracks.

'For how long?' Mary was shocked when she heard that.

'It could be for years.'

'Poor Lar,' Mary felt for her husband. While she often gave out about him, and avoided his amorous approaches, she still loved him.

She continued to go down to the barracks, standing outside in the hope of catching sight of him. Brendan and Bridget came with her, and on a couple of occasions, they did see a large contingent of men being marched out and rushed with the other people after them, but by the time they arrived at the North Wall, Mary had seen every face, and knew Lar wasn't in that particular group. In the end, they never saw him leave, and weren't sure where he was.

In the city, the citizens were faced with the results of the upheaval. Food was extremely scarce, and Mary and Lily hadn't been able to set up their stall in Moore Street yet. But the word went around one morning that the owners had returned to Jacobs, and they were handing out some of the stock still held there to the people. It took quite a while but Mary came back home with a large bag of biscuits, and cakes, and they really enjoyed the treat. She had also received some food from St. Vincent de Paul. She hated having to go and beg, but was forced to put her pride in her pocket and do exactly that.

She went down to Mercer's to see Emily. The hospital was packed with people. She asked at the desk and the woman sent her over to the children's ward.

'Mam?' Emily's thin arms reached for her as soon as she saw her.

'Love,' Mary held her close.

A nurse stood beside her.

'How is she?' Mary asked.

'She's better now,' she said. 'You can take her home.'

Mary was so happy, but at the same time prayed she could look after her as well as the hospital had done.

'Feed her well, she was very undernourished,' she said sharply.

Mary didn't know exactly what *undernourished* meant but knew it had to do with how well she managed to feed her children. She felt guilty.

'We don't want her back in here again.'

Mary nodded, feeling roundly ticked off by the nurse.

'Have you got warm clothes for her? Whatever she came in with has been disposed of in the furnace.'

'I'll go home and get them, I didn't know I could take her today,' Mary said.

'Hurry on then and be back here quickly, we need this bed, as you can see there are a lot of patients and we can't have a child taking up a bed needed by others.'

'Emily is coming home and I have to bring some clothes for her, the hospital threw everything she had into the fire.'

'What?' Bridget was aghast. 'Where will we get more?'

'We'll use one of the twins' dresses,' said Mary.

'But it'll be too big.'

'Won't matter for now, we need a coat too, but I can't find one.' She rooted under the bed. 'Here's one belonging to Dan.'

Bridget found a dress, petticoat, and knickers. 'These should do, although they're a bit light.'

'We'll wrap her up in the coat, we need to keep her warm.'

'Have we any shoes?'

'Here's a little pair of runners.'

'Right, I'm away. Have we any more wood for the fire?'

'I sent Brendan out the back to look for some.'

'It's getting cold.'

'He should be back soon.'

At last Moore Street was open, and Mary, Lily and Bridget were down early at Smithfield Market. They went to their usual supplier, and begged for credit.

'How do you think I paid for these vegetables?' he grumbled.

'We'll have money tomorrow, everyone will want fresh veg now after having little over the past couple of weeks. We'll be sold out and they'll want even more then,' Mary pointed out.

Normally, he wouldn't give credit and they didn't need it, but now it was different.

He grimaced. 'All right, what do you want?'

'Thanks,' Mary's smile was wide and grateful. She didn't bother to mention that there were others giving credit and if he didn't do the same he'd lose his regulars.

'Wonder how my house is?' Lily said as they made their way through the streets.

'I don't know, Mam.'

They went into the back yard.

'There's those shoes Robbie got.' She pointed to them lying in the yard.

'We'd better bring them in before we're caught with them, could find ourselves arrested.' Mary gathered them up.

They went inside and upstairs.

'Robbers must have been in here, it's a terrible mess.' Lily stood looking around. Plaster and brick littered the floors and there was a gaping hole in each wall.

They stared into the neighbour's bedroom.

Mary crossed herself. 'They must have been fighting here.'

'They weren't thinking of us, look at my house? Everything's broken up, how will I get it fixed? I've no money.' Lily was angry.

'We'll help, and the neighbours will get together.'

'I can't live here. When will Eileen be back?'

'Any day now.'

'But what about my things? I think someone's been in here already.'

'Come back with me tonight.'

'If we only had Robbie he'd be the one who would fix this up for me.'

Mary was left without words.

Chapter Eighty-four

James listened to the noises around him. Heavy metal doors banged. Footsteps thumped up and down the stairs. Voices shouted aggressively. The cell smelled of urine, a permanent odour. He sat there, lonely, hating the fact that he couldn't talk to anyone. The hours crawled by. All he did was listen to what was going on around him. The rough accents of the guards as they shouted out orders, the responses of inmates. He would have given anything to talk to someone, or to have a book or a newspaper to read. He spent all of his time thinking of Louise, planning their lives. What they would do if they had children. Where they would live. And the biggest question, would his children live to see the island of Ireland free of the English?

The weather was mild enough but the nights were cold, and James never managed to get warm even lying on the plank under the single grey blanket. Mice and rats scurried, and he spent his time watching out for them and stamping on the ground in an effort to squash them, but not having much success. Still he imagined they were the English and he was getting his own back for Michael.

The isolation was the worst. Wentworth was an enormous place with a large number of prisoners of varying types. James and the other Irishmen were allowed out to walk around the yard for an hour morning and evening but they were not allowed to talk. However, that was difficult for the guards to control even though they walked close to them, watching and listening. James always took a chance. What could they do if he was caught? Put him in solitary? 'How're you?' he asked the man who was walking beside him.

'This no talking stuff is ridiculous,' he murmured out of the corner of his mouth.

'Who's listening?' James tried to keep his expression blank.

'They must think we're going to plan another *Rising*.'

'Not a bad idea.'

The guard came closer.

They stopped talking immediately.

But James spoke every opportunity he got, and enjoyed it, like a schoolboy disobeying the rules. The rest of the time he spent on his own, although he wasn't sure if the other Volunteers were held in single cells around the building, or in shared cells. Lucky beggars if they had company, he thought. Sometimes he tapped the SOS signal *help* on the wall using a button on his jacket and thought that perhaps he could communicate with someone on the other side. But whoever that was didn't pick up but he kept at it in the hope that one day someone would tap back.

He prayed Louise was all right, and that the soldiers weren't abusing the women in Kilmainham Jail. They were rough some of them, and the thought that they might even put a hand on her delicate skin was almost too much for him. His mother and father, sisters and brother at home were on his mind too, and again not knowing how they had managed during the week of the *Rising* caused him a great deal of worry. And even more than that, how was his brother, Maurice. Was he safe? He thought about Michael and deeply regretted his death. Terence was here too, but James hadn't come across him yet. Unable to concentrate on anything particular, his mind continued to go around in crazy circles.

He couldn't sleep, his normal pattern disturbed since the week he had spent in the GPO. He was always hungry too.

There was little food during the *Rising* to go around all the men and he had become used to that as there was so much more happening at the time. He was given a cold porridge-like stuff in the morning, and a watery soup later with biscuits. He ate every last morsel but it simply wasn't enough.

Then there was an improvement in their conditions. Visitors were allowed in to visit the Irishmen. Mostly politicians and people interested in their plight. James learned that there had been an outcry when the executions became known across the world.

Marching around the yard in silence was discontinued, and they were allowed to receive letters and parcels from home. The first one James received was from his mother, the second from Louise. Both arrived on the same day and he tore them open together, reading an alternate line or two of each, so happy. But his eyes widened in shock as he read through the words Liliane had written, and he shouted out loud in pain to hear that his father had died. He crumpled the letter and banged his fists against the wall, knowing massive loss and guilt too that he had been the cause of his father's death.

At the end of June, James and the rest of the Irish were moved again. This time they took a long journey across England into Wales, finally being driven in trucks to an isolated group of buildings in a place called Frongoch. Although they were still incarcerated, there was a certain kind of freedom in the openness of the place. They were living in wooden huts, and while he knew some of the men, others were strangers to him, but he enjoyed the camaraderie. He was glad to find Louise's father, Terence, in the next hut, and was delighted to have an opportunity to get to know the man properly.

They began to organise and decided to make the most of their time in Frongoch to continue with their plans to establish the Irish Republic. Discussions were held on strategy, warfare, and diplomacy. And plans made for the continuing struggle as soon as they were returned home. They wanted to be prepared and James had every intention of being involved in the future.

In the bunk below him was Lar, the man whom he had met on the cattle ship. He was twice James's age, and lived on Cuffe Street with his wife and family. He had been fighting in Jacobs and they became good friends.

Each morning when the steam horn blasted they had to get up immediately. James would shout Lar's name as he passed him on the way down but Lar lay under his blanket without any response. He punched his shoulder. 'Roll call.'

Lar always left it to the very last minute. Could sense when that officer was about to step in the door, and by the time he had arrived in the hut, Lar was standing with every other man. Head up, shoulders back, ready to be counted and once he was up, he never flagged.

'Is it our turn to clean the place?' He would ask James, never able to work out exactly when their turn would come.

'Yes.'

'Damn.'

'It will pass the time,' James laughed.

After breakfast, which wasn't much, a group of men would get down to clean their hut, every inch scrubbed down. After that was the time set aside for receiving letters and parcels. Louise and his mother wrote regularly. To his relief Louise had been released from Kilmainham jail a short time after he had left Dublin himself, and she had returned to work in the Shelbourne Hotel immediately. He had to curb his enthusiasm to write long letters, full of his hopes for the future, so kept them brief. Letters were examined by the military and he was aware that sentences they might not like were struck through, as was the case with the letters they received.

After dinner, the day stretched ahead, filled with opportunities to study the various courses in languages and other subjects which were organised. The Irish in Frongoch had no intention of wasting their time and anyone who had the ability to teach a subject was persuaded to impart their knowledge.

James studied Irish which he loved. There were many members of the GAA held here, and he enjoyed to get out into the fresh air and kick a ball around for exercise.

'Fancy a walk?' he asked Lar.

'Just for half an hour, I'm doing singing.'

'Didn't know you could sing.'

'You haven't heard me, couldn't really call it singing, anyway, I can't do much else ...' Lar seemed ashamed.

For such a hard man, James was surprised. 'What do you mean?'

'I can't ...I don't ...' He kicked the earth with his boot, his eyes lowered.

'What?' James asked, with a grin.

'If I tell you this, you're not to pass it on to anyone else,' Lar warned.

'All right, I won't.'

'Well, no reading or writing so no letters home ...'

James didn't quite grasp what he was talking about at first.

'They don't know where I am.'

'Your family?'

He nodded.

'If you like I can write to them for you?'

'Would you?' he seemed surprised.

'Of course.'

It was their secret. Lar's eldest daughter, Bridget, was able to read his letters and tell his wife, Mary, what he had said.

'I'd like to learn stuff,' he said to James. 'Maybe do some of the things you and the others do, never had much schooling,' he was sheepish.

'What do you fancy?' James laughed. 'There's a big selection. You could learn how to speak French, or Irish, study history, bookkeeping, mathematics ...do a university degree here.'

'See, couldn't do any of them.'

'I'm keen on Irish. A lot of people speak it. Why don't you join in?'

Lar seemed bashful.

'Let's start there, a few words of Irish and maybe some reading and writing in English as well?'

So they began. Quite a number of the men spoke Irish so before long Lar had a smattering of phrases and words. That gave him confidence, and he and James spent the time after they had written letters home to practice his English reading and writing. It meant a lot to him.

James became accustomed to the routine. He occupied his days as much as he could and kept busy, looking forward to the parcels which came from his mother and Louise. Socks, gloves, and scarves knitted with love. And they sent food too. It was so welcome. He treasured every line that they wrote, and in his replies made this place of imprisonment sound as pleasant as he could.

October and November brought autumn wind and rain and they were forced to spend more time inside the hut.

'I've tried to accept that we could be here for years,' James said to Terence whom he had met while walking outside one morning.

'We're hopeful that a political decision will be made to release us.' Terence seemed much more confident these days, brighter.

'Can't wait to get back ...' James admitted.

'Louise will still be there for you, she's a steadfast girl,' Terence said, with a smile.

'I miss her.'

'And why wouldn't you?' His eyes twinkled.

'Could I ...?' James hesitated.

They walked further in silence. It was a bright day, although cold, a clear blue sky above.

'Mr. O'Toole, I wonder ...would you agree ...to allow Louise marry me?' he asked.

'I think you know the answer to that already, James,' Terence said. 'Kathleen and I would be delighted to have you in the family, particularly since ...' he paused. 'Our Michael won't be coming home any more.'

'Thank you.' James was grateful, so happy that Terence had no objection, but sad that he would be taking Michael's place in the O'Toole family.

'You're a lucky man.' Terence said.

'I know.'

'I wish you all the best.' He shook his hand.

'Thank you.'

'All we have to do is get out of here and home where we belong.'

'And hope that we will still have jobs to go to.'

As Christmas approached, James missed Louise and his family more and more, and became dejected as did most of the other men when they contemplated the thought of spending the festive season without their families.

Then, just days before Christmas, it was announced that they were to be released. Men went crazy. Roared. Jumped around. Thumped each other. Euphoric. Among them James, who just couldn't believe this was happening.

Chapter Eighty-five

Anne finished work, climbed on her bicycle and rode over to Cuffe Street. She had called occasionally over the last few months, always anxious to see how little Emily and the other children were doing. She had grown fond of Mary, a woman who came from a very different background to her own, and admired her strength and determination as she faced each day in a life which was hard when compared with the comfort of her own. She left the bicycle in the back hall, and took a large bag off the carrier. This was only the second time she had brought some clothes over, and hoped the family could make use of them. She made her way up to Mary's room. She knocked, and the door was opened immediately by Bridget.

'Miss Montford ...' she stood back to let her in.

'Call me Anne, Bridget,' she said, with a smile.

'Yes, miss.' The girl blushed.

'Anne, it's lovely to see you.' Mary appeared and ushered her inside. 'Sit yourself down.' She brushed the seat of one of the chairs with the piece of cloth she had tucked into the pocket of her apron.

'Thank you.'

'Can I get you a cup of tea?' she offered.

'No thank you, I've had something to eat, and then I'll be going back to the nurses' home.' She always refused anything to eat or drink, conscious of Mary's situation.

'It's lovely to see you.' Mary sat down opposite.

Bridget went across the room to where she was putting the two younger girls to bed.

'How's Emily?'

'She's grand, and already asleep.'

'And the others?'

'Good thanks.'

'Any news of your husband?'

'We had a letter the other day, he's learning to read and write and it was the first one he wrote himself, just a few words, but it's so nice to hear from him. Bridget read it for me.'

'I'm glad. Now I've brought some things for you and they should be nice for Christmas.' She went to fetch the bag which she had left down near the door.

'How good of you. I'm very grateful.'

Anne took out a few items.

'They're so beautiful, we've never had anything so lovely except what you gave us before.'

'I'm only glad to be able to give them to you.' She unfolded a particularly nice plaid skirt in shades of dark green. 'This should fit either you or Bridget.'

'There's something I have to tell you ...I feel so guilty ...but Lar insisted we pawn the other clothes you gave us, I couldn't persuade him to let us keep them, and I wasn't able to tell you I felt so ashamed, I'm sorry.'

'That doesn't matter, maybe this time you could wear them on Christmas Day and pawn them afterwards?' Anne smiled. 'Then take them out again when you need them, that's how it works, isn't it?'

Mary nodded. 'And hope we have the money then.'

'If you get some wear out of them then I'll be glad of that. And there are some dresses for the girls, and trousers and shirts for Brendan. I enquired around my friends and they were delighted to help, so they're all winter clothes, lovely and warm.' She rummaged down in the bag, and took out a coat in a rich shade of dark green wool. 'And this coat will go with the skirt and a white lace blouse. You're going to look lovely. And here's a nice blue dress for Bridget. It belonged to the daughter of a friend of ours who is about the same age.' Anne held the dress up to the girl. 'It's so pretty, and only just a little long, but I'm sure you can take it up, you're so good with the needle.'

Bridget and the boys stared wide-eyed.

'As you're in mourning for Robbie and mightn't be able to wear colours yet perhaps this dress might suit you?' She unfolded a black dress with some pretty trimming. 'And there's one also for Bridget.'

'Thank you so much,' Mary took her hand. 'I'm very grateful to you.'

'It's my pleasure. Why don't you wear this on Christmas Eve when you go to meet your husband?'

'I don't think he'll be home for Christmas.' There was sadness in Mary's voice.

'But the men are being released from the internment camp in Wales, it was in the newspaper, I presumed you already knew.'

'What?' Mary stared at Anne.

At that moment, there was a bang on the door.

Bridget opened it.

'The men are coming home,' Tilly shouted from the landing.

'We've just heard.' Mary jumped up. 'I can't believe it.' She hugged Anne and then Bridget.

'You'll have a wonderful Christmas all together again,' Anne smiled.

'They'll come in on the boat-train on Christmas Eve morning,' Tilly's voice echoed.

Bridget woke the twins to tell them and they gathered around.

'We'll all go to meet him.'

'And wear your new clothes,' Anne suggested.

'I'll have to get my needle and thread out.'

'No better woman.'

'I'm so grateful to you, Anne, such goodness in one person, it's just hard to believe.' Mary touched the soft wool dress.

'I love to help in any way I can, you know that.'

'I pray all the time for your young man, and your brother too.'

'There's something I want to tell you,' Anne felt shy. 'Harry and I are going to get engaged on his next leave.'

'That's lovely for you, I'm delighted.' Mary hugged. 'And you'll be getting married soon after that?'

'Not until I'm fully qualified. Then I can help Harry in his practice.'

'Both of you can settle down to married life and have lots of lovely children.'

'I hope I'll be as good a mother as you are.'

'You will, and they'll be very lucky, those children.'

'I hope so.'

'Happy Christmas dear girl.' Mary kissed her.

Chapter Eighty-six

Kathleen carefully cut around the few printed lines in the newspaper with her scissors. She had spent precious pennies on it so that she could read it herself. The notice which announced that the prisoners in Wales would be released and arrive back on Christmas Eve. She was so delighted that Terence was coming home and couldn't wait to see him. Although they were all still grieving for Michael, it would be so good to put her arms around her husband once again. Hugh was still fighting in France. Putting his life at risk every second. She prayed he would survive and come home to her. She couldn't bear to lose him too, not another of her children.

Even though she had splurged on the newspaper, she was very careful with money these days. Only living on what Louise made in the Shelbourne and the small amount she received from the British Army for Hugh. It was tough going, and difficult to save even a little.

She waited up for Louise, so looking forward to telling her that Terence was coming home, and James too. That would mean everything to her, Kathleen knew that well. But as it grew late, she was worried about the girl coming home on her own through the night streets. The hotel was very busy at this time of the year and she was aware that her daughter had no option but to work on until everything was finished. She closed her eyes then, and dozed a little, but jerked awake when she heard the front door close with a bang. She rushed into the hall waving the piece of paper.

'My love, they're coming home.' She embraced the girl who stood there in the hall looking at her with some puzzlement. Her face pale against the dark coat she wore. Both mother and daughter still in black, mourning Michael.

'Who?'

'Your father, and James of course. Look at the paper, it says so.'

Louise took it from her mother, and stared at the lines written there. 'But we thought it would be years, that's what people said.' she threw her arms around Kathleen. 'It's going to be wonderful to see Father again and James, but what made the British change their minds?'

'Politics, girl, no doubt.'

'I thought I'd never see them again, and that they would disappear like Michael, God rest him.'

'That won't happen. They're well, and have said so in their letters.'

'I don't always believe what they say in their letters, I think it's much harder than they let on.'

'The British censor what they write, you know that.'

Louise nodded.

'Come on, be happy. This is going to be a lovely Christmas.'

Louise wiped her eyes. 'Sorry, I'm reacting very strangely.'

'No, you're not, it's natural.'

'It's just I'm not sure if James will still like me. I dread meeting him. What if he doesn't feel the same way about me as he did before?'

'Wouldn't he be a right fool of a man altogether?'

'I wonder does his mother know he's coming home?'

'I'm sure she does.'

'I'll go over to see her just in case.'

'I didn't know you had been introduced,' Kathleen said.

'We haven't been, but I think, because of the situation, she might be glad to know.'

'If you wish, although I don't like you going out so late, and calling on someone at this hour isn't the height of politeness.'

'I can't go tomorrow, so I'll take a chance and see if she is in.'

Her mother looked doubtful.

'I'll take your bicycle, it won't be so far then.'

'Why don't you write a note and put it in the letter box?' Kathleen suggested. 'So your journey isn't wasted.'

Louise immediately agreed, and penned a short letter.

Chapter Eighty-seven

'It's been lovely to see you this evening,' Liliane smiled at her two sisters. They had become much closer since the death of Matt, calling regularly to each other's homes, all the cousins now firm friends.

'Don't forget you'll be coming over to us for Christmas dinner,' Mimi reminded. 'We'll expect you about four o'clock for drinks.'

'Thank you, I'm looking forward to it, we all are.'

Liliane was delighted. Since being reunited with her sisters again, their lives had changed drastically. Her parents' house on Ailesbury Road had been sold and her share of the money was secure in the bank. But she wasn't inclined to spend rashly. Without Matt, she must raise the family on her own and would need the money to last the rest of her life. She was eternally grateful to Mimi and Etta, and had splurged a little when buying gifts for her sisters and their families. This was the first Christmas they would spend together since she had been a young woman and it had to be marked as special.

The sisters rose to take their leave. They were two attractive women, always dressed in the latest fashions. Feathered hats. Double skirted dresses. Coats with fur collars and cuffs. They smiled, and kissed Liliane, obviously as happy as she was. She saw them out to the front door, no longer self-conscious about her small simple home, compared to Mimi and Etta's palatial mansions in Ballsbridge and Donnybrook. They said a final goodnight and walked down the pathway to where Mimi's black motor car waited, gleaming under the light of the gas lamp. The chauffeur held the door open for them. They climbed in, and the car glided away, Liliane still waving.

She went inside and closed the door, a smile on her face.

After a couple of minutes, there was a knock. She hurried down the hall thinking that perhaps one of her sisters had forgotten something, and was surprised to see a strange girl standing there.

'I apologise for calling so late, Mrs. Wilson,' she paused. 'But I waited until your guests had left before I knocked ...I'm Louise O'Toole, a friend of James, and I called over to let you know James and the prisoners in Wales are coming home on Christmas Eve, I wasn't sure if you knew.'

'Why, thank you,' Liliane said. 'Won't you come in?'

'It's late, perhaps I shouldn't?'

'Please step inside for a moment. This is wonderful news, how did you find out?' Liliane asked.

'It was in the evening newspaper.'

'I was busy today and this evening too and didn't have an opportunity to read the paper and as my sisters were here I wasn't talking to the neighbours.'

Liliane led the way into the sitting room, and they sat down. She offered tea but the young girl declined.

'I must get back, my mother worries.'

'All mothers worry,' Liliane smiled, and tried to put the girl at ease. She was beautiful. Her dark hair in the new shorter hairstyle which was fashionable. And wearing black. She must have lost someone close too, she realised, immediately sympathetic. 'James told me about you.'

Louise blushed.

'I was looking forward to meeting you, so I'm delighted with the opportunity.'

'And I you.'

'We'll have to get to know each other, but I'm sure James will arrange that.'

'I hope so.' Louise stood up. 'I must go.'

'Of course, I don't want to detain you.'

'They are coming in on the early boat-train from Kingstown.'

'I'll be there, and so will his sisters and brothers. Maurice is home on leave, but he will be delighted to see James before he goes back.'

'I'll have to try and get time off work, so I'm not sure.'

'I hope they are generous towards you.'

Louise smiled.

'I look forward to meeting you again, perhaps you might come to tea?' Liliane took her hand.

'Thank you, I'd like that.'

Chapter Eighty-eight

The boat-train from Kingstown arrived into Westland Row railway station, and slowly drew to a halt with a piercing hiss, amid clouds of steam. James hung out of the window of the carriage, astonished to see throngs of people on the platform, yelling, screaming and waving.

'Hey, Terence, Lar, what do you think of this?' he laughed.

'Bloody hell.' Lar took his cap off and began waving it in the air.

'Bit of a difference to when we left Dublin,' Terence said. 'Then they were throwing things at us.'

'Something's changed,' James was staring into the crowd looking for a familiar face, but most especially Louise. He opened the door and stepped out with the others, surrounded immediately by people, some of whom clapped them on the back, and shook their hands. It was difficult to make their way through. 'Don't think we'll find anyone we know in this crush,' he yelled back at Terence and Lar. They said something but it was too noisy to understand and he continued on outside, but it was just as crowded on the street.

'Will we go on home?' James asked, as they stood together.

'It seems strange to be back in Dublin.' Terence looked around him. 'And to remember so many lives given up for the cause of Irish freedom. The executions of our leaders, a savage act.'

'The British won't succeed in putting us down,' muttered James. 'There are still men willing to sacrifice their lives, we'll never give up the fight.' He had changed his viewpoint and now was fully committed to rising up again at the first opportunity.

'There are so many people here, we would have a better chance of establishing the Irish Republic now with such support,' Terence said with a grin.

'The plans are made. We'll get there. It might take time but some day soon there won't be a British soldier in sight on the Dublin streets, or anywhere else in Ireland.' James was confident.

'I hope I live to see that day,' Terence grinned.

'Well, the first thing I want,' Lar said. 'Is a pint. Come on lads, let's celebrate. My mouth's been so dry for months, it won't know what a pint tastes like.'

There was a scream, and a woman threw herself at Lar, followed by a group of children. 'Mary,' he shouted, and hugged her. 'My God, you look beautiful, and who are this lot all dressed up in their Sunday best?' He looked down at the children who clung to him.

James looked at Terence and laughed. 'Don't think he'll be going to the pub now.'

Then someone called his name and he turned around to see Louise push her way through the people and stand smiling at him. 'How are you?' she asked.

'Louise?' He stepped towards her but Terence was closer and already embracing her.

He stayed where he was, feeling a little awkward as Kathleen appeared with the boys. There was a sadness among them, and the talk was all about Michael.

'Only the people at the morgue found a letter from Hugh in his pocket, we'd never have known what happened to him and he'd have been thrown into a common grave, but at least we found our dear boy and were able to give him a proper funeral.' Kathleen clung to Terence.

It was a while before James had a chance to talk to Louise, and then it was just polite conversation.

'Do you think your own family are here?' she asked.

'Haven't seen anyone yet.' James searched the faces gathered around. Suddenly, he spotted a tall man dressed in a British Army uniform.

'There's my brother, Maurice, and Mother,' he shouted. 'Come and meet them,' he brought Louise over to where the family stood.

'I wondered if I'd recognise you it's been so long,' Maurice said, and thumped him on the back.

'And I said James will still be the same James we've always known.' Tears moistened Liliane's eyes, and she threw her arms around him. 'It's so good to see you, son.'

'How have you been since ...father died?' James stuttered. He didn't know what to say exactly, having found it so difficult to come to terms with the loss of Matt.

'It's been very hard.' She bent her head.

He hugged her again. 'I want to introduce you to Louise, this is the girl I told you about, Mother,' he smiled.

'We've already met.' Liliane took her hand. 'And I have to say she's a beautiful girl, and you're lucky to know her.'

'I can't believe this.' James was taken aback.

'I called over to tell your mother that you were coming home, I wasn't sure if she knew,' Louise explained.

'And we're looking forward to getting to know Louise even better soon,' Liliane said and smiled at her.

'Plenty of opportunity for that I hope,' he said.

'And we've a lot to tell you, haven't we Maurice?' she said.

'This is going to be a wonderful Christmas, I can't wait. But come and meet Louise's family, and a friend I made in Frongoch, they're all over there.'

They walked across. James looked at Louise. Their eyes met. He stood close to her.

More introductions were made, and there was plenty of chat between them all.

James took Louise's hand and held it tight. He didn't care who noticed.

'We'll take a cab,' Maurice said eventually.

'That's posh, the tram will do us,' Terence laughed.

'We're going on over to Moore Street, all the family want to see you, Lar, especially Bridget.' Mary put her arm in his.

As they walked, James hung back a little with Louise. 'You've no idea how good it is to see you, I thought about you night and day, and missed you so much. The letters I wrote had nothing in them, nothing, and all I wanted to do was to tell you how much I loved you, but I knew the Brits were going to read them, and I was worried that you might have forgotten me, or met some other fellow, or even got married while I was away. That was the worst, I couldn't get it out of my head.' He put his arm around her waist.

'I thought it would be years before I saw you again, and didn't know if you would feel the same about me so to have you back now is just ...' Her eyes filled with tears.

'How could I change my feelings about you, Louise? That would be impossible. Anyway, I haven't talked to a woman in months, it was all male in Frongoch,' he laughed out loud.

'Am I to be thankful for that?' she asked, with a smile.

'Even if there were women, they couldn't compare with you, my love.' He pressed his lips softly on hers, and they stood there, entwined, in a world of their own ...

**TO MAKE A DONATION TO
LAURALYNN HOUSE**

Children's Sunshine Home/LauraLynn Account
AIB Bank, Sandyford Business Centre,
Foxrock, Dublin 18.

Account No. 32130009
Sort Code: 93-35-70

www.lauralynnhospice.com

Acknowledgements

Many thanks to Military Archives who hold Bureau of Military History Collection.

Many thanks to The Kerryman Ltd.

Many thanks to The Irish Times Ltd.

Many thanks to Cyclone Couriers for all their help over the years.

Many thanks to Southside Storage for their support for LauraLynn.

As always, our very special thanks to Jane and Brendan, knowing you both has changed our lives.

Many thanks to both my family and Arthur's family, our friends and clients, who continue to support our efforts to raise funds for LauraLynn House. And all those generous people who help in various ways but are too numerous to mention. You know who you are and that we appreciate everything you do.

Grateful thanks to all my friends in The Wednesday Group, who give me such valuable critique. Many thanks especially to Muriel Bolger who edited the book on this occasion also, and special thanks to Vivien Hughes who proofed the manuscript. You all know how much we appreciate your generosity.

Special thanks to Martone Design & Print – Yvonne, Martin, Dave. Couldn't do it without you.

Thanks to CPI Group.

Thanks to all at LauraLynn House.

Thanks to Kevin Dempsey Distributors Ltd., and Power Home Products Ltd., for their generosity in supplying product for LauraLynn House.

Special thanks to Nisheeth, of Rasam Indian Restaurant, Glasthule.

Thanks also to Irish Distillers Pernod Ricard. Superquinn. Tesco.

And in Nenagh, our grateful thanks to Walsh Packaging, Nenagh Chamber of Commerce, McLoughlin's Hardware, Cinnamon Alley Restaurant, Jessicas, Irish Computers, Abbey Court Hotel, and Caseys in Toomevara.

And much love to my darling husband, Arthur, without whose love and support this wouldn't be possible.

THE MARRIED WOMAN

Fran O'Brien

Marriage is for ever ...

In their busy lives, Kate and Dermot rush along on parallel lines, seldom coming together to exchange a word or a kiss. To rekindle the love they once knew, Kate struggles to lose weight, has a make-over, buys new clothes, and arranges a romantic trip to Spain with Dermot.

For the third time he cancels and she goes alone.

In Andalucia she meets the artist Jack Linley. He takes her with him into a new world of emotion and for the first time in years she feels like a desirable beautiful woman.

Will life ever be the same again?

THE LIBERATED WOMAN

Fran O'Brien

At last, Kate has made it!

She has ditched her obnoxious husband Dermot and is reunited with her lover, Jack.

Her interior design business goes international and TV appearances bring instant success.

But Dermot hasn't gone away and his problems encroach.

Her brother Pat and family come home from Boston and move in on a supposedly temporary basis.

Her manipulative stepmother Irene is getting married again and Kate is dragged into the extravaganza.

When a secret from the past is revealed Kate has to review her choices ...

ODDS ON LOVE

Fran O'Brien

Bel and Tom seem to be the perfect couple with successful careers, a beautiful home and all the trappings. But underneath the facade cracks appear and damage the basis of their marriage and the deep love they have shared since that first night they met.

Her longing to have a baby creates problems for Tom, who can't deal with the possibility that her failure to conceive may be his fault. His masculinity is questioned and in attempting to deal with his insecurities he is swept up into something far more insidious and dangerous than he could ever have imagined.

Then against all the odds, Bel is thrilled to find out she is pregnant. But she is unable to tell Tom the wonderful news as he doesn't come home that night and disappears mysteriously out of her life leaving her to deal with the fall out.

WHO IS FAYE?

Fran O'Brien

Can the past ever be buried?

Jenny should be fulfilled. She has a successful career, and shares a comfortable life with her husband, Michael, at Ballymoragh Stud.

But increasingly unwelcome memories surface and keep her awake at night.

Is it too late to go back to the source of those fears and confront them?

THE RED CARPET

Fran O'Brien

Lights, Camera, Action.

Amy is raised in the glitzy facade that is Hollywood. Her mother, Maxine, is an Oscar winning actress, and her father, John, a famous film producer. When Amy is eight years old, Maxine is tragically killed.

A grown woman, Amy becomes the focus of John's obsession for her to star in his movies and be as successful as her mother. But Amy's insistence on following her heart, and moving permanently to Ireland, causes a rift between them.

As her daughter, Emma, approaches her eighth birthday, Amy is haunted by the nightmare of what happened on her own eighth birthday.

She determines to find answers to her questions.

FAIRFIELDS

1907 QUEENSTOWN CORK

Set against the backdrop of a family feud and prejudice
Anna and Royal Naval Officer, Mike, fall in love.
They meet secretly at an old cottage
on the shores of the lake at Fairfields.

During that spring and summer their feelings for each other deepen. Blissfully happy, Anna accepts Mike's proposal of marriage, unaware that her family have a different future arranged for her.

**Is their love strong enough to withstand
the turmoil that lies ahead?**

THE PACT

THE POINT OF THE KNIFE PRESSES INTO SOFT SKIN ...

Inspector Grace McKenzie investigates the trafficking of women into Ireland and is drawn under cover into that sinister world.

She is deeply affected by the suffering of one particular woman and her quest for justice re-awakens an unspeakable trauma in her own life.

CAN SHE EVER ESCAPE FROM ITS INFLUENCE AND BE FREE TO LOVE?